DAVID

A Man After God's Own Heart

Gerrie Uys

WESTBOW
P R E S S®
A DIVISION OF THOMAS NELSON
& ZONDERVAN

WestBow Press books may be ordered through booksellers or by contacting:

WestBow Press
A Division of Thomas Nelson & Zondervan
1663 Liberty Drive
Bloomington, IN 47403
www.westbowpress.com
1 (866) 928-1240

ISBN: 978-1-5127-8550-0 (sc)
ISBN: 978-1-5127-8551-7 (hc)
ISBN: 978-1-5127-8549-4 (e)

Library of Congress Control Number: 2017906464

Print information available on the last page.

WestBow Press rev. date: 05/02/2017

Introduction

1.   **ACTS 13: 22** "When he had removed him, he raised up David to be their king, to whom he also testified, 'I have found David the son of Jesse, a man after my heart, who will do all my will."

Special notes:

- All bible quotes was obtained from *Biblegateway.com* and is based on the World English Bible (WEB) Standard.
- The story told in this Novel was based on scripture obtained from the World English Bible out of the books of Samuel, Psalms, Kings and Chronicles.
- If one should study the story of David in the book of Samuel you will find that the story portrayed in this Novel reflects one of true heart and character.
- It is not just the story of David that captures one's attention but the men and woman that surround him in his journey.
- Ultimately the reader comes to understand a deeper relationship between God and man that is portrayed through David.
- I believe it is an early reflection of the Father heart through our saviour Jesus Christ. How else could David be a man after God own heart? Jesus Christ longs for a relationship with every individual no matter our past but rather that we draw on to Him with all of our heart! He should be your first love!
- May the Spirit reveal the heart of the father in this novel through Jesus Christ the saviour. Glory to His name forever!

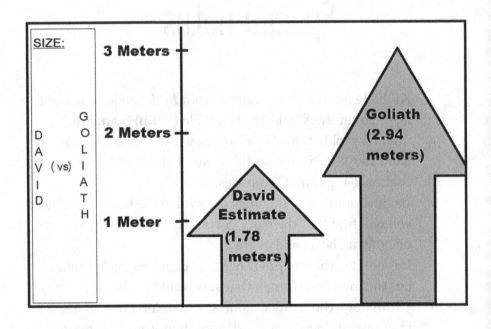

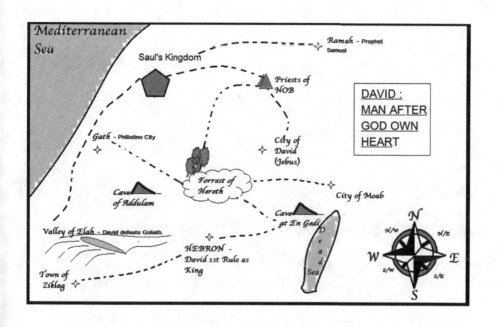

Chapter 1

"Saul!" The word echoes from the stone coble walls.

The prophet gapes at the grass roof of he's dwelling, he's eyes adjusting to the light in the early morning. The sound of the calls of the shepherd boy's and bleating sheep drifts through the desert valley. The rain will come soon and the flocks will be driven to the higher grounds on the hills of Ramah.

The prophet sits up on he's bed and draws the sheep fleece around he's shoulders. Why did Saul not obey Yahweh? The events that came to pass in the passing quarter fills the prophet mind. He seemed so perfect. A tear start to roll down the old man cheek.

"Samuel." The voice penetrates the depths of the prophet mind and body. An intense feeling of love-yet almighty holiness, eminent fear and power-fills the small room and he falls to he's knees.

He remembers the first time when he heard the voice of Yahweh. He was still a small boy and yet he will never grow comfortable with the power and glory of it.

"Samuel, how long still will you mourn for Saul" The voice rumbles through the soul of the prophet like the distant thunder in the depths of the Jericho cliffs and yet it has the gentleness of a whispering breeze playing on the grassy lands of Bethlehem.

"You know I have rejected him as king over Israel." A strand of early morning sunlight filters through the thatch roof and Samuel covers he's head with he's sheep fleece. "Oh Lord! I was thinking about the day in Zuph, when I met him and he's servant. He seemed so flawless. So strong and tall! What will the people of Israel say when they hear that you have rejected their choice?"

A soft breeze blows over the prophet. "Samuel, fill your horn with oil and be on your way. I am sending you to Jesse of Bethlehem. I have chosen one of he's sons to be king." Samuel waits quietly for the Lord to speak again although he can feel he's heart beating much faster in he's chest. The early morning rays of the sun illuminates the grey hair in the prophet's beard.

"Another king for Israel?" Samuel thinks about the look in Saul's eyes when he told him that the Lord rejected him as king. Saul knew that he had done wrong in the eyes of Yahweh but he stood defiantly before Samuel when he met with him. Saul will surely kill the new king. The voice of the most high gently stirs through Samuel's heart

"Don't be afraid. Take a heifer with you and say, 'I have come to sacrifice to the Lord'. Invite Jesse to the sacrifice, and I will show you what to do. You are to anoint for me the one I indicate." Samuel waits for more words of instruction but he feels the presence of Yahweh leaving the room. He slowly rises from the floor. He's heart felt heavy when the Lord announced that Saul will not be king any more but a stirring of joy has yet filled he's heart again.

Saul had sinned. The Lord had chosen yet another servant to be king over Israel. He takes the old water skin from the peg on the wall and enfolds a piece of bread in the sheep fleece. He's mind now wanders back to the day when he's was but a boy in the temple with Eli. Taking up the walking staff in he's strong bony hands he determinately sets of towards Bethlehem. The Lord has spoken. A new king was to be anointed!

Have you heard? Samuel is on he's way to Bethlehem."

The group of elders sitting with Ahiman gives worried nods. "Maybe he is here because he found out of Kenaz conduct?"

The speaker frowns and scratches he's long wispy beard. "What if he announces another plaque from Yahweh?" Ahiman waves he's reed pipe in agitation. A trail of smoke follows he's movements.

"Don't talk like that Sheshai! Samuel has much bigger things to concern himself with than simple few taxes that were raised." Sheshai opens he's mouth as to say something more but Ahiman continues:

"This must be about what happened to King Saul at Shur." Some of the elders nod their heads in agreement. "I heard that he attacked the Amalekites and had a great victory over them. According to he's scribes he gained a lot of cattle and other riches."

Ahiman takes the reed pipe's stem from he's mouth and blows a billowing cloud of smoke in to the air. "I also heard that he spared the leaders of the Amalekite dogs." Sheshai takes the reed pipe from Ahiman. "Why would he spare their lives?" Ahiman stares in the direction of the Southern gate. He had send Migal to stand watch and announce the prophets arrival.

"I heard that the prophet Samuel had gone to visit Saul soon afterwards." Ahiman scratches he's beard. "Yes there are rumours that Samuel told Saul that he was rejected as king by Yahweh."

A shrill voice rings out in the late afternoon "Master!" A young boy comes running from the hill a dust cloud rising behind he's white robes. "Master, the prophet is coming!" Ahiman rewards Migal eagerness with smile and quick ruffle through he's ginger hair. The elders walks to the city gates each one standing in silence with their own thoughts as they await Samuels approach. "He looks tired and irritated"

Ahiman grabs Sheshai by he's shoulder. "Will you be quite Sheshai? Not a word from you or anyone else. I will do the talking." With that Ahiman steps forward waving at Samuel.

"Welcome prophet of Yahweh. Do you come in peace?" Samuel hears the tremble in the elder voice and replies in an emphatic tone. "Yes, in peace; I have come to sacrifice to the Lord."

Samuel stand before the elders of Bethlehem the late afternoon sun setting on the hills. "Consecrate yourself and come to the sacrifice with me." Ahiman bows slightly. "We have erected a tent for you near the eastern slope. We will send someone to take you there." The elder's start of towards their houses some walking in groups and other hurriedly making their way of alone.

Ahiman slowly exhales but the relief that he feels is replaced by curiosity. Why would Samuel come all this way just to sacrifice to the Lord? He almost jumps into the air when Samuel calls out to him.

"Ahiman; I want Jesse and he's sons to come to the sacrifice. Please see that they join us." The curiosity is replaced with a deep frown and Ahiman nods at Samuel. He then hurries away giving instructions to some of the servants that have gathered tasking them with final preparations. Samuel takes the sheep fleece with food and drink and sits down next to the ruins of an old dried up well.

On he's journey he's mind had wandered back over the years. The days when he was in the temple. How strange it all seemed for a little boy. He was brought up in the Temple of Shiloh by the priest Eli. He's mother had prepared him for that day when he was taken to the temple.

He's mother Hannah had explained to him that he was a very special boy. He was a gift from Yahweh. She told him that she had made a promise to Yahweh that she will raise him according to Yahweh's word so that he would abide to Yahweh forever.

He's father Elkhana sat down with him before he went up with the rest of the family for the offering and spoke very gently to him.

He remembered he's father big hands on he's shoulders. He told him that Yahweh will establish He's word in Samuels's life and that Yahweh will lead him and protect him. He's father had squeezed he's shoulder and left for the sacrifice. When they arrived at the temple he's mother brought him before the priest Eli.

Samuel could not remember too much about Eli on that first day accept that he seemed like a serious and strict man.

When Hannah brought him before Eli they went to pray and worshiped before Yahweh and Samuel sat wide eyed staring at all the big rooms in the temple with all the strange new ornaments.

He's mother had held him tight and cried a little before she left and Eli had taken him to he's room when she had gone.

There were many times when he was corrected by Eli for the adventurous exploits. The tomfooleries of a young boy sometimes did not carry the approval of the older man.

Thinking about those days brought some memories back to Samuel that made him smile. He's mother and father came and visited the temple often. When she came she brought scented oil and brushed through he's thick hair. Every year she would make a new robe for him to wear.

He's father and mother continued their visit every year when they came to the yearly sacrifice. Samuel had often missed he's mother. She had told him that she promised Yahweh that a razor would never touch he head and Samuel took pride in specifically looking after he's hair.

He always wore a linen Ephod that he got from he's parents. He did not realize it at the time but he was already ministering the words of Yahweh to the other people in the temple which he had heard from Eli.

Eli taught him wonderful things about Yahweh and told him amazing stories which sparked a burning desire to know more. Stories about a man called Noah that build a mighty boat and took a pair of animals of every kind on to he's boat because Yahweh instructed him so. Samuel use to wonder how Noah managed to get the animals on board especially creatures like lions and bears.

He asked Eli many questions and sometimes it seemed like Eli would grow tired of all the questions but he would always answer. Samuel loved the story of Abraham that had to offer Isaac. He felt that he's mother had also offered him to come to the temple and stay with Eli. He learned to fear Yahweh with a love and reference that can only be explained as awe for the living Creator. He came to know many people that came to the temple and ministered the words that Eli taught him of Yahweh to them.

A man had visited Eli once and Samuel had heard him talking about Eli's two sons Hophni and Phinehas. When the man had left Eli had looked very distraught. Soon after the man had visited Eli; Samuel had he's first true encounter with the Yahweh of Israel.

One night while Samuel was sleeping he heard a voice calling out to him. He sat up groggily in he's bed and then he ran to Eli's bedchamber thinking that it was the old man calling to him. Eli eye sight had become very dim and he frowned at Samuel trying to make out he's form and told him to go back to bed and that he must have dreamed.

He was lying in he's bed wondering if he had imagined it when a second time he heard a voice calling him and again he went to Eli. He was sure it had to be the priest for there was no one else in the temple close to their chambers. Eli mumbled that he was hearing things and he went back to bed again. After the third time this happened though and he came into the priest room, Eli had sat up in he's bed and lit a candle.

He scratched he's beard and after a while he told Samuel to answer when the voice called again because it was the voice of Yahweh calling him. He lit a lamp and waited quietly as Eli had told him. The voice called out to him again.

"Samuel" He had answered as Eli had instructed him saying "Speak Lord for I am your servant."

A presence had filled he's small room that he would never forget and still overwhelms him to this day when the true Yahweh of Israel calls on him. It was a night where Yahweh had brought him a message and one which Samuel had sat listening to fearing the words that was spoken.

The Lord had told him that Eli and he's sons would be punished for Eli's sons had committed terrible sins against the Lord and Eli did nothing to stop it. Their punishment would be death. The voice of Yahweh had spoken to him about Israel and then the presence of Lord had departed from he's room.

The next morning he tried to avoid Eli for he was afraid to tell him what he had heard. Eli had called him and told him to tell him what the Lord had said. The revelation of the words of Yahweh was not wide spread in those days.

The priest had become very white in he's face when he had heard the words spoken but had said nothing accept that Yahweh would do what He seemed was good. The boy did not understand the words of the priest but the word had spread very quickly that the Lord had spoken to Samuel and more people came to the temple to hear the words ministered by Samuel.

A war had broken out and Israel battled against the Philistines and it was that terrible day when a messenger had ran into the temple and told Eli that the ark of Yahweh was captured by the Philistines and that he's sons was killed in the battled.

Eli fell back from the chair on which he was sitting in shock when he heard the news. He fell at and awkward angle and broke he's neck.

Samuel had tried to help the priest but he was too heavy to move and so Eli had died just as the word of Yahweh had predicted.

In those years that followed the Lord had spoken to him often. The people from Israel and as far as Dan to Beer - Sheba came to know Samuel as Yahweh's prophet.

He had come to know the Lord and yet it felt like he still knew nothing. Samuel thoughts are interrupted by the Sheppard boy that he saw running towards the elders as he approached Bethlehem.

The boy casts he's eyes down and Samuel can see that he is nervous. "Sir I have been sent to accompany you to the tent my master has erected for you to stay in." Samuel can't help but to smile at the boy.

"What is your name young man?" The boy swallows and returns the smile widely almost finding it hard to believe that the prophet of Yahweh wanted to know he's name.

"My name is Migal sir" Samuel ruffles the boy's hair and picks up the sheep fleece and he's staff. "Let us then waste no more time sitting here. Let's go to my tent." Samuel thinks about the task the Lord has set before him.

What will the new king be like? The face of Saul comes to Samuels mind once more and he wonders if the new man would be anything like him.

They arrive at a fine white linen tent and Samuel can see that they had prepared the best for him. In a distance not far from the tent Samuel sees two men labouring to erect an altar for the sacrifice.

Migal takes him to the back of the tent where a basin of scented water has been prepared and fresh robes have been laid out. Samuel takes a rock from he's pocket and hands it to the lingering youth. It has the shape of an eagle in flight and he had spotted it on he's journey to Bethlehem.

In he's travels in the years that had past it had become a habit for the prophet to study peculiar looking rocks. The youth can almost not believe he's eyes and Samuel wonders if he's smile could go any wider.

"Thank your Sir!" Samuel laughs and the sound fills the tent. "That will be all for now young Migal. You can go now."

The boy leaves the tent still ogling the rock. Samuel start to wash the dust from he's leather sandals and he's feet in the scented basin.

After he had refreshed himself he changes into the fresh robe that they had laid out for him and then he kneels seeking the Lord.

"Lord please guide me and give me clear understanding for this anointing. I know that you have plans for Israel and I praise your name Yahweh of Abraham and Isaac."

He hears the voices of approaching men and takes a deep breath before stepping out of the tent. The elders approach him and a group of young men together with a few new faces stand before the tent. It must be Jesse with he's sons. Ahiham introduces Jesse before Samuel pointing to a man standing close to him."

As you have instructed Samuel I have gathered Jesse and he's sons." Samuel looks into the face of Jesse. Although Jesse hair is streaked with grey he's appearance is strong and when Samuel makes eye contact the returning stare is that of a humble countenance. The prophet walks over to him and lifts he's hands and places it on Jesses head.

"Jesse; May the blessing of the Lord our Yahweh rest upon you and your family." A bleating sheep breaks the short silence that had fallen upon the crowd.

Migal and an older youth is carrying a young lamb between them. The lamb feet are tied with leather straps and the youths pass by taking the struggling lamb to the men building the altar.

Samuel turns back to the group of men before him.

"Please come for we shall sacrifice to the Lord" Jesse nods at he's sons and they follow the prophet to the altar. He was taken by surprise when Ahiman arrived at he's dwelling asking him and he's sons to come to the outskirts of the city to meet the prophet Samuel to sacrifice to the Lord.

He's sons had all started to talk at once when Ahiman had left and Jesse had raised he's hands to quite them all. It was Eliab he's oldest son that got to speak first.

"Father why do you think the prophet wants us to sacrifice to Yahweh?" This was serious and Jesse had looked at he's oldest son Eliab. He had so many good qualities but he knew that Eliab had an arrogance about him because of these qualities.

All the other young men tried to voice their opinions again and for a second time Jesse raised he's hands. The group of young men grew quit looking at their father. "Patience for we shall know shortly what the Lord has planned on this day my sons. Now go and clean yourselves."

Without another word Jesse had entered he's house. A quite murmur had followed from the group of men and Jesse thoughts went back to the last time he saw Samuel. He had travelled in the caravan with the elders to Ramah to trade some camels. He had known that the elders were about to speak to Samuel about the decision that was reached in the council.

The people of Israel wanted a king. Someone that could lead them into battle and guide them in council was their reasons. Most off all; they wanted a king like the other nations because all the other nations had a king. He was one of the few that did not agree with the desires if Israel to anoint their own king.

They went to Samuel council chambers in Ramah. Samuel had been judging over Israel for as long as Jesse could remember and was a man that feared Yahweh and was fair and just. Jesse had heard complaints from Beersheba where Samuel sons was appointed as judges.

He heard that they were not just and took bribes and perverted justice. This was part of the council's motivation to talk to Samuel about a king. He had conducted he's business in Ramah and had waited outside the council chambers. After a while the elders came out with Samuel. Samuel had stood before them he's long hair billowing in the wind. He had looked sorrowful at the group of elders.

"Remember what I have told you about this king. These are the words of the Lord. "You shall cry out in the day because of the king which you have appointed and the Lord will not hear you. The group of elders had shook their heads and Samuel had told them that he would anoint a king. Soon after that day Saul was appointed as king. The group of men arrive at the altar and Jesse cannot help but to notice Samuel staring at he's sons. Samuel turn towards the group of men studying each son curiously.

"We have come to sacrifice before the Lord." He's eyes rest on Eliab. A tall strong good looking man. This man has the look of a mountain lion. "What is your name?"

Eliab brief hesitation is rather one of astonishment because the prophet addressed him directly but he quickly recovers and answers with a strong proud voice.

"I am Eliab my lord oldest son of my father Jesse." He's voice sound strong and confident. Samuel can hardly contain he's thoughts. He softly prays.

"Surely the Lords anointed stands here before us Lord?" The voice of Yahweh speaks into he's heart.

"Don't look on he's face, or on the height of he's stature, because I have rejected him; for I don't see as man sees. For man looks at the outward appearance, but Yahweh looks at the heart."(1 Samuel 16 v 7)

Samuel turns from Eliab and addresses rest of Jesse sons. One by one they come before Samuel: Abinadab, Shimma, Nathanael, Raddai and Ozem.

Every time Samuel addressed one of Jesse sons he quietly asks the Lord if it is the man he had selected, but the Lord rejects every one of them. When the six sons had passed before Samuel he looks up at Jesse with a slight frown.

"Are these all the sons you have Jesse?"

Jesse had been watching the proceeding with care. He did not understand the interest that Samuel had in sons.

"No, there is still the youngest but he is tending to the sheep up in the mountains" Samuel frowns deeply and the puzzled look in he's eyes does not escape Jesse's attention.

"I want you to send for him for we shall not start the sacrifice until he arrives." Ahiman turns towards Migal. "Run quickly and fetch David and do not waste time boy!"

Chapter 2

A cloud of grey feathers bursts in the blue cloudless sky as the rock strikes the bird on the chest. The young boy puts another rock in he's sling and runs down the mountain towards the spot where he saw the Guinea – fowl fall down.

He lets out a hoot of laughter as he runs and the grazing sheep scatters in all directions as he cuts a path through them.

"That is not fair David!" A dark haired boy races from the opposite slope swinging he's arms at the running boy. The boy's reach the bottom of the slope almost at the same time and David grins at the slender youth.

"Not fair Elika? That was more than fair! You took two shots at it and if you waited any longer it might have died of old age!"

Both boy's hurry along the pathway eager to get to the fallen bird. "There it is!" The red helmet head of the Guinea - fowl can be seen sticking out of a thorny thicket at an awkward angle.

"She is not as big as the bird you took down last week" David prods Elika knowing that he's remark will make he's friend feel better about missing the fowl.

"You are right, but she definitely has a bigger wattle than the one I shot." Their excitement is short lived by a shrill voice calling out to them.

"David!" The boy's turn towards the call on the slope. David shields he's eyes with he's hands from the setting afternoon sun. "It's Migal, I bet you he wants to join us when we take the herd grazing in the southern pastors."

David gives Elika a mischievous grin. "Well maybe we must let him accompany us; we may actually go home with more Guinea – fowl than today."

Before Elika can riposte David takes off towards Migal the Guinea – fowl's head bobbing under he's arm. "Hallo there Migal!"

The youth looks at David with hero worship in he's eyes. During the winter David had come to Migal's rescue when a brown bear had attacked he's herd. David had killed the bear with he's sling but what impressed Migal the most was that David had shown no fear when the bear attacked. He had told Migal afterwards that a strange sensation had come over him and that he could not remember everything up until the point where the brute had taken a last shuddering breath.

Migal notices the blue wattle sticking out under David's arm "Wow, she is a beauty! Can I hold her for a while?" David hands the bird to Migal "Sure; we will be taking the herd to the Southern slopes in two weeks-time, you should accompany us. We can hunt together.

"The youths eyes lights up and he jumps up and down. "Can I really?" David smiles. "Sure. Remember to talk to your father about the grazing." Suddenly as if embarrassed he hands the bird back to David.

"Your father and the elders have requested you to go to him immediately." The smile slips from David's face and a deep worried frown settles on he's forehead. He must have found out about the sheep dung in Eliab's shoe. It was only a little joke. Eliab's face went from a shocking white to a beet purple as he discovered the object of discomfort.

Migal's voice brings David back to reality. "You should go to the west side of the city where they have erected the guest tent; they are waiting for you."

Elika had quietly joined them and now lets out a small whistle. "Was the tent not erected for the prophet Samuel? The elders have been talking about he's visit." Migal pushes out he's chest and with some importance he tells the story of the prophet arrival to the two gawking youths. "He arrived this afternoon. He does not seem like someone that can harm you. I waited for him on the hill. Your father, brothers and the elders are all waiting in the tent with the prophet."

David gives the fowl to Elika and starts of towards the city. "Come by our home tonight before you go to bed, I want to know everything!" David shows no indication that he had heard Elika as he continues towards the city.

It was only a little sheep dung, that's all it was.

Samuel prays silently to Yahweh. The words of the Lord was clear in he's heart. The new king of Israel was to be anointed. The men in the tent had fallen silent. Voices of boy's drift towards the men and a young boy burst into the tent he's voice flushed the sweat drops shinning on he's brow.

The first thing that Samuel notices when David enters the tent is he's ruddy youthful complexion. David looks nervously at he's father.

"I am sorry father; if I had known that I had to attend..." Jesse raise he's hand and David looks from he's father to the prophet. While Samuel studies the young man he silently prays.

"Is he the one Lord?" Samuel continues to study the youth waiting on the Lord. He surely has handsome features. A tanned sanguine skin and clear alert eyes. David heart is beating wildly. Samuel is looking at him very intently without saying a word. He had never seen the prophet but everyone knows that Samuel was Yahweh anointed prophet.

Why was he staring at him like that? Eliab clears he's throat and David had almost not noticed he's brothers. The prophet lips move silently and still he stares at him. The voice of the Lord speaks into Samuels's heart.

"Samuel; rise and anoint him; he is the one" David watches as the prophet takes a horn from a sheep fleece and stares wide eyed as Samuel approaches him.

"David, son of Jesse. He dares not move as the prophet approaches him but feels like the earth is moving under he's feet. "Blessed is the name of the Lord our Yahweh."

Samuel takes the heifer with oil and pours it over David's head. "With this oil I bless you in the name of Yahweh Almighty. The Lord has chosen you to be the new king over Israel."

There is loud gasps and noises uttered of shock from David's brothers and the elders in the tent. Samuel holds up he's hands and the commotion immediately quite down and the prophet of Yahweh continues without any further hesitation.

"The Lord will be with you always. He will guide you and strengthen you in the years to come. Do not let your young heart be troubled for the Lord has a perfect plan for you. Amen"

There is now a stunned silence and although the oil burns David's eyes he had not moved or said anything. The silence is broken by Jesse. "Blessed is the name of the Lord Yahweh Almighty!" May he's will be done!" He's father hands grasp he's shoulders and he's face is smothered in Jesse's tunic by he's embrace.

Samuel turns towards David's silent stricken brothers. "I need to speak to your father and the rest of the elders. Help prepare the lamb. We shall give the sacrifice to the Lord after." The sons of Jesse move towards the tethered lamb and David starts to move in a dream like state following he's brothers.

"Wait David. I want you to stay and listen." Samuel takes he's seat on silk pillows that has been brought by some of the town women facing David, Jesse and the elders. "All the rumours that you have heard is true. Saul was rejected by the Lord as king." Ahiman and Sheshai give a quick glance at one another.

"Jesse; the Lord has chosen David to be the new king of Israel." David stares intently at he's father seeking reassurance and guidance. The full weight of the prophet words had slowly started to sink in and he had never been so scared in he's entire life.

Jesse speaks he's mind with concern noticeable in he's voice. "What about King Saul? If all the rumours are true he will surely kill us all if he should know that David was anointed as king." Every time someone used the word king David heart leaps into he's throat. Samuel lays he's hand on David shoulder but directs he's answer to Jesse.

"Do not be troubled Jesse. Yahweh has rejected Saul as king and is establishing a new king! The journey will surely not be easy. Saul's heart has hardened against the words of the Lord but the Lord will guide your son in the years to come. David has nothing to fear for the Spirit of the Lord has come upon him. Speak to your sons and say none of this to anyone for the Lord shall reveal he's plan in He's own time." Jesse looks into the eyes of the prophet and sees the strength of the Lord.

"Come now let us offer sacrifice to the Lord and do not forget that the Yahweh of Abraham, Isaac and Jacob has chosen a new king today. The time will come when David shall reign as king over Israel."

The song carries through the green pastures. The gentle notes a marching elude to an army of ants scurrying around an anthill. The grazing sheep seems to be hypnotized by the shadows of the wispy clouds drifting by ever so slowly. The last notes of the song die away in the still breeze. David stretches himself out on he's back. The last few weeks had been very exciting and very confusing for the youngster.

Since Samuels anointing everything had changed. He's brothers were the worst and mocked him when they saw him. Just the other night when he had entered the sleeping quarters which he shares with Raddai and Ozem, he saw he's older brothers speaking softly to each other staring in he's direction and sniggering about something.

It was only later when he lay under he's sheep fleece that he had found out why the older brothers acted so apprehensive. He felt small feet scampering over he's back and jumped up in horror. He's two brothers smiled at him and Raddai winked at Ozem

"Is everything all right King David? Anything we can do for you?" They broke out into uncontrolled laughter when David saw the source of he's discomfort he quickly grabbed the sand lizard by its neck and threw it out of the room.

Although he's brothers acted normal around their father, David felt alone and uncertain. He looked forward to the late evenings when he returned from the grazing fields to spend time with he's father. Every night since the anointing they sat together by the by the fire under the desert sky.

He's father recited the teachings about Abraham, Jacob, Moses and Josef. He taught David about the commandments and the stubbornness of he's forefathers in the desert after Yahweh had freed them from Egypt. David had heard these stories a thousand times and more but he sat under the starry desert skies and drank in every word that Jesse spoke. The fire and shadows played tricks on he's eyes and made he's father beard look like a great ball of fire which gave more emphasis on every word that Jesse spoke and everyone listened quietly.

He sat wide eyed as Jesse once again told him about Samson strength and he's final moments when he had crushed the pillars in the temple when he was blind and Yahweh had returned he's power once more. Jesse would always remind them that Yahweh has a perfect plan for he's people. David had found comfort when he heard the story of Moses again. How the Lord had interposed for the pharaohs daughter take care of him for a time. The Lord had watched over Moses to lead he's people out of Egypt's slavery.

The fire cast shadows over Jesse face as he spoke. "Moses was eighty years old when Yahweh appeared to him in a flame of fire in a bush in the wilderness of Mount Sinai." Jesse had paused and looked at he's audience with he's hands raised high above he's head to illustrate the burning bush. "Only after Yahweh had to convince Moses did he go to do Yahweh's biding.

The Lord had kept Moses from harm and he led Israel out of Egypt out of captivity and slavery."

Jesse reminded David that Israel had not listened to the voice of Yahweh and worshiped Idols and that was the reason why they had stayed in the wilderness for forty years.

"The Lord did not turn he's back on Israel! No, He had a plan with us and still has a plan today!" He's father had stopped again and looked directly at him "Yahweh's plan was always to anoint you as king of Israel. It is part of He's perfection as the Creator of all."

David found comfort in these words but the word "king" still weighed heavy on he's heart. If only he could talk to one of he's friends. Elika had fallen ill with serious stomach cramps and could not accompany David to the Southern slopes.

He's father had forbidden him to talk with anyone about the anointment. On the day of the anointing Samuel had told him that the Spirit of Yahweh was upon him. He had told David how Yahweh spoke to him and that he could talk with the Lord whenever he wanted to. He encouraged David to talk to Yahweh and he had found this difficult. How could he talk to the unseen creator of heaven and earth?! Instead he started to sing he's songs to the Lord.

He had been playing the Lyre since he was a small boy. He's mother had taught him lyrics but playing the Lyre came naturally to him.

The bleating sheep brings him out of he's dreams and he stares at the drifting clouds he's fingers draw softly over the strings of the instrument. The sound and the words carries over the grazing flock.

"Yahweh, who may dwell in your sanctuary? Who shall live on your holy hill? He who walks blamelessly and does what is right, and speaks truth in he's heart; He who doesn't slander with he's tongue, nor does evil to he's friend, nor cast slurs against he's fellow man.

In whose eyes a vile man is despised but who honors those who fear Yahweh; he who keeps an oath even when it hurts, and doesn't change; he who doesn't lend out he's money for usury, nor take a bribe against the innocent. He who does these things shall never be shaken." (Psalm 15)

David closes he's eyes and listens to the wind blowing through the grasslands. The combination of the late afternoon breeze and the far - off bleating of the grazing sheep lull's him into a gentle sleep.

"David. Wake up David" David sits up groggily. Who woke him? The wind had picked up twisting the grass in all directions. In the distance a small whirlwind can be seen blowing at the bottom of the plain. There might be a storm brooding and even the sheep seem restless. The voice had sounded so clear or was he just imagining things? The sheep on the far slope start to mill around restively.

David stares at the swaying grasses the wind playing tricks on he's eyes. A sudden movement to he's left catches the corner of David eye and a yellow blur runs into the flock scattering the sheep in all directions.

A lion! David grabs he's staff and start running towards the now panic stricken animals. The brute has singled out a lamb and fells it down nearby an old fallen tree. David runs towards the Lion the wind blowing through he's hair; he's staff raised above he's right shoulder. He jumps onto the fallen log and a battle cry erupts instinctively from he's lips and then with a great leap he jumps directly at the lion.

For a brief moment that seems forever they lock eyes and yellow malicious eyes burns into he's own and another battle cry erupts from the youth lips as he sails through the air. The sudden direct attack had caught the lion off-guard and the predator lays low with the lamb caught in he's massive front paws. David swings he's staff with all he's might striking the predator over the head.

The lion roars in anger and pain. The smell of the human fills he's nostrils and hate burns fiercely in he's mind. He had encountered many humans before and they had thrown him with rocks and sticks but as he grew older he had learned to be more cunning and mostly people run away.

The lion had quickly recovered from he's attack leaving the struggling lamb. The lamb comes back onto its feet and bleats loudly. With very unsteady legs it runs back towards the herd and its calling mother.

David does not take more time to scrutinize and see if the lamb reaches the flock. The lion roars in defiance its tail flicking from side to side. The great mane of the lion blows slightly in the wind and now that the predator is facing him, David sees that he had mistaken the size of the brute.

It is enormous! The lion roars again and the smell of rotting meat and decay hits David in the face the stench almost unbearable. David sees the tail of the Lion straighten a sure sign that it is going to attack and he quickly dives to he's left quickly rolling to he's feet again. The animal had leapt its maw exposed and it misses him by a few inches. David turns and quickly jumps over a fallen log.

He had bought himself only a little time. He nimbly moves around the fallen tree forcing the lion to either come around the side of the fallen log or jump over it. The lion chooses the later and David uses the fallen tree as a shield. David feels the great body of the brute brushing against he's back and the lion front claws rips into he's tunic.

The lion starts mauling the torn piece not realizing that it is only a part of he's clothing. David uses the opportunity and without thinking jumps onto the lions back grabbing the great brute by the mane. The lion rolls onto he's back trying to dislodge the youth and they go down struggling in the grassland. David holds onto the mane with all he's strength but the sheer power of the animal crushes him as it rolls onto he's back driving all the wind from he's lungs.

Dust hangs thick in the air and David gulps for fresh air. The lions struggle becomes even fiercer and in a move trying to dislodge him; the lions head hits him squarely on he's nose. The blow on he's nose causes tears to stream from he's eyes and he blinks rapidly trying to clear the tears from he's eyes.

David can barely hold onto the lion but instinctively he keeps he's fingers locked into the great mane knowing that if he lets go he would surely be mauled by those great paws. He feels he's strength failing. The beast surges upright onto its hind quarters and David feels he's fingers slipping. As he falls to the ground he calls out.

"Yahweh help me!" David hits the ground hard and he waits for claws of the lion to tear into he's body. A blinding light fills he's eyes and David holds up he's hands shielding he's eyes from the brightness. The light drives David to he's knees and the roars of the beast increases close by. David tries to focus he's eyes in the direction of the roaring lion but the light burns into he's eyes and he closes them again tightly.

What was happening? Where did the blinding light come from? Why didn't the lion attack him? David feels a great warmth spreading through he's body and suddenly a great surge of energy engulfs he's whole being. The fear and anxiety that David had felt moments ago disappears and is replaced with a burning fire inside that fills all he's sense. As the warmth continue to surge through him he can feel he's arms, chest and legs filled with new surge of power.

Just as sudden as the bright light had engulfed him it disappears. Although it felt like an eternity it had happened in a matter of seconds. David's whole body is tingling and he's vision had cleared perfectly. The lion stands but a few feet away from him bunched up in a coil of muscle ready to pounce. David does not have much time to wonder why the lion had not attacked him. It comes at him with great ferocity. David has no time to move from the spot and the force in which the predator hits him is astounding!

He falls onto he's back the creature on top of him. The fetid breath is nauseating and saliva drips onto the youths face. The surge of energy increases and he's whole body burns with it .Clarity had filled he's thoughts and without hesitating David grabs the brute on the lower part of its jaw pushing the face away from he's without too much effort! He grabs onto the Mane again and with one foot he pushes into the predators belly using he's momentum he rolls onto he's back throwing the lion over he's head. The creature twists through the air landing a few yards away from him.

David gets back onto he's feet and with a great battle cry he attacks the lion drawing he's shearing knife that he's father had given him from its scabbard. This time it is the lion that has no time to recover and in its surprise the lion rears on its hind legs clawing at the attacker with those powerful front claws. David ducks under one swinging paw and grabs onto the other front leg. The lion struggles but David holds the lion with an iron grip.

He instinctively surges forward with he's shearing knife driving the weapon in below the ribcage of the animal. It is a mighty blow and Lion roars and tries to claw at its attacker but David keeps striking the lion again and again. He feels the sticky substance of the creature over he's arms. The lion hind legs buckle and he's roars are mixed with the sounds of he's own blood filling its lungs. In a final attempt the brute tries to bite down onto David head but it is a feeble attempt and David pushes the lion back with he's shoulder.

The lion falls in the dust and tries to get back onto he's legs but it is a failed attempt. Its legs folds under him and then it gives its final spastic kick and a gurgling roar before its ceases all movement. Warm blood drips from David's brow into he's left eye and he fingers a gash just above he's eye. The tingling surge of energy start to leave he's body and David feels he's muscles relaxing the tingling feeling disappearing. The torn tunic hangs loose around he's frame and he suddenly feels very tired. He's legs buckle under him and he sits on the grass staring at the carcass of the slain predator the dark blood turning the grass into a crimson pool around the fallen creature.

He had called out to Yahweh and miraculously the Lord had given him strength to battle the lion. The familiar story about Samson and the power which Yahweh gave him comes to he's mind as he lies in the grass. The sheep had gathered closer to him staring wide eyed and smelling the air.

"Thank you Lord; for protecting me. I will sing your praises forever and ever." The wind softly blows against he's skin cooling the sweat on he's body. "My right hand has covered you and when you call on me I will answer."

The voice speaks into the heart of David and he closes he's eye lifting he's hands to the heavens.

Chapter 3

The banks of the Jordan River lies thick with mist on the dark murky waters. He knows that it is somewhere out there. All seem so familiar. Somehow he knows that this time there will be no escape. The reeds on the far side of the bank start to move.

It's coming! The water ripples and he has a glimpse of the huge scaly tail. He stands frozen unable to move he's feet. The full moon breaks through the cloudy skies illuminating the horror through the thick rolling mist. It leaves the water edge and he hears the scraping of the beast belly on the wet sand. He tries to run but he's feet are laden by the terror that has gripped him, gnawing talons of fear ripping through he's stomach. The green evil eyes shine through the mist. It comes quickly mouth agape, rows and rows of long filed teeth showing. Its long mouth closes around he's leg and he screams in horror.

"King Saul! Wake up! Wake up!" Saul tries to free himself from the sweat drenched entangled sheets around he's legs. He looks around he's eyes still filled with wild terror. It takes another few seconds before he realizes that he is back in the palace in he's own chambers.

Saul blindly points into a direction. "Gaza; light those lanterns! The stocky servant obeys quickly. "Was it another nightmare your highness?" Mustapha cautiously addresses the king. In the last two quarters he and the other servants had been woken by the terrified screams of their king almost every night. "Don't talk to me about nightmares!

The potion which you gave me was too strong! I cannot awake from this deep sleep! I can still feel those teeth bite into me!" The stocky servant standing at the back of the chamber looks even more horrified than their king. He dreaded coming to the kings chambers at night. Their king had been acting very strangely in the past few months. During the day he had terrible anger outbursts and at night screams of dread filled the king's chambers, dark dreams haunting him. Some servants had fled the palace with dire consequences for the kings guards had brought them back to the palace and they were flogged until their bodies hang lifeless outside the city walls for others to see.

The king's wrath was something no one wanted to face and the word disloyalty and execution was softly spoken among them. Some say that a fluke had come upon the kingdom and others had said that Yahweh had sent an evil spirit to torment the king. Mustapha gives a look at the shivering Gaza standing close by. Something should be done. How long must they all suffer this evil? They had been administering a dosage of herbs to the king every night to try and calm him down and make him sleep without having any disturbing dreams. He had instructed the apostasy to increase the dosage but still the nightmares came.

He approaches the king very wearily. The face of the boy had continuously come into he's mind since he had heard him play he's Lyre at the feast. He had thought long about the proposal which he was about to talk to King Saul about. Every time when the king went into a mad rage he dismissed the idea thinking about how Saul would react to it. An image of the boy's face enters he's mind and once more the sweet music that had such a calming effect on all. It seemed like he could not get the boy out of he's head and somehow he knew that he had to make he's suggestion now.

He glances at he's king seeing a haunted madness in he's eyes. He had decided. The mixed herbs where not helping and he started to fear for he's life.

"My lord, I have found a suitable replacement for Rimah." Saul's frown increases on he's forehead. Rimah was Saul's stable boy but was one of the servants that had fled the palace because of Saul's rage. He was one of the servants that was not captured by the king's soldiers and Mustapha knew it was a sensitive subject. Mustapha continues wearily folding the linen neatly around the king's bed.

"My wife's sister invited me to the harvest feast last week and I saw a very talented man that played the Lyre." Saul stares out into the morning gloom and Mustapha quickly pushes he's advantage. "My sister had said that he's music was like nothing you have ever heard before and when I heard it I must admit that she was right. Saul says nothing. Since the day that Samuel had announced Yahweh's rejection everything had started to change for the worse. The harvest was poor. The enemy kept invading the borders.

Abner; he's General of the Army of Israel had warned Saul that the Philistines where gathering their forces. Mustapha's voice drones into he's subconscious and he only catches the last words spoken. "He killed a lion and the Lord is with him." The words cuts like a sword into Saul heart. He raises from he's bed and stares at Mustapha. He can see the servant trembling.

Saul thinks about the proposal and then gives a tired nod at Mustapha "Yes, get the Lyrist and make sure you show him he's duties and call Abner, I need to talk with him."

Mirages playing on the distant horizon are proof of the ever increasing heat and David closes the Turban tightly around he's head. He takes a swig from the water skin and stares of into the distance. He was walking at a steady pace and was accustomed to traveling through the rugged landscape. The pack on he's back had a balanced weight. He had a lot of time to think about the task that lay ahead in Bethlehem in the service of the king. Every step that he took towards he's destiny to Bethlehem weighed with uncertainties.

He's conversation with he's father the night before he left felt surreal and the comfort he found in he's father words was now gone. He's mind wonders back to the last days spend with he's father and the flock after the anointing by the prophet Samuel. It all had happened so quickly and he had diligently continued with he's daily chores. During the day times with the flock he could almost forget the anointing but was reminded by he's brothers taunting around the campfire meal of the reality and uncertainties that played in he's mind. Time continued to pass by and even he's brothers seemed like they were tired of the jest and jeers and he's life had almost felt normal again. Almost. All that had changed the day when the royal caravan of Saul arrived at their dwelling.

Fear had taken hold of him when he saw the caravan of camels and the royal colors of the Kings soldiers whom accompanied the messenger. At first he had thought that somehow the king had found out about the anointing and came to kill him. He hid away and saw an old man with a sun weathered face and white turban go into the tent and spoke to Jesse for a long time. He's father servants came and watered the horses and camels of the king men. David remained in he's hiding place.

A mountain of questions and considerations played through he's mind and he waited impatiently as the afternoon shadows drew longer. The sun began to set and David rubbed he's tired eyes. He thought that the meeting will never end and he was about to draw another faceless picture in the desert sand when the messenger and Jesse came out of the tent.

Without any further delay the royal caravan left as they came that morning. Soon the dust cloud disappeared and the manure from the camels and stallions were the only trace left behind and conviction that they were even there.

Jesse walked out towards the cooking fires without looking into David's direction and sat down at the place where he sat every evening while the servant prepared the meal. He's father stared into the fire and without looking into he's direction he had called to him.

David eagerly ran to he's father side stumbling over he's own feet. He sat down close to he's father but Jesse did not say another word and continued to stare into the dancing flames of the cooking fire. David knew much better than to ask he's father about the visit and he had to wait patiently for he's father to speak. He's father requested him to put more wood onto the fire and he obeyed without a word although he's mind screamed in anticipation. The shadows around the fire danced and leaped as the flames grew higher. The servants had taken the broth that they prepared form the increasing heat and the ceramic pot summered on a few coals that was scraped aside nearby. In the distance the sound of Guinea fowl finding a roosting spot carries to the men. Jesse clears he's throat and David eagerly looks up at he's father knowing that the drawn silence had come to an end.

"The king has called on you to be a servant at he's palace." David gradually inhales. "Why would he suddenly call on me father? Did he find out about the anointing? What if he wants to kill me?"

Jesse holds up he's hand to stop the rush of words and smiles warmly at he's son "Do not be afraid David for the Lord will never fail you or forsake you. The Lord has gone before you. You were seen and heard by the kings head servant Mustapha playing the Lyre at the harvest last quarter. According to Mustapha they are in need of a new musician for the royal courts and also for the king personal courts. "

David starts to talk again but Jesse gently stops he's son holding up he's hand again. "Remember when Josef was led away as a slave and was taken into the service of Potiphar? He was wrongfully accused of an act which he never committed. Was it not he's own master lustful wife whom made sure he ended up in jail or did God will it? He spent many years in jail and only at the time when the Lord had ordained was he taken from jail.

David intently listens to Jesse as he continues. "The Lord had prepared him in jail for the next part of he's life which Josef served at the right hand position of the pharoah of the land. Yahweh had a special purpose for him and all the things that happened were for a higher purpose for us as Yahweh's people. Many years after he was sold as a slave, Josef family and the rest of the tribe of Israel was looked after in times of great famine. Yahweh had planned all of this to happen and he used Josef in He's plan. Josef was humble and listened to the Lord even in he's times of he's hardship."

David stares deep into he's father eyes the uncertainties somewhat fading from he's mind. Jesse lays he's hands on he's son shoulders. "The Lord has a perfect plan for you. There is a reason why you are called into the king Saul service. You must still honor King Saul for he was also anointed by the hand of the Lord. This is the beginning of your journey.

Walk humbly with Yahweh my son and He will show you the way" David relaxed and stretched out he's legs; the heat of the fire and the voice of he's father lulling him. That was the last evening that he had spent with he's father and the next day he had packed a few belongings. He took the things which he thought may be of use to him. He's most precious belongings he folded neatly into the folds of a new sheep skin. He took he's Lyre, he's sling and written parchments which Jesse had written the laws of Yahweh on. He carefully placed the parchments into the folds of the skin and placed the pack on he's back.

The messenger of the king made it clear that he's main duty would be to entertain the king's royal court with he's Lyre. He's father and brothers waited outside to see him depart.

He kept he's back straight and shoulders up as he greeted he's brothers not showing any of the feelings which was swirling like a desert wind through he's mind. He's father had hugged him fiercely and then he had determinedly started off towards Gibeah looking back once waving at he's father. He did not want to let anyone see the tears in he's eyes and only after he was sure that they could not see him anymore did he stop. For a moment he stood like that staring into the shimmering heat and then he closed he's eyes calling out softly. "Yahweh." He opened he's eyes and then determinedly continued towards Gibeah.

The sun was now at its warmest as he steadily made he's way through the land. He took he's Lyre and played softly he's fingers brushing over the strings. He had played the Lyre in many festivals and he's mother had always said that he had the natural talent for the instrument. Even Miriak complimented him when he played. The thoughts of Miriak made him change he's song again. Miriak is Ahiman's daughter and he had hoped to accompany her to the next desert feast.

The images of the dark haired girl plays in he's mind but is once again replace by thoughts of King Saul and the uncertainties that lay ahead.

The sun started to draw long shadows across the dunes and David decides to make camp before the night falls. He would reach Gibeah in the morning if he continued at he's steady pace. He starts to prepare he's camp for the night by collecting dry wood. The familiar sounds of the coming night fall becomes he's companion blocking out the thoughts of Gibeah and the task that lay ahead. How many times did he not sleep at the side of the sheep folds when he had taken to the slopes? He lay's on he's back drawing warmth from the fire he had made and stares up at the magnificent starry skies.

The lonely sound of a jackal carries far into the desert night and David's yawns putting he's arms behind he's head. He closes he's eyes listening to the crackling sound of the fire and silently prays. "Yahweh please guide me and show me your ways in the new day to come. Thank you for this day's bread."

The dancing candle light flickers against the walls in the council room conjuring untold stories for the wild imagination of the poets and writers. Saul walks restlessly he's eyes searching the unknown.

"Where is Gaza? Did the fool have to swim across the Nile to get me some wine?" Mustapha looks at David. He had warned the boy that the king was in a foul mood. The youth looks calm under the king's outburst. The new white robe they had provided him sits well on he's trimmed sun tanned dark frame. The boy had arrived the previous afternoon and Mustapha was surprised that he was still so young and yet there was something in those green eyes. It was a hidden knowledge and strength.

Mustapha quickly learned that an enthusiastic bright mind hidden behind the youthful appearance. Mustapha was not the only one that took note of David appearance and since the first day that he had spent in the kingdom there was talk about the young musician. The king had been restless the whole day and at the feasting table that afternoon he had requested the services of the acquired musician to come and play after the war council that evening. Mustapha had prepared David the rest of the afternoon and many eyes were on the youth as they made their way to the council chambers. Even Saul took note of David when he entered he's the room because he stopped he's pacing for a moment and stared at the youth and then without a word continued he's pacing. He continued like this for perhaps another hundred breaths and then without a word he sat down on the big satin pillows.

The candle light seems to add more years to the worried face of Saul and no one spoke. The sound of footsteps becomes louder coming down the passage and suddenly a thin bearded servant hurriedly enters the room with a big clay jar that seems to weigh him down.

"Well don't just stand there looking at me! Pour me some wine before you have to go and harvest another vine yard for a jar like that!" Gaza nervously pours a cup for the king and with he's hands shanking. "I apologize for taking so long my king but…" Saul holds up he's hand abruptly ending Gaza's apology. He takes the wine from the shaking servant and irritably waves him away with the other hand. He takes a big sip from the clay cup and lies back onto the pillows. When he addresses Mustapha he's tone sounds much calmer as he stares out of he's window he's words almost inaudible.

"The boy can now entertain me with he's instrument." Saul closes he's eyes thinking about he's general word in the council that afternoon. Abner had forewarned him that the Philistines where breaching the borders of Soco.

A breeze blows into the chambers and the soft touch of the desert wind accompanies the cords of the Lyre filling the chamber as David softly starts to play. The notes flow softly into the spaces of the chamber as he touches the strings. The familiar song tells the story of Moses found by the beautiful Pharaoh's daughter bathing in the Nile. The room seems to be filled by a sweet cinnamon smell, an interlude to this ebullient symphony and Saul's eyelids starts to flutter like the wings of a butterfly. Not one of the servants had moved since David started playing. The music has now grown to a strong burst of notes; the song reaching its crescendo as it explains Yahweh's wrath against the Egyptians. The song draws to an end the sweet melody reminding them all of the promises Yahweh made to he's people.

Mustapha slowly walks towards the door the rest of the servants following he's lead. The last notes ripples through the break of dawn and then dies away. The soft breathing of the king is the only sound left in the room as David exits from the king's war chamber. Mustapha slowly closes the door he's eyes not leaving the frame of he's king. The king had not rested like this in many moons and Mustapha stares at David as seeing him for the first time.

There was something about the boy. When he had started to play the Lyre the room was filled with a presence that every servant had felt and Mustapha knew that it had nothing to do with the music. All of them walked towards the kitchen and the servants murmuring grow into enthusiastic chatter as the progress further away from the king chamber. Some of the servants undisguisedly kept staring at David.

They join the rest of the servants preparing the daily meals and Mustapha orders them to continue their chores. Mustapha pats David on he's shoulder and sits across him slowly shaking he's head. "I have heard before that you could play the Lyre and yet what I heard tonight could not have prepared my ears in a thousand years."

David smiles shyly at Mustapha. "My mother taught me. She died when I was a little boy. Playing the Lyre reminds me of a time when we use to spend our time together as a family. My mother then use to play the Lyre and my father told wonderful stories of Yahweh." It was the first time that Mustapha had heard David speak about Yahweh. He had said the name of Yahweh with so much conviction and fear that the old man was at a loss of words for a short while. What had happened in the king chamber? The old man shakes he's head and he calls one of the servants to he's bidding nodding at David. "You must be starving. Let us sit and have something to eat and then you can tell me more about your family and the stories of Yahweh."

The next morning when David wakes up he feels disorientated. He's first thoughts are to jump from he's bed to start he's morning chores but the soft feel of the silk covers quickly reminds him that he is not at home. He lay's with he's eyes closed listening to the sounds of the palace in the morning hours. Now and again he can hear the servants passing he's room going about their normal duties.

Mustapha had kept him awake until the early morning hours. They had talked about many things and Mustapha had shared he's life story and he's journey in the king service. The candles had started to burn low and Mustapha had stretched and yawned. "We had better go to sleep, tomorrow... I mean today is going to be a busy day."

David was not sure what time it was. He had no idea what other chores he had to perform except to play he's Lyre to King Saul. He hears the sound of approaching footsteps outside he's room followed by a soft rapping on he's bedroom door.

"David? David are you awake?" David rolls from he's bed slipping the sandals onto he's feet. "Uuhhmm yes Mustapha you may enter." Mustapha looks at the youth hiding he's smile. David had quickly found favour with him and he was easy to talk to. He was such a bright young man and maybe he reminded Mustapha of himself when he was but a young man.

The servants had also quickly spread the news that Saul fell instantly asleep after the young shepherd boy played he's Lyre. For those who did not hear the news the previous day quickly heard this because of the servant Gaza loose tongue who spread the story as quickly as the plagues of Egypt. Mustapha was even more surprised that when King Saul had woken up after he's slumber he was in a joyful mood and he spend most of he's early mornings in the gardens before he departed to meet with he's war council. To Mustapha it seemed that the boy was a blessing that he had prayed for and the king seemed more at peace that no one had witnessed in many moons that had passed. David yawns and stretches

"Have I been summoned by the king?" Mustapha ruffles he's hear. "No lad, today the king will be busy with he's war council. It seems that war with the Philistines is inevitable. Let's talk of things less worrying." Mustapha pulls a silk curtain aside sunlight streaming into the room.

The afternoon sun shone brightly and David feels ashamed that he had slept so long. Mustapha seem not notice the boy discomfort and turns to David with a sparkle in he's eyes. "I have come to accompany you to the eastern gardens." He pulls aside the other curtain and continues.

"Jonathan; the kings son have returned with he's army and have requested you to dine with him." David looks at Mustapha with a frown. "Why would he want to dine with me?" The old servant leans against the window sill.

"He is a bit older than you and is also a hunter and a captain in the king army. The two of you have much more in common I realized after our conversation last night." Mustapha winks at David and smiles.

The story that the boy had told him about the lion that he killed and the strange covering power that he had felt during this had intrigued the old man. Mustapha had quietly listened to the whole story and the boy did not sound pompous as he gave account of the battle with the ferocious beast. The old man had felt goose bumps and he's forearms and the prickling feeling at the back of he's neck as David story unfolded.

When Jonathan had arrived early in the morning they had sat together and as always Mustapha gave account of the events that had passed in the young man absence. The king son had seemed much more interested in the news of the new servant and Mustapha had though as much because the word had spread about the young shepherd. Jonathan was quite intrigued by the story of the boy that played the Lyre to he's father and yet was not afraid to kill a lion. Before he had gone to he's chambers he had instructed Mustapha to send the boy to eat with him later in the afternoon.

Mustapha stares intently at the boy as he washes he's face in the scented basin. It was not clear to him yet but he had an inner feeling that there was much more to the arrival of the boy than he or anyone else anticipated. He knew the words that Samuel had spoken over king Saul was already in motion and he wanted to believe that Yahweh would not let them perish but a change would be brought to the kingdom.

The slight breeze tugs gently at the red silk curtains fashioned to keep the sun rays from the veranda. A large oak table is set in the middle of the room and a bronze tray piled with colourful fruit set upon it gleams as the sunlight reflects from it. David attention is drawn to two young servant girls standing at the corner of the table each with their eyes cast down. The sunlight reflects from the tray and plays tricks on David eyes. He walks across to the table and only notices the young man standing at the far end of the veranda overlooking the city when he sits down at the table.

He quickly jumps up again but in the process bumps the wooden table spilling the fruit in the tray. The two servant girls quietly start to pick up the fruit and David runs after a large orange that seems to be finding its way straight to the young man. The man stops the rolling fruit with he's sandal and David quickly stands up from the floor. The man reaches down and picks up the fruit holding it out to David. The first thing David notices about the man is he's wide shoulders with thick dark curly hair coming down he's back. He has golden earrings in both he's ears and before David can say anything the silence in the room is broken as Mustapha clears he's throat.

"My lord. Your father has requested you to join him in he's counsel after breakfast." The smile on the youth lips reflects in he's golden eyes as he turns towards Mustapha clasping he's hands together.

"Ah! Mustapha you old goat! It seems that in my tired state this morning I did not take note of all the changes in the palace."

David stands awkwardly but Jonathan continues. "I see that you have yet again gained a few pounds! It must be the cooking of that last wife you took."

Mustapha almost seem embarrassed by the prince's forwardness but replies with a twinkle in he's eye. "She is a fine cook among other things your majesty"

Jonathan grasp the old man fondly on he's shoulders. "Please make sure that the horses are ready for this afternoon ride. We will take the high route and will be away for a day or two."

Jonathan had turned away from them again staring out into the desert. Mustapha bows and leaves the veranda winking at David. "It has already been arranged my Lord."

David stands quietly staring at the freshly arranged pile of fruit on the tray and almost jumps in surprise when Jonathan address him. "Desert Lions."

David looks at Jonathan with he's eyebrows raised he's confusion clearly showing. "Excuse me your highness?" Jonathan laughter booms out the earrings shaking on the sides of he's shaggy head. "Just call me Jonathan, that is what most of my friends call me."

He turns he's big frame towards the plate of fruit and takes a golden pear from the tray. "Please come and sit with me." A piece of pear is stuck on the side of Jonathan beard and he wipes it with he's back of he's hand the juices glistening in the afternoon sun.

"Desert Lions." This time Jonathan explains he's statement. "I am referring to the hunt. We have been after these brutes for some time now. Sly ruthless animals! They have been pestering the royal herds in the eastern slopes and it was reported last night that some animals were killed again in the valley."

Jonathan summons one of the servant girls holding a clay jug. "You cannot go after one of these monsters without building some strength." David takes an apple from the tray and unconsciously he starts to rub the fruit against he's tunic. The servant girl also fills up he's clay jug.

He takes a sip of his cup and tastes the berries mixed with honey leaving a sweet after taste in the back of he's throat. He was taken completely off-guard when Jonathan spoke of hunting lions. He's temperament for adventure and danger had brought a sense of excitement and he completely forgot that he was dining with King Saul's son. "What is your plan for hunting these killers?" Jonathan studies the young man before him and bites deeply into the pear answering with a mouth full. "Killing it will not be that easy. My men have dug a pit to capture the animal. We will lure it with a freshly killed goat. I have instructed them to rip its bowels out for a nice fresh stench!" The years in the kingdom with he's father had taught Jonathan many things. Especially about the men that served he's father and he became a good judge of character. Now as he surveys the youth with the intelligent green eyes he cannot help but to feel an unexplained sense of mystery and yet intriguing hunger to get to know the young man before him. When he had returned with he's war party in the early morning he had not looked forward to tell he's father about the advancing Philistines. He was surprised that he's father did not burst out in anger and had only instructed him to call on Mustapha and then had advised him to get some rest. Later that morning he had learned from Mustapha of David's arrival and the old servant had explained that after David's recital in the war room Saul had seemed much calmer and had slept without any nightmares. Mustapha had also told him that David was a man of Yahweh. This was not a big surprise to Jonathan. Was

Yahweh still with them? He's father had sinned against Yahweh and now they were punished. He had tried to speak to he's father but he's father had a lot of resentment towards Yahweh. Even the prophet Samuel had not visited them after he's announcement that Yahweh would not have Saul as king anymore. Since that day Saul became very paranoid, thinking that any person might be a threat to him as king. Jonathan had prayed that Yahweh would show them the way. Somehow this young man might be the answer to he's prayers. A tall servant enters onto the veranda. "Sir. King Saul is waiting for you with the generals in the war chambers." Jonathan waves the man away with he's hand a bunch of red grapes in the other. "I am on my way." He finishes the grapes and gets up from the table. One servant girl hands him a cloth that she took from a scented basin. Jonathan wipes he's face and hands with cloth and turns towards David. "Well then I will see you later this afternoon. Make sure that you get some riding shoes from the stable boy's. The rest of our gear will be packed and we will set off just before noon." David gets up from he's chair a big smile on he's face. "We shall go and Yahweh will be with us. Jonathan is somewhat surprised about David assertiveness in he's statement but with a bright smile on he's bearded face he turns towards the hall entrance, whistling a tuneless song.

David had accompanied Mustapha and for the remainder of the afternoon getting all the equipment and supplies ready for the hunt. David's mind was pre-occupied and he thought about he's conversation with Jonathan. He had found an instant liking in the older youth. Although the two of them only had a brief conversation before being interrupted by the servant David knew that he had find connection with Jonathan. Maybe it was a connection of kindred spirit or wild adventurous hearts beating wildly for the excitement for the hunt that lay ahead. He felt a sense of longing for the fresh desert air and the open grazing fields and he was looking forward to get out of the palace. The rest of the afternoon seems to pass too slowly for David. He went down to the royal stables and the boy's supplied him with the fitting riding shoes as Jonathan had advised. He was given a copper brush to tend to the thick black mane of a horse. Jonathan had instructed the boys to prepare this specific mount for him. The animal snorted when David approached shaking its black mane. The muscles on the animal's chest stood out from under its dark bay color. "He's name is Desert Wind." A stable boy which had been busy sweeping one of the stalls walk up to him and leans against the wooden door of another empty pin. "He is one of the kings generals horses and he earned he's name because of he's stamina and he is difficult to see at night." The horse seems to listen to the boy's voice snorting softly and shakings its head. "If he is one of the armies horses why then was he given to me to ride on this expedition?" The boy slowly starts to sweep the floor again and speaks in a more serious tone. "The last general that rode him was killed in battle against the Philistines." He stops and looks back at the steed. "He will not be here for long. My father says the king has been with he's war council and I am sure that someone will take him out into battle again soon." David slowly stretches he's hand out to the steed and talks to him in soft mono tones. The intelligent brown eyes survey him cautiously and he's ears are pointed straight ahead as David continues to speak to him. He slowly rubs the muzzle of the horse and the big animal snorts softly taking in the scent of the young man. The steed seems to relax and David slowly starts brushing the thick mane with he's other hand while continuing to talk to him stroking he's muzzle. The smell of the horse reminds David of times when he's father came to the slopes when he tended the herds. Many times in the early morning hours they would see harras of desert horses roaming the desert plains. They ran freely and with courage an unsung saga of beasts that have survived the harsh desert environment and the hand of the Creator that looked after them. He softly hums a psalm as he continues to brush the steed. Early noon David went back to the palace and sat with Mustapha.

The sun slowly started too decent on the western slopes and David made he's way back to the palace and met with Mustapha in the kitchen. The old servant told him about the battles that Jonathan had fought with Saul against the Philistines. He told him about the victories that Jonathan had accomplished over the Philistine armies and that the Yahweh of Israel had kept he's hand over the young prince. The time seemed to pass quickly now and when the shadows had drawn out across the desert sand one of the stable boy's came to call David to join Jonathan down at the royal stables. David almost knocked Mustapha over as he hurried down the passage way. The old servant shakes he's head and calls after David. "Remember what I said! Do not do anything irresponsible for if you do not return the king will have my head!" David reply comes echoing down the passage. "I will keep my head on my shoulders!"

They rode long after Orion made its appearance in the desert sky. At the edge of the Gilboa Mountain Jonathan calls out to the front men to setup camp for the night. Even after a long ride the men quickly unsaddle their horses and start to make the fires and prepare the camp. They have ridden with Jonathan many times and each had their duties.

"We have almost reached the area where the men have laid out the bait to lore the lion." Jonathan points to the distant edge of the rocky slopes. "We will have a very early start tomorrow morning, how are you keeping up in the saddle?"

David laughs heartedly at Jonathan stretching he's own legs and loosening he's pack from the back of he's saddle. "It is definitely faster than walking up the slopes after the flocks in Rama."

Jonathan takes he's pack from he's mare handing the reigns to a servant. "We must try and surprise them while they are feeding so we must get some rest." The servants had finished preparing their fire and Jonathan lies back against he's saddle looking into the flames. David stares into the fire feeling more at home than he had felt in the passing days. The heat of the fire spreads through he's limbs and he closes he's eyes enjoying the sounds of the desert night. There is an easy silence between him and Jonathan. The occasional call of a jackal with the crackling sound of the fire creates an atmosphere of its own and both youths are left with their thoughts. Jonathan breaks the silence and turns onto he's side facing David across the fire with he's head resting upon he's pack.

"Is there a special girl awaiting your arrival back at home?" David thinks about it for a while before he replies "There is this girl that I wanted to ask to this year's desert feast." Jonathan's laughter booms out into the desert night. "Why do you pull your face like that? It looks like you have bitten into a lemon. Tell me more! Do you love her?"

David laughs shyly. "I don't know, I have never thought about love. I do like her a lot. How about you? Is there anyone special?" Jonathan turns away from David onto he's back staring up at the stars. "Her name is Leola. She is the most beautiful creature this side of the Nile River. She is my father's most trusted war advisors daughter. I think I have always loved her." It is David's turn to jest with Jonathan. "Does she know about this acclaimed love?" Jonathan grunts. "What will she do with a fool like me? No; I have not said anything to her." David turns around taking he's Lyre from he's saddle. "Then my friend we are both fools!" David softly tests the notes of he's Lyre. The tones drift softly into the desert night accompanied by he's strong voice.

"Yahweh, our Lord, how majestic is your name in all the earth, who has set your glory above the heavens! From the lips of babes and infants you have established strength, because of your adversaries, that you might silence the enemy and the avenger. When I consider your heavens, the work of your fingers, the moon and the stars, which you have ordained; what is man that you think of him? What is the son of man that you care for him? For you have made him a little lower than Yahweh, and crowned him with glory and honor. You make him ruler over the works of your hands. You have put all things under he's feet: All sheep and cattle, yes, and the animals of the field. The birds of the sky, the fish of the sea, and whatever passes through the path of the seas. Yahweh, our Lord, how majestic is your name in all the earth!" (Psalm 8)

David sets down he's Lyre next to his saddle and rolls the sheep fleece into a bundle resting he's head upon it. Jonathan mumbles in a sleepy voice. "Mustapha was right. My father shall surly have he's head if something happens to you."

An eerie silence had crept along the ravine of the Gilboa Mountains. The men had stationed themselves on the sides of the rocky path that leads to the fresh carcass of a slaughtered sheep. For the past few weeks fresh bait had been laid out in the branches of an Olive tree that grew on the side of the rocky trail. When they had arrived at the mountain men came and reported that the two black manned lions came to feed readily each morning. The stench of the carcass hangs thick in the air.

David grips the javelin more firmly in he's hands. Except for the men's breathing and the occasional call of a desert Plover all is quite. Before they had taken up their positions Jonathan had laid out he's plan to them. The report was that the Lions came through the pass on the western side of the mountain. Jonathan stationed men on the on either side of the path on the western side as well as men on the eastern side near the carcass. The wind was in their favour. Jonathan's instruction was to wait until the beasts started to feed and then attack them.

David thought about he's last encounter with one of these beasts. He knew about the strength and the speed these ferocious animals had. Once during the wait he thought that the savages had arrived but it was a jackal drawn to the smell of the carcass. The small doglike creature could not reach the carcass raised in the tree and after a while it suddenly looked up sniffing the air and quickly disappeared. David left leg start to cramp and he slowly massages the tight knotted spot gritting he's teeth not making a noise. The pain start to lessen and he reaches to pick up the javelin.

He's breath catches in he's throat. Standing on the rock plate above Jonathan and two of his men at the Western entrance were one of the biggest lions David had ever seen. The silhouette of its massive black main seems to enlarge the brute and bright yellow eyes glare malevolently at the men standing below the rock. Afore David can cry out a warning the beast let's out one mighty roar. The men stand frozen, transfixed in horror. The lion attack's the men standing below the ledge. David runs from behind the rock screaming at the beast trying to get its attention.

Only Jonathan reacts quickly enough jumping into a cleft in the rock face. The cries of the first man dying mixed with another blood curling roar from the lion rips through the morning. It turns its massive jaws yet upon its second victim. Cries of pain mixed with the sound of bones crushing reaches the men's ears and two soldiers with David leave their javelins and run towards the eastern slope. David stumbles over the body of one of the fallen men that was with Jonathan. He cannot make out the face of the mutilated man lying in the grass but runs past the corpse. In the early grey colors of the morning David can see the beast still busy mauling the second soldier that had died.

David hears another blood curling roar and this time from the Eastern side of the slopes. The second lion! The fearful screams of the two soldiers that had left David side are cut of abruptly and without a doubt David knows that they have run into the second Lion. David has no time to think about the soldiers or the other beast because the big black manned Lions suddenly turn around with speed greater than the mind can process and eyes can grasp creating an image of dirty yellow blur in search for its next victim. The lions next target is a man crouched close to the ledge. It is Jonathan!

David calls out to the son of Saul and it almost seems like he is stricken with fear standing motionless. Jonathan waits until the lion is almost upon him and then he strikes out with he's javelin towards the charging creature. He catches the creature high in the chest and the lion crashes into him its momentum carrying both of them over the rocky ledge behind them.

David rushes towards the rocky ledge. For a moment he stands looking at the scene below trying to make out man from beast but the swirling dirt in the early morning rays makes it difficult. The whirling dust cloud passes by and for a moment the back of the animal shows clearly before it is engulfed with the next cloud of dust. David drops the javelin and pulls out the skinning blade that he had gotten from Jesse. "Yahweh give me strength!"

Without hesitation he jumps into the thick dust cloud where he had seen the creature only a few seconds ago landing on-to the back of the lion. The lions surprise is great as David lands on top of him, the weight of the man crushing into the beast. David draws advantage from his position as the stunned animal is still getting to grips with him lodged onto its back. David manage to take a good grip onto the Lions mane the skinning blade still in he's right hand. The lion lets out a throaty roar that mingles with a blood gurgling sound. Jonathan javelin attack must have a fatal outcome! David holds onto the mane of the angry beast and looks around searching franticly for the body of Jonathan but the dust blinds him and he sees no sign of the king son.

David suddenly becomes aware of a feeling welling up deep inside of him. He had last felt it when he defeated the lion while herding his father's sheep. Like a storm the great surge of power covers him and rushes through he's whole body. He's mind becomes composed. He had learned from he's first experience with the Lion. He knew that he should stay clear of its maw and massive paws. He holds onto the infuriating animal with a renewed strength.

The lion shakes its big frame trying in all its might to dislodge David from its back. The beast rears up on its hind legs shaking its massive figure but David holds on with he's renewed strength. The brute suddenly changes tactics and falls onto the ground rolling onto he's back trying to crush David but David pins he's legs under the tummy of the lion avoiding the raking back legs. The animal movement becomes less frantic and David slowly releases he's grip with he's right hand feeling he's way along the creature ribs. When he touches the soft centre part of the creature ribs just behind the front legs of the beast he acts quickly.

He stabs the beast with powerful strikes between the soft areas of the creature ribs. The brute seem to come alive for a second time and with renewed vigour rolls around in the dirt roaring with anger and pain. David feels like he's own ribcage is crushed underneath the weight of the animal but he keeps on stabbing again and again until the dagger penetrates the heart and with one last shudder the beast dies with a spluttering growl. The great body spasms once and then the lion lie still.

David takes in deep gulps of air trying to catch he's breathe. He's right leg is still pinned under the creature. The surge of strength still pulses through him. The deafening sound of another roar brings him back to the realization that there is still a second killer out there. He pulls himself clear from the carcass of this fallen creature and turns towards the sound of the second creature. David shields he's eyes from the early morning sun as he comes around the rocky cleft. The noises of an animal feeding carry towards him. He stops abruptly when he sees a second lion standing over the body of another soldier. This creature is much smaller than the first lion but without a doubt is still big enough to create serious damage. It is as if the lion senses he's stare and without warning it turns towards him.

Its tail sweeps from side to side and then suddenly the tail straightens signalling its intent. David crouches down slightly facing an attack for the second time and readies himself for the impact. The blood of the first lion had made the grip on the shaft of the dagger sticky and he stands he's ground. The power he feels in his body seem to increase in another surge and in the midst of the attack everything slows down. David angles he's blade instinctively holding the dagger lightly and then he hurls the dagger with great strength towards the charging animal. He sees the blade enter the left eye socket of the charging animal and makes a short dive to he's right avoiding the racking claws. The brute front legs collapses under him and it crashes down leaving a great dust cloud around him. The blade must have penetrated the creature's brain and killed him instantly.

For a short time only the voices of men sound distant. As it happened the first time the great surge of energy is suddenly gone leaving David feeling drained. The voices of the men now grow much louder and then suddenly the bloodied face of Jonathan looms into he's tired vision. David notices a deep gash on Jonathan forehead but the latter does not seem to take note of he's own injuries.

He grips David by the shoulder starting to talk uncontrollably. "How did you do that? You may not have the size of a warrior but you sure do not lack anything in courage! That was amazing! How did you know that you would not miss the creature?" David shakes he's head slowly as if awakening from a dream. "Yahweh hand has covered me." Jonathan looks at David seriously. "Praise the name of Yahweh. This is a story that will still be told for generations!"

David slowly turns gesturing towards the bodies of the fallen men. "Not all of us will return to tell the story." The sun had risen noticeably over the horizon and the strewn bodies of the fallen soldiers and the two lions lies still in the rays of the breaking morn. The rays of the sun fall upon the black mane of the bigger lion and it almost seems as if the rays had set it alight. Jonathan softly pats David on he's back. "Yes my brave friend not all will return today but many will live because of your actions here." David gestures at Jonathans face ignoring his last comment. "That looks painful and serious you should tend to it." Jonathan smiles at David wiping the blood from he's forehead with the back of he's hand. "It happened when I fell from the ledge. I struck my head on a rock. It also saved my life because I was knocked unconscious. The brute let me be thinking I was dead but my shield bearer was not that fortunate."

The remaining men had gathered around them. Some was gawking at David with hero admiration while others patted him on the back. Jonathan turns towards the men. "Come let us gather the fallen and prepare the carcasses of the killers." The two carcasses are skinned expertly and when they had completed the task they set out to return back home. Five horses were without riders though.

Chapter 4

"First the pass at Mikas and now they are camping at the borders of Socoh!" Abner does not seem to be taken aback by the Kings outburst. He slowly rises from the table and then turns towards the counsel. "Your Majesty, another thousand men has been deployed to oppose the Philistines. They seem to grow bolder every day."

No one in the room had mentioned it although everyone had been thinking about the Prophet Samuel's last visit to King Saul and the words that he had spoken. It seemed like all the benefit favour they had going for them in battle previously had just disappeared. The prophet Samuel had also disappeared. It did not take long before the word spread that their misfortune had being a curse from the old prophet. Yahweh had left Saul and Israel to the mercy of their enemy. The brown weather worn faces of the men sitting around the war counsel stare at their king with worry and expectancy. "We shall ride to the hills of Socoh near the big tree and set our camp there. Deploy another thousand men. These Philistines need to be taught a lesson once and for all!" In one voice they all hail their King "Long live King Saul!"

"Mustapha! Mustapha where are you!?" Mustapha's opens the flap of he's tent he's bare feet touching the cold desert sand. He yawns once before entering the king tent. As the king head servant Mustapha's tented quarters were close to the king ready to anticipate the King calls.

He enters the tent warily "Yes my lord." Mustapha sees the empty wine kegs standing on the table and Saul has a slight slur when he addresses him. "Bring David, I want him to play something soothing. Where is Gaza! The fool is never around when you need him! I want more wine!" Mustapha stares at the drunken king. "My lord you have given David leave to visit he's family. He will only return tomorrow if all goes well." He takes an involuntarily step towards the entrance as he had notices a mad gleam enter the Kings eyes.

Saul speaks out loudly his tones still slurred. "I will flog the skin from your back myself! Now get Gaza to bring some wine before I break some of your old bones!" Mustapha leaves the tent towards the quarters of the rest of the servants.

He stares out over the star filled desert skies. There are still camp fires burning and many sentries standing around talking in a hushed manner. Mustapha takes a deep breath taking in the fresh crisp night air. All seemed peaceful and quite now but the horror screams of the dying soldiers earlier the day still rings in he's ears. The men had died slowly and painfully and Mustapha knew that they would have to face the giant Philistine again in the morning. Towards the eastern horizon the fires of the enemy also burned and at this distance it seemed like fireflies on the horizon. Mustapha knew Saul had failed to face the threat of the Philistine champion. The men had also lost heart when they saw the defeated look on their king's face after the challenge rang from the Philistine ranks. Mustapha shudder thinking about the men that died during the day. They looked like a bunch of sheep in a lion's den.

The big giant of a man had snapped the neck of one of the Israeli soldiers and the sound of it alone had made Mustapha almost retch. The chanting of the Philistine men continued long after the slaughter. They continued to chant the dreadful name of their champion. Mustapha tries to close he's mind to the recollections without any success he hears the chanting of their champion name.

"Goliath! Goliath!"

It was still early and David had made decent progress as he travelled towards the Israel army camp. He was nearing the valley of Elah where the Israelites were camped and in the distant the smoke of the camp fires hung in the air like a swarm of bees on the horizon. He had travelled to Bethlehem after the king gave him leave to visit he's family and he was overjoyed to see his father and some of his brothers on he's return. Jonathan had given him the stallion Black Desert to make he's journey short. On his arrival, he's brothers admiration for the stallion almost swamped the feelings of hurt and distrust that he had because of the way they had treated him.

It was only later that night he learned that Eliab, Abinadab and Samma he's three elder brothers had also travelled to Socoh to join the Kings army. They sat around the fire under the desert sky and everyone listened to every word he spoke as he described the palace and the activities in King Saul duty. He told them about Jonathan and the hunt that took place. It was clear to Jesse that a bond had formed between David and Jonathan. The mood however was spoiled by the absence of David older three brothers and the Philistine invasion. On the morning of David's departure to Bethlehem Jonathan had also left the city to protect the Northern borders of the kingdom and to evade a further invasion. Saul had ordered he's men to set camp at the Valley of Elah on the borders of Socoh.

Mustapha had given instructions to David to meet with them at the borders of Socoh when he returned. It was the king's direct instruction. A greater invasion from the Philistines was inevitable. A few nights before King Saul had departed; David was summoned to he's chamber to play on his Lyre. The king was drenched in sweat and was mumbling all sorts of insanities. Mustapha told David that the king was haunted by the stories of a champion fighter among the Philistines. He told him that this champion was called Goliath and that he had challenged the whole Israel army every morning to send fighters to oppose him in single combat. This had already continued for twenty eight days and al the Israel fighters that fought the Philistine had been defeated. The Philistine had killed some of the king's most respected fighters.

It almost seemed unreal that one man could cause so much fear in the hearts of Israel and David had felt anger stir up inside of him. On the morning of he's departure to Bethlehem David had stopped to buy tobacco on the market square as a gift to his father. He overheard two of the palace guards talking about the Philistine invasion. He was about to continue on he's journey when he overheard the word "Goliath" and could not help but to stop and listen.

The smaller of the two sentries chattered away excitedly as he described what he had seen. "I will not lie to you Hiram; he is bigger than that brown bear they killed last spring."

The burly man seems to scratch an invisible itch on the side of he's pockmarked face and then with a smirk he jabs the smaller man on the shoulder.

"How would you know Piressa? You never even saw that bear? You were hiding under the blue berry bush; shaking like an old woman."

The smaller man called Piressa seem not to pay much attention the jibe and he continues. "I awoke that morning with the Philistine's war horn sounding. I quickly went out to the defensive lines. The Philistine's were not attacking but I saw a big man come forward from the ranks of those stinking rats!

From a distance the man seemed tall but as he came closer I realized that I had mistaken. This man was a giant! He was more than three meters tall!

He wore a brass helm on he's head that blinded us in the morning light! He also wore some kind of armour that must have weighed more than the mill stone in Oakum's yard. At least sixty kilograms!

He's knees and arms were also protected with brass and he carried the biggest sword that I had ever seen!"

The smirk on Hiram's face was now replaced by a mixture of dread and disbelieve. He was joining the ranks soon and he hoped that the stories of the Philistine warrior were over exaggerated. He did not move a muscle as Piressa continued.

"He also carried a spear. This was no ordinary spear I tell you! I will not lie to you but I think that spears shaft was thicker than a weavers beam and the ugly spear head alone must have weighed about seven kilograms! He came to stand before us and then challenged us to send the finest warriors to do single combat with him. It was awful! Poor Joram never even stood a chance! He's shield was shattered by the first blow of the giant's sword! The blow almost decapitated Joram's left arm. He tried bravely but he was killed by the giant in an instant without any mercy or pity. Afterward the giant placed poor Joram's head on the tip of his spear." The sentry with the pocked face just gaped at the smaller man and the latter continued with his horrible story.

"The next morning the same thing happened. The giant came forward again challenging us to do battle with him. No one really wanted to face the giant but Bersa went and stood before him. It was madness. The giant wasted no time and he chopped off all Bersa's limbs. He left the body parts decomposing in the desert sun. The sounds of the jackals feasting on Bersa's corpse will haunt me forever!"

For a while none of the men had said a word and then the man called Hiram spoke again. "What about King Saul? He is a great warrior. Why did he not face the giant?" David did not wait to hear the reply. He set of towards Bethlehem knowing the answer. The king was haunted by the Philistine champion.

It was the conversation that he brought up with he's father just before he returned that had brought about the swirling emotions and yet a certain excitement as he approached the battle fields. He ponders on the conversation he had with his father.

"Father" David's voice had a slight tremble to it. "I have heard that the Philistine Goliath has been unchallenged for many days now." Smiling at he's son Jesse sat upon the silk pillows resting he's hand on sons arm. David had indeed become more of a man in the last days. He's frame was as lean as leopard and there was extra muscle to he's lean frame. The transformation from boyhood to this passionate young man was evident as he listened to David.

"My son, the Lord will deliver us from this Philistine. Goliath is only a man and Yahweh does not think the way that man does nor does he do the things that men do. No one can challenge the Lord and stand unpunished." The emotions that he felt seem to subside as David took he's father hand smiling lovingly at him. "I know father, it is just that it annoyances me to hear our enemy speak so deliberate against the armies of the living Yahweh."

It was not just the physical transformation that was evident in David but also the way that he's love had grown for the Lord. "David, I want you to take those sacks of grain and bread to you brothers. Also take the cheese we bought from the market and give it to the captain of their thousand. David squeeze's he's father's hand in anticipation. Jesse stared at David for a while. "Don't do anything reckless boy. I have prepared all the supplies and my servant Igaila have packed your horse." David had enjoyed the company of he's father and brothers but he's heart was not as heavy as when he left he's father house the first time.

The wind changes and the stallion neighs softly. "What is it boy?" The sound of a ram battle horn can clearly be heard and David urges the stallion into a gallop down into the valley of Socoh. At a distance David can see the Israel army gather and also sees the illumination of thousands of spears from the Philistines army gleaming in the morning sun. He is stopped by sentries on the Northern side of Socoh as he approaches the Israel camp.

After they glanced at the seal imprinted papyrus document that Mustapha gave him before he left, the sentries explain to him where he will find the king servant quarters and let David through. The Israel camp is in a lot of commotion and soldiers are running towards the front battle lines. David however only sees fear on the faces of the soldiers as he continues towards the servant quarters. He sits up on he's horse trying to get a better view of the enemy but there are too many shields and spears blocking he's view.

"David!? Is that you?" David turns towards the voice and he almost does not recognize he's oldest brothers dust worn face among the soldiers.

"Eliab! How you are doing? What about Abinadab and Samma? Are they here?" Before Eliab can answer a cry from the Philistine ranks can be heard above the noise and the Israel army quiets down to a murmur.

"Look, it is the giant Goliath!" All the stories David heard about the Goliath was not exaggerated at all.

Coming from the ranks is the biggest man David has ever laid his eyes upon. He was at least three meters tall and the coat of mail he is wearing would weigh a horse down. The soldier in the palace never exaggerated when he talked about the size of the weapons the man bared. A shield bearer that seemed small compared to the giant walked before the colossal warrior. The Philistines Goliath slowly makes he's way down the slope close to the front lines of the Israel army. The giant man makes an obscene noise and spits on the ground before the army of Israel. David dismounts from he's horse and without thinking about the steed he moves with Eliab closer to the front rank of the army. As they make their way to the front David can see fear and dismay on the faces of the Israelites. They end their approach close to the front ranks on an elevated rock formation giving David a better view of the Philistine barbarian. The giant points the great spear at the Israel ranks communicating in a slow hoarse voice full of malevolence.

"Why do you still line up for battle? Have I not given you a chance to prove your worth? Is there anyone else among you that will stand against me?"

A complete hush had fallen over the Israel army as if hypnotized by the words that the giant spoke. "If none of you can defeat me how will you defeat our army?" A murmur goes up between the ranks of the Israel army but they quite down again when the giant speaks again. "Today I will offer you our complete surrender! I only ask that your king faces me and if he kills me in battle we will become your servants and surrender."

The words of the giant are lost in the talk among the Israel ranks and the giant holds up he's massive spear to get their attention again.

"I am not finished. If I kill your king you will surrender to us today and become our servants and we will take your woman and give them to real men!" Now a great noise went up from the ranks of the Israel army as they listen to the taunts of the giant. He comes closer to the ranks and stabs he's spear into the air.

"I defy you Israel; I can smell the fear upon your stinking carcasses!" Goliath draws he's sword from he's scabbard taking another step towards the ranks of the Israelites. "Now you stinking jackals, let your king fight me!"

Some of the men take an involuntary step backwards. The words of the men around David carry clearly. "We are doomed! The king will never fight him! This man is unstoppable!" Nods of agreement are seen from the surrounding men and David can't help but to feel frustration and anger growing in him. He turns towards he's brother hoping to see some emotion of courage and faith reflecting upon he's face but he sees the same fear and defeat in he's eyes.

David speaks out loud not towards anyone specific but loud enough for the adjoining men to hear him. "Will no one stand against this giant?" The heads of the men turn towards the youthful voice. "Who does this man think he is to defy the living Yahweh armies?"

Eliab grabs David arm he's brow knotted with anger and frustration. "Be quite David! What nonsense are you talking! These men have been out here for months now! You are but an arrogant Sheppard boy that should be tending the flocks!"

David loosens he's brother grip on he's arm. "This man is not only standing against Israel but against the living Yahweh of Israel!" Eliab grabs David by he's tunic and try to steer him away. "These men are not your sheep! Stop your insolence turn from here and return to your duties!" The tumult attracts more attention and David shakes of he's brother grip and turns towards him in anger.

"Why do you become angry Eliab? We should not stand around and let anyone insult Yahweh like this! These Philistines have no fear for the living Yahweh!" A voice from a man close-by calls out. "I have heard that King Saul will enrich the man greatly that defeats this Philistine! There is even talk of giving he's daughters hand in marriage to such valiant man." The surrounding men start to part away from David as a group of the king soldiers approach Eliab and David.

"David my boy! I was worried about you!" Mustapha comes from the ranks of the approaching soldiers he's weathered face showing a lot of concern. "Your horse came into the camp without a rider and we thought the worst!" David steps out of Mustapha embrace earnestly looking at the older servant. "I need to speak with the king."

"David? What madness is this?" A mixture of disappointment and anger can be heard in the king's voice. Saul had had hoped that someone would take a stand against Goliath but did not expect David to stand before him. "My Lord, I know that you may think I am senseless but let me go and fight this Philistine!" The king puts up he's hand to silent the talk among the men that had erupted in the tented area.

"You are a Sheppard boy and have not yet been accomplished in the arts of war. This giant has been a warrior since he's youth. He is three times your size and has defeated some of my finest warriors! You are no match for Goliath; he will kill you in a heartbeat. Why do put yourself in such peril?"

A silence falls upon the king's tent and every warrior and counsellor has their eyes on David. "My king; many was the time when I tended to my father's flock where a lion or a bear came and took a lamb and ran into the undergrowth. I followed the beast and struck it with my staff. When the beast turned on me I grabbed it by its mane and killed it! Yahweh has delivered me from the Lion and from the bear, He will also deliver me from this Philistine for no one who defies the army of the living Yahweh will be left standing!" King Saul moves uncomfortably in he's seat. David had spoken with such zeal about Yahweh. Saul knew all too well about David and Jonathan excursion with the lions. He knew that there was something different about the young man.

He had also heard the challenge form the Philistine champion and knew that he would be mocked as a coward if he did not fight Goliath. He knew that he did not stand a chance against this warrior. He was rejected as king by Yahweh. The prophet Samuel had told him that the Lord would not spare him. He's mind wanders back to that day at Gilgal. They had defeated the Amalekites. What a glorious battle! Instead of destroying everything as Yahweh had instructed them he could not bring himself to destroy some of the fat livestock and he kept some for himself. He had also decided to spare the life of Agag the king of the Amalekites. Soon afterwards Samuel came to him bringing the ruined words of Yahweh. Saul had hardened he's heart when Samuel spoke with him and had torn a piece of the prophet garment in anger and screamed at him to leave he's sight and felt no remorse.

The people of Israel spoke of the deeds of their ruler among themselves. Soon rumours of treachery were heard and some of he's higher ranking guards were believed to be trading with the enemy. It was because of this that their borders had weakened. The word spread quickly and soon the neighbouring adversaries started to invade the borders of Israel.

Saul looked up at the young man standing before him. He was tired and desperate. The war was relentless and he did not want to die. Saul scratches he's beard and then addresses David loudly for all to hear.

"David; I grant you your wish but cannot take responsibility for your death." The men in the tent start to talk again and Saul raise he's hand for silence. "I will not let you go into battle without any protection. You must prepare as a real warrior would. Agur; get this young man my amour, a helm and my sword!"

The soldier disappears from the king's tent returning a short while later bearing bronze amour, a long sword and a bronze helm tucked under he's arm. David looks at the weapons of choice and he reluctantly takes the helm from the soldier.

"My king I do not think I will be able to wear this." He dons the helm and the visor section obscures he's view and quickly removes it again.

Saul moves around unnervingly. He did not want he's men to think that he was sending David to be slaughtered without any weapons or protection. Mustapha approaches David with real concern showing in he's leather creased face. "I think you should try the armour and sword at least." Two guards approach him and tie the armour around he's body. The sword belt is secured around he's amour and David takes a few steps forward looking very uncomfortable. "I cannot walk with this amour. I am not used to its weight and it will only slow me down. Take it off."

Saul nods he's head slowly and they quickly exonerate the sword and amour. "How will you face this barbarian without protection or weapons to fight with?" David takes he's leather pouch from he's shoulder and takes out a sling holding it up for all the men to see. "I have used this when I was herding my sheep and I will use it again."

Some of the men laugh nervously while others shake their heads in pity and disbelieve. A soldier burst into the king tent panting heavily, patches of sweat showing under he's arms. The stench of he's unwashed body fills the tent and Saul glares at him irritably.

"I am sorry my lord but the Philistine giant has warned that their army will advance if no one has come forward by noon!" Saul takes a quick glance at David. "Tell them that we will send a warrior from our ranks." The soldier looks uncertainly at David with eyes wide in disbelieve and then hastily he leaves the tent. Saul again addresses David "If you believe that Yahweh will protect you then so it shall be. I wash my hands from all guilt should your blood be spilled today." The king now addresses his trusted servant. "Mustapha take a company of guards and walk with David." David turns away from Saul following Mustapha out from the king tent.

Saul rubs he's eyes wearily the haunted look on his face even more evident than before.

Mustapha had not spoken much accept giving instructions to the soldiers accompanying them down to the battle ground. The messenger that had entered the tent had not wasted any time to spread the word of what he had heard and seen in the king tent and about David fighting the Philistine. As he pass the ranks with David slightly behind him he can hear the Israel men softly conversing with one another, whispering David's name in anxious tones. Mustapha suspicion is affirmed that the messengers has a wagging tongue. Some of the men pats him on the shoulder and hears someone talking louder than they perhaps should have. "Poor fool."

David seems to be oblivious to he's surroundings. He quietly prays while they are walking. "Yahweh, you know my heart and can see what I have gotten myself into. I put my trust in you and ask you to deliver me from this Philistine and let Israel know that you are the true God of Israel." Mustapha misinterprets the solemn expression on David's face and gently pats him on the shoulder. "Do not listen to their cowardly words boy." David shrugs but Mustapha stops in front of him. "I do not know why you have decided to do such a foolish thing like this?" The old man almost seems close to tears. David stares out into the distance for a short while before he replies. "This man is not only standing against Israel but he is defying the true living God of Israel Mustapha. I go because I believe that Yahweh will fight for us and goes before me."

They had reached the bottom slopes of the valley close to the brook. The sound of water squabbling over the rocks in the brook can be heard and suddenly David's throat feels parched. The buzz among the men had now grown more quite in the distance as they had walked away from the front lines of the Israel army in the direction of the Philistine army. Mustapha walks quietly besides David. The old man stops staring at the Philistine army and squeezes David's shoulder. "May Yahweh be with you David son of Jesse." He turns back towards the Israel front lines leaving David at the brook in bottom of the valley. David slowly makes he's way down the brook and only once he stares back after Mustapha. The old man had joined the ranks at the front line of the soldiers; he's old frame almost unnoticeable among the armoured soldiers. He continues down the brook staring at the Philistine hordes.

Suddenly a great cheer comes from the Philistines and the men part rank as their champion Goliath makes he's way down the valley for a second time. The man is really enormous standing head; shoulders and torso above the rest of the men. David takes a deep breath. He bows down at the water stream and takes a drink from the clear water. The sound of the running water over the rocks can now barely be heard over the cheering Philistine men. David digs into the stream with he's bare hands and scoops up some sand and stones from the bright stream. He washes the sand away and selects five smooth stones which he places in he's Sheppard bag. He takes one last quaff of water and then he steps over the brook and continues down the valley.

The sand crunch under he's leather sandals. He fastens the strap of his Sheppard bag around he's shoulder; his left hand encircling the grip of the sling concealed in the folds of the bag. Goliath and he's arms bearer had made their way down the slope. The size of the man grows with every step he takes closer towards him. The Philistine frowns as he comes closer to David and then he stops. The cheering Philistine army has now grown silent and with a great booming voice Goliath calls out to David pointing he's great sword in he's direction.

"Boy! Why have you come down here? Where is your chosen fighter?" David looks up at the Philistine. He's long hair and shaggy beard with he's great bulk gives him the appearance of a mountain bear. A light breeze tucks at the untidy beard of the giant. David responds speaking clear and unhurriedly.

"I am David the servant of the living Yahweh of Israel and I have come to battle with you for the Lord is my rock!"

Goliath nudges he's shield bearer he's booming laughter ringing out. "Did you hear that Goram? Look at the boy! He wants to fight me! By Dagon he thinks I am a dog for he comes to beat me with he's stick!" Goliaths tone changes and sounds more evil and malicious than any other voice David had ever heard. "I swear by Dagon that you will die today and I will give your flesh to the vultures and the jackal will feast on your bones tonight!" There was no movement from both the Philistine and Israel armies; the men were listening to the conversation echoing in the valley below.

David has become familiar with the surging energy and fire that he had felt twice before. He knew it was Yahweh's covering power. It suddenly engulfs him again without any warning. He feels he's body and mind strengthen and all fear disappeared from him.

"You are a big man Goliath!" David stares at the giant unwaveringly. "You come to me with a sword, with a spear, and with a javelin; but I come to you in the name of Yahweh of Armies, the God of the armies of Israel, whom you have defied. Today, Yahweh will deliver you into my hand. I will strike you, and take your head from off you. I will give the dead bodies of the army of the Philistines today to the birds of the sky, and to the wild animals of the earth; that all the earth may know that there is a God in Israel." (1 Samuel 17 v 45)

David sees the anger growing in the Philistine. He carefully feels around in the bag with he's concealed hand selecting a rock that was picked up at the brook.

"All this assembly may know that Yahweh doesn't save with sword and spear; for the battle is Yahweh's, and he will give you into our hand." (1 Samuel 17 v 47)

The big man shakes with rage and anger. No one has talked to him in this manner ever! He raise he's sword over he's head and screams attacking David.

"Die you arrogant boy!"

David drops he's Sheppard bag from he's shoulder, pulling out the sling with he's concealed hand. In one practiced move he quickly places the smooth rock he had selected into the rough patch of the sling.

A great roar comes from the camp of the Philistines and the drawn sword of Goliath gleams brightly in the sun as he moves towards David. David quickly swings the slingshot over he's head the whirling sound increasing with each swing.

Ssshhhwwirr, sshhhwwwirrrrr, shhwirrrrrrrrrrrr.

He looks into the eyes of the attacking man seeing the hatred burning there and then with a snap he releases the sling.

The smooth stone cannot be seen as it travels through the air but when the rock hits the running man on the forehead just below he's helm between he's eyes the sound cracks like thunder.

The big man instantly comes to almost a complete standstill. He's eyes bulge from he's shaggy head in surprise.

Like when the wind depart from a giant sail of a merchant ship Goliath stumbles falling at David's feet dust and sand flying in all directions. David rushes towards the fallen man side and lifts the enormous sword from the giants twitching fingers. The giant Philistine groans again and he groggily tries to push himself to he's feet. David swings the sword in an arch like motion and with one mighty swing he cuts into the trunk of the giant neck.

Twice more he completes this action and then Goliaths head rolls into the sand the light in he's eyes fading. The headless corpse twitches for a moment before it lies still on the ground. The shocked silence that follows is almost overwhelming and then suddenly the men of the Israel army let's out a great roar and comes screaming down the valley, their battle cry crushing over the Philistine hordes. The Philistines quickly turn and start to flee in panic. The Israel men run past David leaving him with the corpse. He drops the sword beside the corpse of the fallen giant and stares after the attacking Israel army. As before the energy that had engulfed he's body fades again and slowly sinks down on he's knees.

"Thank you Yahweh."

David had retired to he's own tent. The feeling of loneliness had become stronger as the night had progressed. The men were still celebrating; their laughter booming out into the desert night. He was summoned before King Saul after the Israel army pursue ended and had returned to the camp. The men had cheered him and although King Saul seemed overjoyed with the victory; there was hidden depths in he's eyes when congratulated David. He handed him the shield of Goliath as a victory prize and the men cheered mightily! All the attention made David feel apprehensive. Had they not heard that it was Yahweh who had delivered them from the Philistines sword? He encountered his brothers and he tried to speak with them.

Eliab ignored him completely but Abinadab, and Shimma let him sit with them. David was not sure if it was only because of the attention that he's presence attracted to their table; but it felt good to at least sit with people he knew. Everyone wanted to know how it felt to stand in front of the giant. One of the soldiers drunkenly also made mention of the lions that was killed by David when he accompanied Jonathan. David recognized the speaker as one of the soldiers whom had escorted them on the hunt. The conversation went into a different direction after the soldier mentioned the hunt and the sizes of the teeth and claws of the slain beasts grew as the wine flowed. Later some of his other brothers Nathanael, Raddai and Ozem also joined them returning from a scouting party.

They embraced David when they saw him and soon got caught up in the celebrations of the men. The noise grew as the men drank more and he decided to sneak away from the burning fires and went to the tent they had erected for him which at least was well away from celebrating men. David did not fail to notice that he's tent had moved away from the servant's quarters into the inner ring of Saul most trusted men. A small fire that was made outside the opening of he's tent burns lowly and his eyes feel tired as he stares into the dying embers. A shadow falls outside he's tent opening and he hopes that it is not one of the king's soldiers looking for him.

"David. David are you in there?" The voice of Jonathan is surprisingly unexpected for David had not seen Jonathan at the festivities. He walks out of the tent and with unfeigned excitement he speaks to the larger man. "Jonathan! It is good to see you!" The two men embrace each other with a heartfelt brotherly love. Jonathan puts a few logs onto the dying fire and then puts he's sword over he's lap as he crosses he's legs to sit down. The smoke from the new logs casts shadows across the bearded face of Jonathan. The big man speaks while prodding the coals with a dried out branch. "Lions, bears and giants! What is next my friend? You say you are a shepherd and yet seem to be much more than this? Indeed a mystery to me."

Jonathan had brought a jug of wine with him and he had now poured some into two clay cups. David smiles at Jonathan as he takes the wine from him. "I have done nothing. It was Yahweh who delivered the Philistine into my hands and into the hands of Israel." Jonathan looks at David with an earnest expression. "You are a very unusual man David. Many men have spoken about Yahweh but it seems like you are a man close to Yahweh's heart."

David takes a sip out of he's clay cup and places the cup on the desert sand. "I do not understand why Yahweh have chosen to be merciful and gracious like this and protect me against the Lion and now the giant warrior. I know this; He's ways are not our ways and He's doing not ours." The flames lick hungry at the new burning logs. The ring of light which the fire makes lights up the surrounding camp area. David sees Jonathan face is covered with dust and grime but also a deep frown edged in he's forehead. Jonathan looks up seeing David concern and if reading he's mind he takes another sip out of he's cup and clears he's throat.

"David. I respect my father but he is a man that does not easily forgive. He has become a very infuriated frustrated man." David stares at Jonathan attentively as he continues. "He will not take too kindly in he's heart that you have stood triumphantly before the Philistines today. I warn you that you should tread carefully from now on and I only say this because of our true bond of friendship that I feel." Jonathan stands up and takes the armour that he is wearing off and hands it to David. "What are you doing?" Jonathan ignores the question and takes he's sword, bow and belt and hands it to David. "You have become a dear friend to me David. I see Yahweh strength in you. You have once again stood in the face of danger and you have given glory to Yahweh. I have come to love you as a brother and a friend. I hereby give you these garments and weapons as a covenant between your house and my house."

For a while David seem to be at a loss of words but then he stands up raising he's clay cup. "Your father was anointed as king by Yahweh and I will honor that. Yahweh will go before me." David raises he's cup to he's lips.

"We will be brothers forever my friend for Yahweh has knitted our souls together! Jonathan raises he's cup in union.

"You have my friendship and loyalty forever my brother!"

Chapter 5.

The clay cup smashes against the far wall missing Mustapha by a few inches. "Did you hear them sing? They adore him!" Mustapha can see the madness gleaming in Saul's eyes. It all started on their arrival back from the slaughter of the Philistines army. As the king's army came near the cities of Israel the women had come to the roads with tambourines and other musical instruments and they had sung and danced. At first the king smiled and waved but as they drew near Mustapha heard the words that started the jealous psychosis. "Saul has slain he's thousands and David will slay ten thousands!" Saul did not say a word but a deep hatred had grown inside him when he heard these words. Mustapha recognized that the King had a murderous intent. He had seen this in King Saul eyes before. Mustapha pours another cup of wine and is startled when David enters the king chamber.

He's hands shake uncontrollably and he spills some wine. Saul had summoned David to play the Lyre and Mustapha hides he's uneasiness by cleaning the wine smiling at David. As always the boy closes he's eyes as he start to play the sweet tones drifting through the night. Mustapha stares at Saul seeing him reach for he's spear stroking the shaft. Twice during the respite he's hands curled along the shaft and Mustapha knew what Saul was thinking. Saul wanted to kill David. Saul suddenly sat up and again grabbed hold of the shaft he's eyes burning with hatred. Mustapha gasps loudly he's eyes locked on Saul and he stumbles over a rug. In the process he knocks over a jar standing close to the king.

Saul hurls the spear towards David but the sound of the breaking jar brings David out of his reverie. In a matter of seconds he summed up what was happening and ducked to he's left as the shaft came flying through the air missing him by mere inches. David jumps up and runs from the room. Saul does not move another muscle but keeps on staring in direction David had fled from the room like a man possessed. The breaking jar and commotion had attracted more attention to the king's chamber than anticipated. Merab, Saul's oldest daughter walks into the room with a frown on her forehead. She sees the broken jar and stares at Mustapha and again at her father.

"Is everything alright father?" Saul stares at Merab. It seems like he noticed her for the very first time ever. With the mad sheen in his eyes he nods he's head. Mustapha voice breaks through the uncomfortable silence. "It is just a broken jar my dear." Saul continues to stare at Merab a wide grin appearing on he's bearded face and he repeats Mustapha words. "Just a broken jar, everything is just fine my dear." Merab leaves the chamber and Saul mumbles to himself and then he breaks out in an uncontrollable laughter and Mustapha quietly leaves he's chambers.

The mad laughter of Saul follows him down the hallway and brings goose bumps to the old servants flesh.

Early the next day it becomes clear to Mustapha why Saul suddenly seemed more relaxed after Merab had visited him. He called on all he's trusted advisors and discussed the plan he had with them. The king wanted to give Merab to David as he's wife.

"I will give him Merab and will make him Captain over the army of Israel as a sign of my favour. " All but Mustapha in the chamber give cheer to the announcement. Mustapha knows that Saul intent is to let David fight all Saul enemies. As the king son in law the eyes and favour of the people will return to the king. After David defeated the Philistine champion he had become a sworn enemy of the Philistines. It was Bron the king's war advisor that carefully pointed out the flaw in the plan.

"My King is Merab not promised to Adriel the Meholathite as wife?" It seemed as if Saul was going to lose he's temper with Bron but then Gaza spoke up with a tight voice. "Your highness. What about Michal? My wife had spoken to me recently and she had mentioned the Michal was quite smitten with David. She had been singing songs about him while my wife was tending to her." Saul seemed to relax and smile at the mysterious ways of women. Then it shall be arranged. We will have a wedding and David shall become the captain of the Israel army! The men cheered again and shortly after they left the king chamber. All except Mustapha had gone and King Saul spoke to him in an imperturbable tone.

The palace was filled with the people from all over Israel. The story of David defeating the Philistine champion had spread like wild fire throughout the kingdom and everybody wanted to see the new conqueror of Israel. It was going to be an extra special day because they would be witness to the king giving he's daughters hand to the young champion. They could not wait to indulge in the festivities and they could already taste the wine and meat! Time seem to drag out ever so slowly. David was the only one who felt that the days were speeding by. He sat in a chamber close to the main stage that was setup for the festivities waiting to be summoned into the king presence. He listens to the sound of the large crowd outside and he's mind wonders back pondering the last few days.

Mustapha had come and told him that Saul was going to give he's daughter hand in marriage to him. Saul had prepared Mustapha and told him not to say anything else to David. The King had spoken in riddles talking about a dowry and David being promoted as the captain over the Israel army. Saul however told him only to speak to David about becoming he's son in law. Mustapha had spoken to David in a heavy heart knowing that Saul intention wasn't true and honourable. David was surprised and did not want to accept the proposal.

"I can't marry her Mustapha! I am poor and a lightly esteemed man!" As Saul had coached him Mustapha had answered David. "You have found delight in the king's eyes! You have defeated Goliath and therefore the king wants to honour you. King Saul had promised he's daughter hand in marriage to whoever defeated the giant and the Philistine army was driven back from our borders. It will not be an honourable act if you try and deny the creed that the king has declared as an act of he's good will."

Even as he spoke these words, he felt a sense of gloom but hid it well behind a big smile. "She is not hard on the eyes my boy and has a bright young mind. You could have done worse."

David felt he's palms starting to sweat he's heart pounding wildly. Matrimony! He had seen Michal a few times before and it was true she was striking but getting married to her was a different state of affairs all together. He felt more nervous than when he faced Goliath.

"The King will make this special announcement before the entire Israel a few weeks from now. Soon thereafter Michal will be your wife." Mustapha turned from the boy and left David to he's own thoughts. It suddenly seemed like the whole kingdom was in uproar. The preparation for the wedding announcement festival was evident and a new tunic was tailored for David that he had to fit and try on a few times before the tailor seemed satisfied. Since Mustapha spoke with David, he also did not go about he's normal duties. Although nobody was rude the other servants treated him differently with a sense of awe and reverence. Everywhere David went he experienced an atmosphere of jubilance among the people. The women giggled softly behind their hands whenever he was near and the men showed a silent respect sometimes nodding at him while others refrained from making eye contact.

One morning as he came down to the kitchen he overheard two maid servants discussing the wedlock. He could not see the faces of the woman as their backs were turned towards him but the servant to he's left chattered away excitedly.

"The days are dragging by so slowly!" The girl to his right reprimanded but without any real sternness. "Come now we still have a lot of work to do. People are coming as far as Heshbon and you know that is why the king gave more time to ensure all people have enough time to arrive!"

David had turned away from the exchange not wanting to impose and spoil the mood in the kitchen. There were certainly a lot of people coming to the wedlock and it seemed like Saul had invited all of Israel. Mustapha had told David that he's father and family were on their way and that he had prepared a tent for them in the inner sanctum of the palace.

The day had arrived and David continue to pace around his own chambers like a caged animal. Seven days before the wedlock he was told not to enter the Southern section of the gardens anymore. He had spent the last few afternoons taking his much-loved stallion Desert Wind out into the fast open spaces. He had found a spot where he could just let he's thoughts roam. It was an old drinking well where the Sheppard's brought their flocks and he sat there listening to the bleating of the thirsty animals lazily grazing the pastures. Here he would stare out over the hills taking he's Lyre and singing along the tunes with he's eyes closed.

"Praise awaits you, our Yahweh, in Zion; to you our vows will be fulfilled. You who answers prayer, to you all people will come. When we were overwhelmed by sins, you forgave our transgressions. Blessed are those you choose and bring near to live in your courts. We are filled with the good things of your house, of your holy temple. You answer us with awesome and righteous deeds, Yahweh our Saviour."

The hours had seemed to pass too swiftly and before long he would steer the stallion back slowly into the setting sun. The stallion knew the route back and with a soft neigh he would start the journey back towards the palace. The king actions was indeed a mystery to him as he was reminded of the evening when he was summoned by Saul to play the Lyre in he's chambers and the mysterious actions of the king when he threw the spear at him. He had ran from the chamber that night in fear and was reminded off Jonathan words about his father. Mustapha was the one that came the next day and had assured him everything was in order.

A couple of days ago his own father had arrived together with all his brothers. David had almost spent every moment with them that was allowed. Jesse had once again reminded him that Yahweh had planned every step of the way for him.

He's thoughts are interrupted as a servant walks into the chamber.

"The king awaits you." David takes a deep breath and follows the servant. He walks out of the chamber into the front hall area of the prepared ceremony tent. He is stunned by a sudden upsurge of ovation and cheering as the people get their first sight of the Israel victor. The cheering continues as he gradually walks towards the raised stage where the King was seated for the ceremony. David stares straight ahead as the people continue their encouraging as he steadily ascents the steps towards where Saul sits staring at David from he's white silk pillows. He's youngest daughter sits at he's feet keeping her face modestly covered and bowed. He stops in front of the king and cannot help to notice Michal fleeting stare from underneath the veil her dark eyes locking with he's for a diminutive moment.

A ram horn blows and the king arises lifting he's hands and the crowd quite down. Saul start to speak: "As you all know this man has come into the house of Israel as my personal servant. He pauses for a moment staring at David and then continues. He became known among the servants in the palace as one of the finest musicians." The crowd had gone dead silent hanging on to Saul's every word. "He has shown he's dedication and bravery towards Israel when he defeated the Philistine champion Goliath!" Now the crowd shouted greatly at the mention of the astonishing defeat. Saul turns towards David raising he's hands again and the crowd quiets down. "As per my own creed. I bestow my favour on you David by giving you my youngest daughter as your wife and therefore making you my son in law."

David stare at the king and then speaks with a clear voice as Mustapha had coached him but adding some of he's own reprieve. "I am not worthy of your favour your majesty for it was Yahweh who defeated the Philistine and not me. I am but a Sheppard boy and I have no dowry to give for your daughters hand in marriage."

Saul smiles tightly but continues hurriedly. "From this day forth you will also be a captain of one thousand men!" The crowd now burst into a loud cheer and Saul looks into David's eyes. There is something that makes him feel uneasy in those green depths of the youth eyes gazing back at him. This was the moment that he had been waiting for. He would give Michal to David and make him the captain of a thousand of he's men and then send him into battle with the Philistines. He knew that it would be the perfect plan. Like a Ferret stalking a Guinee-fowl it may be a snare to him. For a moment he's hatred is undisguised as he stares at David. The hand of the Philistines will surly rise against David!

The ram horn blows again and the crowd once again turns silent but not completely, an exciting mummer can be heard as Saul once again continues. "I will make you captain over a thousand of my men and because you have no dowry you and your men will go on an assignment to take vengeance on my enemies!" The crowd had quieted down completely to hear the king decree. "For my daughters hand in marriage I require one hundred Philistine foreskins!" David stares at the king. He had not expected the king announcement. The duty to become the captain over a thousand men was a great honour and responsibility. Something inside of him stirred. The battle with Goliath had awakened something deep within him. The only other time when he had felt so alive was when he battled with the bear and the lion. Something about going in to battle with the Philistines excites him even more. He looks a Saul and sees an expression upon the king's face that he cannot decipher. Saul realizes David scrutiny and he smiles easily and takes Michal by her hand lifting her to her feet.

"What do you say David? Will you advance upon this offer and take my daughters hand bringing the dowry I have requested?" Michal stares shyly at David and the young man returns her gaze with a broad smile. "I accept! As the king wishes it will be done!" Saul breathes a sigh of relief. The Israel crowd again exploded in hoots and cheers. Saul again turns to the crowd and raises he's voice above the noise but more for the servants close to him.

"Prepare the food. We shall feast now."

Dozens of small camp fires lay spread out across the desert floor. Earlier David and he's men had passed through the valley of Elah and had approached the borders of Ekron. David's scouting party had come back with the news that a small Philistine war party was making its way to Ekron. The city of Gath was close by. After the defeat of Goliath the reports came that the Philistines drew all the way back to Ekron and Gath. The cycle moon had risen over the valley not shedding much light and had moved away to the East as the morning hours crept along.

David sat silently waiting on the scouts to give a final report on the number of men in the valley below. The fires burned lower and the booming laughter still rang out as the Philistine soldiers continued their festivities into the still desert morning hours. A shadow moved in the darkness to David's left and a burly figure makes he's appearance soon afterwards. "Captain the scouts have returned." David recognizes the whispering voice of Abdi he's general. He stares at the outlines of the man as he slowly makes his way down the slope of the dune. They stop abruptly and David stares into the face of the man before him trying to see he's eyes in the darkness. Some clouds had drifted in front of the cycle moon and David can only make out the outline of Abdi huge beard. Abdi settle close to David on the dune and continues in a soft tone. "The men have reported that there are definitely more than a hundred men down below. What is your command?"

David scratches the stubble of he's own beard thinking about the charge he was to perform. Saul had asked for a hundred foreskins as a dowry and yet the urge to do battle again was now more overwhelming than the sweet face of Micah. David once again feels the excitement building inside knowing that the fight would start soon. He turns he's face towards the fires below the dune, listening to the drunken men laughter. "Tell the men that we will attack at the first rays of dawn. I want you to ready a hundred and fifty of the men. The rest will wait here and only advance on my signal should we need them. I will lead the attack." He could not tell the expression on Abdi's face and when the general answered him it was a sure response. "I will ready the men Captain." David lies on he's back trying to find some calm before the attack. It would soon be dawn and he would need all he's vitality. It would only be the second time that he would face the brutality of killing and slaying another man.

He touches the sword belt that he had received from Jonathan putting he's hand on the hilt. "Yahweh I ask that you grant me the strength to overcome and win this battle tonight. Yahweh please cover me in battle." The clouds drift away from the moon as the time passes and the fires had now burned out below. There was no more laughter to be heard from the men below. An eerie silence followed that was occasionally broken by the bark of a jackal close by. David slowly makes he's way down the dune and stands before the two hundred men that had accompanied him. In the darkness of the morning David could only make out the frontline of the men but he knew he's command would be passed among the men.

"On my order: quickly but quietly advance towards the Philistine's. The scouting party will go before us and take down the few sentries stationed to keep an eye open for danger. When you hear the sound of the ram horn attack and slay the enemy." The only way that David can see that the men acknowledge he's command is the sword arms of the frontline raised in union. David canters down the dune advancing towards the sleeping Philistine camp. The skies are starting to turn a murky grey as dawn approach and the outlines of the scouting party can be seen attacking the sentries stationed about twenty meters away from the camp. David witnesses the collapse of one of the sentries and takes the ram's horn around he's neck and blows loudly onto it.

Like a swarm of Locust flying into a cornfield he's men hits the camp area. Some men die in their sleep but yet there are some veteran fighters that wakes up and tries to counter the Israel army surprise attack. David sprint past a sleeping body thrusting he's sword into the lying man exposing neck and turns just in time to deflect the sword of an attacking Philistine soldier. He turns quickly blocking yet another blow from the soldier. David can now see the clear outlines of the attacking man face and realizes that the man is much older than him. A nasty scar runs from the man brow down the left side of he's upper lip giving the Philistines a more menacing appearance. The soldier again wordlessly attacks cutting expertly at David left shoulder and at the last moment he twists he's arm almost thrusting he's sword into David stomach. David quickly jumps away to he's right the sword edge cutting into he's side. He realizes that he is facing a seasoned experienced warrior.

The soldier grins at him staring at the side where he had drawn blood and attacks again with new vigour. David blocks every thrust and the heavy breathing and metallic clang of swords is the only sounds as the two men engage in a silent dance of death. David feels he's heart quicken and a renew strength filling he's being and for a moment the movements of he's opponent seems to become predictably clear and slow. David blocks another blow to he's head and then he drops he's shoulders stumbling to he's left faking weariness exposing he's left flank. When the warrior see David stumble the older warrior over excitedly step in for the kill.

As when a leopard silently exposes its tummy for a hunting pack of dogs before it rakes its back claws tearing out their entrails so David exposes he's whole midsection of he's body. The Philistine lifts he's sword with both hands planning to perform the dying blow. David sees the opportunity and quickly reverses he's sword arm cutting across the soldier tummy. The man grabs he's stomach trying to keep the cut closed falling on to he's knees surprise showing in he's widened eyes. David thrusts the sword through the Philistine's neck and quickly turns looking for the next attack.

A man runs at him with a javelin and David ducks and rolls just in time the spear tip tucking at he's tunic tearing of a piece out of he's robe. David attacks the man cutting through muscle in he's calf. The soldier screams and try to get back onto he's feet but the cut had severed a sinew and he's leg buckles underneath him. David delivers a death blow piercing he's sword through the soldier a last dying scream erupting from the man lips.

A blow explodes at the base of he's skull and David is knocked off he's feet. Blackness threatens to engulf all he's senses but he fights the urge to give in to the nothingness and turns onto he's back lifting he's sword arm protecting he's face. A blow hits against he's sword arm and he's fingers feel numb making it hard to hold onto he's sword hilt. He squints into the rising sun staring at the outlines of a burly soldier just in time to see a swinging wooden club aimed at head. He blocks the heavy blow and kicks the man on he's knee cap with all he's might hearing a sickening crack! The soldier drops the club and David cuts through he's artery on the left side of he's neck. The man fall face forward into the sand.

David slowly rises from the sand shaking he's head groggily. All around him the screams of dying men can be heard and just as quickly as the attack had started it ends. David sees some of he's men performing dying blows to Philistine men lying in the sand and as he had instructed lifting their tunics and taking their foreskins. He turns the fallen soldier onto he's back and stares into the lifeless eyes now filled with grains of sand. A few seconds ago there was life in those eyes. David lifts the tunic of the man he had just slaughtered and performs the act king Saul had instructed. The blood of the dead man covers he's hands and he stands to walk to the previous body of the man that he had killed to perform the same task yet again.

The Philistines are all uncircumcised not sharing in the promise that Yahweh made with Abraham and as the gruesome task continues David thinks back on the day when he's painful circumcision had taken place. Abdi seeks out he's company reporting that they had suffered only five loses. "We have killed more than two hundred Philistine men here today captain. No one escaped but another Philistine party may cross this way soon."

David gives instruction to gather the fallen comrades and move out towards Gibeah. Only when the moon slowly rises again they setup camp and the men prepare fires to cook a meal. The fires lights up the dirt and blood covered features of the men sitting around them lost in their own thoughts. It had been a long bloody day and the men's voices blend with the cracking fires and the call of a lonely night owl. Some are enjoying roast breads and dried fish for their evening meal and others merely stare into the flames thinking about their return to their families. Abdi scratches a few coals aside and then lies on he's back closing he's eyes. David stares out into the fast heavens and talks to no one in particular.

"We shall return tomorrow our duty done and yet are we victors?" Abdi opens he's eyes and stares at he's captain. "The Philistines have been slain and you have outperformed the king command. Is that goat skin of yours not filled with two hundred Philistine foreskins? David takes a swig from a clay jug and wipes he's mouth with the back of he's hand but says nothing. Abdi continues "You have become the king next of kin by marrying he's daughter. The people of Israel love you. Very soon we shall stand together at the City walls of Beer – Sheba and chase these Philistine dogs to their own land and stinking cities once and for all!"

David looks into the dancing flames smiling at Abdi last words. It was true that he had taken more foreskins than what Saul had required. Every raid they had fought with a new passion and hunger and he knew that the men had come to respect him as a combatant and leader. He had prayed to Yahweh every time before they had engaged in battle but felt a growing hunger to fight and a blood thirst that could not be contained fuelling he's craving for war. He could not trust himself to respond to Abdi for he feared that the desire for more bloodshed would be heard in he's voice.

"I want him dead!" There is a shocked silence in Saul's war chamber. Jonathan moves uneasy in he's chair. "He was supposed to be killed by the Philistines! He comes back and he taunts me openly before the people. The people of Israel all see him as a mighty warrior and what about me? All I hear is David this and David that! David slays ten thousands! I am sick of that name! He has invaded my house and is married to my daughter!" Jonathan opens he's mouth to remind he's father that the wedlock between David and Michal was he's idea. He is cut off by the thumping sound of Saul fist brutally slamming into the wooden oak table the men are sitting at. He turns towards Jonathan "I don't want to hear it! I don't want my own son speaking out against me as well! I want David dead! I want you to kill him!" Saul storms out of the war chamber and Jonathan and the rest of the servants rise from the table.

Jonathan knows that there will be no stopping he's father for he was set in he's way. "Mustapha; you and Gaza go and look for David in the kitchen and I will go and look in he's quarters." Jonathan knows that David is in neither place but at the royal stables for he had spoken to him earlier that morning. He was aiding the stable boy's with Saul's new pair of breeding war horses. David loved horses and he and Jonathan often went riding on these magnificent creatures when they were flying the trained hawks or hunting for desert Oryx. He did not want Gaza or Mustapha to be in trouble for he was about to go directly against he's father orders. He hurries along the path that leads to the stables and start calling out to David as he still approached.

"David! David I must talk to you!" David comes around the corner of the paddock door and almost runs into Jonathan. "What is wrong Jonathan? You sound like the Philistines are attacking our borders!" Jonathan takes David by he's elbow and leads him out of sight. "It is worse than an invasion from the enemy my brother." David frowns at the worried look on Jonathan face. "What is it my brother?" Jonathan scratches he's beard and tries to avoid eye contact "It is my father, he wants you dead." The whining of a horse in the paddock is the only sound and it hangs between the two men like early morning mist. "What have I done now to anger your father Jonathan? Have I not done all that he has asked me to do?" Jonathan looks as stricken as David and the big man sighs deeply before he replies.

"I know. He has been tormented since..." Jonathan sighs deeply. "Well since the prophet Samuel came and told him that he was rejected as the Lords chosen king. He is worried that another king will take he's place soon." David stares at the paddock hiding he's face from Jonathan. Jonathan misinterprets he's action as one of resentment and quickly continues. "Do not go home to Michal tonight. My father will most surely look for you. I want you to hide in the field near the old thorny bush just for the night. I will talk with my father tonight and tomorrow morning my father and I will take a walk in the field where you are. I will continue to speak in high favour of you with my father. I will remind him of all the things you have done. He knows that you have brought about a great deliverance for Israel when you battled Goliath. I will send Mustapha to bring you food and water. David thinks about the words of he's friend. The Lord had always delivered him. "I will do as you instruct."

Jonathan breath another sight but this time one of relief. "Hide well my brother for my father will surely kill you if he finds you today. Go now David, I will go to Michal and tell her of our plans. Wait for me in the morning."

David stares at the big stone known as Ezel. Many moons had come and gone after that day at the stables when Jonathan had warned him of he's father's murderous plans. He thinks back upon that day that Jonathan had ordered him to wait in the field. He had waited and quietly listened as Jonathan spoke to Saul reminding him of the things that he had done for Israel. At the time the words Jonathan spoke had touched Saul because he had taken mercy on him. He had apologized to Jonathan and that evening David returned to Michal and he was allowed to roam freely in the palace. He enjoyed life with he's wife and again on the king instruction went into battle when the Philistines tried to invade the borders of Israel. Many nights were spent under the starry skies and he and he's men protected the borders of the invading Philistines. The Lord gave him victory in all the battles that he engaged and he relentlessly fought the wars that waged between the Philistines and the armies of Israel. Upon he's return to Gibeah the people gathered outside the city gates to welcome the men and again songs of victory and praises was heaped upon him. The songwriters sang songs and also the Philistines knew David by he's striking red beard and fierce green eyes. They hated him but also started to show respect and since he's presence the border attacks had quieted down.

He had returned to he's wife after the war and sometimes continued he's duties and played the Lyre to comfort Saul troublesome sleep.

It was a day like that while playing he's lyre that had brought about the situation that he was in. Again he had to rely on Jonathan for a signal here at the rock of Ezel. He's mind travels back to that perilous day in the court yard tending to the king. For a second time it became clear what the king murderous intentions was. Just like the time before he's announcement as captain over a thousand. Again he had played the Lyre and this time one of the servant let out blood curling scream. David had instinctively moved he's body to the right dropping the lyre and a loud thump hit the wall where he had just been sitting. He turned he's head and saw the shaft of a spear still quivering from the impact sticking out of the wall. He had turned towards Saul and the face that he saw was a murderous face deprived of sanity. It was then that David made a final decision and he knew he had to flee in fear for he's life.

He had gone home and spoke to Michal about he's close encounter with her father. He told her about the first time before their wedlock when Saul had also attempted to take his life. The night was dawning and someone had knocked on their door. A servant send by Mustapha had come and warned David that the king would invade he's sleeping quarters that night. At first Michal had broken down in tears but after the servant came to warn them about the king plan Michal had devised a clever plan. She had taken goat's hair and some of he's clothes and laid out an appearance of him in their bed. Although time had passed the conversation they had before he fled was still fresh in he's memory. "I will let you down the window so that you can escape. My father will be furious when he finds this appearance of you in our bed. This is the only way because he's spies will inform him if you leave now and follow you my husband. Go and I will wait for you."

David had felt he's love and devotion grow for he's wife. He had come to find that Michal love was as true as her word. "What about you? As you have said, your father will be furious when he finds that you had let me escape?" Michal had spoken with inordinate devotion. "I will tell him that you gave me no choice and threatened to take my life." He had kissed her then and fled from Saul's madness.

He received word from he's father that he should meet with Samuel in Naioth in Ramah. It was the first time that he had seen the prophet again since he's anointing and at first he was nervous to speak with the prophet. Samuel however comforted him and reminded David that Yahweh plan could not be ruined by any man. He reaffirmed the words that was spoken over him and that he should wait patiently upon the Lord. He stayed at Naioth for more than a month and although occasionally he had grown restless he learned to abide in the words that Yahweh had spoken especially when he again witnessed Yahweh power. During he's period in Naioth Saul's men came looking for him. It was then that a strange thing had happened and he had then witnessed Yahweh's power again. Every time one of Saul men came looking for him they would enter into Ramah and is was as if they were blinded and they could not see him. Even stranger yet was that as soon as they had come into city they would start to prophesize and honor the name of the living Yahweh.

Samuel explained to him that when The Spirit of Yahweh came upon them that no other word would come from their mouths and that was a sign that the Lord was with him. This must have enraged Saul even more and he quickly learned that David was indeed at Ramah. One morning a herdsman came running to them telling them that Saul and he's army was advancing towards Ramah. David had hidden in Samuel's house but to everyone astonishment the Spirit of the Lord also came upon Saul when he entered Ramah. He started prophesying and when he saw Samuel he started to take off he's clothes before him. All day long he continued to prophesize naked. That evening the convoy left Ramah and the people of Ramah was mystified by this and asked if Saul was also among the prophets.

David did not say anything. The prophet Samuel words rang true. He knew that Yahweh was protecting him. Soon afterwards it had come about for a second time that he had to rely on Jonathan help. His heart again became restless and he had hoped that Saul might have changed he's mind after Ramah so he wrote a letter to Jonathan. He asked him to plea with he's father yet again. In he's letter he spoke about their oath and that he would treat the house of Jonathan with kindness and he and Jonathan will be brothers in heart and soul until their dying day. Michal had also send him word that it was time for the new moon feast in Bethlehem. David wrote to Jonathan asking him to plead he's case before he's father. He wanted to see he's wife and tend to the sacrifice in Bethlehem. A week ago he had received a letter form Jonathan and because of the content of this letter David was once again hiding in the field close to the stone of Ezel waiting for Jonathan sign as per he's instruction.

David takes the parchment from he's bag the words of Jonathan had brought tears and hope: My brother and friend in the Lord. Praise Yahweh for you are well! Your sincerity towards my father has touched me deeply even after all that he has done to you. I have decided to act in your absence and I will again address my father. As you know the new moon feast will be in two week time. I will bring your request to go to the feast in Bethlehem under my father attention without harm befalling you. If my father becomes angry when I put forward your request I will let you know by a sure sign.

The day after the new moon feast I will come to the field at the stone of Ezel. You must hide in the field by the stone. I will then take three arrows and pretend as if I am practicing my shots shooting at a target. I will have a servant with me to collect the arrows I have shot.

Now David, after I have shot the arrows I will instruct the servant to collect them. If you hear me say:

"The arrows are to your side boy get them and come!" Then you should know that my father have let you safe passage to Gibeah. If you hear me say to the lad: "The arrows are beyond you boy!" Then you must go your own way for my father is still out to kill you. I also stand by our covenant with you and promise that between my house and the house of David my kindness will never be cut off. May the Lord require all these things as He has done to you David? I miss you dearly my brother. Until we meet again. Jonathan.

David had been hiding in the field since the new moon had come. He was tired and hoped that the news that Jonathan brought was good. The afternoon sun was setting and he lies back on the grass waiting patiently. He hears the exiting chatter of small boy's and when he looks out behind the rock he sees Jonathan approach he's arrow slung over he's shoulder two young servant boy's accompanying him.

David looks at Jonathan as he draws he's bow and shoots the arrows one by one. After the third arrow the boy's run into the field to collect the arrows. The one boy was very close to where the arrows had flown and then he hears Jonathan speak out. "Boy, is the arrow not beyond you?" David feels he's legs go numb. Saul had shown no mercy. He hears Jonathan speak again. "Hurry up boy, collect all the arrows and let's head back to the city." Jonathan and the boy start walking back toward the palace. Just before they disappear into an entrance in the wall Jonathan looks back over he's shoulder. David cannot see he's facial expression but waves at him. Jonathan nods he's head and then disappears into the entrance. The breeze pulls slightly at David's beard. The overwhelming feeling of sorrow and helplessness threatens to engulf him.

He slowly turns south heading towards Nob.

Chapter 6

The white linen ephods of the priests working in the fields blends with the durra they are reaping. Standing on the balcony of the temple of Nob; Ahimelech stares of into the distance. The number of young men that had come to the temple had grown in the past years and people now referred to Nob as the city of the priests. Nob was not really a city. The town lay about a mile north east of Jebus. There were eighty five priests that stayed in Nob and that was almost more than the rest of the population in the town.

In the distance Ahimelech sees a single figure approaching the town gates. How crazy, Ahimelech thinks to himself. No one should travel alone these parts. Why did the man not travel with the company of a caravan? Why was he traveling alone during the heat of the day? Ahimelech's attention wanders from the single figure to a group of herdsman standing near the pillars at the temples entrance. The men had arrived a few days ago and a tall man introduced himself as the leader. He had the appearance of a vulture and when Ahimelech spoke with him he had declared that he was the chief herdsman of King Saul.

He's traveling companions all looked like a rogue pack of Hyenas. Ahimelech did not like the men for they were rude, loud and brutal. They had chased some of the other sheep herders away from the water well just outside the temple gates. They had also been over friendly with the woman going to the water well and bared more than just their yellow teeth. Some of the older priests had tried to talk to them. They were made fun off and one afternoon one of the older priests broke he's arm after he intervened when the group harassed some women at the well. The group of men described their behaviour as having a bit of fun and the priest injury as he's own misfortune. Ahimelech shakes he's head again. Some people just never learn.

He's attention turns back to the single figure coming across another dune now much closer than before.

It seems like a young man with a bright red beard. He's beard seem to catch fire in the afternoon sun. The group of herdsmen walks out to the stranger and Ahimelech sadly shakes he's head. It would not be a pleasant reception for the stranger. He calls out to one of the younger priests. "Be ready to go out and treat that man after he is beaten." He walks to the west side of the temple to have a better view and worriedly looks upon the stranger.

"Like a bird walking into the mouth of a Jackal." He thinks to himself.

"Lord please protect him."

Doeg scratches a scab on the side of he's face and swats at an irritating fly that seemed to find its way into he's left nostril all the time. They had been waiting patiently for the lonesome traveller to approach the gate of Nob. The traveller was still too far away to clearly see he's appearance but they waited expectantly trying to see if anyone else travelled with him. It had been more than a full moon cycle that they had been away from Gibeah travelling between the herds.

He belches loudly. The sour smell of the wine he drank not disturbing him at all. Gadar walks over to him handing him the goatskin full of water. "We should have travelled after the caravan this morning. I saw a few pretty little things among the tribes of the Amalekites." Doeg takes a small dagger from he's pouch and tries to clean the dried blood under he's nails. Gadar takes a step backwards when he sees the dagger. Doeg was a betting man. He easily lost he's temper and that was something that Gadar knew all too well. They had left Gibeah a few days ago but did not leave without spilling blood. It was not the first time that they had killed.

Doeg was the king head herdsman and did not raise through the ranks because of he's honesty. He had quickly made himself a reputation among the other herdsmen as a killer and a thief. It was their duty to take stock of the king entire livestock and this enterprise alone was not enriching. Doeg and he's companions found ways to enrich themselves.

"We wait for this fool and then leave for Gibeah in the morning." The lonesome traveller was now much closer and Doeg saw that he had a bushy red beard showing behind the face cover. The man looks tired and yet; there is something about him that Doeg finds disturbing. The man is now a hundred paces away and Doeg and he's men moves forward towards the stranger. Gadar moves in union to he's left accompanied by three other cohorts approaching David in a small half-moon encircling the traveller.

The traveller stops before the group without uttering a word. Doeg stares at the stranger and sees clear green eyes staring back at him from behind the face cover. It does not seem if the traveller has much but Doeg knows that a small pouch of money can easily be hidden in the folds of a man robes. He slowly draws he's dagger; the small group of herders following he's example. "Hand over your money pouch and you may enter the city." David stares at the tall man with the crooked teeth not saying a word. Gadar moves closer to David swinging he's club into the palm of he's hand. The slapping sound makes a corpulent noise. "Are you deaf? Hand over the pouch!" Doeg nods at Gadar and the latter moves in quickly raising the club above he's head.

David waits unto the last moment of impact before he's bends down onto he's left knee scooping some sand into he's right hand. He twists he's upper body taking the impact of the club on he's left shoulder rolling with the blow. He turns towards the attacking man he's hand snakes out throwing the sand into he's attacker eyes. Gadar instinctively covers he's face trying to rub out the burning sand from he's eyes. David moves like a dancer kicking Gadar on he's left knee the sound of the kneecap dislocating heard clearly. Gadar screams he's stinging eyes forgotten as he grabs he's dislocated knee.

David picks up the fallen club lying next to the collapsed body and blocks a blow from one of the other attackers. The man eyes widen as David reverses the club and with a short jab, knocks he's breath out hitting him squarely at the pit of he's stomach.

Doeg waits for the right moment and as David turns he's back to fend off another attack from he's two remaining fighting men he moves in the dagger hilt glimmering in the sunlight. He stabs he's dagger with all he's might bringing down the weapon into David exposed back. The dagger finds its way into flesh and the scream of a man is cut abruptly by the gurgling sound of a chest wound. Doeg stares in unbelief at the hilt of he's dagger protruding from one of he's own men. David had knowingly grabbed onto one of the remaining attackers and pulled him into the path of Doeg attacking thrust. He uses the man as a shield and pushes the body into the remaining attacker the latter stumbling as the body crashes into him.

Doeg looks around in dismay at the strewn bodies of he's men and fear grips him as he faces David. "Spare my life for I am the king head heard man! If you kill me soldiers will come looking for you and when they find you they will kill you." He stares into the green eyes of the eyes of the stranger and feels a cold shiver down he's spine. David points the club at the fallen men. "Take these worthless sheep dung with you and leave this place!" Two of the men help Gadar to he's feet supporting he's body weight as he nurses he's dislocated knee. Doeg moves towards the fallen man that got stabbed with he's dagger. The lifeless eyes stare back at him and he tries to wrench the dagger from the dead man chest. "Leave it!"

David raises the club again. A voice suddenly cries out. "Please don't!" A young man dressed in white robes runs towards them. An old man with white robes is just a few yards behind him. The young man kneels at the dead man body and then with huge eyes he turns towards the older approaching man. "I think he is dead." The older man approaches them and David sees that both men are priests. The older man bows down and touches the dead soldiers slightly at the base of he's neck and then turn towards the younger priest. "Tend to these men wounds and get someone to prepare this man body for burial." The younger priest slowly responds as if in a dreamlike state. Ahimelech looks at the dust wary traveller standing before him. He had seen him twice before. Once in the king tent just before he battled the giant Philistine. When he got married to the king daughter he had seen him for a second time. Fear grips the old man. What was David doing in Nob?

He is sure that the man standing before him recognizes him as well those green eyes burning like fire staring into he's own. First the kings head herdsman and now the king's exiled son in law. The word had spread and Ahimelech knew that Saul was trying to kill David. The whole Israel knew. More priests come to the gate to assist with the injured and fallen man. Ahimelech never takes he's eyes of David "I saw these men attack you but I must know: what is your business in Nob?"

David drops the club into the sand and turns he's back towards the priest taking a few steps back. He bends and picks up a folded sheep skin that he had dropped unnoticed just as Doeg and he's men had blocked he's way. He had slept a little in the last few days and he was as ravenous as a desert lion. He had left Gibeah knowing that he might not ever see Jonathan or Michal again. He felt that the turn of the events of he's life were starting to take their toll. Just three years ago he was tending to he's father flock. Now he was a condemned man. He was an innocent man on the run trying to escape the king's wrath.

He had made he's way to Nob because of the instruction that Samuel had given him. He had told him that if he was in trouble again that he should go to Nob and seek the elder of the temple. He had travelled without sleep for days and some nights. During the scorching days he kept looking over he's shoulder into the distance for the dust cloud of Saul's riders. He could hardly sleep at night fearing that Saul's men might surprise him. He lay freezing not risking the heat of a fire, hardly sleeping fearing that Saul's men might creep upon him. He turns back towards the old priest. He had seen him before. The old priest stares at him with a mixture of surprise and yet suspicion. Was he not David the slayer of ten thousand men? King Saul exiled son in law. Surely they priests knew who he was? He turns towards the older man again. "I am here on business for the king." David looks at the priest reaction to he's words.

"Ahimelech face becomes apprehensive. "You are welcome to stay son of Jesse. May the Lord's blessing be upon you in whatever endeavours await you." Doeg eyes widen in disbelieve when he hears the old priests speak to David. He should have known it was the king exiled son in law! Those eyes should have been a giveaway. He had looked into those eyes before. It was when they had gone to slay the pair of desert lions a few years ago! He shivers when he's mind wanders back to the day. The men enter the gates of Nob and David's stomach turns as the fresh smell of bread fills the air. "That smells good; give me five loafs of bread or whatever can be found to eat." The old priest looks nervously at David. "That is not common bread. The bread you smell is holy bread." The priest sees the facial expression of David change and continues hurriedly.

"The only way that you may have some of it is if you have kept yourself from the arms of a women." David stares at the priest he's hunger almost overpowering his sound reasons. "I have not seen any women for the last three days let alone to be found in the arms of one!" Ahimelech turns towards one of the younger priests. "Get this man some bread and bring us some wine." The priest hurries along to the temple entrance and shortly thereafter he returns with some loaves of steaming bread, a clay jug and some cups. The body of the fallen man was taken away and the injured men left accompanied by some of the younger priests to be treated.

Doeg was the only one left of the party that attacked David. Ahimelech offer some wine to him and he takes the jug without any ceremony. He pours himself a cup and downs it and then refills it again before passing the jug along. David eyes the Edomite prudently. This was Saul head herdsman. He had known that it was him when the Edomite had blocked he's path. He had thought that he had been discovered but kept quite when a demand was made for he's purse. He had quickly realized that the head herdsman had not known who he was but he could see now that that this notion had changed.

Doeg tears off a chunk of bread and stuffs it into he's mouth. He cannot believe he's good fortune! He sat with the most wanted man in Israel. He was already envisioning how the king was going to reward him when he told him about the whereabouts of he's wanted son in law. For a moment he started to daydream about the riches that Saul was going to bestow upon him. The voices of the conversing men bring him back to his current reality. He should find out all that he can about David whereabouts.

He focuses he's attention to the conversation between the priest and the king son in law. David bites into another chunk of bread and speaks to the priest with he's mouth full.

"I had to leave the kings tent in haste for he's business required some urgency." He takes a sip of wine and clears he's throat.

"I am in need of a sword or a spear. Would you be able to supply me with such a weapon or any weapon at all?" Ahimelech scratches he's beard a look of amusement spreads on his face. David request was so ironic! The old priest scratches he's beard he's brow notches in deep ponder. "Come follow me."

David follows the old man into the temple. Doeg follows them at a distance. Ahimelech leads David into a cellar with wine jars stacked closely together. They enter another room behind the cellar and the air in the chamber is very cool. David takes a deep breath enjoying the cool of the chamber after the excoriating heat.

A blue dyed Ephod hangs against the corner wall in the chamber. Ahimelech walks towards the Ephod and stops before it. "After you killed the Philistine champion Goliath, a young soldier brought a sword to the temple claiming that it was the very sword you cut the man called Goliath's head from he's shoulders.

Ahimelech removes the Ephod and takes out an object covered with a dark cloth. He unwraps the object partially exposing the hilt of a sword. David walks over to where the priest is, staring at the partly exposed weapon. He takes the sword out of the priest hands and un-wraps the weapon completely. There is no mistake. This was the sword of the giant Philistine.

There was none like it. He takes the heavy weapon and swings it through the air the weapon making a whooshing sound as it cuts through the air. "Thank you Ahimelech, I will take this sword with me for there may be danger on my expedition and I need to be on my way." Ahimelech feels relief as he realizes that David will not be staying for the night. Outside the chamber Doeg slowly backs away from the talking men. He slips out of the temple and sets of in the direction of Gibeah.

The flowers on the branches of the tamarisk tree stirs slightly in the wind. Saul had travelled north of Gibeah with he's men and had setup camp awaiting news from he's spies on David whereabouts. He is in a rage-full mood pacing under the tree. "My own son has betrayed me! Have anyone else made a covenant with the son of Jesse?

Will he give you fields and vineyards? Will he make you captain of thousands? Why can no one find David?" The men standing close to the king turn their heads from him to avoid he's angry gaze. The soldiers part way when a dust worn traveller makes he's way to the king. Mustapha recognizes the king's chief herdsman as he stumbles before the king's feet. Doeg appearance matches he's evil demeanour.

He's clothing and face are dirty but he's eyes gleam with malice! The king's mood seems to darken as Doeg approaches. "Why are you here you foul smelling man? Have I not commanded you to find new grazing fields for the heard?"

Doeg cowers before Saul. "Your majesty, I bring good news. I have seen the son of Jesse." Saul's whole composure changes and he suddenly sits up like an eager child awaiting he's supper. "Well then, do not just stand there looking pitiful! Where did you see him?" Doeg draws more audacity from the king's exited voice but he's throat feels swollen form thirst. He starts to cough uncontrollably. Saul calls a servant over to them with an irate voice. "Give him some water!"

Mustapha hands a clay goblet to the coughing man and he tilts the cup hastily spilling more water onto he's dust worn robe than he could drink. It takes an interval before he continues with he's story. "We were staying over in Nob and the day before yesterday. We were preparing to move the flocks away from Nob and were station close to the gates of the City. We saw a man came from the desert to the temple of the priests of Nob.

There was something familiar about the man and when he spoke to the old priest I saw that it was your son in law." Doeg takes another drink from the jar and continues his story. "I of course immediately recognized him when he entered the city gates and that is why I followed him. My suspicion was confirmed when he started to talk to the old priest Ahimelech. I heard the old goat say he's name and followed them into the temple. I saw Ahimelech the son of Ahitub gave David some of the temples bread as well as the sword of Goliath.

If I had more men with me I would have tried to apprehend him. Instead I sneaked out of the palace and came here as fast as I could to tell you great king." Saul sits back in he's chair. He never really liked Doeg but at least here was a man that was prepared to follow him even if it meant paying him to do so.

"You did well by coming here to tell me. Was he seeking refuge in Nob?" The herdsman seems to squirm like a puppy at the attention he received and the audience. "No your majesty, he took the bread and a sword that the priest gave him and then said that he was leaving. He did not say where he was going but seemed in a hurry." Saul smiles broadly. "A sword?" He relaxes back into the pillows of he's chair. "Doeg take some men with you. I want you to send for Ahimelech. He must not come alone but let all of he's father house come to me. It is going to be a glorious day indeed!"

The City of Gath stands like a fortress in the night. The Philistine soldiers escorting David did not let their watchfulness slip. One would nudge him with a spear shaft every time he seemed to slow down. An unfamiliar feeling creeps upon David.

Perhaps he felt fear? It was a thick feeling that sat in the back of he's throat and in the pit of he's stomach. It was like the experience of being aware that a leopard was stalking it's pray in the dark but with the knowledge that he was the prey! Was it because of the sheer height of the men walking beside him? Was it because he was captured and brought into the Philistine's stronghold? The same Philistine's that he had met so many times on the battle field in the past few quarters. The time when he defeated Goliath suddenly seemed a like a faraway memory.

"Move along!" The guard shoves him into the small of he's back. After he had left the city of Nob he had thought about where he was going next. Ironic enough it was the sword that he's that he got from the priest that made him decide to go to the Philistine's. "If King Saul wants me dead then who better to join than the people that wants the king dead? I will hide among the king enemy" He's plan seemed like a great idea at the time. He had buried the sword he got from the priest as soon as he had the city in sight. There was no need to draw unnecessary attention to himself. He had approached the city walls with he's hands raised above he's head but the guards brutally attacked him and dragged him into the inner sanctum of the city. He was half stunned by the attack and suddenly he's plan seemed like the most foolish thing that he had done in he's entire life. The guards half dragged him along and he tried to keep count of the numerous doors they had entered through.

David lost all sense of direction and when he had felt strong enough he started to walk by himself again the guards prodding him all the way. They enter into a long dark passage and the sounds of laughing men grow louder as they continue. They round another corner and suddenly they enter a bright lit chamber. A long wooden table is set in the middle of the room and a big fire burns brightly. The shadows of the men that sit at the tables dance against the clay walls. No one seems to take notice of the trio as they enter. David however stares at the man sitting at the head of the table. He had seen that trident beard in the Philistine's war party before. This was Achish the king of Gath. The fear David had felt had now increased and he has to make an effort to keep himself from trying to break free and escape. The man on David's left side approaches the king and talks to him holding he's mouth close to the king ear. The king looks in David's direction. The laughter and noise die down as the king slowly rises from he's chair. He approaches David and comes to a stop an arms-length away from him. The men around the table had all turned towards David now. David feels the sweat running from he's brow and back. "What is your business in the city of Gath? Why were you outside the city walls? Are you a spy? " The ice in the king's voice does not escape David. An idea broods in he's mind. "I need to act at the right time." He thinks to himself. He had worn the same clothes the last two weeks and he's clothes were full of dirt and sweat. He's beard had grown much longer and profuse since he's departure from Nob and he was sure that king Achish did not recognize him. The king stares at him and strokes he's own trident beard. "I am sure we have met before. I never forget a face I have seen on the battlefield." The king's eyes stare coldly into he's. It reminds David of the specie of king Cobra that he had seen on the market squares of Jebus. "Majesty I have also seen this man before." The speaker a bald man with lots of scars on he's flat ugly face has now left the table staring intently at David. "I am almost sure this is David slayer of Philistine armies!" The sarcasm drips from the man's voice. "David?" The king now also stares at David he's face devoid of any emotion. "The same David they sing about? What was the song? Oh yes! Saul has slain he's thousands and David he's ten thousands." David stares into Achish eyes. Those eyes spell death. If he admits to the truth he will surly die. Time to act on the short formulated plan.

He falls down on his knees and he starts to froth from he's mouth the salvia falling down into he's beard. This is the last thing that Achish and his men expected. The King of Gath jumps back bumping into scar face. David rolls he's eyes and then he starts to crawl on his hands and knees in the dirt. He crawls toward the men sitting at the table and they open a path for him like Moses through the sea. David pulls himself up onto the table he's eyes still rolling making animal like sounds. He launches himself back against the door they had entered as if in a spasm. He starts to scratch at the wooden door increasing he's growls.

"What madness is this?" Achish voice had raised a note or two. "This man is possessed by Dagon's devils! Get him out of here or we all will become impotent, and our women barren!" The two guards that brought David into the city rushes towards him and the last thing that David remembers is the pain as a wooden spear shaft cracks against he's skull and then there is total darkness...

"Now hear me son of Ahitub!" Ahimelech's eyes are wide with fear but he tries to conceal it as he gawks at the speaker.

When Doeg had arrived back at Nob with the king soldiers he knew it spelled trouble. Doeg had told him that he and the rest of the priests were summoned by King Saul. He knew that something was amiss. He expected something bad but did not expect to see the king in such a dark mood. He now feared for the worst. Saul continues his brash address. "I want to know why you conspired against me. I know that you gave David a sword and some bread at the temple. What else did he tell you? Do you know where he went? Why did you help the enemy of your king?"

Ahimelech shakes he's head in fear faltering over his prattling words. "I did not know that David was your sworn enemy your majesty. When he came out of the desert and asked for help I did not think twice about he's requests. Is he not your son in law? When you asked him to do your biding he did not hesitate for who is as faithful as your servant David?"

Saul rises from he's chair. "You fool! You have conspired against the king! You and your whole house will surely die! Kill them! Kill all the priests! They have chosen to take the side of David! They have conspired against me and did not tell me where David had fled!"

The guards standing in the king's chamber have not moved a muscle since the king's outburst. "I said kill them all! Why are you just standing there?" Mustapha looks at the mad eyes of the king and the trembling priest. He knows that the men were not eager to raise their swords against the priests of Yahweh. They feared Saul but to kill a priest seemed outrages.

"Are all of you cowards?" Saul had completely lost control and in desperation he turns towards Doeg. "How about you Doeg? Whose side are you on?" Doeg scrambles towards the king's chair and takes Saul sword from he's hands. Without a word he turns towards Ahimelech and stabs the sword trough he's throat. The old priest grabs the sword but Doeg withdraws the blade cutting into the old man hands. Two severed fingers fall onto the ground and Saul's mad laughter mixes with the dying priest gurgling scream. "Now after you have killed all of these worthless traitors I want you to take a band of men and go to the city of Nob.

Kill every living thing in the city! Let all know that king Saul will not tolerate traitors!

Chapter 7

The wind hollers through the open mouth of the cave. Somewhere the dripping of water can be heard in the background. The wounds on David's face and head had started to heal. The walloping that he received by the Philistines hands while he was unconscious was without mercy. When he awoke he found himself outside the gates of Gath every part of he's body was hurting and there was a dried clot of blood at the back of his head. He was afraid that the soldiers might come back to give him another beating or even worse. He got up and stumbled onward into the desert.

He collected the sword of Goliath that he had buried before he was captured and headed into the desert. The morning glow showed on the horizon and he kept on walking until the sun rose high in the sky. He's thirst was unbearable but he kept on walking until the salty air of the Mediterranean Sea greeted he's nostrils.

This only made him thirstier. David slowly continued down the coast line until he reached a sheer cliff rock hanging out over the sea. He climbed the rock face and while climbing he stumbled upon the opening of the cave he found himself in. At first he was too tired to explore he's surroundings and he lay in the coolness of the enclosure. After a while he's curiosity got the better of him. The mouth of the cave was very narrow. He used he's a tinder box and lit a part of cloth mixed with fat to explore the cave. He found water coming out against the rock wall of the cave. To he's surprise when he tasted it was sweet and refreshing. He closed he's eyes and drank until he's stomach felt like it would burst. He was bone wary and tired and made himself comfortable near the entrance of the cave. He fell asleep and only awoke during the cold of the morning hours. He's body was stiff and he's stomach ached. He had not eaten in the last few days and he felt weak and he's wounds hurt profoundly. He lay still listening to the sound of the waves crashing against the rock cliff below. The sound below felt like his only companion to his lonely thoughts. Everything just seemed to get worse by the day. What happened? The thoughts of loneliness and despair become too much and David quietly cries and talks to Yahweh.

"I will bless Yahweh at all times. He's praise will always be in my mouth. My soul shall boast in Yahweh. The humble shall hear of it, and be glad. Oh magnify Yahweh with me. Let us exalt he's name together.

I sought Yahweh, and he answered me, and delivered me from all my fears. They looked to him, and were radiant. Their faces shall never be covered with shame. This poor man cried, and Yahweh heard him, and saved him out of all he's troubles. Yahweh's angels encamps around those who fear him, and delivers them.

Oh taste and see that Yahweh is good. Blessed is the man who takes refuge in him. H fear Yahweh, you he's saints, for there is no lack with those who fear him. The young lions do lack, and suffer hunger, but those who seek Yahweh shall not lack any good thing.

Come you children, listen to me. I will teach you the fear of Yahweh. Who is someone who desires life, and loves many days, that he may see good? Keep your tongue from evil, and your lips from speaking lies. Depart from evil, and do good. Seek peace, and pursue it. Yahweh's eyes are towards the righteous. He's ears listen to their cry.

Yahweh face is against those who do evil, to cut off their memory from the earth. The righteous cry, and Yahweh hears, and he delivers them out of all their troubles. Yahweh is near to those who have a broken heart, and saves those who have a crushed spirit. Many are the afflictions of the righteous, but Yahweh delivers him out of them all. He protects all of he's bones.

Not one of them is broken. Evil shall kill the wicked. Those who hate the righteous shall be condemned. Yahweh redeems the soul of he's servants. None of those who take refuge in him shall be condemned." (Psalm 34)

A soft wind sweeps into the cave and David hears the words that he's soul had thirsted for. His grieve gives way to joy and the comfort that the words bring. "Do not be afraid for I am with you son of Jesse".

A breeze picks up the loose grains of sand and blows it across the coastal sands.

The Oryx stand relaxed grazing on the scattered sea grass knolls. Their beautiful horns shine in the early morning sun and with a quick swing of their black wispy tails they chase away the irritating flies. David had been stalking after these animals for the last hour. The wind was in he's favour but he had to move slowly behind the dunes for the cover was not that good. The Oryx faces look like it has been painted with black and white paint. The almost identical horns of the Oryx are long and straight looking like two black spears.

When he was younger, he and he's brothers had learned very quickly how deadly those horns could be. Once they went hunting with their father and Jesse had taught them how to kill these magnificent beasts. "You have to make sure that you creep up very close to them. Hunting these animals requires patience and speed for they are as swift as the desert wind." He and he's brothers had made a semi - circle around the group of animals. They made sure that they were standing down the wind blowing from the eastern direction slightly from where the animals stood. As per their father instruction they would creep up to them as close as they could and then would sit and wait behind a dune. He's father would then instruct him to go around and approach from the other side of the circle in the same direction as the wind making sure the animals picked up he's scent.

When the animals smelled the approaching person they normally stood still, their big ears turning in every direction trying to see the danger. Eliab; David's oldest brother would give the signal and he would start running towards the Oryx clapping he's hands making a great noise. The animals would flee right in the direction where the semi- circle of men crouched. As soon as the animals came among them they would jump up and try to spear a fleeing animal. The best way to bring down one of these animals would be to spear the Oryx just behind where he's fore legs and he's ribs met. The spear would be driven through he's lungs and it would be a mortal wound. After one of their first hunts a big male went down with a spear sticking from he's side. They all had whooped and screamed with excitement and they had rushed in on the big animal. When they tried to move closer to give the Oryx the death stab the beast had suddenly jumped up and used those spear like antlers to defend itself.

Every time one of them tried to rush in to finish the beast it would turn he's head towards the person fending with those antlers. When one of them came too close the Oryx would then drop he's head between he's shoulders attacking the person the great antlers acting as spears. Shammah had almost been stabbed when he had stumbled in the way of the attacking Oryx. Was it not that Abinadab and Eliab came in from the side to give the Oryx the death thrust Shammah might have been mortally wounded. The boy's had learned on that day that they should never be on the receiving side of those antlers.

David is brought back to the present by the movement before him. It was going to be difficult trying to hunt these great beasts alone. David trusted the Lord. He had laid he's heart bare before the Lord and felt at peace again. He tests the weight of the spear in his hand. He had crafted it with the sword of Goliath from a branch of a thorn tree near the cave.

Suddenly without warning the pack of animals burst into a wild run coming directly at where David was positioned. David crouches low behind the dune. The wind was blowing in the opposite direction and would not give his scent away. An Oryx almost runs into David but swerves swiftly when it spots the man crouched lowly. David speedily stabs he's spear into the flank of the fleeing animal feeling that familiar feeling as the spear passes through the ribcage into the lung capacity. The Oryx goes down heavily kicking up a dust cloud.

David is about to run to the fallen animal when he notices a man standing at the top of the dune where the animals came running from. That must have been the reason why they have become spooked. David's spear is still embedded in the side of the Oryx and he has nothing left to defend himself. He had left the great sword in the cave because it would have only slowed him down. The man moves to his left and only then does David notice another Oryx felled down. David spots two arrows sticking from its flank. The approaching man kneels down at the Oryx extracting the arrows from the carcass.

David notices that the man is well build, he's forearms flexing with muscle as he extract the arrows. The complexion of the man is darker than he's own reminding David of some of the Arab traders that he had seen near Jebus. The man puts the arrows in some sort of a holder hanging behind he's back. He takes the bow and hangs it around he's shoulder and then he stands smiling at David.

"That was a pretty impressive throw. I did not expect you to fell the Oryx" The man's Hebrew is perfect and he's voice sounds genuine. "My name is Benaiah the son of Jehoiada." David had heard this name "Jehoiada" before. Jahoiada was a known man from Kabzeel. Jesse had traded with him before. The tall man turns towards the Oryx. He takes a long knife from a sheath hanging by he's side and starts to skin the animal. David walks over to Banaiah and sits on the other side of the Oryx.

"I am David son of Jesse the Bethlehemite." At the mention of he's name, Benaiah raises an eyebrow but without missing a stroke continues with the bloody work. David stares at the carcass before him but he saw the look on the man face when he had introduced himself.

"Do you live around these parts?" The escaping sound of gas hissing followed by a bit of a stench erupts as Benaiah cuts through the Oryx's entrails. Benaiah answers without looking at him "I live of the land but am far from home." Benaiah digs a hole in the sand and picks up the entrails burying it in the hole that he had dug. "Don't want a lion on our trail, do we?

Benaiah stops for a moment looking into David face. "I have not seen any footprints or evidence of other company. Why are you alone in this desolate place? Are you an outcast?" The question came without accusation. The knife gleams in the sunlight and Benaiah expertly continues to skin the Oryx not immediately responding to David question. Only the sound of the knife cutting into the flesh is audible. Benaiah response is pacified.

"When a man is alone in this part of the desert do you normally assume him to be an outcast?" Benaiah stops the skinning process. He establishes direct eye-contact with David.

"I know who you are son of Jesse. I know that King Saul is trying to kill you. I have come to pledge my allegiance." David is astounded by he's words. "Pledge your allegiance? Why?" Benaiah returns the knife to its sheath.

"Many stories have spread through Israel and two moons ago a prophet came and spoke to my father. He told me to come and seek you in the desert and pledge my alliance for you are the chosen king of Israel.

The Lord is preparing a mighty army for Israel.

The tall trees sway lightly in the wind. David rises slowly listening to the pecking sound of a woodpecker echoing through the still forest. He walked away from the camp early before the sun had risen thinking about the words that Abiathar had spoken the day before. The young priest had found them where they were camped out in the forest Hereth.

Abiathar's news was shocking. How could King Saul have done something so horrendous? David had listened to the exhausted priest account and only prodded gently with a few questions of he's own. "What about the rest of Nob?" he had asked. The dust covered priest bright blue eyes became moist as he continued.

"All of them were struck with the edge of Doeg and he's men swords. The men, woman, children, nursing infants, oxen, donkeys and sheep where all killed. King Saul allowed me to escape the brutal assault and he knows you are camped here in Hereth."

David had told the son of Ahimelech to take shelter with him and he's group of men. The priest had then handed him a package. "I brought this and the Lord will reveal himself when you wear this and call the name of the Lord." David quietly un-rap the package covered in the sheep-fleece. The emeralds on the Ephod reflect slightly in the moonlit sky. "Is this not meant for the High priest?" Ahimelech had only beamed and looked him earnestly in the eyes when her responded. "Seek the Lord Yahweh with all your heart and He will answer you."

David could not sleep that night. He left the tree platform and slowly descended down the narrow forest path. Some of the men had already woken. Their cooking fires are evident and he sees white clouds of wispy smoke drifting through the trees. They were almost three hundred men now.

A few days after he had met Benaiah, more men came to find him. He's father and brothers had also sought him out while in the city of Moab. He had met the king of Moab. King Mizpah. The king welcomed the great conqueror of the Philistine armies into he's city with open arms. David knew that the Philistines were also Moab common enemy.

His father had told him that Saul had send soldiers to look for him. Jesse decided to leave their home and it was the prophet Samuel who shared insight on David whereabouts. While they spend time in the stronghold of Moab more men sought him out. David was soon to learn that most of them were sought by authority in essence outlawed and hunted for tribunal. Some had accrued debt that they could not pay. Others had had been detached from their communities and were hunted by the authority. Each person had a different story why they wanted to stay with David's group. David never asked them too many questions but gave all asylum. David felt the presence of Yahweh stir he's heart and he felt compassion for the men that came to him. These men had hardened faces. Some of them looked like desert dwellers and yet some were craftsmen and shepherds while other remained somewhat of a mystery to him. Many brought their wives and children and at first David had wondered if it was good to have woman and children. He had learned that if a man had he's family with him that he had more rectitude to live up to so he allowed them to come. There were men pledged their allegiance but decided to leave their wives and children in Moab. Some men were a paradox to him. The man called Benaiah was one of these men. David had enquired about he's wife and if he had children. He had looked David in the eyes and spoke with he's gruff voice. "There is someone here in Moab but I will return for her when the time is right." That was all that Benaiah had to say about he's mystery woman. He saw Benaiah often depart the company of the men wandering of into the inner city of Moab only to return in the morning hours. He did not question the big man but found he's actions strange. David made a decision to stay in the stronghold of Moab for a bit longer and fight with the king of Moab. The time went by swiftly and on a day when the armies of Israel and of Moab departed the king gave David a strange looking dagger. The hilt was made of a hard white substance that Mizpah called ivory. "This is a token of my friendship young David. You are a brave young man and should you require my service do not be afraid to call on me." One night while sitting around a fire, Jesse had used the knife to cut some beef of an Oryx that they had grilled and had told David about the great beasts that carried the white ivory. David had listened intently to Jesse story and wanted to lay he's eyes on one of the beasts. The weeks went by and David was also visited by a prophet called Gad. Samuel had send him and he spoke in earnest with David "David the Lord Yahweh has spoken these words to He's servant David. Do not stay in the stronghold; depart and go to the land of Judah." David felt confused but he spoke to he's father and soon after the prophet had spoken to him he went to speak to king Mizpah. The king was disappointed to hear of their departure but Mizpah had sworn he's alliance to David. After a long festive night David and he's men had left the stronghold and had travelled South West towards the forest of Hereth. They had setup camp and more men had joined them.

As he now continues through the forest in the early morning hours he hears the droning sound of a large water mass. He had reached a place in the forest where the water falling onto the rocks of a large waterfall almost drowned out all the sounds of the forest in the early morning hours. He makes he's way down close to the big clear pool side the misty spray of water forming droplets on he's beard and brow.

He takes the Ephod and hang it around he's shoulders and kneels next to the pool speaking softly.

"Lord in You I take refuge. You have said flee to the forest of Hereth and I have done that. The wicked are bending their bows and setting their arrow against the city of Keilah. Lord what shall I do? You examine the righteous but the wicked, those who love violence you hate. Lord You are righteous and just. I wait on you."

David's hair and beard is completely soaked by the falling water cloud. In the rumble of the water he hears a voice.

"Let Eleazar son of Dodai, the man with the blades take refuge with you. I will command you about the city of Keilah."

David takes the Ephod from he's shoulders and brushes he's fingers through he's wet hair. The Lord had spoken and he would soon meet another stranger. "Eleazar."

"The fighting started early in the morning an hour before day break." Eleazar leans on he's two long swords, he's hawk like eyes fixed on he's new leader. The man moved effortlessly and commanded so much respect but it was not just he's human stature that commanded respect, it was something more. It was the presence of the Yahweh of Israel. He returns he's gaze to the fighting below. Without looking at David he addresses he's lately accepted leader.

"They easily broke through the defences of the men of Keilah." He points at another group of attacking soldiers in the distance with he's one long sword the blade gleaming in the early morning sun. The soldiers below overpower the group of defending men standing at the harvest floor. As a front ranked combatant standing in line with the fighting men Eleazar exclaims loudly. "They are robbing the threshing floors! Shall we attack now?"

David looks at the Benjamite shaking he's head. "Give it some time Eleazar. Yahweh has shown us the way. We will attack on the West side of the gate shortly. Ready the group of men."

Eleazar gaze moves towards another division of men below. He turns away from David and then slides down the rope to the ground. The craftsmen had strengthened the wooden platforms high up in the trees for shelter and protection against man and beast. The creation was simple but it served its purpose.

The tall warrior moves quietly through the assembled men waiting for David's further instruction. He had never felt the need to follow anyone. He was Eleazar the son of Dodai. He had no rules and chose to share he's line of expertise with those who paid well. He's reputation as a slayer and bounty hunter also preceded him.

He shakes he's head as to clear the cob webs creeping into he's mind. He's plan was to kill David and yet it ended when he had the dream. After that he had met David and he's first impression was that of a man that commanded great respect. He could not put he's finger on it. Because of the dream he knew that this was a man that was going to be a great king. The meeting with David was somehow overshadowed by the man that had appeared in his dream. The man had filled him with an emotion of fear and yet overpowering love. Goose bumps crawl along he's neck again. The eyes of the man burned bright and without a word commanded great fear. Still there was a gentle mercy when the man spoke to him that overpowered and brought his presence in excellence. The image of the man that spoke to him was still imprinted so fresh in he's memory.

The sounds of fighting down below again draw he's attention and he can feel the blood rushing through he's veins eagerly waiting to draw he's blades. So how did he find himself in the service of an outlawed yet to be king? It had been he's mission to kill David and yet here he was ready to wage war with the man. It was the Yahweh of Israel that made all the difference. He's mind wanders, reminiscing the past days that had brought him to this moment and place.

He was traveling through Jebus when he had heard about the reward offered by King Saul to kill and bring the head of David the king son in law. He had decided to take the job. Why not? He had killed for much less intriguing stories. The bounty was desirable! The king soldiers that read the decree made it clear that Saul would pay in gold for the man's head but much more if he was brought alive.

For him personally it was not about the riches anymore. Every silver piece he had earned was drenched in blood. He had experienced many restless nights seeing he's victims lifeless eyes staring back at him. How many lives had he taken? He did not feel remorse but lately something was prodding him at the depths of he's inner man. The riches had become a burden. He had fictitious friends and bought desire without love. He had hunted after innumerable of prizes. Every-time it seemed that it was the exhilaration of the bounty that prevailed.

He had taken to challenge and set out to do what he did best. He followed he's usual subterfuge when he started to look for David. First He visited the surrounding towns. He joined the men after they came from the fields at night and listened to the stories told around the campfires. He spent he's nights like this for the next couple of days sometimes also visiting the nearby taverns.

It also came as no surprise that the first time he heard David's name was in one of the small taverns that he visited outside the City of Moab. He heard some men speak of the brigand like some sort of a conqueror. He was sitting at a wooden table listening to a group of men that had drunk a fair amount of ale. The men were loud enough and when the name David suddenly rang-out above the noises of the tavern he was almost unsure if he had heard properly. The ale was flowing and they were talking louder. He had heard many tales when men were intoxicated and always the tales were exaggerated. The men were talking about the act when David slayed a giant called Goliath.

This was not the first time that he had heard about this exploit. Eleazar stared at one of the men with he's back slightly turned towards him voicing he's slurred opinion. The man ended he's account and slammed he's jug of ale on the table declaring that he had decided to join David and he's group of men. For a moment Eleazer had pondered those words. What group of men? He also found it interesting that the men talked about joining David. He would have thought that the men would have tried and collect on the bounty rather than join the fugitive. He smiled inwardly.

Not all men are killers. He would soon collect the bounty himself. The mood of the men sounded less audacious. It was the right moment to join the group and he did so by offering them an extra round of the hot brewing ale.

The night was no longer young and the men accepted he's offer without riposte. They did not try to reason why they received free drinks from the tall dark stranger. Soon they seemed to forget that he was a stranger in their midst and drew him into the conversation. Eleazar took the opportunity and steered the conversation back to David. He admitted that he heard about the story of the giant Philistine defeat at the hands of David. The men did not mind to be drawn back into this discussion. The night drew along and the men made no secret that David was building an army who they would soon join. Eleazar gamble to join the group of men paid off. One of the man to he's right secretively leaned towards him. The man's breath could have spurned a lion's attack. He whispered (well it was barely a whisper) that he knew the whereabouts of David and he's men. He threw he's arm around Eleazar shoulder and grinned proudly and announced that he's brother had joined David in the forest of Hereth.

It was the information that he needed and after another round of beer he left the group of men with some objection of feigned friendship. He sought the young harlot he saw at the tavern door when he had arrived. He woke up the next morning he's mouth feeling as dry as the desert sand. He's head was pounding like a thousand garrison horses thundering through the plains. The woman had left he's side before he woke and he preferred this because he did not like long emotional departures.

He took a long drink from a water well and washed he's face. He tried to eat a little oatmeal which he mixed with the water and felt he's stomach settle. He packed up he's belongings and took he's long blades draping them across he's back in the scabbards that an old blacksmith had made on he's request. The pounding headache seemed much more bearable as he recalled the events of the previous night.

"Hereth" He spoke the name softly. He would travel to Judah and then to the forest Hereth at Keilah. He had taken he's sheepskin pack and without looking back he travelled towards Judah. As he continued the heat of the sun took care of the previous night antic's as he sweated out most of the brew. In he's mind the encounter with David continuously played itself out and although the outcome was him killing the man there was an uncertainty about he's thought process. He knew that it would not be easy to kill him. As he had gathered the man was surrounded by he's own men. He must have some experience in combat if even some of the claims against the Philistine giant was true. He thought about the words of the man the previous night. Suddenly it became much easier and clearer to him. He would enter David's camp and spend time with the men and get close to him before he acted.

That night he slept on the soft needles of pine trees. It would take another day maybe two before he entered David's camp. He was tired and fell asleep instantly. He dreamed about he's mother and then realized deep in he's subconscious that she was murdered and the scene changed. He was walking very warily in a dark forest. He immediately knew that he was stalking the man that brought him on this quest. The man they called David. He felt out of breath and was trying to control the rhythm of he's breathing. He pushed through thick branches and then suddenly staggered into a clearing in the forest. He looked up into the sky and only saw thick clouds, the moonlight concealed behind a thick blanket of clouds. He looked straight ahead and spotted a silhouette of a man standing close to him.

The moonlight broke through the clouds and the face of the man before him was illuminated portraying a bearded face. "David." He just knew it had to be him! He uttered the name but no audible word was spoken. He had expected David to be bigger, taller and somewhat older. He stared at the bearded face and then experienced a certain fear for the man standing before him. He was not accustomed to the feeling but there was something about the man that was overpowering. He decided to move into a different position and walked down an embankment along the river close to where David was standing. He continued at a safe distance to make he's way towards David using the undergrowth close to the river to hide him. He drew he's long swords; the moonlight reflecting on the blades. Everything seemed to slow down. He experienced a moment were he knew he was dreaming and it became very clear to him that he had fallen asleep on the forest floor. Was he still dreaming? Everything felt so real? He could not see David anymore and it seemed like the forest had engulfed him in its thick branches. He continued through the thicket and again he entered into another clearing in the forest. There was a vibrant sound of a stream squabbling over the mountain rocks. The figure of David appeared again close to the stream. He kneeled on he's one knee and scooped up water with he's hands. Eleazar started to creep closer. A silence had fallen upon the forest and even the stream was quite. He's hair stood out on the back of he's neck. There was sudden movement to he's left and he turned he's attention to the moving object. He crept closer to where he saw the movement. A bright light exploded from the branches ahead of him and he covered he's face with he's forearms the swords pointing into the air. He strained to see against the blinding light and made out a silhouette of an enormous man standing close to a tree just behind the mountain stream. He could not see the man's face and Eleazar felt all the hair on he's body stand at end. The man slowly walked towards him and Eleazar tried to move back but he could not move at all. Eleazar had never been a superstitious being but he knew with he's whole heart that this was not an ordinary man. The man drew near and Eleazar felt he's breathing increase and tried to lift he's swords but to no avail. The man face became clear and what he looked upon made he's tongue stuck to the inside of he's mouth. The man's eyes burned like crystals and Eleazar felt he's knees weaken. He tried to lift he's arms again but he could not move. Eleazar tried to move he's head away from the fierce stare but he could not. Then the man spoke to him "Eleazar son of Dodai. The Lord sees you. You must not harm David for he is the Lord's anointed King" Eleazar could not get a word out. The man spoke again "You will be one of King David's men. You will be a leader and the Lord of Abraham, Isaac and Jacob has selected you. The Lord will strengthen you and you will stand by David side." Eleazar did not try to speak anymore. The man touched he's shoulder. "Now awake mighty warrior. You are chosen by the Ancient of Days. Go and find David." He woke up the burning eyes of the man were imprinted in he's memory and the hair on he's fore arms stood at end again. He sat up staring at the half moon shining through the branches of the forest floor. He looked around him but there was no trace of any movement as far as he could see. It was in the early morning hours and the lonely hoot of an owl greeted him.

He decided to get up and continue. Who was the man that he saw in he's dream? How did He know he's name? Why did the man command him not to kill David?

"David." He uttered the name he's voice traveling much further in the early morning. He felt different after he had said he's name but why? Who was this Ancient of Days? Then it dawned on him as sure as he had ever felt about anything before in he's life. He knew that he was not going to kill David. He's thoughts were occupied by he's vision and he continued deeper into the forest. He's years and experience as an assassin had honed he's senses and instinctively he knew someone was close by in the forest ahead. He's had learned to trust the skills he had acquired over the years and he now followed this instinct immediately. He dropped to he's left knee and rolled behind a tree both long swords drawn. Was it the man with the burning eyes?

A few feet away he saw a big man leaning against a tree obscured by some low hanging branches. He was normal, well at least he's eyes seemed human but he was also enormous. A rumbling voice spoke out into the cold of the morning.

"You will have no need for those." The man spat out the piece of grass he was chewing. He looked calm and did not sound surprised to see him. He was definitely a warrior. The scars on he's huge forearms give him away. Eleazar switches the balance of he's sword not wanting to come too close to the man arms reach should he need to use he's weapons. The man draws another stem of grass from the ground and lazily continues to chew the one end of the stem. He stares at Eleazar with a certain amusement and again gestures he's head looking at he's blades.

"I said: You will have no need for those." The man did not use a threatening tone in he's voice when he spoke. There was also no fear but composure in his countenance. He said nothing after that and continued to stare at Eleazar. He's jaw moved slowly chewing one end of the grass producing from he's teeth. Eleazar did not drop he's blades.

"I am Eleazar Son of Dodi. I have come to seek out the man they call David." Benaiah scratches he's beard, still staring at Eleazar. David had told him to come to the forest and meet with a tall man with blades.

"Bring him to the camp and tell him that the Ancient of Days had already prepared he's way." Benaiah knew Yahweh had spoken to David and obeyed without asking questions.

Benaiah continues in the same intonation. "He said you will come." Eleazar frowns at the big man shaking he's head. "Who are you talking about?" Benaiah turns towards the denser forest cove and starts to walk. Eleazar was in two minds about putting he's sword away and then Benaiah spoke again and that made all the difference. "I am Benaiah. Follow me and do not fret for the Ancient of days said you will come." Eleazar drops he's swords to he's sides the hair on he's arms standing at end again. "Who is this Ancient of days?" Benaiah stops and turns back towards Eleazar. "He is the one and only true Yahweh. He is the Yahweh of Abraham, Isaac, Moses and Israel." Without another word Benaiah turns and walks further into the forest. The big man continued quietly taken into account he's great bulk. Eleazar was amazed how such a big man moved so quietly through the dense forest. He kept pace with the man making sure that he did not sound like a herd of stampeding water buffalo through the forest.

They continued until the sun had risen just above the line of the forest trees. Benaiah slowed down and gave a long whistle followed by two shorter whistles. In the distance Eleazar heard someone respond in the same manner. They made their way down a game path and the noise of water falling into a pool became audible. The trees seemed denser and there was a lot of plants growing in the shaded forest surroundings that covered the forest floor. The trunks of the trees where thicker and the bark was darker than the trees higher up the slope where they came from. They rounded another bend in the game trail that rapidly descended into a basin of trees. It was quite astounding and it seemed like a forest within a forest. The subordinate branches of the trees stood level with them as they continued down the steep path. Unexpectedly they stood at the edge of a camp settlement. Eleazar looked around him taking in the scene before him. There were groups of people as far as he could see. There must have been more than two hundred people on the forest floor. Some of them where sitting around small fires sheltered by river stones and yet others were busy with crafting work that seemed like spears and swords.

Eleazar was astounded to see woman in the area and even children playing around. It was only then that Eleazar noticed movement up in the canopy of the trees. There were people in the trees! He looked up and saw elevated stilts with wooden platforms in many of the surrounding trees. Eleazar followed Benaiah and a very few people took notice of them as they continued. The came to a stop at some stilts and Benaiah started to climb pegs that protruded from the trees.

"I hope you are not afraid of heights." The big man said as he looked down at him from the elevated platform he was lifting he's bulk onto. Eleazar climbed nimbly and climbed onto a wide platform with robust structures that was created upon them for shelter. Benaiah walked past the structures and they came out onto a second clearing with another crafted platform. "This must be used as a lookout point." Eleazar thought to himself. Another man with a sword made he's way towards Benaiah and glanced at him for a moment as the men conversed. Both of them walked towards the end of the platform that was screened by a huge branch and Eleazar heard Benaiah talk. Shortly after Benaiah returned and behind him a man with a ruddy face and red beard followed him and came and stood before him. There was a great sword hanging from a scabbard on he's side that almost dwarfed he's appearance.

He's green eyes sparkled brightly and a smile showed on his bearded face. Eleazar realized that although he had never seen he's face before there was an assertive knowing that it was David. It seemed like David read he's mind but did not say a word to him. David turns toward Benaiah and the other soldier on the platform.

"Leave us for a while." The two men set of towards the edge of the platform and without a word Benaiah great bulk disappears from he's view followed by the other soldier. David points at pillows propped up against the wooden rail. "Please sit down." Eleazar sits down folding both he's swords across he's lap he's eyes never leaving David. David moves towards a pillow across the platform and in a similar fashion folds the giant sword across he's lap. "Welcome Eleazar son of Dodi." David speaks with the authority of a leader that has commanded great armies in battle.

Eleazar is reminded of the stories he had heard that David had slain thousands upon thousands of Philistine soldiers when he was in Saul service. The young man eyes also never left he's and he almost bowed he's head to David but thought better of it. "How is it that you know my name?" David acknowledges the question with a droll smile and yet again he speaks with a calm yet commanding tone. "The one true Yahweh has shown me that you will come." Eleazar think about he's own dream but does not give any words to this memory, instead he's frown increases and he feels more confused than before. "Where is this one true Yahweh?" As he asks the question, Eleazar hands instinctively move towards he's swords, he's hands touching the hilts of the blades. He did not want to be slain over a dispute over Yahweh. David however ignores the motion and pauses a moment before he answers. "Why should the nations ask us, Where is your God? Our Yahweh is in heaven; He does whatever He wishes." David spoke with zeal and Eleazar moves around uncomfortably. "I have seen many gods. The Philistines worship their god and yet no worth seem to come from it. Why is your Yahweh different?" David's left eyebrow lifts slightly but he calmly answers. "Their gods are made of silver and gold, formed by human hands. They have mouths, but cannot speak, and eyes but cannot see. They have ears, but cannot hear, and noses, but cannot smell. They have hands, but cannot feel, and feet but cannot walk; they cannot make a sound. David pauses for a moment. "All these are gods that are dead but not the Ancient of days" Eleazar shivers. "Why do you call him that?" David stretches he's left leg out the giant blade scraping against the wooden platform. "Yahweh covers himself with light as with a garment. He stretches out the heavens like a curtain. He makes he's messengers winds; he's servants flames of fire. He laid the foundation of the earth, that it should not be moved forever." (Psalm 104 v 2 – 5) Eleazar moves uncomfortably. "It is Yahweh, who is enthroned from old, who does not change." Eleazar gets up from he's pillow and paces the wooden deck the emotions running wild in he's inner being. "I have heard the stories of the Yahweh of Israel. I have heard great testimonies of the wonders that He has performed that one surely can only believe if you could see it. I have heard that He has punished he's own people and that they dwelled in the desert for forty years. I am a man that have killed many. I will surely be killed by this Yahweh if he knows my ways!" Eleazar looks at David with searching eyes. "We have all sinned, even as our descendants did; we have done wrong and acted wickedly. When our descendants were in Egypt, they gave no thought to He's miracles; they did not remember He's many kindnesses, and they rebelled by the Red sea. Yet He saved them for He's name sake, to make He's mighty power known." Eleazar shoulders slumps and for the first time ever in he's life there is a feeling of deepened remorse. "If it is true that the Yahweh of Israel is the only one true Yahweh then I must leave this place for He will rebuke me." David stands up from the pillows and faces Eleazar directly. "Where will you flee from the Spirit? Can you flee from Yahweh's presence? Yahweh has called you to be here. He knows everything about you Eleazar. The Lord is forgiving and good, abounding in love to all who call to Him." Eleazar shakes he's head. "He does not know me?" David smile broadly. "Was it not Yahweh that told you that you must not kill me?" Eleazar seem shocked by David words. "You know that I wanted to kill you? How is this possible?" A voice below the platform calls out to David. David peers over the side. A voice calls out from below. "The Philistines have gathered close to the City! They will surely attack tomorrow!" David looks at Eleazar before he calls down to the orator. "Make sure that the men that are watching the tree lines close to the City give reports as the day continues. Assemble the rest of the men I will come down shortly." David again turns he's attention to Eleazar. "Yahweh has searched your heart and knows your ways. Let the Lord teach you He's ways and rely on He's faithfulness." Eleazar again sees the man in he's dream. He was called to be here. David sees the emotion on the slayers face. "Accept the true God of Israel and you shall be changed forever. Repent of your ways and let He's way become yours." Eleazar frowns. "How can it be that easy?" David smiles a robust smile. "He's way is not our way my friend." There was something else that the man in the wood radiated and suddenly Eleazar knew what he had felt. It was an intense overwhelming love. He blinks away the tears and swallows noisily. "I accept the Yahweh of Israel to be the only true Yahweh." Eleazar draws he's blades and holds them close to he's chest. "I will be your servant and fight by your side!" David acknowledges Eleazar pledge as he had done with so many others that the Lord had send. "Come let us prepare for the battle that will come in the morning."

The shouts of the Philistine army and the people in the city of Keilah resonances out in the early morning hours. The scouts had reported that the west-wing had just being penetrated. David had received reports the previous day that advancing Philistine army were about two-thousand men strong.

There was panic among the people of Keilah. They were farmers and not fighting men. David saw them draw people into the inner sanctum. A few fighting men made their way to the West and stationed themselves upon the city walls. It was early in the morning just before the breaking of the dawn and David again went on he's knees with the Ephod that Abiathar gave him around he's shoulders.

When he spoke to Yahweh it was one of the most intimate and holy things that he had ever felt. Yahweh's presence was so overwhelming that it sometimes took him an hour to stand on he's feet again. David knew that Yahweh had heard he's cries on the day in the cave of Adullam. He had felt that the Lord had renewed him. Every day since then he had stood before the Lord and Yahweh spoke to him. He enquired from the Lord and waited on Yahweh to tell him what to do.

When Eleazar informed him that the Philistine army was attacking he knew that he's own men were outnumbered. David had become angry for the people of Keilah had been kind to them. He had assembled the men the day before and told them that they might have to defend the city of Keilah. After he had spoken the reaction that he received was what he had expected.

"David's men said to him, "Behold, we are afraid here in Judah. How much more than if we go to Keilah against the armies of the Philistines?" (1 Samuel 23 v 3) The men had looked at their leader for an answer. "The Lord will go before us. Did Yahweh not give us favour when we fought in Moab?"

He had introduced Eleazar to the men and gave him command over a group of men that would defend the Western City gates. Kneeling he waits quietly putting every thought out of he's mind waiting on the presence of the Lord.

"Lord; shall we go and attack these Philistine's now?" The voice that sounds like the roar of the sea yet has the gentle touch of the morning mist upon a flower speaks to David. "Go and attack the Philistines, and save Keilah." The thoughts of the men's fear enter David's mind but the Lord speaks again.

"Arise, go down to Keilah. I will deliver the Philistines into your hands." The fear that David had felt disappears and makes way for something else...the same feeling he had felt when he had faced the giant Goliath.

"Men, you shall be victorious! You shall strike the Philistines with a mighty blow for the Lord has spoken this!"

When David came from he's tree platform he had spoken to all the assembled men and they had stood quietly before David listening intently to every word he spoke. There was a certain glow on David's face that radiated power. The sun was breaking through the tree branches. The rays outlined the figures of the attacking Philistines army. Although David had spent a short time enquiring before the Lord it felt to him like many hours had passed since he enquired before the Lord. David saw that the Philistines placed guards close to the main gate leading to the outer sanctum of the city.

He saw that a coup of only about a thousand five hundred men were send to attack the City. The rest of the Philistine's would still be below the forest edge at the Eastern side of the forest. David had received reports from he's scouts that they had an enormous herd of livestock at their encampment and knew that they would still look after these possessions.

David knew that Philistine army were returning to their own city and that Keilah was part of a raid that stood between them and their homes. He knew that the remainder of the army that stayed behind would not engage if a command was not given.

"Eleazar take the men to the Western gate." Eleazer slightly nods and sets of towards the gate. David reprised the words that the Lord had brought screaming after the men led by Eleazer. "Remember! Yahweh is with you!" David walked to the front lines of the assembled men. All-together there number was estimated as six hundred men. Benaiah accompanied him and flanked his left shoulder. The Philistine soldiers that were left to guard the main gate spotted David and he's men. They had made their way to the edge of the forest. A roar went up from them as they turned and assembled. David raised the massive sword of Goliath and it shone in the early morning sun. "Yahweh! Let them know that it is your hand, that you, Yahweh have done it! You will give victory!" Benaiah looks at David. He's face shines with a magnificent glow. When David had spoken the name of Yahweh, Benaiah had felt something running through he's whole being. The men must have felt the same for suddenly their eyes lit up with the hunger for battle and they raise their swords baying for the Philistine's blood.

David starts running towards the Philistine army, Benaiah keeping pace with his leader and both men screaming the name of Yahweh.

The Philistines stand at the walls of Keilah awaiting the opposing group of men running at them. Genitah looks at the men running towards his army. He had been one of the captains for this Northern region of the Philistine army for the last seven years.

When one of he's soldiers came to tell him about a group of men that was armed assembling at the forest edge he became afraid. He had thought that it was King Saul and he's armies.

They had taken the front City walls and he's men were advancing into the inner sanctum of the city where the people of Keilah would all be assembled. The sentries had called out and warned him of an advancing group of men and he did not want to gamble with he's sure victory. He rallied all the men and they assembled in the outer sanctum of the city. Genitah knew that he would not receive any other assistance from the rest of the assembled Philistine army in the forest. They were waiting on the victory horn to sound.

He saw that the advancing group was smaller than anticipated. Then he saw another thing that thrilled him and also put his mind at ease. They did not wear the rubicund colors which represented King Saul on their chests. He felt much more relieved. He walked over to the South side of the city wall to get a better look at the advancing men.

What he saw was not a mighty army but a group of men, not more than perhaps five hundred and maybe less running towards the city. He's relief was short lived as he pondered the strategy of the advancing men. Why would these men attack the city? Did they also want to raid Keilah? They must have seen he's own army advance. Were more men hiding in the forest? He again looked at the men and could now make out a war cry. It sounded like they called on the name of their god? He had heard that name before. "Yahweh." It was the name that the young boy had called upon when the champion Goliath was slain! Yes he can clearly make out their call now. "Yahweh! Yahweh!" The advancing men did not slow done but it seemed that they increased their pace as they ran towards his men. It was plain suicide! He's army was at least a thousand eight hundred men strong and outnumbered them by almost three to one. He turns towards one of he's generals standing at the way side. "Defend the gates!" There were about a hundred men outside the gates of Keilah. "Rally the rest of the men. We will take the inner sanctum of Keilah as soon as we have dealt with these fools!" Genitah returns he's observation to the group streaming out of the forest.

He sees more of he's men streaming out of the city gates and in no time there were almost a thousand men guarding the City gates. He fervently awaits the point where the armies will clash. The Philistines would run over them like a stampeding buffalo herd. The two armies meet and for a few moments Genitah cannot make out the difference between he's men and the enemy. He's soldiers should be breaking through the front ranks any moment now.

Genitah looks at the fighting men and a deep frown start to appear on his forehead. Something is amiss. The men had not broken through the line yet as he had expected they would. Commotion on the opposite line among his own ranks draws his attention. He must be mistaken! The Philistines ranks are suddenly broken and a man with a fiery beard stands in the midst of his men swaying a massive sword from side to side. A group of about fifty Philistine men rush towards the man. Genitah stares at the group. That should be the end of him.

A great roar erupts from the Western gate distracting him for a moment. Genitah turns he's attention to the commotion and sees another smaller group of men attacking the Western gate. A dark skinned man with two long blades seem to lead the attack. Genitah stand astounded as he sees he's fighting men falling to the swords of the dark skinned man. He screams a command to one of his officers his voice slightly higher pitched than he intended it to be. "Atub! Send men to the Western gate!" The soldier turns around hurriedly. "My Lord we have send all the men to defend the main gates!"

Genitah turns around seeking the group of men that attacked the bearded man certain now that they would have advanced. What he sees brings a feeling into the pit of his stomach that he had not experienced for some period. Fear! The bearded man was still standing where he had last seen him but not only was he still fighting; there were hordes of Philistine bodies sewn around him. How could this be? The man was supposed to be dead! No one could survive an onslaught like that and still be fighting with such vigour! The Philistine army was starting to fall back before he's eyes.

Benaiah saw the hordes of Philistine stream through the gates of Keila. He was good with he's sword but never before had he experienced such agility and strength. It was as if something had taken over he's body. When they clashed with the first line of attackers he stood bravely swinging he's sword at every attack. He broke through the first line of defence and without much effort. He had continued to fight the bodies of men starting to pile up almost blocking he's path. The Philistines kept coming and somehow he had kept swinging he's blade. David stood not far from him a pile of bodies surrounding him also. He must have experienced the same type of strength and unfailing energy that Benaiah experienced.

He's gaze sweeps towards the Western gate and he sees Eleazar fighting the hordes as they stream out of the gate. The dark warrior blades shun every now and then, Philistine men falling around him. He turns back towards David and sees their leader swinging the giant sword cutting into the enemy relentlessly.

When the first wave of attack on the Philistines men sounded; David felt Yahweh's presence come over him. It was the same overwhelming feeling he felt when he fought against Goliath. He had experienced the same feeling every time he had fought in battle thereafter and he knew he was in the presence of Yahweh. David continues to swing he's sword left and right the steel hacking through the bodies of the Philistines.

A bearded man runs at him an axe raised above he's head. David ducks under the swing, cutting into the man's stomach and then he faces the next soldier. The Philistines come at them wave upon wave attacking the men. David's and the men continue to stand their ground like a rock enduring the battement of a flooding river. He blocks a wild cut aimed at he's throat. He steps to his left and drives the giant sword through the Philistines left eye almost decapitating half of the man's face. The soldier falls down he's dying scream cut short by David sword. He readies himself for the next attack but there was no one attacking anymore. He turns to he's left and sees Benaiah covered in blood. Eleazar stands almost two hundred paces away and David only recognized him by he's tall figure and the blades that he wields.

Around them were the bodies of more than a thousand men, maybe more. Eleazar approaches David. "There are still men inside the City. I saw them upon the city walls." David sees questions in those fierce eyes. "Today we were outnumbered at least three to one. We fought these Philistine and killed them without growing weary. When I look around us it seems like we did not lose a single soldier." The tall warrior shakes his head in astonishment. "I did not keep count but I know that today at least a hundred men fell by my own sword."

Most of David men had now gathered around them. They had the same look of astonishment on their faces as Eleazar has. Eleazer continued to speak his voice in wonderment of their surroundings. "Today I have experienced something that I would not be able to explain. It is a mystery and resonates the stories I have heard about Yahweh."

David walks towards the warrior placing he's hand on Eleazar's arm. "The fool has said in he's heart, there is no God." (Psalm 14 v 1) It is not over yet. Come let us enter the gates of Keilah."

"Yahweh has delivered him into my hands, for he has shut himself in by entering a town that has gates and bars."

Saul combs he's fingers through he's bushy beard and stares malevolently out into the dark. "Abner; I want you to send some spies to the city of Keilah. Take this message to them. I will take our armies to stand against David and he's men. If the people of Keilah do not deliver them we shall crush the city with all in it. We are not the Philistine army we shall crush them like ants."

Between the invading armies of the Philistines and continued hunt for David, Saul did not get much rest. He had tried to find David but every time it seemed that he's son in law was one step ahead. The days that followed seem to draw out slowly and Saul became anxious to hear from the men he sent to Keilah. When they returned the news that they bore was once again not what he wanted to hear. David and he's men had left the city of Keilah during the early morning hours. This action somehow managed to escape the attention of Saul's men. The king was furious. Two of the spies were beheaded before they could even speak another word. The rest of the group cowered in fear before Saul.

After the report was received at Keilah; Saul tried more than ever to seek after David. Not long after this Saul was again confronted with Philistines armies trying to breach the borders. During the months that followed he battled with the Philistines but the face of David was always present in he's mind. Even while he was on the battle field he's spies continued to report to him. At first it had seemed that David had vanished but while Saul and he's men were camping at Gilbeah; some men of the Ziphites came to Saul with information about the whereabouts of David. The Ziphites acted upon the reward that Saul had promised to anyone that might help him find David. The Ziphites men told Saul that David was hiding in the strongholds in the woods, in the hill of Hachilah in the South of Jeshimon. This time Saul told the man that they should go and spy on David. They should seek out every hiding place that he might flee to for David had become very crafty.

Time passed and soon the Ziphite men came back and told Saul that David had fled to the wilderness of Moan. Saul went and pursued after him. After many days of traveling Saul came to the mountain side at Moan. He was informed that David and he's men were indeed just on the other side of the mountain. They knew about he's presence and were fleeing from them. One of the Ziphite men came to report back later that afternoon.

"Sire, we are closing in on David and he's men!" If you look at the horizon you will see the dust rising from the fleeing group." Saul was about to give instruction to pursue with all their forces but there was commotion among the west ranks and soon a messenger arrived and came to Saul with a message from Abner. He saw the general's mark on the parchment and knew it was serious. Saul took the parchment and read the dreaded words. "The Philistines are invading the main land. All forces are needed to battle and haste should be made to counter this invasion." Saul looked into the distance and saw the dust that the Ziphite spy had pointed out. He was so close and yet he knew that he could not ignore the message from Abner. He turned towards he's men. "We will return to Gibeah! The Philistines have invaded the land!" The Ziphite men that were among Saul's men groaned and one man that had reported David's whereabouts spoke up. "What about David? We are so close! It is only these rocks on the plain that separate us from them." Saul looked into the distance. "We are close indeed. How ironic?" Saul thought to himself. Again it seems like David escapes by the hand of the Philistine undoing. "I will call this place Sela Hammahlekoth for it was only the rocks that separated us today from spilling he's blood. We cannot ignore the attack on us by the Philistines. We will return soon and David will have no one that will save him."

It was then that Saul turned back from pursuing David and went to fight the Philistines. The war against the invading Philistine armies raged for a full quarter and he managed to push back the Philistine armies but not without heavy losses. Saul then returned to Gibeah. On he's return he immediately sought news from the Ziphite spies on David whereabouts. The men reported that David was in the Desert of En Gedi. Saul was still in a fighting mood so when the men spoke he jumped up from he's chair and started giving the orders.

"Abner! I want three thousand of our best men. We will go to the Desert of En Gedi and this time David will not escape!"

It was quite in the cave except for the breathing of David's assembled men. The air inside the cave was much cooler than the outside and the drop in temperature was welcome after their hasty retreat.

It was without warning that Saul and he's men had arrived here at "The Rocks of the wild Goats" as it was called by all the Sheppard's. He had not expected Saul to come seeking him so soon after the war with the Philistines but should have expected it. The sweat pours freely from David's brow. The cool air coming from the recess of the cave blows over he's crown and David sits quietly waiting, listening for the arrival of Saul and he's army.

David and he's men had travelled all over En Gedi. In the year that passed David had escaped narrowly a few times from the armies of Saul. He had enquired from the Lord if the people of Keilah would deliver them to Saul and Yahweh had told him that they would. He had fled into the wilderness of Ziph and while he was in the Wilderness of Ziph Jonathan had come to him. They had prayed together and Jonathan promised once again that he would stand by David's side. He had travelled to Moan and it was here that Saul had almost caught up with him and he's men. They had seen the army of Saul in the distance and he was surprised to learn that Saul had returned to Gibeah because of an invading Philistine army.

Yahweh had once again gone before them. He and he's men had travelled to En Gedi and they had found the recesses in the caves and he and he's group which was just over six hundred stayed in the recesses of the cave. The land had enough for them to live from and they had found favour in the sight of some of the Sheppard's whom they had protected while their herds where grazing. In response to their services they had received meat from the herders. When they had found the caves David stood astonished staring at the inner sanctum and creation there off. The caves stretched out over an enormous part of the Judean Mountains. When they explored the caves they found that there were many different divisions inside the fast spaces under the mountain.

Some parts had led them directly to the Dead Sea. Another part of the cave had led them into an Oasis that was hidden from the outside observers view. This was one of David favourite discoveries. The area had an opening into the mountain that had been formed by a waterfall that filled a big pool and had the sweetest water. It was a natural window inside the mountain. The sound of the water falling from the rocks into the clear pools of the cave was blocked out by the surrounding rock walls of its natural splendour. At night time David had spent lying on the rock-floor looking at the starts illuminating brightly in the En Gedi skies. They had found that there were many other chambers inside the inner sanctum of the caves. Most of the inner cambers were connected by passages leading in and out of into smaller created spaces. Some passages led to the outside of the mountain that were much higher on the face of the mountain side and could not be seen from the ground. It was the same for David and he's men when they had first come to the caves. They were unaware of the other entrances on the rock face of the Judean Mountain and had entered in by the most obvious entrance on the face of the mountain. It was the Eastern face entrance and it was from this point that they had entered the recesses of the caves. They had continued to explore the inner sanctums of the caves and soon the recesses at the caves at En Gedi became their next stronghold.

When the lookout sentry arrived and told him that Saul and a company of men had arrived at the sheepfolds by the road they retreated into the deeper sanctum of the explored cavern. David did not expect Saul and he's men to find them here for it had taken them many days to explore the fast spaces in the underground rock caverns. The main entrance to the cave on the Eastern side of the Judean Mountain range would be the most likely place for Saul and he's men to enter into the caves. They had retreated into the most secret area in the explored sanctums and David trusted that Yahweh would not deliver him into the hands of Saul. David's raises his hand. He gave clear instruction to he's captains of the army that they should be quite and wait on he's order.

They sat quietly in the cave listening. There was not a sound accept the dripping of water from the cave roof. A baby hungry cries were heard at the back of the cavern but its mother must have quickly made a plan to feed it for the cries dies away as quickly as it had started. David called Benaiah, Jashobeam and Eleazar to him. They had become he's most entrusted captains and as time continued a brotherly bond had developed among them.

"Come let's go and see how many men have entered the caves mouth at the eastern entrance close to the sheepfolds." He gave further instruction to Abishai and Shammah the commanders over a separate order of he's men. The instruction was to keep the rest of the men, woman and children hidden and subdued until they returned. David advanced into the darkness the men following. The four men slowly make their way down the passage wall inside the cave, the darkness of the cave totally engulfing them. It was too risky to burn a torch. They knew their way inside the cave but David led the men slowly throughout the dark maze to ensure that they did not stumble upon any of Saul's men. He conversed with he's men as they continued in a very soft low tone. Every time he wanted them to stop, he would stretch out he's hand close behind him and touch Eleazar who was the closest to him.

When they stopped they would all stand still in the darkness and listened for any sound that that would forewarn them of Saul and he's approaching men. They continued towards the Eastern side of the caves and after almost an hour David could see a dim light illuminating the walls of the cave. As he continued he turned towards the men behind him and he could now clearly make out the features of Eleazar whom was the closest to him. This meant that they were close to the Eastern entrance of the cave. The light coming in from the outside of the enormous mouth entrance of the cave close to the sheepfold gives enough light for him to see movement ahead of them. David signals he's men to stand still.

The sound of leather sandals crunching on the sand pebbles, voices and horses neighing, caries through the cave passage. The breeze coming from the outside also brings the smells of unwashed bodies and the beasts that Saul and he's army are traveling upon. It was like David had suspected. The enormous caves and hidden entrances on the rock face of the Judean mountain's had brought Saul and he's army right to the Eastern side of the mountain. Saul would setup camp and will wait on he's generals to advise him how to best approach the search for David and he's men. David turns he's face towards he's group of men and indicates with he's head to follow him. "Come let's get a better view point." David turns into an entrance on the right hand side of the passage. As they enter into the passage they are once again engulfed in complete darkness. They continue through the darkness the path ascending with a few turns to the left and right. Eleazar stay close to David; Benaiah and Jashobeam following nearby.

The passage that David is leading them on is well known to all of them. The passage would first take them deeper into the mountain. Then they would eventually come out much higher on a ledge about hundred meters away from the main Eastern entrance. Eleazar knows that David want a better vantage point of Saul and he's men without the risk of being discovered. A light ahead of them reveals that they had reached their destination. The men slowly approach the ledge. David creeps down. At first on he's hands and knees and then on he's stomach edging closer the edge of the cave mouth the group of men following he's lead. David stares out over the ledge.

The sun had started to set in the West and the shadows from the Judean Mountain draw out over the desert floor before him. David looks down towards the Eastern entrance. There are large groups of men encamped all the way from the entrance stretching into the desert. The men below had started to prepare their cooking fires and David could make out the much larger tent of Saul and he's servants in the middle of the entourage below. It was a much larger group of men than David had anticipated almost three thousand men according to he's quick calculations. Eleazar takes up the space to he's left. He whistles softly and takes a deep breath. "Saul seems determined to get to you this time." David shrugs and keeps he's eyes on the hordes below. "Saul will not give up until he has found me." The sadness in he's voice did not go by unnoticed. Eleazar silently wonders why David still felt concern towards the man that had been trying to kill him in the past couple of years.

David moves back into the cave trusting the cover of the ledge for cover from below. "Jashobeam, I want you to stay here and report to me when you see Saul and he's group of men entering the cave mouth." He pats Jashobeam on the shoulder and starts back down the path they came from. "Come let's go back. I want to deploy groups of our men at various places inside the caves. If we have to hold off three thousand men we will do it on our terms. We will force them to fight in the narrow passages making the numbers even." David slowly makes he's way down the path that was now descending. He's thoughts consumed by Saul and he's men. Why did Saul continue this madness? When will it ever end? They continue their descending route but David brings them to a sudden halt.

David heard a scraping noise up ahead. Unmistakably the passage is filled with a dim light that could only mean one thing! Somebody with a torch has stepped into passage where they were. David and he's men crouch down slowly and retreat back into the passage away from the approaching light. They crouch down behind a twist in the passage where they came from. The men hold their breath as they hear approaching feet. David silently takes he's dagger from he's sheath and gapes out from behind the bend.

He can make out the form of a soldier. The man seems to be alone and soon he's unexpected arrival is made known to them. He bends down and puts the torch against the passage wall. He opens the front of he's robes and the stench of urine fills David's nostrils. The man has a big gait and if David stretches out he's hand he can almost touch him. The shadows caused by the torch against the wall plays tricks on David's eyes as he stares at the bearded man. The soldier turns he's face towards them as the sound of the urine splatters against the cavern wall. He stares into the darkness of the passage. David takes a sharp breath as the light of the torch exposes the man's features. It was King Saul! David cannot believe he's eyes. Eleazar whispers into David's ear. "Is that who I think it is?" David keeps he's eyes on the man before him not responding to Eleazar. Saul features had changed since the last time David had seen him. He's eyes seemed sunken and a more prominent grey featured in he's bearded face. Eleazar again whispers close to he's ear. "The Lord has delivered your enemy in your hands. You should kill him now." The dagger suddenly weights down very heavily in David hand. This was still the Lord anointed. Who was he to judge and make a decision to take Saul's life? He turns he's face away from Saul and whispers back at Eleazar. "I will not stretch out my hand against my lord Saul, for he is the Lords anointed." Before Eleazar can respond David slowly creeps closer towards Saul; the dagger still in he's right hand. Saul turns away from him towards the torch he's whole back exposed to David. He busies himself with the effort of closing he's robe. David slowly reaches out towards Saul. He takes hold of the king's heavy robe and silently cuts at the corner of the red satin robe. Saul lingers for another while and then without looking back he picks up the torch and walks out of the passage of the cave. The light of the torch start to fade and David stares at the piece that he cut of Saul's robe. Without saying anything to the men he walks after Saul.

Eleazar tries to grab onto David's robe but is too late and David disappears into the darkness after Saul. Eleazar mind races wildly. What was David going to do? "Benaiah, we must follow David he has gone after Saul!" Benaiah was still behind the bend hidden from all that had transpired but the alarm in Eleazar voice jolts him into motion. The two of them hurriedly continue down the passage in the cave until they reach the area where the passage joins the main cavern leading to the Eastern entrance. They turn towards the main passage and Eleazar sees David form far ahead of them. It was too late.

Eleazar and Benaiah reaches the Eastern Cave and sees David running out of the cave entrance calling after Saul. "My lord the King!" Saul stops in alarm. The two guards on either side of Saul quickly turn towards David with their spears raised. Eleazar realizes that the guards must have been with him in the cavern and gave him he's privacy when nature called.

David falls on he's knees pressing he's face on the ground and continues calling out to Saul. "Why do you listen to men's words, saying 'Behold, David seeks to harm you?" The sun had completely set over the mountains and although David could see Saul clearly in the light of the torch he was bathed in darkness.

"Behold, today your eyes have seen how Yahweh had delivered you today into my hand in the cave. Some urged me to kill you; but I spared you; and I said, I will not stretch out my hand against my lord; for he is Yahweh's anointed." (1 Samuel 24 v 9.

Saul walks closer to the voice coming out of the darkness holding the torch higher in the air and sees David is lying face down on the ground.

"Is this your voice my son David?" David lifts he's face he's red beard seems to catch fire as the torch shines upon he's face. "King Saul, in my hand is the corner of your robe." David lifts the piece of garment he had cut from Saul robe in he's hand so that Saul can clearly see it. "I had cut it off when you were in the cave and yet I did not kill you." Saul takes he's own garment in he's hand lifting he's robe he can clearly see where the peace was cut off.

"Why do you, great king of Israel come after me?" David stands up from the dirt the tears rolls down he's cheeks leaving a dirt path on he's face. "Why do you pursue me? I am but a dead dog? A flea? Let the Lord be the judge between you and me, and see and plead my case, and deliver me out of your hand."

Saul feels very weary. He stares at the bearded face before him and he suddenly feels old and tired. He had tried everything in he's power to get to David. He had spent more than six years trying to find David. He had sought after David because he knew that Yahweh had rejected him as the king. He knew that David was anointed as the new king. He had known this for some time but did not want to accept he's own failure. It had dawned on him that when the prophet Samuel had told him that he would be king no more. He knew and feared that a new king would rise. Who else than the man that had the favour of Yahweh upon him? Who else than the man that slayed their enemy with hand of Yahweh? Who else than the man that the people sang songs about? Who else than the man standing before him? Now seeing David like this before him he becomes emotional and he starts to weep

"You are more righteous than I; for you have rewarded me with good, whereas I have rewarded you with evil. And you have shown this day how you have dealt with me. May the Lord reward you for when a man finds he's enemy and lets him get away safely he is surely not my enemy?" Saul turns he's face away from David and stares into the darkness. A large group of men had walked closer to the conversing men now standing behind Saul. Their torches held high so that the figures of Eleazar, Benaiah and Jashobeam who had now joined the latter men could clearly be seen at the mouth of the cave. The grey in Saul beard looks like snow, capped on the Syrian mountains. He draws a deep breath and looks at David. "David; I know that you were anointed as the new king over Israel. You are a righteous man and the kingdom of Israel shall be established in your hand."

David stands rooted staring at Saul. This was the first time ever that king Saul mentioned the fact that he had knowledge of the anointing by the prophet Samuel. Standing before him was the man that hated him and hunted him endlessly. To hear him say the words that was uttered must have been very testing for Saul to speak. Saul does not give time for David to react. He walks closer and puts he's hands on David shoulders. "David; I want you to swear to me by the Lord that you will not cut of my descendants after me and that you will not destroy my name from my father house. Swear it now!" David looks into the eyes of the man that has pursued after him for so long. He sees nothing but sorrow and a brokenness in the eyes of Saul. "I swear it King Saul." Without a word Saul turns away from David. "Get the horses ready, we are leaving this place!" Saul moves of towards the men below and does not look back he's men following and readying themselves for the journey back to Gibeah.

Eleazar, Benaiah and Jashobeam join David side. Eleazar stares at the departing men shaking he's head. "You are indeed a merciful man David. You know that even if Saul has shown mercy today that he can still not be trusted? The nature of this rule is like a new pride of male Lions and soon he will have the raging madness upon him and then will come after you again." David stares in the direction where Saul and he's men are breaking camp. "I know but Yahweh will deliver me from he's hand if it is He's will."

The whole of Israel had gathered in mourning. The news had spread like wild fire. The prophet Samuel was dead.

The people of Israel lamented for him and David had come down to Ramah weeping for Samuel. He travelled only with Jashobeam and Eleazar by he's side instructing Benaiah, Abishai and Shammah to break up their camp in the caves at En Gedi. They had been scouting the land down in the wilderness of Paran and David instructed them to move towards Paran. When the news of the prophets death had reached David he had not hesitated to come to Ramah for Samuel was God's prophet and anointed. He had instructed David in God's way. He had taught David to listen to Yahweh commandments and David had grown in the knowledge of the Lord every day.

Since that day when David and Saul had spoken at the cave on the Rocks of the wild Goats David and he's men had continued to live in their stronghold. King Saul had gone back to Gibeah but David always kept a guarded eye. As time progressed David had heard a lot of stories. Some tales sounded farfetched but most stories that he heard was true and confirmed by different sources. King Saul had become a ruthless tyrant. He was losing more and more to the Philistine armies and Israel was in terror. Now the prophet Samuel had passed away and the people of Israel had despair in their eyes.

David had lamented the state of the people. Had everyone forgotten about the Lord? The mourning lasted for three days and then David returned to he's men in the wilderness in Paran.

Chapter 7

"The shearing has started my Lord. The servant stares wearily at he's master and continues hurriedly. "I have send word to all the Sheppard's asking them to work without rest until all the shearing has been done as you have requested." The man takes another swig from the wine jar and then without warning he throws the clay cup at the servant standing before him.

"It was not a request! It was a command! Do I not pay them with my kindness? They should be thankful that they have the work I have provided for them!" The servant picks up the pieces of the cup that narrowly missed him. He did not look up in the eyes of Nabal for the man was in a foul mood. He did not want to be whipped like Gittan. The man's back looked like it had been mauled by a Leopard.

"Where is that wretch of a wife of mine? Stop crawling around in the dirt you worm and go and find her! Someone get me another jug of wine! Nabal sits back on he's pillows under he's tent. He was waiting for the report from the South. Rashar and he's men were doing a stock count and Nabal was sure that the numbers would have increased significantly since the last season. Things were looking expectant for Nabal and he was looking forward to the feast that was being prepared. The only thing that might still spoil this wonderful day was the person approaching him. He's wife Abigail. Nabal got her when he bought the piece of land on the eastern slopes of Carmel. He had paid highly for her but the price still did not match her beauty. Her father Nariff had almost seem relieved when he handed the raven haired, green eyed daughter to Nabal. Abigail was beautiful but what interested Nabal most was that Nariff had told him that he's daughter was a skilled horse trader. He had listened intently to Nariff and decided to make the purchase. Nariff was true to he's word and in time, Nabal had quickly learned that behind the beauty was an intelligent mind. What the man did not mention was that the woman also came with a quick tongue. She also prayed to an invisible god she called: Yahweh.

At first it did not bother him but she then told him that Yahweh would not forsake her and he had forbidden her to talk of this Yahweh. When he had met her it was clear from the onset that she did not agree with her father, choosing him as her husband. Nabal had he's own way to deal with her stubbornness and the first night of their wedlock when they had left Jezreel he took the whip to her. He was shocked when she had fought back and almost lost he's left eye when her nails raked into he's face leaving blood streaming down he's cheek. He had called some of he's men into their tent and on he's instruction they had held her naked body down. He saw the shame in her eyes as the men stared hungry at her beauty and smiled inwardly. Without warning she spat into he's face and he's anger erupted. He grabbed her by her neck and started to strangle her and would have killed her if Rashar he's right hand man had not stopped him.

"You will certainly lose the pastures that you have received from Nariff as a gift! Do not kill her but rather let the men have their way with her!" Nabal had thought about this and saw the fear in Abigail's eyes when Rashar had suggested this. He had seen the lust in Rashar eyes when he had first laid he's eyes upon her. "Take the bamboo staff and give her twenty lashings but do not let blood break her skin or you will be next!" He had seen the disappointment in Rashar eyes. "When you are finished with her bring her back to me." The men had dragged Abigail from he's tent and her screams of anguish rang out in the desert night. Later he's men had brought her to him. He saw big welts on her back also covering her bottom but there was no blood. Rashar was a professional. Her head was hanging her hair covering her face and he had lifted her chin staring into her eyes. He had expected to see a brokenness but was taken aback when he saw hatred and pride in those eyes. He grabbed her hair and whispered into her ear. "You will obey me. If you do anything that angers me again I will surly give you to Rashar and he's men."

Abigail had looked into he's snake like eyes and knew that he would be true to his word. She hated him and knew that her father had given her to Nabal because it was the way and the tradition of their people. Her father was also a prosperous business man and she knew just as her sister before he acted as per their tradition. He had prepared her and taught her that her feelings did not matter in this case. Many men had come before Nabal but her father had never approved of any of them. When Nabal had come she had seen the look in her father eyes and she knew that her father had approved of him. As she suspected he was a rich man that traded in live-stock and high breeding horses. She had send one of her maid servants Ariel, to go out and spy on Nabal's caravan. When the servant had returned she at first seemed desponded to share what she had learned and seen about Nabal. Abigail had looked at her and sternly instructed her to tell her what she had seen.

Ariel told her that she had entered Nabal's camp and witness Nabal's men dragging a woman from he's tent. Abigail did not press her on how she gained entrance into the servant camp. She knew that Ariel was a Greek prostitute that was captured and had a reputation among the men. Ariel continued and told her that she had asked the man she was with what had happened to the woman that came out of the tent. The man only laughed and when the soldiers passed close to their tent she saw blood streaming from the woman face. The man had drawn her to him saying that it was what happened to those whom shared Nabal's bed. Abigail had thanked Ariel for her amenity and dismissed her. For the rest of the day she prepared herself in the best way possible to meet with Nabal. She had learned from her mother about the God of Israel:

Yahweh He was the one and true God and she prayed to him asking him to protect her. Her father had warned her not to show rejection towards Nabal in any way. She knew that in some way her father was glad to be rid of her because she reminded him so much of her mother. She had thought about the early years. Her father's heart was not like this always. She had thought about a time when he could not see any reason why she could not go out to hunt with her brothers, fly a hawk with them and accompany them to the market place to see the magnificent animals on display. Her father was a horse trader and since the first time that she had laid her eyes on one of these magnificent beasts she fell in love with them.

She had continuously disobeyed her mother instruction not to engage in the activities with the boy's. These activities always seemed so much more fun than the picking of sheaves or the preparation of food. Her father held her mother hugging her from behind and with a sparkle in he's eyes. He would always speak firmly with her when they had found out that she had once again gone off with her brothers but with no true conviction. She use to follow her brothers at a safe distance and only when she knew that they would not turn back she revealed her presence. It was especially difficult for them to return home when they had to meet with their father at the market place. They would normally make a huge commotion and threatened to feed her to a mountain bear but always it was Obed the oldest of the group that would interpose for her. They would meet their father in the market place and he would always give her a knowing nod. They would then all sit quietly as men brought the horses that was captured in the desert into an enclosed ring.

The animals would snort and neigh nervously as they were herded into the ring kicking and bucking. She would always stare in awe at the powerful legs and mane covered necks of these great creatures. Her father had selected only some of the finest mares. He needed them to breed and treated them with love and admiration. When they had purchased these fine animals more than a day travel from Jezreel; her father would often bring the mares that he had purchased inside the family tent. This was for shelter and protection from theft and predators. Abigail had quickly learned that the big animals had the gentle ability to form a cooperative relationship with humans. She had discovered that the desert horse breed had a good-natured, quick to learn, and willing to please nature. The animals also had a high spirit and alertness needed in a horse used for raiding and war. It was because of this deeper knowledge that her father had acquired he's early wealth. She quickly learned the combination of willingness and sensitivity required to handle the horses with aptitude and respect. It seemed like her father had finally given up on raising her the same as her older sisters and had soon allowed her to accompany him and her brothers on all he's trades. It was in those final years entering into womanhood that she was educated in the finer trades and crafts of the magnificent animals and found the business interesting and easy to understand. Soon her father saw that she had a keen natural eye and an ingenious mind.

He would let her speak with him out of sight of the other men asking her for her opinion. She would point out the refined, wedge-shaped heads and broad foreheads of some of the smaller mares. Other mares where identified by their large eyes, large nostrils, and small muzzles. Most of the purer breed desert mares displayed a distinctive concave profile with a slight forehead bulge between their eyes. He father believed that it was these trademarks that separated the true breeding mares from other mares to adapt in the dry desert climate. As time progressed she grew in confidence and would point out other distinctive features. She looked at the shape of the hips of the mares which was deep, well-angled with well laid-back shoulders. She developed an ever keener eye than her father and saw that within the breed that there were variations. Some mares had wider, more powerfully muscled hindquarters suitable for intense bursts running, while others had longer, leaner muscles which was better suited for long stretches where endurance was needed. She became immiscible and she even accompanied her father to the biggest auctions held in the market places in the city of Jebus.

All this had changed when her mother had died. When her mother died her father withdrew from her and she somehow felt it was her fault that he felt so much pain. Her mother had died when a plague had struck Jezreel. She had prayed to Yahweh and asked why her mother had died. She did not find any answers but there was a peace inside her heart because her mother had told her that they would see one another again one day in the Kingdom of Yahweh. She missed her mother. Her father soon had seem to forget the times they shared. He did not take keen interest in the trades anymore and stayed away from the market place. It was her oldest brother that continued the trade and she continue to accompany him. A couple of years passed and she changed into a young woman. It was too soon that her father instructed her that the time was ready for her to be wed. She knew that when Nabal had arrived that something in her father's demeanour was different. He had shared more personal details of her trading skills but as always it was her beauty that seem to capture Nabal immediately.

Abigail had known that her beauty which sometimes felt like a curse would be enough to persuade Nabal. That was if her father buoyant information did not convince him. The morning after the servant had shared what she had witnessed in Nabal camp her father had instructed her to ready herself for wedlock. She was presented to Nabal and got married in their old customs. Nabal had acted he's part while they were still in Jezreel and she only experienced he's harsh demeanour when they had left the place she called home. As soon as they had left the gates of Jezreel the man that was now her husband had rode up to the front of the caravan where she was seated on a horses back. He harshly gave instruction to some men not to let her out of their sight.

He had looked at her in a way that she had come to know as stubborn pride. She loathed the idea that they would be together that night and although her mother had instructed her in all the duties of a wife before she died it was the idea of him touching her that she had found loathsome. She was shocked when he had entered their tent that evening with a horsewhip in he's hands and without warning he had lashed out at her. She instinctively reacted and afterwards she had felt irritated at her own ill-discipline. She had told herself to stay calm and to submit to him in the best possible way and then plan her escape. Instead she had lost her temper. She had endured the beating the men had given her and felt Rashar stinking breath close to her face. She had feared Rashar more than she had feared Nabal. She had seen a ruthlessness in him when he had made the vulgar suggestion to Nabal to hand her over to him and his men. She again prayed that Yahweh would protect her and felt meek and alone.

When they had arrived in Moab she was taken to the Harem where Nabal kept all he's other wife's. She was also not looked upon kindly when she had entered the Harem for her beauty dwarfed the rest of the woman in the sanctum. An old woman called Sarai looked after her and took her under her wing in the Harem. She explained her duties to Abigail. Sarai also believed in the Yahweh of Israel. She had prayed with her and told her that she should continue to trust in Yahweh even when it seemed like he did not listen to her prayers. They formed a close bond and she prayed with Sarai every night. With Sarai careful instruction Abigail rather kept to herself. For a few weeks she did not see Nabal and when the guards called on her it was unexpected. The other woman in the Harem almost seemed relieved that it was not one of them that was called upon. She told herself that she would not act out again as she had done before. Sarai prayed with her and she left the Harem. She was surprised to learn that Nabal called on her to accompany him to a market meeting where they were peddling horses. As they entered into the market place it became apparent that he was also using her to dazzle the men with her beauty.

Like a prized possession he was showing her off but he also knew that she had a deep knowledge in the trade of the animals he had come to acquire. He had instructed her to keep quite as they walked through the market place. She did as she was told and did not say a word. The men in the market place reacted to her beauty in the same manner in which she was well accustomed to when she grew up and men first laid their eyes upon her. Some gasped and pointed and spoke in a vulgar way but she never gave any indication that she heard their lewd remarks. She had sat down on the pillows under the shade of the tent that was erected for her and Nabal. She enjoyed the sun and when the first lot of animals was presented she could not help but to examine the stock before her with her keen well trained eyes. Soon she saw two mares that had the distinctive trades that would give fine offspring. Nabal had watched her carefully and he turned he's head slightly towards her and had enquired "Which ones?" She hesitated only for a moment and then pointed out a mare with white markings above her knees and then another mare with a grey skin but with distinctive markings on her face. Nabal had quietly pointed out the horses to Rashar and the purchase was made. They had travelled back to Carmel and Nabal had again called her to he's bedchamber. He did not take the whip to her but she knew it was a test. He was rough and she had endured the pain putting her mind elsewhere. He did not send her back to the Harem again but gave her close quarters to he's chambers. She had cried that night and felt that Yahweh had comforted her in her heart. She came to know Nabal as a ruthless hard man but she knew that he would certainly give her to Rashar and he's men if she disobeyed him again. The thoughts of escape never left her mind but she continued to trust that Yahweh would show her the way and she waited patiently for the right time. It was if Nabal had suspected that she wanted to escape for he kept a close eye on her. He instructed Rashar to follow her when she went to the market places for flowers and fresh fruit. Nabal was a wealthy man and was known in the surrounding areas of Moab. When the second year of their wedlock approached Abigail knew that the season again presented itself and the large herds of sheep that Nabal had possessed needed to be sheared. She knew that it was just after the shearing that he would arrange for a feast as he had done the year before. This was her best chance.

Abigail knew that he would send Rashad and he's men to visit the regions and get an accurate count of the live- stock from the herdsmen as he had done before. Nabal had also asked her to take over the preparations for the feast and it was with this in mind that hope flared inside of her. She did not want to draw unnecessary attention to herself and submitted to Nabal every request. At night time she would lie awake and in her mind she prepared herself to escape from Maon and Nabal for good.

Abigail now approached Nabal warily. She had seen her husband throw the clay cup at the servant and she knew that he would test her tenacity. "My lord you have called me?" Nabal looks at Abigail stroking he's long wispy beard. The woman had brought him good fortune in he's horse trading and was still the most beautiful woman in Moan. He knew that Abigail despised him and kept her under close watch. Even when Rashar left he had asked Gittan to report her whereabouts to him. He had felt that something was amiss put could not put he's finger on it. The woman had become more submissive to he's requests and that alarmed him even more. "Woman. Have you looked to it that the tents are well prepared? You know that Roben will arrive shortly. He's caravan is still a day travel from us but I expect everything to be perfect when they arrive."

Nabal reaches for her stroking her hip. "I expect you to be on your best behaviour." Abigail does not respond immediately and it takes all her commitment not to pull away from he's touch. Nabal stares at Abigail .Those green eyes still captivated him and suddenly Nabal feels a stirring lusting after her. Abigail recognizes the look in Nabal eyes and she bites back the retort she had for her scoundrel husband. "The servants are still preparing some of the silk dressings for the visitor tent my lord. I have come to enquire about the arrival time of your guests and now you have answered my question."

Nabal is again taken by surprise by he's wife's calm and submissive demeanour. She was up to something. He had received word from a messenger that the final count was made in the South.

He felt at ease because he knew that Rashar would be back in Moan by nightfall. He drops he's hand from her hip, picking up a cup that the servant had replaced and had filled with new wine. He enjoyed it when Abigail resisted him and her submissive demeanour made him feel uneasy. He'd rather spend he's energy on another jug of wine. He takes a quaff from the cup. "Abigail, Rashar will also return tonight. Please inform me when he arrives." Nabal continue to stare into her eyes and Abigail keeps her face from showing any expression. The disappointment must surely show in her eyes but she turns away from Nabal towards a group of ten men that have entered the court yard with the servant Gittan leading them.

She looks at Gittan her heart going out to the scrawny servant. Rashar had beat him badly and she had sent her maidservants to give him treatment in secret. Nabal also turns he's gaze away from Abigail towards the unfamiliar men that are led by the servant Gittan. Nabal notices that Gittan is still walking with a slight limp. *That will teach the fool.* Nabal silently thinks to himself. The servant wearily approaches him. "Eh… my lord. These men want to talk to you" The group of men look like a bunch of desert nomads and are quite young.

Nabal's anger starts to boil. "Why have you not enquired from me first if I wanted to see anyone Gittan? I will deal with you later! Your incompetence has no end it seems!" Nabal points to the young men. "What is your business here? Speak! I have important guest arriving shortly!" One of the young men steps forward standing next to the servant Gittan. "My lord. Peace be to you, peace to your house and peace to all that you have. I come and speak on behalf of our Lord David the son of Jesse." Nabal knuckles turn white as he grips the side of the wooden chair he sits upon not trying to hide the irritation he feels as the young man continues. "We were in the desert and we looked after your shepherds and their herds. When the shearers arrived we did them no harm and we took no bounty from your heard. We were well behaved towards your men always. We have heard that a feast day has come and now we ask you to give to us whatever you can spare and comes to your hand and give to us and our Lord David."

Nabal cannot contain he's anger any longer and blurts out. "David! Who is this son of Jesse? There are many servants that break away from their masters! Should I feed all that comes on to my land? I can look after my own herd! I will not give away my meat and bread to men that I do not know! Away with all of you! Get of my land you curs! The young man seems taken aback by the outburst but recovers quickly keeping he's face neutral. "As you wish my Lord." Nabal reaches for the jug of wine taking another big gulp drenching he's anger with the filled clay cup. The young man leave the gates of Carmel. Abigail stands in the front portal of the gardens waiting on Gittan to return after he had led the group of young men to the gate. She does not have to wait long and soon the figure of the servant appears. "Gittan; Gittan!" Her voice sounds loud in her own ears and she turns around suspecting Rashad to stand behind her but no one is there. The servant Gittan sees her standing behind the pillar in the garden and looks around nervously as he approaches her. "My lady?" Abigail squeezes he's shoulder reassuringly. "Tell me more about the group of men that was just here." Gittan adoration for Abigail shows clearly. She had only been kind to him. He looks around one more time and then softly responds to Abigail question. "These men came from the wilderness of Paran. They came with a message from their Lord David." Abigail frown increases. "David? King Saul outlawed son in law?" Abigail had heard about David and he's men. It came about when she had visited Gibeah with Nabal. King Saul had returned from perusing David. She had quietly sat and listened to one of Nabal men stationed in Gibeah telling one of the servants about how Saul had pursued David and how Saul life was spared. She had heard that David wife was given to another man and she felt unfamiliar emotions stir inside. How could the king kill he's son in law and give he's wife away?

Gittan brings her back to the moment nodding he's head excitedly. "Yes my lady! When I was at the outskirts of Paran with the shearers he's men were very good to us and we were not hurt. They looked after us and there was no theft or wild animals that attacked the herds while they were with us. They were like a wall to us during the day time and night time while we were keeping the sheep." Abigail laughter rings out spontaneously. "It sounds like you enjoyed their company." Gittan laughs shyly. "We all did my lady." Abigail hesitates for a moment. "Did you see David?" Gittan shakes he's head. "No my lady, he was not with the group of men but the men that was with us spoke with admiration and vigour of him." Gittan suddenly seem worried and Abigail notices the change that has come upon him. "What is it Gittan?" Gittan does not look her in the eyes and speaks almost whispering. "Our Lord Nabal is a scoundrel. He did not take kindly to the request of David's men. I have heard that David have fought battles in the wilderness of Paran and have succeeded in all of them. I do not think that he will take kind to our Lord's harshness." Abigail considers Gittan words carefully and she feels a stirring inside of her that she had come to trust as Yahweh guiding her.

She closes her eyes for a while asking Yahweh to confirm her thoughts and suddenly it all seem clear to her. She did not have much time for Rashad and he's men would surly return any moment. "Make haste Gittan. Go to the kitchen where they are preparing the bread for the feast and ask the them to keep two hundred loaves aside, take two skins of wine and also let them take five sheep that are being prepared and load it on the donkeys." Gittan stare at Abigail with wide eyes. "Do not waste time Gittan! Oh and let them take five Seahs of roasted grain from the store, one hundred clusters of raisins, and two hundred cakes of figs and also load it on the donkeys." Gittan turns away from Abigail towards the preparation quarters to follow her instructions.

He quickly turns back again when Abigail calls after him. "Gittan! Take the food and some servants and go before me and head towards the wilderness in Paran. I am coming after you!"

"Every man gird your sword!" David swings he's sword on he's back and continues he's voice strained with anger. "Two hundred men will accompany me and two hundred will stay behind to look after the supplies!"

David walks towards he's camel and Eleazar flanks him from the right. "David. Two hundred men? Do you think we need such a fast number of men for this farmer and he's people?" David does not ease he's stride as he replies. "In vain I have protected all that this fellow has in the wilderness. Nothing was missed and he has repaid my good with he's evil and foul mouth! May Yahweh do the same to my enemies if I leave even one male alive of all that belongs to him!" Eleazar knows better than to argue with their leader and walks towards he's own camel.

They rode for at least an hour into the night when they heard Maspur a young scout's voice "Draw your swords! Enemy ahead!" David draws he's sword. The blade glimmers in the moonlight. "Wait on my instruction! Flank to the left!" A cool breeze plays on he's face and he can make out dark images in the night. The blood pumps in he's veins as he readies himself for battle.

Suddenly a sweet and strong voice calls out from a distance and for a moment David is taken off-guard for he did not except to hear a woman's voice in the midst of battle. "My lord David! My lord!" David holds he's fist in the air, to signal the men to stop. He stares out into the night trying to make out the person who was calling he's name. A small group of people emerge from the darkness over a dune with what seems like a large pack of donkeys. A dark haired woman climbs of a donkey and falls to her face in the sand. "My Lord. This great iniquity let it be on me! Please let me speak with you! Let your maidservant speak and listen to my words!" David moves forward weary of a trap. "What madness is this? What are you talking about woman?" David is taken aback when the woman lifts her face from the sand for her beauty almost blinds out the beauty of the moon that shines through the clouds of the desert night. "I am but your maidservant and this man Nabal who has caused you to take he's life; is as he's name says: a shameless fool!"

Why then will you act against Yahweh's will and take vengeance into your own hands?

I know that Yahweh has protected you from those who seek your life. Please do not spill a fool's blood in anger for again Yahweh will fight this battle for you." The anger and bloodlust in David's head fades away with every word the woman speaks. He finds himself staring at the woman before him. The rest of he's fighting party have become oblivious to him. The dark haired women turns her face towards the pack of donkeys and people guarding them. "I have brought you and your men two hundred loaves of bread, two skins of wine, five sheep already dressed, five sheaves of roasted grain, one hundred clusters of raisins, and two hundred cakes of figs and loaded them on donkeys. Please forgive the trespasses of your maidservant. The Lord will surly make your house strong for I know that you fight the Lord battles and evil is not found in you."

The woman beautiful face shines with moist and she takes a strand of hair from her face. "I know that you have shown mercy before. I know that Saul has risen to pursue you and seek your life. It shall come to pass that the Lord will do all that he has spoken over you and you will become ruler over all of Israel."

David did not even realize that he still had the broad sword in he's hands and must look a fearsome sight. The woman does not seemed to notice. "Why will you then shed blood tonight without cause my Lord? The Lord will deal with Nabal and when He does, do not forget your maidservant." The woman hangs her head almost as if the last words were too abrupt. David sheathes the broad sword and slowly walks towards the woman. She looks up as he approaches and again David feels as if someone has given him a blow to the stomach. Her beauty was enchanting, leaving him without any spoken word. As if coming out of a deep slumber, he looks around him seeing he's men swords gleaming in the moonlight. He had almost gone and wiped out an entire family without enquiring from the Lord. Realization dawns on him that he would have sinned against Yahweh should he have continued with he's vengeance. He looks at the woman before him.

"Blessed is the Lord Yahweh of Israel who sent you to meet with me! Blessed is your advice for you have kept me today from spilling blood and avenging myself with my own hand. Blessed are you!" David continues to stare at Abigail. Who are you and why do you plead the case for this man called Nabal?"

The penetrating look of David makes Abigail feel vulnerable and she bows her head again. "I am but your maidservant and the wife of Nabal." David feels a stab of pain in he's heart but no emotion shows as he speaks to Abigail. "Go back to your house for I have heeded your voice and esteemed your request." He takes one last look at the woman before him and then turns to Eleazar. "Give ten men instruction to make sure that she returns safely to her home." Without another word he walks back to he's Camel.

Long after Abigail and her servants had left David stand staring in the direction of their departure. "The men feel that it was wise of you to listen to the woman." Eleazar sits next to David staring at the stars and for a while there are no words between them. David stretches himself out on the sand he's gaze now also at the skies. "Is it ever wise to listen to any woman Eleazar? Why did the Lord instruct this beautiful married woman to cross my path? Now there are more things I do not understand." Eleazar smiles he's white teeth in contrast to he's dark skin. "If you try and understand the things of a woman it will bring you great distress, heartache and sleepless nights."

Eleazar rubs over he's tummy. "I have eaten too much fig cakes." David again turns he's gaze into the direction Abigail and he's men had left. "I am not hungry." Eleazar laughs heartedly.

A harsh knock on her door makes Abigail jump from her bed. She enfolds herself within the satin folds of the linen on her bed and stares at the door. The door suddenly opens and the figure of Rashad fills the doorway. He stares at the curves of her body and Abigail draws the sheets tightly around her shoulders. He's malevolent eyes stares into her own and she almost feels like a prey hypnotized by a cobra. Abigail fears that her nightly exploits had been uncovered but Rashad only lingers in the doorway for another few more seconds. "Our lord Nabal wants to see you." He takes a final glance at her covered body and then leaves the room. She sighs a huge breath of relief as the door closes. Her heart weighs heavily in her chest. What now Yahweh?

She again felt an unfamiliar stirring in her heart when she had laid eyes upon David in the desert. Was it all over? What was Yahweh's plan? The chance of her escaping was in ruins. When she and the servants had returned she had thought about heading south but knew that she would not have enough time and that Nabal would send Rashad to find her. When she came into the house she was surprised to find that Rashad and he's men had not yet returned to Carmel. The guests was still streaming in towards the erected tent. The fires were burning bright and Abigail went to see if the servants had taken the prepared dishes to the serving tables. The dressed sheep carcasses was hanging over the fire pits and there was a jovial mood in the air. Abigail had then joined Nabal's table and it seemed like he had taken the preparations for the feast as a natural excuse for her late arrival.

She ate the food that was prepared and later when the men took out their pipes all the woman left the table. She withdrew to her sleeping quarters. When she left the table, Nabal was in high spirit and very drunk.

She takes an ivory comb that Nabal had given her and start to brush her hair in the reflection of the copper mirror. She wonders what Nabal wants but was not that concerned. She was pleased that she had not been found out for if that was the situation Rashad would have acted differently. Her mind again drift to the previous night. When she had returned to her sleeping quarters she could not find sleep. The bearded face of David was in her thoughts and she twisted and turned but could not escape those piercing green eyes. She knew that David could have been her way out of Carmel.

What if she had left him to destroy Nabal? It had dawned on her that he would easily have killed her as well.

Yahweh please do not let me think about my own hearts adoptions. What is your heart desire? She yawned and felt tired as she continued to brush her raven hair. She looks at herself in the copper mirror and the image reflecting back at her seemed tired and helpless. Her shoulders drop in despair. She could not go on like this. "Yahweh please help me." Another knock startles her thoughts. "Who is it?" She dreads to hear to voice of Rashad again but the muffled voice of Gittan greets her. "My lady. The lord Nabal have retired to he's sleeping quarters. He waits for you." He must still feel the after effects of the brew that intoxicated him: Abigail thinks to herself and replies softly. "Does Rashad know?" She hears movement behind the door and then Gittan's soft response. "It does not seem so my lady." She walks back to the copper mirror and calls out louder into the direction of the closed door. "I will be there shortly, thank you Gittan." She takes a deep breath and after another few strokes through her hair she places the comb on the chair. She rises and starts of towards Nabal sleeping chambers.

She opens the door of her chambers and looks to her left and right and is welcomed by an empty passage. The house is quite accept for the sounds down the passage coming from the kitchen where the servants were cleaning the aftermath of the previous night festivities. She makes her way further down the passage until she reaches Nabal door. The sounds of the kitchen activities was no longer audible. She knocks softly on the door and is greeted by a low grunt.

"Who is it?" She takes another breath. "It is Abigail my lord." She hears movement behind the heavy door and then Nabal reply. "Enter." She opens the door and walks into the semi-dark chamber of Nabal. The chamber reeks of sweat and alcohol and she feels the bile rising in her throat. Nabal is prompted on he's bed by pillows filled with goose feathers behind him. He's hair is unwashed and the stubble on he's face speaks of the absence of a blade that had touched he's cheeks. The white satin pillows appears in contrast with he's red face and Abigail moves closer quietly.

"You summoned me my lord." Nabal stares at her through bloodshot eyes but there was something else in those eyes. "It has come to my attention that you took food that was being prepared for the feast from the kitchen yesterday. I have also heard that some supplies was taken from the storeroom. What did you do with it?" Abigail feels like a fist had hit her in her stomach.

"He knows." She thinks to herself. Someone must have reported that the food was taken from the kitchen. Why did Rashad not act upon the information when she saw him earlier? She continues to stare at him trying to rationalize her thoughts. He must have only found out. Nabal grabs Abigail arm twisting it painfully he's mouth drawn into a snarl. "Answer me! What did you do with the food that you took from the stores and the kitchen?" Abigail tries to free her arm from Nabal's grip but it is like the jaws of a Hyena. Too late she notices that Nabal had drawn a dagger from its sheath that hang next to he's bed and he lashes out towards her face. She blocks the blow with her free arm and the blade cuts into her arm. She screams out and winches in pain. It is as if the pain opens up a floodgate of emotions and memories that she had kept inside since the night of her wedding and it engulfs her being. She stares into the bloodshot eyes of Nabal. His fingers was pressing hard around the cut in her arm and suddenly she screams out. "I gave it all away! I took it all and gave it to David! I met with him in the desert and begged that he would spare our lives for your foolishness!"

It seems like an invisible hand had struck Nabal across he's face. He's face was blood red and he's mouth opens and closes without any sound coming out accept a strange gurgling sound. He looked like a gutted fish on dry land. He stretches out he's hands towards her and then clutches he's chest falling back onto the goose feather filled pillows without making any further movement. Abigail stares at him in disbelieve. Nabal lies very still on he's bed. She approaches him very wearily and she puts her hand under he's nose to feel if he was still breathing. She could make out a slight breath on the back of her palm. The wound on her arm bleeds profoundly and she tries to wipe it on the satins sheets leaving a red smear across the white linen. What has happened? "Nabal. Nabal!" She shakes he's shoulders but he does not respond. She hears footsteps approaching the closed door and the voice of Rashad calling out.

"My Lord? Is everything in order?" She looks around hurriedly and she sees the blade that Nabal used to attack her lying on the floor. She quickly picks up the blade and hides behind the door. Rashad burst into the room and she sees him enter walking to the bed with he's back towards her calling out to Nabal. "My Lord!" She knows that she must act quickly and hesitates for a moment only. She silently stalks up behind him the blade raised high.

Rashad spins around he's natural instincts warning him. He grabs onto her raised arm wrist and wrestles the blade from her grasp. He knocks her from her feet hitting her against the side of her head with an open hand. She falls onto her back and then tries helplessly to get away from him but he straddles her like a horse. "I will first have you!" After I am done I will call on my men to have their way with you! Your death will be slow and painfully!"

She feels him pulling her dress high above her waist but the loss of blood from the gash in her arm makes her feel lightheaded and the face above her becomes blurred. Yahweh help me. She regains her conciseness and tries with one last effort to push him off her. Suddenly Rashad body goes ridged and he's eyes bulges out of he's skull. He reaches behind him and then he's eyes turns inwards and he falls heavily onto her. He's weight crushes her and she panics for a moment that she would suffocate. She feels two hands grabbing onto her shoulder and hears the familiar voice of Gittan. "It's going to be all right my lady." She stares at the body of Rashad lying close to her a scimitar sword sticking out between he's shoulder blades. She turns her face slowly towards Gittan. She tries to say something but then she falls into a deep dark pit and all the pain is gone.

The gait of the donkey sways from side to side and the wound in Abigail arm pulls making her grimace with pain. Gittan looks at her with a worried expression on he's face walking close to the animal she sat on.

"We should have waited my lady. You are not strong enough." Abigail smiles wearily at her servant. He had saved her life. "I am fine Gittan." She looks at the rest of the group and sees David messengers scouting ahead. The course of her life had completely changed in the last few days.

She had regained consciousness later the evening on the same day that she had passed out in Nabal's room. At first she could not remember anything but it all came flooding back to her like the Nile River flooding its banks. She tried to sit up in her bed but two hands had gently pressed her down into her pillows. It was Gittan and she had meekly asked him for water. When he had returned he had sat down and gently explained to her that Nabal was still alive but unconscious. She was shocked to hear that her husband was still alive and tears welled up in her eyes. Gittan explained that a healer had come from Dan to look at him and was tending to him. She had laid quietly listening to her servant and then she had enquired about Rashad. Gittan told her that Rashad was dead. The tears rolled down her cheeks again and but this time it was tears of relieve.

Gittan told her that he had heard her cries in Nabal's room. He had seen Rashad enter Nabal's room and followed him closely. He had panicked when he saw Rashad on top of her. He had taken one of the soldier's scimitar swords and killed Rashad with it. The news of Nabal state and Rashad death brought mixed feelings but she was still tired and she had fallen asleep again. She had only woken the next day.

This time when she opened her eyes and her servant Ariel was sitting next to her bed. Ariel had told Abigail that Nabal was still unconscious. She did not keep from telling Abigail that the whole household rejoiced because of Rashad's death. Abigail had reprimanded her but without real conviction in her tone. Ariel had told her that the healer that came from Dan would also come and tend her wounds.

Abigail had stayed in her room for another day. When the healer came he gently put new dressings on her wound. He was an old man and without looking into her face while he was changing the dressing on her arm he had explained that Nabal had a heart attack. He explained that the chances of he's recovery was very slim. She looked away not trying to show any emotion. For so long she had wondered and made plans to escape from Nabal and Rashad. She could almost not imagine what her live would be without them. Another thought came to her mind and fear gripped her. She knew that Nabal's brother Kesh would be the next in line to take all that he owned which included her according to their tradition.

"O Yahweh. I know you saved me. I wait on you for you will direct my ways." Later that day she had left her room. She encountered many of the servants and although Nabal was unconscious and Rashad was dead the household had a joyful visage. Abigail could not blame them.

A messenger arrived and announced that Kesh was coming to Carmel. She knew that it would take Kesh at least fifteen days before he would reach Carmel. It was on the tenth day however after Nabal had fallen unconscious that the healer had come out of Nabal room shaking he's head. He had looked at no one in particular but explained that Nabal had a second heart attack. He then looked straight at her. "Nabal is dead."

She did not feel any emotion. The day was far from over and she gave instruction to prepare Nabal body. She knew that he's brother would look after the arrangements for he's burial and that the body had to stay preserved until he's arrival. Gittan had arrived later that afternoon with a broad smile on he's face. "My lady. There are people here to talk with you." She had frowned upon him but knew that he would protect her with he's life and showed no fear. She had walked out into the court yard and was surprised to see the same young men that came to Nabal's court the first time asking him for food now standing before her. The same young man that spoke to Nabal came forward addressing her. He cleared he's throat and without further hesitation he spoke.

"My lady, David has sent us to you to take you to him and to become he's wife." She stood frozen and felt like she did not hear the young man correctly. She did not even seem to take notice of Ariel's joy full interjection although she stood next to her. David wanted her as he's wife? How could he? She was certainly not a maiden anymore? The young man then moved closer and repeated himself. "My lady, you must prepare yourself and come with us. Arrange with your servants and pack all your belongings for surely David awaits you if you accept he's offer."

She had asked the Lord to prepare her way but she could almost not believe what she had heard. "Yahweh is this your way for me?" The stirring in her heart quietens her thoughts and she bows her head before the men of David and addressed no one in particular. "Here is your maidservant, a servant to wash the feet of the servants of my lord. I will come with you." The young men boyishly bellows and she blushes in the late afternoon sun.

She had gathered very few things and only five of her servants of which Ariel and Gittan was part off to accompany her. They did not take any of the horses but Gittan had prepared a few donkeys that he owned according to he's own testimony. A yell rings out ahead and she blocks out the sun with her forearm staring ahead of her.

A figure stands on the dune ahead of her the wind blowing through he's golden hair. Bearded men surrounding the figure of David. She sighs inwardly a feeling of joy overwhelming her. Thank you Yahweh.

Chapter 8

"There is a man from the Ziphites my king, claiming that they know the whereabouts of David. He claims that he is back in he's stronghold in the hill of Hachilah, opposite Jeshimon." Saul frowns at Abner. The war against the Philistines were on the brink of a calamity. He and he's men were camped at Gibeah where they were holding against the Philistines.

On every campaign the losses were greater and the men's morale was truncated. Samuel was dead and rumours began to surface that David's army of men were becoming greater and greater every day. He and he's band of men had defeated a great multitude armies wherever he went and Saul became more restless. That day that he had seen David at the cave he had felt a strange sense of shame and remorse for he's actions against he's son in law. He told no one of he's feelings and soon they turned into a penitence that was rotting away on the inside. Thinking back on that day now only angers him for he should have killed him! David was nobody to him anymore! He had given he's daughter Michal's hand to Palti the son of Laish from Gallim. He had even sent a messenger to David with the word that he's marriage to Michal had ended. He had done so in hope that it would lure him towards Gibeah but without any effect. Saul became more agitated every day. He's mind was constantly occupied with David, and the Philistine hordes.

"Let's gather the men Abner. Choose three thousand of our best. We shall go down to the wilderness of Ziph."

The woman lying in the crook of David arm truly astonishes him. Never before had he experienced any emotions like the ones he felt towards Abigail.

She stirs in her sleep and a strand of her raven hair falls across her face. The past few weeks had been weeks of utter revelation and joy and the most happiest since he left Gibeah.

The day the messenger arrived at their camp with the news that Nabal had died had brought mixed emotions to David. He and he's band of men were readying themselves to go to the stronghold in Ziph. The same servant that had previously accompanied Abigail in the dessert arrived at their camp. It was the morning before they started their journey to Hachilah. The message that he brought took David by surprise.

Nabal had died. David listened to the man as he explained what had happened and the anger stirred inside when he heard about the man Rashad that attacked Abigail. The servant had explained that Nabal had a heart attack. He recounted how Nabal was struck with a second heart ten days after the first attack and had died.

David had felt anxious for he knew that Nabal brothers or closest kin would lay claim to all Nabal's assets. He did not care about Nabal earthly possessions and only one question remained. What of Abigail? He did not think twice but called on Joasim the messenger the come and wait by he's tent. He went inside he's tent and prayed. "Blessed is Yahweh, who has pleaded the cause of my reproach from the hand of Nabal, and has kept back he's servant from evil. Yahweh has returned the evil doing of Nabal on he's own head." (1 Samuel 25 v 39) "Grant me Abigail as my own wife." He came out of he's tent and gave the messenger a message of he's own to deliver to Abigail. He had send some of the younger warriors with the Joasim if they encountered any hostility.

All day long he had waited in anticipation for he's messenger to return with the hopes that Abigail would be with them. He could not wait any longer and rode out on he's camel as the sun drew long shadows over the dunes. He saw a group approaching in the distance but could not make out the figure of Abigail for sure. He stood on the dune and waited patiently. He's messengers had returned. They were not alone. She rode on a donkey with five of her servants surrounding her. He stood on the dune he's heart beating wildly. That night under the desert stars before Yahweh and before the eyes of all he's men David and Abigail stood holding hands.

The priest Abiathar read out the words of how Yahweh created Adam and Eve to be friends and have union with him. He reminded them that it was because they were disobedient that Yahweh anger arose and drove them out of the garden. He spoke of the covenant that Yahweh made with Moses. "Therefore the Lord wants you to keep every commandment which I command you today. Love the Lord your Yahweh and serve Him with all your heart and with your soul." They listened intently to Abiathar but kept on staring at one another with admiration and undisguised interest.

That night the camp fires burned bright and they feasted under the clear star filled desert skies. They went to their tent and their marriage was sealed according to God own instruction when they became one. Long afterwards the lay together and began to speak to one another telling their stories since their childhood. They never slept and too soon the rays of the sun had crept over the dunes in the desert. They had prepared to move towards Hachilah and David arose from the tent and kissed Abigail on her soft lips. "We will continue our conversation my beautiful desert flower but first we need to move camp." Abigail stared at David lazily and yawned. "It is going to be a long day indeed my husband and lord but I am looking forward to continue were we have ended our conversation today." Abigail stood up and David hesitated for another moment longer taking in her beauty before he left the tent.

The men had gathered all their belongings and the camels were packed. They gathered themselves and David gave the command and they made their way towards Ziph. They travelled for a few days and entered the hills of Hachilah. David's men and their families made their preparations to settle in their new environment. They cut down some of the trees and made structures which protected them against the elements during the day and night. The men continued to train under the close instruction of Jashobeam, Eleazar, Benaiah, Abishai and Shammah their captains. David received news that the Philistines were threatening to invade the borders at Gilboa. There was also a rumour that Saul and three thousand elect soldiers were heading towards Ziph.

Benaiah came to David one evening and without much emotion he announced his leave of absence. "It is time for me to return to Moab." David looked earnestly at the broad shouldered warrior. He had become very close to him. Maybe it was also because Benaiah was the first man that the Lord brought into he's army of men. "Is it Abishai cooking that drives you back to Moab? Is it perhaps the strangers that came into our camp two days ago that has influenced this decision?" The big man moves uncomfortably. "There is something that I need to get in Moab and then I shall return." David smiles. "Is this something perhaps... someone?" It was if the big man was wrestling with he's inner thoughts. It seemed like he finally had made a decision for he sat down and took a deep breath and then he started to talk.

"I did not even know her name the first time I had laid eyes on her. It was just after I met you and we had come from the desert into Moab." Benaiah searched David face but the former kept silent and he continues. "We were in the city for about two weeks and men and their families were joining us. I was in the market place and there was a group of young slave girls that had been brought into Moab from an Amalekite merchant caravan. The Amalekites traded on the old Egyptian trading routes. One of their particular interests were young slave girls that the Egyptians sold." The big man moved uncomfortably.

"These woman were very beautiful and some came from the cities across the seas. Normally the merchants would sell them as slaves to the richest bidders." Benaiah cleared he's throat and then he continued. "It sometimes happens that the king would take interest in these girls and buy a girl for he's harem and keep her for a while and then sell her again."

162

David stared at Benaiah in silence only nodding he's head allowing the big man to continue. "I saw her standing naked on the slave block and she seemed so small and fragile while men were baying and whistling at her. She was not more than two meters from me and I tried to avert my eyes from her beauty but shamefully kept on staring at her.

She had suddenly looked up straight into my eyes. She looked at me and I felt that we were the only two people in the market place. It was if she wanted to say something to me but then the crowd had suddenly grown subdued and it was king Mizpah soldiers that had caused the crowd reaction. I saw one of king Mizpah advisors speak with the merchant and the girl was taken away. She continued to stare at me even when they started to take her away. I felt frustrated that the king had acquired her. As you are aware king Mizpah is not a young man anymore and he has a harem full of wives.

For the rest of the day I could not get her face out of my mind. I was taken by surprise when I saw her sitting at the king table when we dined with king Mizpah that evening." David runs he's hand through he's thick beard. He recalled some of the memories of that evening and that the men that accompanied him commented on the young girl beauty sitting with the king of Moab. Benaiah speaks again interrupting he's thoughts. "At first she did not seem to notice me and I barely touched the food that they had brought us.

I perceived though that she had gazed into my direction once, her eye pleading. She however did not look into my direction again for the remainder of the evening after that. I tried to persuade her in my inner most being to look at me again but as the night drew it was in vain. It was only later that evening when the old king had announced that he would retire that she drew my attention. She made a gesture with her hands but most of it was obstructed by the angle of my view and I did not understand. It was only when one of the other female servants brought more wine that her odd behaviour was explained."

The two men conversation is interrupted by the sound of crunching soles on the desert sand. The footfalls of an approaching person becomes louder and the two men can make out the silhouette of a soldier that comes running towards them. As the man approaches David recognizes the soldier as a man called Adino. He was still a youngster but had proven himself in battle. He slows down as he approaches the two men. He takes a few moments to catch he's breathing before he addresses David. "My Lord, the spies have returned from the hills and would like an audience with you." David had expected their return but not so soon. "All right Adino. Ask Shammah to gather Abishai, Jashobeam and Eleazar, I will join them shortly."

Benaiah clears he's throat staring in the direction of the departing soldier. "I know that you have more serious things to deal with than to listen to my plight for a concubine. I must make this journey and will return if it is Yahweh will." The sound of a jackal sounds lonely and unnerving in the distance. David gestures in understanding and prompts the warrior to finish he's account. "Benaiah; what did the servant tell you in king Moab's hall when she approached you?"

The big man rubs the thick leather straps on he's forearms and spits onto the ground. "The servant told me that the girls name is Takisha." The big man stays quite for a while and David prompts him with a grin. "That was it? She told you her name is Takisha and how did you respond?" Benaiah utters with a grunt and folds he's arms on he's chest. "No, I did not even have time to respond and the slave girl left our table in haste. Only later that evening when the most men were intoxicated with the wine the same servant came to our table and spoke with me again. She told me that Takisha would like to meet me in the gardens of the Sanhedrin court at midnight." David smiles in amusement at he's brother in arms sitting opposite him. "At this point you still did not talk or even give your name to the servant?" Benaiah lifts he's arms up in the air as a sign of utter hopelessness. "There was no time I tell you. I was still kind of at a loss for words. I mean she wanted to meet in the king's concubine court." David burst out in laughter. "Yes, there is that part of course!"

The big man good-humoured laughter rises in the still of the night and both men eye each other before another bout of laughter erupts into the night. Benaiah big body shakes with suppressed laughter and he wipes the tears streaming down he's cheek with the back of he's hand. He felt a sense of relief that he could share he's story with David. David speaks again amid he's laughter.

"And? Did you meet her in the Sanhedrin court?" Benaiah nods he's head in acknowledgement. "I was led by the maidservant who brought me the message. She distracted some of the guards at the court yard entrance and I sneaked past and we made our way towards the sanctum. She led me to a well close to main gardens. Behind the well it seemed like thick foliage had overgrown the wall. We walked right up to the wall and the maid servant disappeared into the thick foliage hanging on the side of the wall. It was then that I saw that there was a natural hidden space behind the foliage.

I followed and to my astonishment walked into a big enough space that could almost house four people. Later I would learn that the room was connected to the Sanhedrin and only few knew about it. The room was lit up with candles that could not be seen from the outside because of the foliage. It was not the sanctuary that captured my attention but the woman that stood with the maid servant.

It was her. It was Takisha"

David stretches he's legs out before him. "Now I know why and where you disappeared to every night when we stayed in Moab." Benaiah face seemed pained. "Yes. I did see her almost every night after our first meeting. That first meeting will stay with me forever though. The servant that led me there quickly left and the girl just started to weep. I did not know what to do so I did what came naturally and held her closely while she wept. The weeping became sobs and she started to talk to me.

She told me that she came from a city near Greece far across the ocean. She had travelled with her father whom was a spice merchant on he's dhow when an Egyptian war ship attacked them. She explained that her father was beheaded right in front of her and that the Egyptian men took her aboard their own vessel. She did not know for how long she was on the ship but when they reached land she was taken and held captive. It was not long before woman came and took her to a bath house. They cleaned her, dressed her and painted her face the way that Egyptian woman do. She was then taken towards a caravan outside the city by a group of men. An Amalekite merchant came and examined her face and her body they way that you look at animals when you buy them in the market place. She did not understand what the men were saying. She saw that the men that had brought her received a bulging pouch from the Amalekite Merchant. The Egyptian men left her with the merchant. The merchant then took her and spoke to her but she could not understand him.

He then spoke in Greek and told her that he would not harm her but that they were in for a long journey. They travelled for days at end until they had reached the city walls of Moab. It was here where she saw me and she just knew when she saw me that I was a respectable man."

The warrior sitting before David sighs deeply. "Respectable man she said but I knew she was mistaken. There I was talking to the King of Moab's newly acquired concubine in secret. She did not belong to me. I could not help it though and we talked and talked. I knew that we had little time and although it seemed only like moments ago, the servant girl returned too soon. She told us that the sun would soon rise and that the guards were changing shifts.

It was the best time for me to depart. I could not get her out of my mind and I did not even sleep during that day. I saw her again that evening and we met at the same place every evening from thereon until I heard that we would depart from Moab. She cried when I told her and wanted to come with me. We planned her escape and I would come and take her the following evening. That evening when I came into the courtyard I saw that something was amiss. There were some of Mizpah men standing close to the well.

As I retreated a hand touched my shoulder. I turned around ready to defend myself but saw the tearful face of the servant girl that had brought me to Takisha. The girl told me that one of the other girls had told Mizpah's guards that Takisha had met with a man in the courtyard every evening. She told me that the King of Moab wanted to capture me alive. I knew then that he did not know who I was for if he did he would have spoken to you."

Benaiah slams he's fist in the palm of he's big hand. "I should have gone after her that night!" David allows Benaiah anger to simmer. "Why did you not come to me?" Benaiah stares at the stars above them and sighs deeply again. "Deep inside me, I knew that she belonged to king Moab. I also knew that you had found favour in the king's eyes. You had left your father and mother behind in Moab." The big man stands up dusting the desert sand from he's legs. "I needed time to think .Away from Moab, away from her." David also rises from the sand. "In time the pain that I felt became more tolerable."

The big man stares at the star filled skies. "It was the right choice my friend but what made you change your mind to decide to return?" Benaiah face David again with a determined look in he's eyes. "My heart was foolish and before I left Moab I had spoken to the servant girl and told her to take this message to Takisha. I made her a promise that I would never forget her and that I would return for her if Yahweh allowed it."

The high pitched bleating sound of a group of camels close by interposes the men conversation. They will be fed soon and could smell water for miles away.

Benaiah exhales raucously. "As time progressed in her absence I knew that it was foolish and that she belonged to king Mizpah. That all changed a few days ago.

As you so readily observed, a group of people arrived here as we came to the hills of Hachilah. It was the slave girl that introduced me to Takisha together with a male travel companion. She explained that King Mizpah had sold Takisha and that in just a few moons she would be taken from Moab to the city of Gaza by some of King Mizpah men." David scratches he's beard. He knew that the king had free rule to trade slaves and material if they chose to obtain something in return. He had been in the presence of Saul many times when King Saul had traded some of the woman that they had captured on the routes of Judah. King Mizpah had paid for Takisha. She belonged to him therefore if he wanted to sell her he could.

"You know that they will not just allow you to walk out of Moab with the girl." Benaiah smiles determinedly. "I really hope that they will give a good account of themselves when I meet with them." The men stare at each other for a moment longer. David reaches out and grips Benaiah by he's shoulder. "Go with Yahweh brother and return soon!"

Benaiah takes the sheep flees across he's shoulder and moves of into darkness. David stares after the man until the darkness completely swallows he's bulk. "Lord please deliver him from he's enemies. Be a fortress against those who attack him."

David moves towards the middle of the camp where a big fire illuminates the faces of the men he had called together. They expression on Eleazar face tells him what he had expected all along when he had heard of the spies hasty return and yet he still asks the question. "So it is true? Is he here?"

Eleazar speaks for the group. "Yes my lord, he is encamped below the hill of Hachilah."

David strokes he's beard he's frown increasing on he's forehead. Why would Saul not let him be?

The wind picks up and hollers through the rocky mountain landscape. The two men move quietly across the cloudless, starlight filled mountain area heading towards the outskirts of the camp.

They had scouted the area just before sunset. David explained he's plan to Abishai using rocks to illustrate Saul camp layout and Rock Hyrax faeces to illustrate their infiltration plan.

Abishai grinned at David from underneath he's dark smeared face. The Rock Hyrax faeces was also used to ensure that their faces would blend in with the cover of the night. "We will move quietly my lord but I hope the smell does not wake anyone up."

David winks at Abishai but he only sees a row of white teeth giving indication that he had heard him. David had met with he's chiefs the previous night and decided that only one man should accompany him on the task that lay before them. He knew that all the men would volunteer but at the end he asked Abishai to accompany him.

He had brought into remembrance the night that he had dubbed a night of total irrationality. The man with fierce blue eyes and braided hair had handed him the skin of water drawn from the well at Jebus. This was close to where the Philistines were encamped. It was irrational but David had to admit at the time that it took real courage! It happened when David and he's men where in the stronghold in Adullam and the army of the Philistines encamped in the Valley of Rephaim.

One evening while the men had gather around talking about the events of the day, David had made a comment: "We will go from Adullam tomorrow. If it were not for the Philistine army that where encamped at Jebus we would have stopped and gotten supplies from there. O' how sweet it would have been to drink water from the well of Jebus again."

At the time David did not realize that the words that he had spoken would be taken up literally to encourage a small group of men to do the unthinkable. Benaiah the son of Jehoiada, Shammoth the Harorite and Abishai had crept into the Philistine camp in the middle of the night and had drawn water from the well in the midst of the enemy.

In the early morning hours David was awoken by commotion from the Philistine camp and much later Abishai, Benaiah and Shammoth came back into the camp full of mirth like youngsters on their first hunt. Abishai had presented the skin of water to David. He had no words and felt angry at their recklessness and yet loyalty and courage beamed from their countenance.

He had taken the skin and in front of the men he had poured the water onto the ground. He had then explained to them that he could not drink the water for their lives were much more worth than he's foolish requests. He told them that it would be as if he would be drinking their blood. They had gone to bed and after much deliberation later that day he had praised the men for their courage and appointed them as chiefs over the army.

This was but one of the many brave deeds that these men had performed over the last years and he's army had grown with courage and wisdom day by day.

So it was that he and Abishai made their way towards Saul camp. A bat flies low over their heads as the two men creep towards the camp. The shrill screeching noise echoes through the cloudless night as the creature navigates its way in the darkness. The two men pause for a while listening to the winged creature and then continue to creep forward. They try and spot the sentries that they had seen earlier. They were scouting the camp and saw the sentries who were stationed on the furthest side of the camp. David stares into the night. He was sure that they were on the right track. He had used a big boulder on the mountain they had come from as he's beacon. He stares back and can still make out the silhouette of the rock in the dim starlight.

They lay and wait patiently. The sentries would make their presence known soon. They wait for a long time and David begins to think that he had made an error. The clouds break for a moment and Abishai nudges he's shoulder whispering into he's ear. "Look, there by the fallen tree." David stares into the direction Abishai is point towards. He makes out a figure against the fallen tree. The person head seems slumped forward and David frowns in the dark. He turns he's face towards Abishai and whispers back. "These men will be killed if Saul were to find out that they were sleeping."

The men creep toward the fallen log and David keeps a trained eye out for the second sentry. He does not have to search too long though because as he creeps closer he can see the body of a second man hidden by the branch of the fallen tree. It was very peculiar that both sentries slept the way that they did.

David recollects when he was in Saul regiment that the men that kept watch was severely punished if they were found sleeping. The men that were entrusted with this duty feared the king wrath and it was an odd sight to see both men sleeping. The two men slip past the sleeping men. Smoke from the burned out cooking fires drifts slowly into the night air. The grunting noise of a camel makes the two men stop in their tracks. They wait for a while scanning the area and then continue. They make their way through the camp.

An eerie silence had fallen upon the camp. David listens intently but all that they could hear was the deep breathing noises of sleeping men and some snores reverberating in the still of the night. They made their way towards the middle of the camp where they had seen the royal tent erected. It was not hard to find the enclosure where Saul slept. The tent erected in the middle of the camp stood out because of its bulk and a small fire still burned lowly. The two men slowly approach the tent.

Shadows of sleeping men dances in the fire light and seem to be the only thing moving inside the circle of men. David stares at the tent. The tents side walls are open for night air to pass through. David sees Abner son of Ner, the commander of Saul army and then spots Saul sleeping close by. A spear is stuck in the ground close to Saul's head. Abishai reaches for spear and in he's haste trips over a man close to Saul. David stares in horror and Abishai freezes on the spot. The man only mumbles but does not even move he's eyelids. David stares at all the men before him and frowns deeply and softly whispers ratifying he's own suspicion.

"The Lord has put these men in a deep sleep Abishai. That is why the sentries are sleeping." Abishai again reaches for the spear close to Saul head. David grabs he's tunic and pulls him back whispering in he's ear. "What are you doing?" Abishai turns towards David. "Yahweh has delivered this man in your hands my lord. Let me strike him with the spear!"

David looks at the man lying on the ground and then softly replies. "No Abishai. We shall not stretch our hand out against the Lords anointed. As the Lord lives, the Lord shall strike him, or he's day shall come to die, or he shall go out to battle and perish."

David pulls the spear out of the ground and also takes a jug of water standing next to Saul's head. He stares at Saul for some time and then beckons for Abishai to follow him. They slowly make their way out of the camp. It is an uneasy experience. They leave the camp and no man even stirs. David again uses the boulder as a beacon. After a great distance climb into the hills he stops and looks back at the camp. The light had changed and soon the dawn will break.

He stares at the embers of the fire where Saul tent is erected. He puts he's hands on either side of he's mouth and calls out in the early morning hours.

"King Saul! Abner!" The words rolls down the hills the resonance deafening into the camp below.

"King Saul! Abner!"

It seem like David's voice have the desired effect for the two men sees movement in the camp below and they can even make out a stirring around King Saul's tent. The voice of Abner calls back to the men on the hill.

"Who are you men calling out to the king?" David waits for the reverberation to die down and then calls back to the Abner. "Are you not a man? Are you not a great general? And yet why have you and your men not guarded your king through the night?"

David pauses for some effect before he continues. With me is the king's jug of water and he's spear that lay by he's head. I have come into your camp and I have taken these items!" David can make out some commotion around the tent and they must now have seen that the spear and jug was missing. The unmistakable figure of King Saul come and stands next to Abner.

"Is that your voice my son David?" The voice of Saul sounds tired and old. "Yes my king it is me." David trains he's eyes and gives instruction to Abishai. "Go up to the ridge and make sure that no one flanks us." He stares down at the camp and can still see Saul standing next to Abner. "I came in the middle of the night and took your spear and the jug of water which stood by your head. I could have taken your life king Saul and yet I have not lifted my hand against the Lords anointed." David pauses again for a moment. "Why do you still seek the live of your servant David?"

For a while there is no answer. David sees Abner move with the king but after about twenty paces both men stop. The dawn was breaking and the suns first rays greeted them on the mountain. They men below was still too far away to see the emotions on their faces but the silence is broken by Saul's deep voice. "Again you spare my life? You could surly have taken the spear and driven it through my heart." It is quite between the men for a while before David responds.

"I am but a flea my king! The king of Israel have come out to hunt me as one hunts a partridge in the mountain. I am not worth all this trouble my king." There is another silence before Saul responds. "David, again I have sinned. Return with me for I will seek you're life no longer. You have shown me today that you value my life." A fresh morning breeze tangles David's hair sweeping some locks into he's face. The words that Saul spoke feels empty. He knows that Saul will pursue him still. David lifts the spear that he had taken from the camp. "Here is the king spear! Let one of your young men come and get it!" He's words carries to the men in the valley below. "My life is in the hands of the Lord. He value's all life. I will wait on the Lord for He will deliver me out of tribulation!" With that David turns back making he's way up the mountain towards Abishai. The words of King Saul echo's through the hills and follows him as he ascends. "May you be blessed my son David! You shall do great things and still prevail!"

Chapter 9

The Philistine king sees David enter into the hallway and smiles inwardly. Achish was dumbstruck when a sentry had come to him a few months ago and announced that David wanted to speak with him. At first Achish had though that it was a trap and he had send out he's scouts before he decided to meet with David. The men returned and reported that David and he's army of men which was about seven hundred strong with women and children were all encamped just outside the city of Gath. Why will David put himself and he's men with their families at risk like this? David exploits was well known to him and he remembered the day when the youth fooled him to believe that he was possessed, scratching on the walls, spitting into he's beard acting all infatuated and crazy. He did not recognize David then and it was only later that he learned that it was David indeed that had stood before him and he's men.

He did not hold a grudge against him however and admired the recourse fullness and courage of the warrior. In fact it was David who made it easier for them in the past few years for he had conquered many of the enemies bordering the Philistine lands extending to Shur and Egypt. He was intrigued by David's request to meet with him but even more dumbfound when the warrior spoke and requested passage to live among them.

Achish knew that Saul still pursued the young warrior and after listening to David plea he had found that he even enjoyed the young man more. They sat together and after three days of discussion he proclaimed the terms of their bargain and gave them passage to the city of Gath.

At first the Philistine men treated the group with a lot of hostility but David was a man that was true he's word and he had promised the king that he would raid the neighbouring cities and help defend the land.

David and he's men dwelled in the city Gath with the Philistine king and he's men. King Achish send he's spies to accompany David on he's wars to their neighbouring enemies. Every time he received great reports of success and triumph. David found great favour in the eyes king Achish son of Maoch. After almost a year that David and his men had spent in the city; David came and urgently requested an audience with the king. King Achish eagerly invited him in to he's banquet.

The request that David brought before him was excessive indeed but the king did not see any reason why he should not grant David he's request. The men sat at the banquet and Achish was in a jovial mood. He sat listening with a mellow heart to David request although some of the other Philistines did not seem pleased with David words.

"If I now have found favour in your eyes king Achish, give my men and me a place in some town in the country of the Philistines that we may dwell there?" Achish takes a drink out of he's wine goblet and summons the servants with a raised hand for another jug. "Since your arrival in Gath there have been many battles that you have waged against our enemies and you have conquered them all!"

The Philistine men sitting with their king acknowledges the truth of their king's words. Achish silently studies the man with the ruddy red beard before him and continues. "At first you conquered the Geshurites, and then the Girzites and you have been a constant thorn in the side of the Amalekites. I have heard that you are planning to go as far as Egypt in the land of Shur and also wage war against our enemies there?" David acknowledges the kings last remark by nodding he's head. "You have not spared any man or woman when you raided the lands. Always you have brought the sheep, oxen, camel's donkeys and apparel back to me." Servants enter the great hall replacing the old jugs of wine with full containers and some of the men eagerly pour more wine into their goblets.

King Achish wait for the servants to depart. He slowly rises from he's chair and although he still addresses David he stares at all the men sitting around the table when he speaks. "David you assuredly know that the time will come when I gather all the Philistine armies to draw against Israel?" It was completely silent in the big hall and all the men now stared at David.

David clears he's throat. "King Achish, your enemies have become our enemies. Surely you have seen and know what your servant can do?" The men around the table turn their gazes upon their king. Achish raises he's goblet. "David I give you and your men the land of Ziklag to dwell in and do as you please." The Philistine men around the table murmur and some shake their heads but Achish blazing eyes quiets their discontent. "Furthermore I make you one of my chief guardians forever!"

The king raises he's goblet and the men around the table all stand with raises goblets some of the malevolent stares not escaping David.

Yahweh gave David and he's men strength and great victories. The battles that they fought became the stories that Philistine and Israel fathers told their young in the evenings around the camp fires.

The stories of mighty men.

David's mighty men!

Achish never doubted David's loyalty and he always reminded himself that the people of Israel would abhor him because he fought with the Philistines. David had been staying in the land that Achish had given them for a year and four months. In those days the

Philistines started to gather their armies to go to war with Israel but David continued to wage war against the Amalekite tribes in the land of old as far as Shur. Day by day David's army grew and some men from the tribe of Benjamin and Judah defected from Saul to join David army. Some Gadites also joined the stronghold, mighty men of valour, men trained for battle who could handle shield and spear whose faces where like the faces of lions and were as swift as gazelle's!

When the sons of Benjamin and Judah came to David's stronghold David went out to meet them and told them that if they came in peace to help him and he's army he would unite with them in he's heart. If they would betray him Yahweh would punish them for their ways. As he was speaking the Holy Spirit came upon Amasai, chief of the captains of Judah and he said.

"We are yours, David, and on your side, you son of Jesse. Peace, peace be to you, and peace be to your helpers; for your God helps you" (1 Chronicles 12 v 18)

The day came when the Philistines armies gathered at Aphek to fight against Israel encamped at Jezreel.

David was summoned.

Benaiah stares at the gridlocked wall. The screams of dying men can be heard above the cheering of the crowd. Soon he will enter the arena. In the distance the roaring of an animal rises above the screams of the crowd.

Benaiah feels no fear. In he's mind he sees the sinuous face of the adoration of he's life, Takisha. The winter cold seeps in through the stone walls and the big man rubs he's hands together for warmth. The sound of keys turning opening a sell door echoes in the passage and the feet of soldiers approaching in the distance announces that the time had arrived.

It will all be over soon; he thinks to himself. They had almost escaped the hands of King Mizpah of Moab. Now he had to participate in the king's cruel encounter with all odds stacked against him.

There was a shimmer of hope as long as he was still alive. All seemed so distant since he and David had sat on the dune that evening before he departed.

He had travelled towards Moab after he had left David and the rest of the troop. He had carefully planned he's way and when he arrived in Moab he kept a very low profile. He was just one of the crowd and did not reveal he's identity to anyone. He only made contact with Shizen, the servant girl that had brought him the message when he was still with David at the hill of Hachilah. She told him that the caravan would leave for the city of Gaza within the cycle of the next moon. Then they would travel up the Nile River making the exchange with the traders. King Mizpah was selling Takisha among other entities for spices coming from the trade routes from the north.

At first he thought that he would speak with Mizpah and try and buy her from him but he's hopes was completely dashed when he heard the trading price which the king would obtain for Takisha. The price was far greater than two years good earned wages and he had varied feelings when he heard this. To him she was far more worth than the asking price and yet he did not have that amount of coinage. He started to think about other alternatives but in the end he knew that he's best chance would be to escape with Takisha from the city of Moab. He knew that he would have to plan the escape before she left Moab because the king would guard the caravan heavily. He thought extensively and firmly about their escape and trusted no one with he's plans but he had to get the message through to Takisha. He's only direct connection to Takisha was Shizen henceforth he started to share the plan with her trusting her to relay he's exact instructions to he's beloved.

Only afterwards when he was captured and had an audience with the king did he realize how foolish he's plans were. The king guard had kept a close eye on Shizen and knew when he had entered the city. They knew of he's exact whereabouts and waited on the precise moment to seize him. It happened one evening when he returned to the inn where he stayed. It was shortly after he had met with Shizen close by the market square. He was clubbed over the head by an unseen assailant. When he had awoken he's hands and feet were tied very tightly and he's vision was blinded by a cloth tied around he's head. It had felt like he's head would explode from the pain were the weapon had struck him.

He was lying on he's back on a stone cobbled floor. The harsh winter cold was intensified on the cobbled floor. The cold crept into he's bones and he started to shake uncontrollably. He must have passed out because he awoke with a startle when ice water splashed into he's face. He had opened he's eyes and saw that the blind fold had been removed. He stared into the fierce faces of the king guard.

"On your feet treacherous thief! The king wants to see your ugly mug before you are fed to the lions!" He was taken from the enclosure where he was kept. Confirmation of what he suspected all along became evident as they left the enclosure. He was kept in the dungeon underneath the city walls. The guards roughly man handled him. When he entered the great hallway where he and David together with other men had a feasted with king Mizpah; he's thoughts was still only off Takisha.

"Bow down you cur!"

He got hit on the small of he's back with the shaft of a spear and stumbled onto he's one knee.

"Do not lift your hands against him!"

It was the familiar voice of king Mizpah. Benaiah looked up and saw the king sitting on a bear skin on a huge stone crafted chair. The flames of a fire in an enormous hearth, threw shadows across the bearded face of King Mizpah. The king moved forward the light of the flames illuminating he's thick brow. "Indeed; it is the mighty general of the bodyguard of David." The fire burning in the hall casts shadows dancing across walls. The pain throbbing in Benaiah he's head felt like it was going to explode behind he's eyelids. "Did you think that you could just walk out of Moab with one of my consort's?" Benaiah wanted to speak out but there was something about the king demeanour that made him keep quiet. "I know what you are thinking great general. Why would the king be interested to capture a man who wanted to steal a consort that he was about to sell?" The king slowly stands up from the bear skin and Benaiah sees the head of the mighty felled creature draped over the upright stone of he's chair. Mizpah continued. "I do not seek the pleasures of the youth anymore. I chose Takisha mainly because she was a beauty that I had not seen before and I was rather interested in her. When I first learned that someone had visited her in secret I was angry but also bemused. I had wondered who would be so bold as to enter the Sanhedrin."

The king walks towards the fire stretching out he's hands towards the heat. "I knew that someone would be able to share information on the rogue that met with my newly acquired wife. It was not long before my men found out about the young servant girl that helped you in the Sanhedrin." King Mizpah turns from the fire and come to stand before him. "I must admit that I was not that surprised to find out that it was one of the mighty warriors of David that met in secret with Takisha. I was never going to trade her general but used the servant with the news to lure you back here." The king turns away from Benaiah. The frown on Benaiah face had increased since the king had started to talk. He could not understand why king Mizpah was so calm.

King Mizpah back was turned towards him. As if he had read Benaiah thoughts he had continued. "The colosseum games have started. You know that the most prized Moab fighters compete against man and beast." The king pauses and again turns he's face towards Benaiah. "Kings and leaders come from all over to see these men compete." The king had once again come to a standstill before him. "General, the games will be different this year. The people will remember this year as the year when a mighty Hebrew general stood in the face of man and beast! A mighty man of David! You will stand against the lion like heroes of Moab!"

Benaiah still did not say a word but he's jaw was clenched as he continued to listen to the king. "All is not lost general. Fight you will fight for sure for you have acted treacherously dishonouring me." Mizpah pauses for a moment. "If you win against man and beast I will set you free and you can take the young Takisha with you." The words hang between the men. Benaiah can almost not trust the words of the king. He knows that he's chances are slim and yet there was a chance. Mizpah mind seem to have drifted. "I was also once young and foolish and in love."

The king eagerly turned towards him. "What do you say general? Is your admiration for this woman resilient enough?" Benaiah takes a deep breath. "I will fight and if Yahweh wills it I will surmount." Mizpah smiles broadly. "Yes; you will need this Yahweh of yours aid if you are going to walk out of the colosseum alive." Mizpah beckons the guards. "Take him back to he's cell. Feed him properly. The games starts tomorrow." With that said the conversation was over and the king turned away from him. He was taken back to the cell and was fed as per king instruction. He had prayed to the Yahweh of Abraham, Jacob, Josef and Moses as David had done before the battle at Keilah.

He had pleaded that Yahweh would forgive he's young foolish heart and then he had fallen asleep.

The memory of all that had happened since he was captured fades away. He hears feet approaching down the corridor that stops abruptly before he's cell door.

A key turns heavily in its padlock. The sounds of the cheering crowds erupts again somewhere above him. He had listened to these sounds since he's return from the king's chamber a fortnight ago.

"Yahweh please help me for I will either be in Sheol or with my dearest Takisha tonight."

The guards enter he's cell carrying spears and they escort him out. In the distance and he hears the screams of dying men. The guards nudges him forward and continue past a few cell doors. They enter a wider passage and Benaiah sees a light shining in the distance of the passage. The guards continue their stride their spears pointing at the vitals of he's back. The sound of the jeering crowd swells as they continue towards the light. They reach the end of the passage and the light almost blinds Benaiah as they exit the passage. Benaiah is greeted by a deafening sound of the baying crowd their voices crashing over him. The sun reflects severely from the snow covered arena and he lifts he's arms shielding he's eyes from the glare in the snow filled arena. The cold seem to seep into he's every bone and he blinks rapidly taking in the scene before him.

Benaiah sees two guards placed on either side of the passage that he had just entered through into the arena. Another set of guards can be seen standing at an exit across from him. Judging by the dark drag marks and dark stains in the snow leading towards the exit; Benaiah does not have to guess to know that the bodies of the men he heard screaming before was dragged through the same exit.

A sudden roar erupts coming from the earth to he's left and he involuntary jumps to he's right. The guards that escorted him also retract their steps and he is left alone in the middle of the arena. The roar erupts again and the arena is filled with the baying of the crowd. Benaiah stares in the direction where the roaring comes from and sees the dark edge of a man-made pit. He winces thinking about the danger in the pit. Many of the screams he had heard must have come from the men that had faced the terror down in the depths where the roars erupts from. The sound of drums starting to pound seem to quite the crowd and the snarling sound of the animal is also drowned out by the timeous pounding. Just as sudden as the pounding had started it abruptly ends and an eerie silence befalls the arena.

The voice of man suddenly fill the arena. "The accused general of David stands before you because he tried to steal one of the king's consorts!" The crowd erupts again. Benaiah again shields he's eyes against the sun and sees a man dressed in a dark turban standing on a platform on the left side of the arena addressing the crowds. It is not the man that draws he's attention though but the figures seated to the left of the man. The unmistakable figure of King Mizpah is seen surrounded by servants but it is the small figure sitting below the king that catches he's full attention.

Takisha!

The voice of the man on the platform booms out again and the crowd quiets down. "It was only because David had shown great service to the king that our king has decided that should the general be victorious in he's battles that the king grant both the general and this woman (The man pointed towards Takisha) their freedom." The crowd erupted again and this time they hailed the name of king Mizpah. The man standing on the platform raises he's hand for silence again and the crowd noise dies down to a murmur. "Should the general fail today the same fate that he suffers will follow the woman!" Benaiah screams out in anger but he's voice was lost in the roar of the crowd. The announcer again raises he's hands. "The challenge for such conniving deed is defeating man and beast!" Without any further warning two enormous men enter the arena through the area guarded by the soldiers across from the entrance he came in. Benaiah recognizes the men known as the Lion faced Moabite warriors. He looks into the faces of the approaching warriors and is again reminded why they carried the name: Men with Faces of Lions.

When David had first brought them to Moab after they had defeated the Philistines at Keilah they had met the elite soldiers of Moab. It was not only the ferocity that they fought and trained with that earned them the name. It was all the battle scars in their faces that resembled the faces of lions that had seen many battles. While they stayed in Moab, Benaiah had heard many stories about these men; but a specific story had stayed with him and he had uncovered gruesome witnessed to some of it. They had returned from the palace one evening and passed a weapons bearer that had accompanied some of the Moabite Lion warriors earlier that day. He was dragging a big heavy bag behind him and Benaiah and Eleazar stopped to receive news of a report of an invasion on the Southern borders of the Moabite city. The weapons bearer had stopped and given them an account that ten of the Moabite elite Lion faced warriors had torn into a band of hundred men that tried to invade the borders and defeated them in a matter of moments. It was than then that Benaiah had notice a dark wet patch in the sand where the man had dragged the bag. When he had enquired what was in the bag the weapons bearer opened the bag partially and the lifeless eyes of beheaded men stared back at him. Benaiah had witnessed many horrific things on the battleground but somehow those lifeless eyes had stayed with him. Shortly after they had met with the weapons bearer, the group of Moabite warriors that returned from battle had passed them. It was the look in their eyes that made him realize that these warriors were different for their eyes seemed as lifeless as the beheaded men he had then witnessed.

The two warriors approaching him now does not make any sound and the look in their eyes again remind Benaiah why they were compared to men with the faces of Lions. The expression in their eyes was deadly and almost a pool of black emptiness. The men each bare their weapon of choice; a heavy double headed axe that gleams in the winter sunlight. Benaiah is not fooled by the heavy look of the weapons in their hands for he had seen the warriors wield them with ease. The two men slowly approach him and take a crouched stance on either side of him each at least fifteen feet away from him. An eerie silence had befallen the arena. "Yahweh please forgive me the arrogance of my youth and help me today." Benaiah crouches down on he's knees and digs deep into the snow covered ground. He scoops a fist full of mud into he's right hand and stays in a crouched position. He's body starts to tingle and a sudden burst of energy fills he's being as it had happened when they had fought at Keilah. The attack is without warning and both the Moabite warriors move in silently with an unmatched swiftness. Benaiah rolls on he's left shoulder encountering the Moabite attack from he's right. An axe flashes past he's face thumping into the soft covered earth where he had been moments before. The crowd squeals wildly but Benaiah is oblivious to the noise in the arena. He turns slowly exposing he's back knowing that the other warrior was close but it was a chance he had to take. He's senses is heightened and he hears the soft shoes of the other warrior in the snow behind him approaching above the baying crowd and he ducks to he's right the axe head burying itself into he's snow by he's side. He quickly rolls to he's left onto the axe shaft trapping the blade under the weight of he's body. He feels the edge of the axe blade cutting into he's left flank but he's hand quickly snakes out around the shaft of the axe pulling the Moabite towards him. He stands face to face with one of the Moabite warriors the man eyes blazing with hatred.

Benaiah throws the mud that he had picked up when he was crouching down, with a mighty force into the warriors face standing before him. The man stumbles back; momentarily blinded by the force of the mud. Without any hesitation Benaiah swings the big axe in a wide arch and brings it down onto the base of the man skull. He hears the sickening crack of vertebrae and the lifeless form of the Moabite drops down onto the snow before him. The crowd had now gone crazy and it was now difficult to hear anything in the arena. He's next action was instinctively. Instead of turning around to face the other warrior he dives in behind the fallen man body lying before him. The meaty thump of an axe burying itself into meat sounds behind him. Benaiah scrambles up from behind the fallen body and sees the second warrior trying to loosen he's axe from he's fallen comrades back. Benaiah had dropped he's axe when he had dived in behind the fallen Moabite body. He takes advantage of the struggling warrior actions trying to loosen he's axe and steps towards him punching the man in the face with a sickening blow that would have felled a buffalo. This was the Lion faced warriors of Moab though! Instead of falling as Benaiah had hoped for the man only takes a step backwards shaking his head. He then advances again leaving the axe he had tried to get behind coming at Benaiah with fortitude. Benaiah did not expect the quick reaction and too late he feels a fist explode against the side of he's head. A thousand stars fills he's vision and when the real world appears again he finds himself on he's back in the snow.

He lifts he's head and sees the warrior running at him. Benaiah kicks out with both he's legs when the warrior is almost upon him sending the man flying back into the snow. Benaiah stands up groggily. He sees the edge of the pit where he heard the animal roaring from looming behind the fallen warrior. The Moabite had quickly risen and again made an attempt to retrieves the axe from he's fallen companions back. The man wrestles the axe clear from the fallen body and before the warrior turns Benaiah does the unthinkable. He runs with full force hitting the warrior in the small of he's back sending them both flying over the edge of the pit into the unknown. Benaiah hits he's head against something hard and he shakes he's head groggily. He feels the body of the Moabite moving under him but it is the deafening roars behind him that quickly brings him to he's senses. He slowly turns he's head not making any quick movement. He's sight is filled by a big black mane. Another roar explodes in the enclosure and the fetid breath of the beast close by fills he's nostrils.

The Moabite under him starts to move franticly and Benaiah slowly rolls of the man lying beneath him. The Moabite sits up and shakes he's head seeming oblivious to the danger close to them in the bottom of the pit. A trickle of blood runs down the side of the Moabites face and he shakes he's head once more before he's eyes come to rest on the figure of Benaiah. When he sees Benaiah he screams out in anger moving towards him. The lion growls lowly and paws the ground before the men. The Moabites reaction when he sees the lion is instinctively triggered and he turns and tries to scramble up the side of the pit to no avail. This time the lion does not mock charge and in one fluid motion with a straight tail the brute attacks the scrambling Moabite. Its big maw closes around the shoulder of the Moabite warrior and he continues to scream as the lion drags him to the ground. Benaiah stares in horror at the scene before him and then starts looking around him for a possible escape. He's eyes captures an object lying close by. It is the shaft of the double headed axe lying at an awkward angle. It was the weapon that the Moabite had in he's hands when he took him down into the pit. The Moabite cries out again but this time he is much weaker and Benaiah moves slowly towards the axe not trying to draw the attention of the lion. He becomes aware of the noise of the crowd above them knowing that they would have heard the dying screams of the man that the lion was mauling. He had almost reached the axe but the lion suddenly turns and comes straight at him. Benaiah grabs the shaft of the axe and swings the weapon directly into the face of the ferocious animal. He hears a tooth snap as the massive double headed axe connects the charging animal; the force throwing Benaiah to the ground. Benaiah holds onto the axe shaft with both he's hands and pushes it out horizontally keeping the massive jaws above him at bay. He violently twists the shaft of the axe. The blade of the weapon connects the brute on the side of its face and the animal roars out in pain and retrieves for a moment. Benaiah come to stand on he's feet looking at the indicator of the next attack from the injured beast which comes very quickly. With another roar the lion runs at him. Benaiah hesitates only for a moment before he swings the axe down in a mighty arch onto the skull of the animal. The one front paw of the animal hits him against he's left shoulder numbing he's arm. The animal crouches before him blood streaming form its nostrils. Benaiah rises the axe with he's right hand screaming as the lion attacks for a third time. "Yahweh!" He brings downs the axe with great strength; power surging through he's body. The blade buries itself in the forehead of the brute driving in deep between its yellow eyes instantly killing it. Benaiah falls against the side of the pit breathing deeply. "Thank you Yahweh, thank you."

He hears voices above him. Only when he looks up he becomes aware of faces looking down at him from above the pit. The man that had announced he's fate earlier voice rings out above him. "The Hebrew has slain the two lion like heroes of Moab! He has also gone down the pit and killed a lion on this snowy day!" A wooden ladder is lowered down into the pit and he is ordered to climb out of the pit. As he climbs out of the pit a great cheer arise from the crowd. He slowly moves away from the edge of the pit and sees that

King Mizpah had come into the arena surrounded by some of he's men. For a moment he wishes that he had not left the axe behind in the pit but al is suspicion is forgotten when he sees her running to him. Takisha throws her arms around him and he winches in pain he's left arm a reminder of the battle that he had just fought. "We are free to be together!" The words seem unreal but when Benaiah sees the face of king Mizpah he knows that they are true. The king holds he's hand in the air and the crowd goes silent. "Blessed be the Yahweh of Benaiah who delivered He's servant from the hands of he's enemy and the jaws of this creature. Therefore I make a decree that anyone that speaks out against the Yahweh of Benaiah he shall be cut into pieces! Your Yahweh is surly the true Yahweh because there is no other Yahweh that can deliver like this!" King Mizpah walks over to him and speaks in a softer tone but still loud enough for the surrounding men to hear. "You are free to leave Moab with this woman. May you have a sanctified life."

The crowd again erupts as the kings final words are spoken hailing the name of king Mizpah!

The mist drifts away slowly over the escarpment as the sun rays creeps over the valley of Aphek. As far as David could see, he saw men arriving and they were already more than ten thousand men. The valley had started to fill early before the sun had set and the smell of the horses and sweat of human bodies mingle in the morning breeze. David and he's men are at the rear of the armies just behind Achish army. It did not elude him when a group of riders had approached Achish. There were a lot of murmur and angry talk among the men and they continued to point in he's direction. It was clear that the Philistine lords were unhappy with he's presence. David decided to approach Achish and the men in conversation. A tall warrior with broad shoulders and thick arms also approached Achish riding a beautiful black Arabian horse.

David had seen him before and knew that the prince of Ashdod did not keep him in high esteem.

Bilahim the prince of Ashdod dismounts and speaks to Achish "I speak for the rest of the Philistines princes as well. I put this concern before you, appointed by the tribes as spokesmen for our tribe. What are these Hebrews doing here?" He looks directly at David. "Is he not Saul's servant?" Achish clears he's throat and speaks out. "Yes it is David. Once he was Saul's son in law. Once he even defeated one of our greatest warriors but he has stayed with me for this last few years and never have I found fault in him since he had arrived here." Bilahim shakes he's head in anger. "Let this fellow return to the place that you have given to him! He cannot be trusted! This is a good opportunity to show he's master that he is still loyal! Is it not this David that they sang about in the dance: Saul has slain he's thousands, and David he's ten thousands?" Achish looks at the commander before him and back at David and he shrugs he's shoulders in submissiveness. Bilahim and Achish walks away from the group and parleys quietly for an instant. The men continue their discussion and then Bilahim mounts he's stallion looking at David once more; hatred burning in he's eyes. He then turns he's stallion and rides away with the group of men that accompanied him. David waits silently as Achish approaches.

"David, I want you and your men to return to Ziklag when the dawn breaks. This battle shall not be fought with you in our midst." David looks at Achish in frustration. "What have I done wrong? Have we not proven our loyalty to you?" Achish raises he's hand to silence David "You have proven your loyalty and I have found no evil in you. The lords of the Philistines do not approve of you being here. As you well know they represent the regents of Gaza, Ashkelon, Ashdod and Ekron and have power over the region according to our ways." Achish sighed heavily and embraced David. "I know that you are good in my sight, as an angel of God. Notwithstanding what the princes of the Philistines have said, 'He shall not go up with us to the battle. Therefore now rise up early in the morning with the servants of your lord who have come with you; and as soon as you are up early in the morning, and have light, depart. (1 Samuel 29 v 9) I will send word and meet with you soon."

Achish and he's men departed to Jezreel and left David and he's men. In morning David and he's men rose early and departed to Ziklag. It was a three day journey back to Ziklag and David and he's men looked forward to see their wives and children again.

The whole of Israel was assembled at Gilboa. When Saul had heard that the Philistines was pitched at Shunem he send out he's scouts. When they had reported a host of the Philistine armies Saul was afraid and he's heart was dazed. "I don't know what else to do? Samuel is dead and the Philistines are threatening to take a hold over the whole of Israel!"

Abinadab Saul's eldest son looks at he's father seeing the madness shining in he's eyes. "You where the one that put the mediums and Spiritism out of the land father! There is no prophets to help you now. I know where we can go to speak to a woman who can consult with the spirits!" Saul looks at he's son a flicker of hope showing in he's eyes. "Where is this medium?" Abinadab takes he's father by the shoulder leading him to he's pillows "She is in En Dor. I will give the servants the command to ready the horses tonight so that we can travel there. You better disguise yourself father. We do not want anyone to recognize the king of Israel consulting with mediums."

The little clay hut smells like herbs and garlic. Saul enters the small dwelling but he can't help but to shun away from the old woman's repulsive face. Saul has an old head cloth wrapped around he's head. He had put kohl around he's eyes to disguise himself. "I want you to conduct with a séance for me. One that I will name." The old woman looks at Saul and then frowns "You know that if I do this

I could be killed. Saul has cut off all the mediums of this land and why would I put myself in such peril?"

He gave the old wench three gold coins that made her face crackle with a smile. "Whom shall I bring up for you?" It was only Saul and Abinadab in the dwelling. The other servants waited outside. The wind hollers through a hole in the roof and Saul feels an uneasy restlessness upon him. "Bring up Samuel for me." Suddenly the old woman falls on her knees crying out horribly. She looks up at Saul fear showing in hear eyes. "You have deceived me! You are King Saul!" Saul takes a step backwards. "How do you know this woman? What did you see? Do not be afraid for no punishment shall come upon you." The woman shakes her head from side to side. "I see an old man coming up with a mantle!"

Suddenly the voice of the woman alters and Saul falls to he's knees. The voice of the prophet Samuel speaks again. "Why do you disturb me?" Saul does not look up but answers. "I am greatly distressed! The Philistines are threatening to take Israel! I have no prophets that can help me and Yahweh has deserted me! Therefore I have called upon you so that you may reveal to me what to do." The voice of Samuel fills the hut. "The Lord has left you for you have sinned! He will give the kingdom in the hand of David as He has spoken by me. The Lord will deliver Israel with you in the hand of the Philistines. Tomorrow you and your sons will die and Israel will be in the Philistines hands. "

An anguished cry comes from the throat of Saul and cannot rise for the news is too dreadful. He had not eaten that whole day and night and now was completely drained. The old women approaches Saul anxiety showing in hear face "My lord you have come to me asking this of me and I have heeded to your request. Rest for a while and let me prepare some food for you." Saul shrugs off the woman's hand. "I will not eat. I am dead already."

Abinadab walks over to he's father he's face pale in the candle light. "Father please let us eat something. We need the strength. We will find another medium, one that can give us a better omen."

Saul slowly gets to he's feet. Suddenly he looks twenty years older. They sit at the table while the woman prepares the food.

Saul did not say anything anymore.

It was the third day on their return to Ziklag and the men became more boisterous as they drew closer to the town. The men had hungered for war but after they made their way back from Aphek it seemed that everyone agreed that spending time with their families was much more in their favour than the brutal ways of war.

Most of the young men that joined David army had found themselves wife's while they stayed in Gath. As young men often did they were the ones making jokes their youth full countenance yearning with the expectations of the young married life. David had send a scouting party ahead of them. They were making good time and would reach Ziklag before the midday. "People approaching from the west!" The voice of one of the men rang out in the early morning hours. David reigned in he's horse and held he's hands up in the air. The group of men grouped together as they had trained and fought the last couple of years. The front line men armed with spears formed a semi-circle and Abishai their general called them to order. Shammah gave order to the rear of the army that formed a squadron and held their spears and swords ready for their general's command. Eleazar and he's men formed the core of the army ready to attack and their swords gleamed in the early rays of the sun. The scout called out again. "It seems like it is only a single caravan." David put he's hand over he's brow staring into the distance. A single caravan indeed was approaching them and by the likes of it he saw four camels. "Flank them from the east. Be careful of a tail ambush!" The men had quieted down to a murmur. David saw the horses approach the caravan from the east and soon it became obvious that the people on the camels had noticed the men approaching them for the leader stopped the caravan. David continued to stare in the distance and it seemed like there was a short exchange between the leader of the caravan and the men he had send. Soon the caravan and he's men started to move again towards them and as they drew closer David smile grew broader and he dismounted he's steed. "Benaiah!" The bearded warrior climbed of the bulky animal he rode and the men embraced laughing with joy. Benaiah beard had grown into a thick bush and he's face had the appearance of an old grizzly bear. In he's left hand he held a Sheppard staff and if David did not know any better he would have mistaken him for one of the Sheppard's tending the sheep in Ziklag.

The men seemed oblivious of everyone else around them and soon Eleazar and Shammah also came closer and embraced the bear like figure of Benaiah their joyful exchange resounding in the desert morning. It only dawned on David after Benaiah kept staring at the caravan behind him seemingly uncomfortable; that there was three woman sitting on the camels behind him. The woman were all veiled and Benaiah approached the first camel and held out he's hand towards the woman perched on top of it. "David, this is my wife Takisha." The woman bows lowly before David and when she uncovers her veil David recognizes the girl he had once seen in king Mizpah hall. David clasp he's left hand on Benaiah shoulder and the men embrace again. "Time has passed my friend but it seems like yesterday since you departed on your quest. From what I can gather it was a success!" Benaiah seem to frown earnestly. "It has had it challenges but I will tell you about it tonight when we sit next to a fire." The men laugh like children and Benaiah grumbling voice trails off as another voice cries out in the early morning hours. "Scouts approaching!" David sees a blanket of dust approaching from the west and makes out he's scouts red color head garment trailing in the wind. The men ride with urgency and David feels a knot in he's stomach. The men are still at a distance but one of the men strong young voice carries in the morning hours "There is a thick blanket of smoke hanging over the town of Ziklag!"

The horses come to stop before them, the steed flanks gleaming from sweat and the horses neigh nervously. "It seems like the town has been raided my lord!" David thoughts whirls and the sweet face of he's wife Abigail comes to his mind. "Come! Let us not waste time! Every man make haste!" Most of the men were running and moving as fast as they could while David and the generals rode their horses towards the city. They seemed like a trail of ants scurrying down the valley. Time seem to pass slowly but soon they approached Ziklag. They saw a thick dark cloud of smoke hanging over the town as it had been reported. The men now cried out and ran franticly towards the burning city. David makes he's way towards he's own home and he's stomach drops when he sees the thatched roof laying in smoulders. He enters the dwelling.

The smoke from the burning roof burns he's eyes making it hard to breathe. Some of the roof had collapsed in to the interior of the house and David searches franticly between the smouldering rubble for any sign of he's wife. He winches as he burns he's hands when he takes hold of a beam that had fallen across the entrance of their bedroom. He pushes the smouldering log without ceremony and continues he's dreadful search for a smouldering corpse but is relieved when he finds none. He sees a copper spearhead lying in the entrance of he's house sticking out between the rubble. He picks up the spearhead and studies it carefully. The edges are barbed. "Amalekites!" He's wife was taken! The spearhead spelled it out! The Amalekites took their women while they were off to battle the Israelites! David falls on he's knees in the dirt and ashes.

"Vindicate me, O Yahweh. And plead my cause against an unworthy nation." David gets up from the dust, tears rolling from he's face. The air is filled with the men's cries of anger and anguish. David sees the men all around their anguish showing on their root smeared faces. A group of men approach him and a front man scream out. "We have fought for you and we have bled for you! Now our woman and children have died because of you!" David looks up at the man who speaks to him. It was the fierce red bearded warrior Atait from the Gadites holding he's spear before him. Indeed he's men had fought like lions and could handle their shield and spears like it was a part of their bodies. More men start to surround him roaring in agreement and David see some of the men pick up stones. The burly figure of Benaiah appears. He makes he's way through the throng and he faces Atait holding the long Sheppard staff across he's chest.

He's loud voice boom out. "All of us have lost our wives and children today! How can you blame David for this misfortune? He has also lost he's wife!" David puts he's hand on Benaiah shoulder and addresses the men before him. "Wait brothers! Yahweh has not forsaken us! We are all grief stricken and things seem for the worse but Yahweh will hear us!"

Atait lowers he's spear and the grumbling dies down. The men stand before David awaiting he's next command. David calls Abiathar the priest, Ahimelech's son. "Bring the ephod here to me." Abiathar makes he's way through the men carrying the Ephod covered by a sheep fleece. David takes the fleece covered Ephod from Abiathar and turns towards Benaiah. "I will return soon brother for I will enquire our ways before the Lord."

David walks of towards the edge of the town and finds a place under an Acacia tree. The wind picks up and the black smoke seem to lift from the city. David stares at the ruins smouldering in the wind. He takes the Ephod from the sheep covered fleece and drapes the golden Ephod on he's shoulders. He falls onto he's knees on the desert floor weeping. "Lord! You are my Yahweh! I have come to know you as a righteous Yahweh! These men have done what is wrong in your eyes and as sure as the day breaks we will follow them if you will it! Can we pursue this Amalekite troop? Shall we be able to overtake them and be victorious?" In the stillness of David's soul he hears the thundering voice of Yahweh speak to him.

"Pursue; for you will surely overtake them, and will without fail recover all."(1 Samuel 30 v 8) The thunder in he's soul quiets down.

David lifts the Ephod from he's shoulders and stands up from the ground. He wipes he's face and sets of back towards the men a determined look on he's face. The men eagerly await he's return. David can see that there is still some among them that look ready to turn their grief towards him. He lifts he's hands and the men face him waiting on he's instruction. "I have enquired from the Lord. We shall go after the Amalekite troop and take from them what they have taken from us and more!

Yahweh Almighty has spoken and we shall be victorious! Praise and glory to He's name!"

The men had travelled unyielding in their stride. Their grim eyes show fortitude under their dust weary faces. They had come to the brook Besor and the group stops some drinking from the brook and others filing their water skins. One of the captains Joelah comes forth approaching David.

"The men are tired. Should we not rest for a while and then continue?" David stares at Joelah. He was one of the older men in the army and the group of men with him also were more advanced in their years. David turns away from Joelah staring into the direction where the Amalekites went.

"Let the men that are too tired stay here. We will continue to pursue after the Amalekites and find them before this day is done." David turns towards he's men.

"If any of you men want to rest let them stay; but those who want to continue gather your swords and come!" The red bearded warrior Atait looks at Joelah and he's men in disgust. He turns away from them with a set determined look on he's face. "The Gadites will continue! This Yahweh of yours is stronger than any Yahweh that we have served!"

He looks into the horizon looking almost boyish. "I want to taste that woman's cooking before this day is done!" David pats the warrior on he's back. "We shall brother!" The men start to depart and David observes almost two hundred men that stay behind. The rest of the men continue after the Amalekite's. David had also started to feel weary but he takes he's pouch from he's shoulder and reaches into the bag for a honey comb. He breaks off a piece and sucks on the honey comb. He feels he's energy returning. He looks at the rest if the group travelling with him. They had travelled for most of the day but the men continued resiliently. A horse rider calls out from the front line. "My Lord!" David sees that a group of he's men had deviated from the road and was standing next to something in the grass. David approaches and sees a young man lying in the field he's body covered with lashes.

"He must have taken more than thirty." One of the men observes dryly. Abiathar puts he's hand on the man face and the young man groans softly.

"He is still alive!" David stares at the bloody body of the man. "Clean he's wounds and give him something to eat and drink. This is the work of the Amalekites! He might be valuable to us." They set of again and they continue at the murderous pace. Much later when the sun start to set in the West Abiathar calls for David. He directs him towards the figure of a man slouched across the saddle of a horse close by. "We cleaned he's wounds and gave him some bread; water; a piece of cake, figs and raisins. It seems like he's strength is coming back to him. Maybe it is because he is still a youngster."

David canters closer to the horse carrying the young man they had rescued. The man look up, he's eyes seem clear and he speaks as David approaches and yet his throat still sounds parched. David leans in closer to the man listening to he's croaked voice. "Thank you for the food and drink for I have had nothing for three days." David again notices that he was still very young and Abiathar was right. This was most probably why he was still alive. "Tell me where are from? Who did this to you?" The young man unhooks the water skin from the saddle of the horse and takes a drink from the water skin before he replies. "My name is Zopath. I come from Egypt but was enslaved by the Amalekites. I have served them well and have always tried to please my masters. Three days ago I fell sick. At first my masters did not take notice but my bowels made it difficult for me to keep up. When they had raided Ziklag they kept at a steady pace and when I fell behind I was whipped and left in the desert without food or drink to die."

There was a stir of anger inside David but he keeps quite allowing the man to continue. "They made their invasion to the Southern area of the Cherethites and the Southern area of Caleb and then came back burning Ziklag with fire." The man must have seen the anger in David eyes when he spoke of Ziklag because he quickly explains.

"Our duties were to tend to the woman and children taken after the raids and provide them with food and drink on the journey back but we were always treated with the same neglect as the rest of the slaves."

David takes a deep breath and relaxes a bit. He can see that the man seem worried about he's fate. "Can you lead us down to where the Amalekites are?" A shadow falls on the youths face. "If I do; swear to me that you will not kill me or deliver me back into the hands of my master?" The question was honest and the young man stared at David with huge eyes fear showing in them. David touches the man arm lightly making sure he did not inflict any pain on the fresh covered lashes.

"From this day you belong to the house of David and you will only be a servant of the living Yahweh." The young man stares at David and the uncertainty seem to leave he's face.

"I will lead you along the high path towards the dwelling place of the Amalekites and we will be unnoticed in the wilderness." David smiles at the youth and spurs he's mount calling Abishai who was leading the men. "Let the youth ride with you and listen to he's direction. Keep your eyes peeled. We will certainly see our families before day break."

Zopath was true to he's words and they had continued on a path that was not familiar to David. They travelled until the girdle of Orion showed in the Northern skies. They came down a mountain pass into a valley and David soon saw that Zopath had lead them straight into the trail close to where the Amalekites were encamped.

The darkness provided enough cover for the men to go unobserved and David could hear that the Amalekite camp was in elated mood. They were spread out all across the valley below them the camping fires burning bright. Benaiah moves in next to David speaking in disgust. "They are eating and drinking and dancing. They are revelling in the abundant spoils they had taken from Ziklag and the land of Judah. We are outnumbered at least by three thousand."

David stares at the valley below. "We shall attack when twilight comes and they are lulled by the drink and spend their energy." They sit watching the men dance and drink and David wonders about Abigail.

He gathers he's generals and instruct them on he's plan to attack when the morning dawns. Afterwards the men move away from him to inform the rest of the men. Soon they had quietened down the sound of the celebrating Amalekites invading their hushed thoughts. The sounds below become more subdued as the evening draws by. Much later the men would occasionally still hear drunken laughter. The air become more chilled as the morning draws near and the men stir in anticipation. The time had come. The group that would execute the first part of the invasion gather close to David drawing their swords silently. They come down the hill still in the cover of darkness. David kills he's first man the only audible sound, the air hissing out from a severed thorax. As per David instruction the group of men continue their silent assassination and for some time no sound is uttered. Then suddenly a scream from a dying man pierces the early morning hours. David know that soon the element of their surprise attack will be over. There was a commotion in the Amalekite camp but still no one seemed to notice they were under attack. A voice call out in the darkness of the morning hours.

"Who walks there?" David stabs the man in the throat he's arms flailing to he's sides before he falls on he's face down in the dirt. Men move in the darkness to he's left. Suddenly a voice screams out.

"We are under attack!"

David had coached he's men to take final advantage under the cover of darkness if they were to be discovered. Darkness still surround the men and as per he's instruction they attack without a word. The sounds of swords, shields and dying men fills the morning.

David swings the broad side of the massive blade against a head of another Amalekite looming before him. The Amalekite camp stirred like a serpent awakening ready to strike and men were quickly gathering all around them. David takes the Ramshorn hanging by he's side and blows loudly the sound booming above the fighting men.

As per he's instruction, some of he's men on the far side of the camp started to beat their spears against their shields causing a distraction. He and the men that came into the camp start to retreat up on the rocky hills where they had come from. He had stationed archers up on the hills and gave them instruction to shoot at the enemy as soon as they heard a second blow on the ram's horn. The first rays of the sun had exposed the darkness. The grey dawn announces the birth of a new day. David can make out the forms of Amalekite following the retreating men. David lifts the horn to he's mouth and for a second time that morning he blows as loud as he can. Suddenly the air is filled by a mortal noise of arrows in flight. Men scream as they are met by a noxious sting of arrows.

David and he's men continue to retreat and soon they find themselves behind the curve in mountain slope. They do not waste time but quickly drink water from their skins. It was always one of the things that happened in battle that one's mouth would become very dry. The men ready themselves and then as he had instructed they flank the group of Amalekites coming up the mountain slope. The attack is so unexpected that more than a hundred men are killed before they know that they are under attack again. David and he's men continue the attack and each time they retreat behind the line of archers. The sun stretches its rays across the valley and bodies lay scattered all throughout the valley.

The Amalekites camp seem to be in panic and David and he's men attack again. They keep the attacking coup of men to the minimum and hitting the most vulnerable sides of the enemy down in the valley. The archers continue their assault keeping the hordes at bay. The archers had become skilled over time and their arrows find the mark almost every time they venture up the slope. David continues he's strategy and soon the sun was directly above them in the desert sky. David takes a swig out of he's water skin and notices that the Amalekite ranks were reduced at least to half of their troop.

A war drum beats loudly below them in the valley. David sees the Amalekites retreating behind a new formed rank. Out of the rank comes an Egyptian man of great height at least more than two and a half meters. The Amalekites army withdraw well behind the man. This was the practice of war. The Amalekites wanted their strongest warrior to face the giant standing in the valley below. Should the Egyptian win the Amalekites men morale will be lifted and David knows that they would attack with new ferocity. David stares at the giant and sees the man has a spear in he's hand the size of a young oak tree. David eye catches movement from he's own ranks. He sees Benaiah dropping he's sword and he's shield, taking only he's Sheppard staff in he's right hand running towards the Egyptian. David calls after him but he seem oblivious to David's voice as he runs out to meet the Egyptian.

David and he's men dare not follow and they all stare at the two men in the valley below. Although Benaiah was much shorter than the Egyptian he was broad shouldered and well-muscled. David did not feel terror for Benaiah for he believed that the Yahweh was with him. The men start to circle each other and the Egyptian stabs at Benaiah's head. A great cheer erupts from the Amalekites. The spear head flashes by he's skull with the speed of a Cobra strike! Benaiah drop to he's left knee reaching out with he's Shepard staff towards the Egyptians legs. He hooks the crook of the staff around the Egyptians left ankle throwing him off balance. The Egyptian lose he's footing and for a moment he's arms cart wheels to keep he's balance.

Benaiah takes the opportunity and hits the man in the chest with the butt end of he's staff. The Egyptian stumbles back and now a great roar erupts from David's men. Benaiah drops he's staff and advances while the Egyptian tries to regain he's balance. He grabs onto the spear mighty in the Egyptians hand and tries to wrestle it from the big man. The Egyptian quickly regain he's balance and before Benaiah can rip the weapon from he's grasp he grabs on to the spear with both hands.

The two men come face to face standing chest to chest each one trying to unsettle the others footing while the wrestle holding onto the shaft of the spear. The Egyptian is a fierce man and towers over Benaiah like an Elephant bull. Benaiah look into the eyes of the Egyptian and sees a murderous rage burning there. He feels he's power starting to fail the spear slipping from he's grasp. He knows that it will be over should he lose he's grip on the weapon. The Egyptian sees the uncertainty in Benaiah's eyes and pushes into he's opponent using all he's strength. Benaiah's back start to arch dangerously. Benaiah screams out but not in pain! "Yahweh is my strength I shall not fail!" The Egyptian had anticipated the sound of Benaiah spine snapping and a cry for mercy. He is completely perplexed after Benaiah call. Benaiah feels raw power surging through him. He starts to shake the Egyptian holding on to the spear like a rag doll. Fear now shows in the big man eyes. Benaiah tears the spear from he's hands and with one swift movement he stabs him through the sternum. The man stands awkwardly for a few seconds longer he's mouth opening and closing. The big man falls down the last breathing sound escaping from he's dying lungs. This was too much for the Amalekites. Men start to run for their camels. David gives the command. "Go after them! Do not let anyone escape!" The men pursue without hesitation like a pack of wild dogs chasing their query. The Amalekites had left their captives in the middle of the camp. Some of the Amalekite men run towards these captives and ensure a bargain of hostages but David's men are upon them within a matter of seconds. Other Amalekite men throw their hands in the air as a sign of submission but David's men run them through with sword and spear like a wave crashing over the shores.

The fight is over very brutally and quickly and the men turn towards the captives untying their bonds. David searches for Abigail looking for her raven hair among the group. He sees her helping another women to her feet. Their eyes meet. She embraces the woman and then slowly walk towards him. "My lord you have come." Abigail face is covered with dirt and the tears streaming down her face creates narrow smears down her cheeks. David takes Abigail into he's arms. "The Lord has delivered you from the Amalekites praise Yahweh!" All around David men reunited with their wives laughter and tears mixing indeed a strange face to see the dirt smeared woman with the bloody warriors. Atait approaches David with a big bosomed woman by he's side. "My lord. Some of the Amalekites had fled on their Camels. All our woman and children have been taken count of and there is no loses on our side. Shall we pursue the Amalekites?" David smiles at the burly warrior. "No do not pursue them." To the left of the men a huge heard of sheep, camels and cattle can be seen as far as the eyes stretches. The animals escaped their attention as they came from the ravines side when they attacked the Amalekites. "Yahweh has blessed us for we have not taken any loss and gained in abundance in the spoils of war. Gather the men and instruct them to round up all the animals and take all the belongings that is left. The evening is already upon us. We shall move away from here and setup camp before darkness completely dawns upon us. Tomorrow we shall return to the Brook Besor for there is a lot of work to be done in Ziklag." They make haste and move away from the battlefield strewn with dead bodies of the Amalekites taking all the possessions with them. They made camp not far from there and early that morning David, he's men and all their families that was taken returned to Ziklag. As they drew near to the Brook Besor they were greeted by the men that stayed behind. "What a glorious victory! Praise Yahweh!" Men run towards their families and the embrace and shouts for joy is almost as ecstatic as the previous day reunion. A group of men that had being helping with the herding of the cattle and sheep approaches David. A tall warrior from the tribe of Rachal with a bloodied armband addresses him. The man turns towards the group of men behind him and point at the approaching herds. "We fought hard and put our lives in danger. The herds and stock taken should not be shared with the men that stayed behind at the brook." They must have decided that the man must be the speaker for David can see the nervous tension in he's eyes. Eleazar and some other men had moved in behind the group of men standing before David. The tall warrior points towards the group that stayed behind.

"They did not risk their lives for their own families! We all saw the shame on some of their own women's faces when they had returned and reunited this morning." The people had heard the statements that the warrior was making and more had gathered now. Some men shake their heads in agreement to the warrior statement while others wait on David to speak. David looks at the people standing before him "My brothers! Who has delivered our families from the Amalekites? Was it in our own strength? No it was because Yahweh had delivered them into our hands! Can we then make a claim and take all the blessing that the Lord has given us and decide who is worth the blessing and who is not! Did the men that stayed behind do a lesser duty in the Lord's eyes by watching the supplies? No they did not!" The man standing in front of David seem defiant but David stares him squarely in the eyes and continue to speak out so that all can hear him. "From this day on this will be an ordinance for Israel! Every man and woman will be rewarded equally for when Yahweh blesses he wants to bless us all!" David points towards the tall warrior. "When we reach Ziklag you and your men will take some of the spoils to those who are in Aroer, those who are in Siphmoth and Eshtemoa." The warrior seems like he wants to make some objection but is silenced by David further instructions. "We shall share with those in Rachal and also those in the cities of the Jerahmeelites and the Kenites. You will take some of the spoils all the way to Hormaha, Chorashan, Athach and Hebron."

The tall warrior now seemed subdued by David ordinance and he and the group of men that had first approach David slowly retreated from the circle. "They should be watched." Eleazar leans on he's spear he's dark eyes following the group of men. "As soon as they get their share they will forget all about this. Come now let us go for we need to reach Ziklag before the sun sets."

The dust clogs heavily on the steed and the horse turns he's eyes nervously towards the approaching rider the whites in he's eyes in contrast to he's hide.

"King Saul! The last defence has fallen! The Philistines have killed all our men at the Mount Gilboa!" The words cut into the heart of Saul and he turns he's horse back towards the east. Jonathan points towards a dust cloud approaching. "Father! The Philistines are coming we better flee!" The words of Jonathan seem illusory. The battle had been fierce and the Philistines kept on attacking wave after wave. Saul saw he's men go down and he's sons turn away from the battle; riding behind the last defence. Saul looked over he's shoulder and saw the rising dust cloud two hundred meters from them. The Philistines were coming at pace!

"Come! Ride towards the mountain!" He's sons Abinadab and Malchishua rode to he's right just in front of him together with he's arms bearer. Jonathan was making up the rear and when he saw the Philistine masses were gaining he turned he's horse towards the army. Saul sees Jonathan action and turns he's steed towards he's son.

"What are you doing?" Jonathan draws he's sword and comes to an abrupt stop. Saul also come to a stop he's horse snorting nervously he's eyes rolling and nostrils flaring.

"This is it father! We are all going to die here today! We cannot outrun them!" Although death was charging down on them Jonathan sounded unafraid. Saul stared at the approaching danger and could make out the outlines of horse and rider. He's older sons had also stopped and drawn their swords. The Philistine army had seen the pack of riders. The archers let go of their first volley of arrows. An arrow hit Abinadab squarely in he's chest and then another hit him in he's stomach and he goes down in the dirt.

The arrows strike the horses that the men are sitting on and Malchishua is thrown by he's horse after an arrow hits him in the flank. The horse falls down heavily and Malchishua rolls away from the danger of being struck by a kicking hoof. Abinadab cries out in pain and Malchishua crawls towards he's fallen brother. Saul, he's arms bearer and Jonathan take shelter behind the fallen animals. A second volley of arrows follows and the men duck behind the body of the horses and yet another cry goes up. Saul turns towards where Abinadab and Malchishua are lying and he sees an arrow shaft sticking out on the left side of he's Malchishua head. Abinadab also lie very still a few more arrows sticking out of he's back. Saul tries to utter some words he's mouth agape but he falls with he's face in the sand trying to escape the horror bearing down on them. Saul feels a sudden sting and a burning sensation in he's back. He tries to turn he's head but knows that he is hit.

Jonathan is also wounded an arrow protruding from he's chest. Saul sees Jonathan getting up and walking towards the approaching enemy. "Is that all you worms are going to do! Sit behind your archers and not even give me a decent fight!" Blood was bubbling out of he's mouth and although Jonathan though he had screamed at the enemy he's voice came out as a whisper. The damage was done and he feels he's legs weakening. He stares at the shaft protruding from he's upper body. He grabs the tail of the shaft and he brake's it off. He knees buckle and he and falls in the sand lying on he's side. He tries to get a better grip on he's sword but realizes that he is not holding the weapon anymore. Jonathan stares into the sky. For a moment he can almost hear the sweet sound of David's lyre again and then he draws he's last breath. Saul stares out from behind the fallen horse. He sees Jonathan go down. The pain in he's back had spread out like a wild fire and he can barely lift he's upper body. He's arms bearer lay beside him whimpering in fear and pain. "Hushai, I want you to draw your sword and thrust it into me." Hushai looks at the king as if he had asked him to do dance naked in the sun before him. "I cannot do that your highness." Saul's face twists in pain as he gets to he's knees. "You coward!" He slowly pulls he's own sword from the scabbard and places the hilt against a rock in the sand. Holding the blade point in he's sternum Saul looks across the desert at the Philistines. The leading men saw that their pray was not going to die by their hand and they come running towards them. Saul closes he's eyes and then with all he's weight he falls into he's own sword. When the first Philistine soldier arrives at Saul's dead body he sees the king's arms bearer had also fallen into he's own sword. All the light had faded from Saul's eyes.

King Saul of Israel was dead. The Philistine drew he's sword and cut the head from Saul's body as he had been instructed.

Chapter 10

Two days had gone by since their return to Ziklag. With all of their homes destroyed, David's army had erected tents just outside the ruins of the city that was Ziklag.

Eleazar approaches him and sits with him on the wall of one of the ruined houses. David stares of into the distance. The sun will be setting soon and the desert would suddenly be transformed. David loves this time of the day. Soon the stars will appear in sky. The color of the setting sun becomes a glow of bright orange that fills the escarpment. The sound of Guinea-Fowl can be heard all over the rocky plains and the cooking fires around the tented camp burn brightly. It's a comforting feeling and David is brought back to the moment by Eleazar's sudden movement. The tall warrior had come to he's feet he's hand on he's sword hilt staring at a group of men approaching from the Western wall. It was the scouts that David had placed on the exterior perimeters should the Amalekites plan a retaliation coup.

In their midst David see a stranger. As they approach David can see that the stranger clothes are torn and dust covers he's head. The sign of a mourning man! David climbs down from the wall and approaches he's men. He stops right in he's tracks when he sees the object that the man is carrying in he's left hand. David's anger flares up and before he could contain he's emotions he lashes out at the man.

"Where did you get that?!" He can barely control he's voice. The man falls to he's knees. David's eyes are still on the familiar crown in the man left hand but he dares not to touch it!

"This cannot be true!" David thinks to himself as he continue to stare at Saul's crown. The golden colors flicker softly as the dying rays of the sun falls on the crown. The wings of the two angels touching each other almost seem to come to life. It is unmistakably the crown of Israel. There is only one crown that resembles the symbol of the Ark. David cannot bare it any longer and reaches out and takes the crown from the trembling man hands. Another item falls from the man outstretched hand. The bracelet that Saul always wore falls into the dirt. David battles to get he's anger under control.

"Get up! Where did you get this?" The man quickly gets up as Eleazar nudges him with he's spear tip. The man stares at them with huge bewildered eyes.

"Wait! Wait! I was just trying to pass by the outskirts to avoid the terrible battle when he saw me!" David grabs the man by he's tattered robe. "What are you talking about? Who called you?" The man looks from Eleazar to David. "King Saul my lord. When I approached him I saw that he's sons were already dead." David feels the blood drain from he's face. "Jonathan? Dead?" David let go of the man robe. He stares at the golden crown in he's hands and he's own voice sounds as if it comes from far away. "Tell me exactly what happened."

The man seem to draw strength from David actions and only Eleazar sees the blaze in David eyes. "I am but a wandering Amalekite and I was making my way from the mount Gilboa trying to evade the Philistine hordes." Eleazar grimace under he's breath. "Yea right! Wandering Amalekite! Fleeing Amalekite is most probably the correct way to describe himself. The man most probably had part in the raid at Ziklag." Eleazar shakes he's head. He could tell that the man thought that he was pleasing David by bearing the news he brought. Eleazar kept quiet but the man almost assuredly delivered he's last message.

"I ran away from the hordes and came close to the foot of the Gilboa Mountain when I saw fallen men and close by a man leaning on he's spear. When the man leaning on he's spear saw me he called me over. I was very afraid and but the man's tone sounded like a man that was used to command authority. As I approached the man I saw the royal crown and knew that it was King Saul." The man licks over he's dry lips seeming more nervous than ever. "The king asked me who I was and I replied by telling him that I was an Amalekite. The king then took he's sword and handed it to me and ordered me to kill him. He was badly wounded and I thought that he would not live anyway. So I took the sword and I killed him. I took he's crown and he's bracelet for I knew that you would be pleased if I bring it to you my lord." David stares into the man's eyes he's whole face drained of any emotion. "How do you know that the Kings sons were also dead?"

The man takes some of he's torn cloth into he's hands wiping the dirt from he's face. "They lay close to the king and the resemblance they displayed to the fallen king was too striking not to phantom their relation." David sees the faces of Saul sons in he's mind. He knew them all well and while he was in the king service there where many times when they all had gathered in the great hall planning war or enjoying a meal together. David toneless voice sounds hollow in he's own ears.

"Describe these men to me." The Amalekite scratches he's dirt covered head. "A tall man with golden hair."

Ishvi. David thinks to himself.

"A man with a pocked face."

David shakes his head in acknowledgement. "That must be Malchishua!"

"Then there was a big man with a bush of dark hair and a beard. At first I almost did not see him because he lay away from the others the bodies of Philistine men almost covering him. He lay with he's face in the dirt he's drawn sword still in he's hand."

The tears well up in David's eyes but he rapidly blinks them away. It had to be Jonathan. Something inside David feels like it is tearing. He turns away from the Amalekite he's voice sounding stone cold. "You killed the king. You lifted your hands against the Lords anointed without thinking twice." The Amalekite realizes that he's fate may be different than what he envisaged and he tremors before David.

"My Lord I only did what..." David turns around and faces the man again. "Silence! You only did what was in your best interest! No one can lift he's hand against the Lord's anointed and live! Kill him!" A young warrior that David had noticed before on the battle field had already moved into position and quickly steps forward. He's spear pierces the Amalekites heart before the man can utter another word. David tears he's clothes and turns away from the men before him. Now that Saul was dead he was supposed to feel relieved but all he feels is heaviness in he's heart. The other men standing around David follow their leader example and also tear their clothes in mourning. The word spread throughout the camp. King Saul and he's sons were dead. The fire in the camps burn lowly and later that night the tones of David's Lyre could be heard carrying across the valley of Ziklag. It is a song written in memory of King Saul and Jonathan. David's men listened to their leader's voice as he laments over Saul and Jonathan.

"Your glory, Israel was slain on your high places! How the mighty have fallen! Don't tell it in Gath. Don't publish it in the streets of Ashkelon, lest the daughters of the Philistines rejoice, lest the daughters of the uncircumcised triumph. You mountains of Gilboa, let there be new dew or rain on you, and no fields of offerings; for there the shield of the mighty was defiled and cast away. The shield of Saul was not anointed with oil. From the blood of the slain, from the fat of the mighty, Jonathan's bow didn't turn back. Saul's sword didn't return empty. Saul and Jonathan were lovey and pleasant in their lives. In their death, they were not divided, they were swifter than eagles. They were stronger than lions. You daughters of Israel weep over Saul, who clothed you delicately in scarlet, who put ornaments of gold on your clothing. How the mighty have fallen in the middle of battle! Jonathan was slain on your high places. I am distressed for you, my brother Jonathan. You have been very pleasant to me. Your love to me was wonderful, passing the love of women. How the mighty have fallen and the weapons of war have perished!" (2 Samuel 1 verse 19 – 27)* *This song was written in the book of Jashar.*

"I have heard that David and he's men are coming to Hebron." Etam looks at each of the elders before he continues.

"The prophet Samuel anointed David as the King almost fourteen years ago. He was kept from this eminence because of Saul. Now Saul is dead." The men sitting in the tent nod their heads in approval and Naarah voices he's thoughts.

"Rumours are spreading that Abner have taken Ishbosheth to Mahanaiam and that he has made him king over Gilead, the Ashurites, Jezreel, Ephraim, Benjamin and the whole of Israel." Shobal paces around in the tent. "It is not rumours. Huram the son of Benjamin has taken he's whole family and moved to Mahanaiam. I confronted him and he said that he's family was going to give honor to the new king since Saul was killed. What does the tribe of Judah say?"

A slight breeze tugs at the wispy beard of Etam. "Perez, Hur, Hezron and Shobal have all confirmed that the tribe of Judah wants David to take he's rightful place as king as the prophet Samuel has proclaimed through the living Yahweh." Murmurs of agreement rises from the elders gathered in the tent. Etam stares out over the tents in the valley. "I have heard that the Philistines have dishonoured the body of King Saul and that he's head was cut from he's body. He's body was fastened in the temples of those Yahweh-less men and they worshipped their idols!" The elders all shake their heads some with tear filled eyes. Etam continues. "I then heard that David planned to revenge king Saul death and get he's body for burial. The people of Jabesh Gilead however had heard what the Philistine had done. Before David send he's men some of the valiant men from Jabesh Gilead had marched through the night to Beth Shan. They sneaked into Beth Shan and took the bodies of King Saul and he's sons from the wall and took them back to Jabesh. The bodies were burned at Jabesh and the remaining bones were buried under a Tamarisk tree. The people of Jabesh fasted for seven days after this was done."

Etam takes the reed pipe from he's mouth a cloud of white smoke billowing from he's bearded mouth. He stares at the smoke drifting into the air and then lays the pipe down on he's lap. "Let the families of Judah know that David and he's men will be arriving in Hebron. Send word to the rest of Israel and let them know that David will rightfully be anointed as king over Israel and that anyone who heeds the voice of the prophet Samuel and the living Yahweh of Israel is welcome to celebrate the appointment of the new king of Israel."

David walks with Eleazar; behind him he's two wives Ahinoam and Abigail and the rest of men, women and children follow. He's heart was still heavy and he dealt with he's emotions quietly. He would not see Jonathan again. After he received the news of the death of Saul and he's sons he had called a group of he's men together to draw up towards Beth Shan for he had heard that they had fastened the bodies of Saul and he's sons against the city wall. He was greatly angered and the act for revenge overwhelmed every thought. He had almost killed the messenger when he unexpectedly made an appearance as they made their way to Beth Shan. Two of he's men had dragged the messenger before him and the man cried for mercy.

The man had explained that he had been send by the elders from the city of Jabesh and that the bodies of Saul and he's sons were taken from Beth Shan. David had attentively listened to the man and only after he had heard the whole story he again realized how close he was to killing the man that had brought the good news. He instructed the man to tell the elders of Jabesh that they would have he's protection over their land as long as he lived. They had made camp in the desert that night and David enquired from Lord what He had to do. Yahweh had told him to move up to Hebron. Yahweh had told him that the time had come and that he would take he's place as the new king of Israel. The following morning they had broken up their camp and made their way towards Hebron. The years had come and the years had gone by. The youth that faced Goliath seemed like a distant memory. He was replaced by a thirty year old man that had fought many battles and now walked in front of a six hundred men army. David had called he's captains and explained what the Lord had told him. The men had had all shown respect as their leader shared the news and one by one they touched the hem of David battle dress as they left the tent. They had travelled even before the break of dawn and they continued towards Hebron throughout the morning. Abigail had prepared a white robe for him to wear and she had spoken words of encouragement and wisdom as she had done in the past few months together. The sun sat in the middle of the skies. Like a mirage playing on the desert horizon the city of Hebron suddenly loomed in the distance. They make their way towards the city and in the far distance David hears the sound of Sophars blowing. He puts he's hand over he's eyes to shade the rays of the afternoon sun and sees the gates of the city open. People come streaming out of the gates waving white and blue banners. David stop and stare at the gathering crowd. It is not the crowd itself that made him stop but the words they were singing. "The Lord has chosen a king! The Lord has chosen a King! Israel open your gates to the King! King David! King David!" The people come streaming around David and he's men. Soon David's men joins the people of Hebron in singing with such sentiment and passion that David eyelids stings with tears. A group of elders approaches through the throng. An old man with a grey wispy beard holds up he's hands and the people quite down. "Welcome son of Jesse! Anointed King of Israel! Yahweh has chosen you to be King by the words of the prophet Samuel." Etam takes a horn of scented oil from he's shoulder and pours the oil out over David's head. "May the Lord protect you and keep you as King over Israel. Amen." The people of Hebron burst into union again the blue and white banners waving in the wind. " The Lord has chosen a king! The Lord has chosen a King! Israel open your gates to the King! King David! King David!"

Chapter 11

"It has almost been seven years since he had become king. Judah is growing stronger and stronger! The war between the house of David and of my father has been raging for too long and needs to come to an end!" The wine in Ish-bosheth hand spills over the clay cup but he does not seem to notice.

"Why is it that David and he's men are more victorious and my men are getting weaker and weaker Abner? Does the houses of Gilead, the Ashurites, Jezreel, Ephraim, Benjamin and the whole of Israel not stand behind me? Abner looks at Ish-bosheth no emotion shows on he's sun tanned leathered face. When Saul died Abner was afraid that David would come after him. He gathered the remaining men of the houses Gilead, the Ashurites, Jezreel, Ephraim, Benjamin and Israel. Most of these men had been fighting for Saul and Abner had been their commander. It was easy to convince them that Ish-bosheth was king as Saul predecessor. Ish-bosheth was next in line after the older three sons of Saul had died with him. From the first day Abner knew that Ish-bosheth was a weakling. He relied heavily on the old war commander.

"I am going to Gibeon my Lord. We have been challenged by Joab son of Zeruiah in the old traditional ways. Twelve of our young warriors will do face to face combat and whoever loses shall return defeated." Ish-bosheth holds he's cup towards one of the servant to be refilled. "Do not disappoint me Abner. Return victoriously and I will reward you greatly!" Some of the drink again spills from the youth's cup onto he's robe but again it goes unnoticed. "Go now and give me a full report of the account!"

Abner turns away from Ish-bosheth. Since he was chosen as king he had not even once accompanied them into battle. The men saw this. A lot of talking was going on behind Ish-bosheth back. He had heard that the elders from the tribes of Gilead, the Azurites, Jezreel, Ephraim, Benjamin and Israel were talking about David and the words prophesied by Samuel. Abner walked down the passage thinking of David. Did he hate him? No it was not hate but fear that had driven him to anoint Ish-bosheth. The remainder of Saul's men looked up to him for guidance and he had made an instinctive call.

The darkness had fallen on the city and the passage was illuminated by burning lamps filled with animal fat. Out of the shadows a slender figure approaches him. She walks gracefully towards him. Abner feels the touch of her warm hand on he's battle scarred forearm and feels more alive than he had ever felt before. Rizpah beauty still captivated him. She still looked the same way that she had many years when he had met her the first time in the king chambers. She was one of Saul's concubines. It was because of the close relationship between Saul and he's most trusted general that their first encounter was one that he would not forget. The king had called him to he's personal chambers when he had heard that the Philistines invaded. It was on this specific night that he found the king in a very dark sombre mood. Saul had seemed to forget that there was still women in he's chamber and it was not the first time that Abner had arrived in the king chamber when the woman that was entertaining the king had not left. It was the first time however that he had seen Rizpah and from the moment they locked eyes he knew that her face would be embedded in he's memory forever. Abner did not have a wife or any children of he's own. That night something started between the two of them and although Abner never lay as much as a finger on Rizpah while Saul was still alive both of them felt it. They would stare at one another and sometimes would make eye contact only briefly and yet he always felt the same. After Saul death; Abner had taken Rizpah with him and they got married in secret.

She cupped he's bearded face and looked into he's eyes. "Will you be gone for long?" Her husky voice stirs something in him and he pulls her closer to him. "Only as long as it takes to defeat the adolescents at Gibeon." Rizpah hides her face in Abner's chest her arms curls around he's neck. "These wars will never end. You are an ancient man." Abner takes her hands into he's own and pulls her after him with a mischievous grin on he's face. "Undeniably wise but not ancient."

Abner ran at a steady pace. The spear in he's hand did not hamper him at all. All the years of battle had taught him that you should always try to keep the advantage and the weapon felt as another part of he's moving body.

He realized that he might need to use it soon. He looked behind him and saw the youth still in full pursuit. He had warned the youth twice now and somehow knew that the chase would not end well for the youngster. He's own breath and the crunching of the pebbles underneath the feet of the man that was pursuing him, leather sandals was the only sounds in he's ears. It had been a long and bloody day. Early that morning they had met at the pool of Gibeon. Abner and he's men had sat on the one side of the pool and Joab sat at the other side of the pool. Joab was accompanied by he's younger brothers Abishai and Asahel. The look on Asahel face was very hostile indeed but Abner spoke to Joab. As per the initiation customs between the once united tribes Abner made the suggestion that some of the young men fight hand to hand with their bare fists. Joab had agreed and twelve men from the tribe of Benjamin and under Ish-Bosheth son of Saul and twelve for David. There was a tense atmosphere and very soon the fight was heated. It was one of the men from the side of David camp that screamed out in alarm and Abner saw one of he's men blade glimmering in the sun light.

"You fool!" but Abner words were drowned out by Joab command. Joab had also seen the glimmer of the blade. Joab gave the command the men from David acted swiftly and took their daggers from the sleeves. They engaged with his men and the fight became bloody. The men from David grabbed their opponents by their heads and thrust their daggers into the Benjamites sides. Abner had no choice and gave the command for the rest of he's men to attack. Joab blew the war trumpet and the rest of David's men also engaged. They fighting was fierce and soon David men began to push back the men of Ish-Bosheth.

Abner knew that they had to retreat and blew he's trumpet for he's men to fall back. He retrieved with them. He started making he's way up the hill of Ammah and took a turn on the side of the hill and got separated from the rest of the fleeing men. It was then that he noticed a young man from David group of men that was following close behind him. Abner kept running at a steady pace and it was not long before he recognized he's pursuer. It was Asahel the son of Zeruiah; Joab and Abishai younger brother. Abner looked behind him and saw that the youth was gaining on him. He had called out twice to the youth.

"Is that you Asahel?" The youth continued he's stride and called back after Abner.

"It is indeed mighty general!" Abner did not slow down and the arrogance and sneer in Asahel voice also did not go by unnoticed. Abner steadied himself as he climbed a steeper rocky slope but called back behind him as he climbed. "Stop pursuing me! Why should I strike you down? Not so long ago our tribes stood together in the face of adversity! How will I face your brothers if I kill you?"

Asahel laughter rings out much closer behind him. "I can see you are tiring old man! I will chase you and cut you down! The earth shall soak up your blood!" By the sound in Asahel voice Abner knew that he did not have a choice anymore. Kill or be killed. The big builder on the side of the path stands out as a beacon. Abner slows down he's pace and fakes stumbling behind the big builder on the side of the path. He swiftly turns the spear in he's grasp the butt end protruding out before him.

Just as he had expected. Asahel saw the stumble as the moment to quickly move in and take advantage. The youth look of surprise is quickly replaced with a grimace of death. He runs into the butt end of Abner spear, the shear speed and force driving the spear through he's stomach and comes out on the other side of he's back. The eyes of Asahel lose their light and Abner wrestles the spear from the limp body. He had killed many men that had tried to kill him before and again the outcome was the same. He turns away from the body and continues up the hill at a steady pace.

The sun was setting and soon it would be dark. Abner reached the top of the hill close to the path of the desert and he saw the rest of he's remaining men had gathered. They were all waiting on him. The men reception is short lived. One of the men point at two figures making their way up the hill. Abner can almost not make out the figures because of the fading light. It is only because he had fought with the men coming up the hill that he recognizes them and calls out. "Joab! Abishai! Must the sword kill forever?"

The two figures come to a standstill and Abner can make out their faces. "Asahel was killed by your spear! We will avenge our brother death!"

The men surrounding Abner look at their commander waiting on he's response. Abner look back at the men. They were only few now. Abner estimated that more than three hundred of he's men were killed. Abner turned back to the figures below him and shouted back to Joab.

"I have killed Asahel but because he would have killed me. I asked him twice to turn away from me. Surely you know that if you continue this will only end in sorrow. How many of our brothers still have to die today? Will you continue to kill your own brothers?" The two figures below him stand quietly and then Joab responds.

"As surly as Yahweh lives. We will not chase you anymore today. Joab hits he's fist in he's palm.

"However Abner, you will pay for what you have done! You will surely die I swear this!" Joab laughs bitterly.

"This day I have made a promise and I will keep it!" The two figures turn away from the group of men. In the distance Abner hears the ram's horn blowing a signal that the chase was stopped.

"You have disgraced my father! Why have you gone to my father's concubine behind my back? " Ish-bosheth tries to sound intimidating but the words had come out in quite a high tone.

Abner had become quite a force in the household of Saul and the men had more respect for him than they had for their king. Abner looks at Ish-bosheth with distain, he's anger getting the better of him. He knew that Ish- Bosheth was still angry because of their heavy losses that they had suffered at the pool of Gibeon.

"Am I a dog Ish-bosheth? I have shown loyalty to the house of Saul! When I could have I did not delivered you in the hands of David! I have fought for you and now you charge me with a petty thing as this woman!"

Ish – Bosheth cowers at the angry words of the old war commander. Abner continues he's anger still fuelled. "May Yahweh do to me as He should have. I will make sure that Yahweh promise happens. I will surely transfer the kingdom from the house of Saul and setup the Kingdom of David over Israel!" He storms out of the chamber leaving Ish – Bosheth without looking back. Ish –Bosheth is too afraid to say anything and hoped that Abner would calm down. Abner was he's stranglehold on the kingdom and he feared him.

Abner storms into he's chambers calling one of the servants to him. "Send a messenger to my chambers and then go and find the woman Rizpah and sent her to me." He paces around in he's chambers he's mind racing. Since the day Asahel was killed Abner had been in two minds over he's loyalty towards Ish – bosheth. Why did the arrogant youth not turn back when he had ordered him to do so? He takes a piece of papyrus and starts to write on it.

When the messenger arrives Abner hands the roll of papyrus to him. "I want you to deliver this to King David.

Do not talk to anyone but make haste and return with the king's response."

The soldiers coming into Hebron are greeted by their fellow men with calls of joy and laughter. The raid that Joab led had been successful and the spoils had been plentiful. Since David had been announced king over Judah no wars had been lost and Hebron became more prosperous than ever.

Abishai embraces he's brother. "Your victory came to us two days ago! Welcome back brother!" Joab holds he's brother by he's shoulder he's facial expression serious. "I have heard that Abner have made a covenant with King David. Is this true?"

Abishai sighs a hurtful expression showing on he's face. "It is so my brother. Abner has gone to all the elders of Israel speaking the words of the prophet Samuel. He spoke of the foretold prophesy that David will lead Israel and save them from the hands of the Philistines and all of Israel's enemies." Joab takes a seat on a wooden chair. "That was the words spoken by Samuel but why the covenant with Abner? What about Ish – Bosheth?"

The men's voices and laughter had increased and all around them the men that had returned were drinking wine and talking about the raid. "Anber had told David that he will bring the whole of Israel to him. He has gone out and spoken to the elders of Israel and the elders of Benjamin. The king accepted the peace with Abner and shortly after this he sent a message to Ish – Bosheth. Joab raises he's brows "Ish - Bosheth?" Why would King David want to talk with him?" One of the men had set a jar of wine before them and Abishai fills the clay cups while continuing he's story. "This was what David had required before he would see Abner. He had told Abner that he would do nothing behind Ish – Bosheth's back and that he wanted peace with him."

Joab smashes he's fist on the table, some of the men around them stare at their captain. "Meet with him! He killed our brother!" Abishai takes he's brother by he's elbow. "That is not all my brother. We all knew that Ish – Bosheth was fearful of Abner. The whole of Israel have respect for Saul's old war captain. He has not even protested against Abner's treachery. Ish – Bosheth has been drowning himself with the drink since he had become king.

Joab fills he's cup for the second time not interrupting he's brother again. "A few days ago Abner arrived with Michal, Saul youngest daughter and twenty of he's men." Joab wipes the wine running down he's chin. "Michal? Saul daughter?" Abishai takes a swig of he's clay cup and then continues. "Yes, it was one of David requirements that he had send to Ish – Bosheth that he would return Michal he's first wife to him." Joab was slowly shaking he's head but he did not interrupt Abishai as he spoke. "The king spoke with Abner for more than a day and then yesterday Abner and he's men left Hebron to return to Ish - Bosheth."

Joab suddenly sits up and looks into the direction of Jebus. "That means that they are still close by!" Abishai puts he's hand on he's older brother's arm. "Do not even think about it. King David had sent Abner away in peace." Suddenly there is a sly smile on Joab's face.

"Send a messenger after Abner and tell him that king David wants him to return. I must go and report to King David on our raid. Do not let Abner enter the city gates but let him wait by the gate. Do not let him see you. I will return shortly."

The afternoon breeze tucks slightly at the Egyptian silk curtains in the council chamber. David quietly looks at the man sitting across from him eating a piece of bread. The bearded warrior had walked into he's chamber and David could see that he was in a troublesome mood. He knew that Joab came to talk to him about Abner. David was truly surprised when the messenger brought him the papyrus scroll that Abner had written to him. After receiving Abner message David had spoken to Yahweh asking Him for wisdom and he found peace in he's heart. He sent a message of he's own back to Abner. He also wrote a separate message in which he addressed Ish – Bosheth. Among other things he had required that Michal was returned to him. Not only was Michal he's first wife bit he had to kill more than a fair portion of Philistines to obtain Saul daughters hand in marriage. He also wanted to make it clear to Abner that he would not deal traitorously behind Ish – Bosheth's back but that this covenant with the house of Israel would be made clear to all.

He had respected Saul when he was king for Yahweh had chosen him. He had also loved Jonathan as he's own brother. Ish – Bosheth might have opposed him but he was still a direct descendant of Saul. A few days after he had send he's retorting message he had heard from the council. Abner had kept he's word and had gone and spoken to the elders of Israel and Benjamin. Two days ago a messenger came to him and announced that Abner and twenty of he's men with he's first wife Michal were making their way towards Hebron.

He had started he's preparations for a feast and when Abner arrived he had greeted him with peace in the name of the Lord. Michal had traditionally shown him respect as her first husband and departed to her chambers that he had prepared for her. He would have time to speak with her later. Abner told David that he had done as he had said and that the elders of Israel had been reminded of the prophesied words that Samuel had spoken. He told David that the elders had come together and that they would arrive in Hebron within the next few days to address him.

"They have gathered and will soon come to Hebron. Yahweh has proclaimed this through the prophet and you will be king over all Israel." Soon after they had conversed about these matters the feast started. It was as if the years fell away and they sat and spoke of old times. They sat until the fires burned low and the red embers of the fire winked at them.

Abner had told him that he would prepare he's house and come to Hebron with the elders. The next morning Abner and he's men had left and David said farewell with peace in he's heart. Abner would return soon and David knew that the war commander would be valuable. He had heard the commotion when Joab had returned from he's raid. He had expected him to oppose the covenant he had made with Abner. Soon after David had heard of he's arrival it was announced that the bearded warrior wanted an audience with him. The servants brought some fresh bread and David thanked the Lord. David wiped he's beard with he's hand and after the servants departed he spoke with Joab. "I have heard that you and your men fought well. There were no losses and the enemy has scattered further to the North" Joab shakes he's head in agreement. "Yes my king. The Philistines have been driven back." David looks intently at Joab. He could see that Joab was masking he's annoyance.

"It is good. Soon we will embark on a greater challenge. We will conquer Jebus." Joab seems to be taken completely by surprise. "Jebus? Those arrogant Jebusites have been in Jebus since I can remember. Jebus is their stronghold and a fortress. How will you go about this?"

David strokes he's beard. "We shall talk about all this soon. I know that is not the reason you came here today Joab. You have heard that Abner came to Hebron. I have made a covenant with him and he's house hold."

Joab seem to lose control of the resentment that he had kept at bay.

"What have you done? Why did you do such a thing? You know that he will never keep he's word but will deceive you!

Joab stands up from the chair he was sitting on and stares out through the window into the desert.

"He only came here so that he could observe our movements and find out everything that we are doing!" David can see that there will be no reasoning with Joab. "I know that you are still hurt by your brother's death Joab. I have known Abner for a long time and he feels regret that the young Asahel was killed. He told me that he tried to reason with your brother but to no avail."

Joab keeps quiet for a long time standing with he's back towards David. He turns back towards he's king with a neutral expression on he's face and shrugs he's shoulders making he's way out of the chambers.

"I have had a long journey and I am tired. I am going to rest now." He bows he's head towards David and leaves the room.

Abner was surprised when the messenger came after them. He had never seen the man before but the man wore the blue arm band that most men wore in David's army.

When the messenger caught up with them he told him that King David had wanted him to return to Hebron. Abner did not know what to make of it but knew that it had to be important. The meeting with David had reaffirmed a bond that he once knew when David was but a youth in the service of Saul. He turned back without any questions. The hot desert wind blow against he's face and he enjoys a moment of utter peace.

He would return to Ish – Bosheth and make him an offer to come with the elders of Israel when they came to reunite Israel under David kingdom. He's mind shifted and a wry smile plays on he's face as he thinks about Rizpah. He planned on surprising her and asking for her hand in marriage for a second time but this time as a public announcement. He did not want to spend he's years fighting anymore and had seen enough of war. Maybe he would get a few sheep and become a farmer.

He was not far from the gates of Hebron and in the distance he made out a group of men. They must be merchants he thought to himself. The men at the gate seem familiar and a feeling of alarm arises inside Abner. Over the years he had come to trust the intuitive feeling and it saved him from many certain defeats.

He's sentiment is affirmed as he gets closer. He sees Joab and Abishai standing by the gate with some men. None of the men are armed and Joab waves at Anbner, perhaps a sign of peace? David must have spoken to Joab. He feels he's misgiving falter. He would be able to tell Joab face to face that he never wanted to kill Asahel. Abner stops in front of the men and Joab moves towards him.

"Abner. I have heard that you have made a covenant with King David." The war commander takes him by the shoulder and leads him to the side of the gate. Suddenly Abner feels very old and he wants to plea with Joab explaining the death of Asahel to him "I come in peace Joab and I am..." The hot excruciating pain that Abner feels in he's stomach cuts of he's final words. Joab stabs and stabs again and again. Abner falls on he's knees he's tearful eyes focused on Joab. He takes one last breath and then he dies.

The elders together with all the tribes of Israel came and gathered at Hebron. They came and united by the words that was spoken by the prophet Samuel. The words that he had received by Yahweh. The elder from each tribe of Israel acted as a spokesperson and came forth repeating the words of Yahweh that He had spoken through the prophet Samuel. "You shall shepherd my people Israel, and be ruler over Israel."

The numbers were great and al the tribes came before David. The sons of Judah with six thousand eight hundred men armed with spear and shield. The sons of Simeon, seven thousand one hundred mighty men of valour. Sons of Levi, four thousand six hundred men. Jehoiada, the leader of the Aaronites with him three thousand seven hundred. The young warrior Zadok brought twenty two captains and pledged he's allegiance. From the sons of Benjamin, relatives of Saul came three thousand men. The sons of Ephraim brought twenty thousand valour men. Of the half tribe of Manasseh came eighteen thousand. The tribe of Issachar brought two hundred chiefs. Zebulun brought fifty thousand men. Naphtali brought one thousand captains and thirty seven thousand with shield and spear. The Danites came with twenty eight thousand six hundred and the Asher with forty thousand men. The Reubenites and Gadites and the half tribe of Manasseh from the other side of the Jordan brought hundred and twenty thousand. One by one the tribe leaders and elders came before David and spoke before the whole Israel.

"Indeed we are Your bone and your flesh."

People came from as far away as Issachar, Zebulun and Naphtali brought food and oxen with provisions of flour, cakes of figs and raisins, wine and oil and sheep in abundance for the joy was great in Israel.

David stares at the gathered masses. He thinks back on the day that Samuel anointed him as king. The words that Yahweh had spoken had come to pass. "Great is the Lord, and greatly to be praised."

He's own men that he had fought many battles with had also presented their allegiance before him as the anointed king. When Joab and he's men stood before him David searched the face of the commander but it was set out as cold as stone. The commander and he's men also pledged allegiance but David felt very uneasy with Joab. When he had heard that Joab had killed Abner he had torn he's clothes in mourning. He had called upon Joab and had commanded him and he's men to do the same. He had lamented over Abner grieving he's treacherous death. Abner had died because of a man's un-forgiveness without he's hands been neither bound nor he's feet been in ruins.

He had walked behind the coffin of Abner and refused to eat until the next day. All of Hebron knew Abner for he was the war general of Saul. The stories of he's early years in the kings command was well known by all. It was just after the death of Abner that the tribes of Israel came to pay respect to the fallen general. The news first got worse because a day after the death of Abner two men came to Hebron with Ish – bosheth head wrapped in goat skin.

They had murdered him thinking that they were going to acquire his approval for their actions from David.

The men stood before him with the ghastly remains and David was again reminded of the way that Saul and Jonathan's death was announced to him. David did not hesitate and the men were immediately taken to be executed. David had ordered he's men to cut off their feet and hands and they were hanged at the pool in Hebron. He further gave instruction that the remains of Ish – Bosheth be buried in the tomb of Abner. So came the death of Abner, Ish – Bosheth and that of two wicked men that had taken the life of a righteous man. It came to pass that David became king over the whole of Israel and that the tribes of Judah and the rest of Israel reunited as the Ancient of Days had prepared it.

Glory to He's Holy Name forever and ever all the inhabitants of the earth rejoice!

Chapter 12

Aranhima looks down at the war party encamped close to the gates. The Israelites have not moved much since their arrival at the city. Standing on one of the watchtower platforms on wall of the city of Jebus he feels a pang of fear stabbing at he's heart. What if they did invade Jebus?

The masses of the Israelites seemed much greater but he realized that it was something else that kept bothering him. He sees some of the sentries come to attention and he recognizes the Jebusite war general Madelic approaching. The general speaks but to no one specific.

"Look at them! They are just sitting out there watching us! They are fools! They will never enter the city! Even our blind and lame will repel them!"

The surrounding men laugh at their general's jest.

"They will soon have a taste of the fierce hospitality of the Jebusites and then they will turn their camels and run back to their stinking hole they came from!"

The general steps onto the watch tower platform cooping he's hand over he's mouth. Aranhima swallows loudly. He had followed the general in many battles but he had heard about David and he's men. He had heard that it was the Israelites god, Yahweh that went before them that gave success. No one had ever laid their eyes upon this Yahweh and yet how could it be that a small army could defeat so many men? He makes a sign against he's chest to overcome he's superstitious feeling and stares at he's general standing on the platform before the men encamped below.

Madelic screams in a booming voice! "Children of Israel! Why do you want to die here? You will not enter into this city!" The men below seem unresponsive. "You are not even a match for our lame and blind sitting before the gates!"

A cloud of dust driven by the desert wind rises behind the Israel army and the Israel men cover their faces. The war general looks at the army before him and shakes he's head. He makes a last malicious gesture towards them before he faces Aranhima and the rest of the men.

"They will soon grow tired and return to their city. It is then that we will go after them and kill them all!"

"The water shafts by the spring would be the best way to enter. Nobody will suspect us coming this way for it is far too dangerous." The men nod their heads in agreement. With their eyes fixed on their king the men sit in silence while David explains he's plan to them.

"The shafts are slippery and will be very treacherous in the dark. There will be no place for errors. We will enter the shafts three hours before daybreak." David look at the men sitting before him. Some faces are new but the eyes of Eleazar and Benaiah meet he's own determined countenance with no fear showing in them. David examines the room. Some are still very young but these men are the best of the tribes. Men of valour and honor. Before he had left Hebron he had asked the elders of all the tribes to meet with him. He had explained to them that they would take the city called Jebus where the Jebusites had built a stronghold over more than an epoch. The elders had not raised any demurral to the thought-provoking plan.

Joab points to the wooden blocks on the table. "The shafts lead to two wells. One is at the South-end near the gardens. The other is in the middle of the court yard. The men that reach the well in the court yard must kill the guards at the gates and open the gates from the inside. David keenly observes Joab as he explains the plan that he had discussed with the war commander. David had called the men together and had told them that whoever would lead the attack against the Jebusites would become commander-in-chief. There were a few hands that went up in acknowledgement to he's challenge like Eleazar, Benaiah and Abishai but it was Joab hand that went up first, and so he received the command. "The men entering through the well at the gardens must flank the court yard as soon as we enter through the gates taking them by surprise." The men grin at each other like a pack of Hyena's. David steps forward. "Yes it is dangerous but have we not encountered danger before? Yahweh will keep you and protect you."

All eyes were fixed again on their king. Many of the men had never fought with David before but all sat with eager admiration and listened to the thirty year old bearded warrior.

"In the past we have fought bravely against each other but now we fight for something greater. We united as one great tribe. We stand before Yahweh almighty. Sons of Israel you belong to Yahweh! Tonight I make you chiefs and captains over your tribes. Yahweh is with you!"

Madelic awakes with a jerk. Screams fill the hallways close to he's quarters. He draws he's sword hanging from he's scabbard next to he's bed and pulls on a tunic made of Jackal skin. The sound of clashing swords fill the air and he slowly opens the wooden door staring out into the passage. He can see the shadows of men fighting in the lantern lights hanging in the antechamber.

How did the Israelites get into the fortress? "I will have those guards at the wall hanged upside down!" He thinks to himself. He slowly closes he's door and is about to hinge he's lock when something slams into the door. The side of the door hits him squarely on he's chest knocking him from he's feet. He's sword falls from he's grasp and he quickly scrambles to he's feet searching for he's fallen weapon.

Standing in the door is the silhouette of a man with a colossal sword in he's hands. He expects the figure to attack but he just stands there with the sword drawn. Madelic fingers closes on the hilt of he's own sword and he slowly rise from the floor.

"Who are you?" A scream of a dying man rends through the morning air in the hall behind the silhouetted man. Madelic wipes the sweat from he's brow with the back of he's hand. The light shining from the outside had cast a shadow over the man's face and Madelic feels the unseen eyes staring at him. He is about to ask another question but is cut short by the man's deep voice.

"You were arrogant today and said that the lame and the blind will keep us from the city. The Lord gave you and your men into our hands and Jebus now belongs to Israel." Madelic raises he's sword and attacks the dark figure screaming out loud. "Never!" He stabs at the dark figure and the sound of metal against metal fills the chamber as sword come upon sword. He was used to fighting in closed quarters and he continues he's sword Riposte. The man before him counters every attack and Madelic slowly feels the energy draining from he's right arm. The confidence that he had felt had also started make way for a feeling that he had not being accustomed to. Terror! He starts with a fresh attack and bumps into a wooden table close by. The distraction is diminutive but suddenly Madelic feels a warm sticky substance dripping down he's thy. He's legs feels like heavy logs and cannot support he's weight anymore. He stares up into the face of he's attacker and he's eyes are met by a set of olive green coloured ones.

"Who are you?" He slowly falls to the ground and the last words he hears comes as a murmur to him.

"I am David, king of Israel."

The fire burns lowly in the furnace and the smell of the smoke mixes with the smell of fresh cedar wood. David stares into the blue ebbing flames. The word had spread very quickly that he and he's men had taken the stronghold of Jebus. The men had run into the streets of the fortress and with one loud accord that was soon taken up by everyone standing within earshot they had screamed out. "Jebus has fallen! Long live the City of David! Long live King David!"

A few weeks after the fortress and City was taken a big caravan with messengers from the king Hiram of Tyre announced their arrival. An emissary asked an audience with David and told him that their king had sent them with carpenters and masons to build a bastion for him. Ships, horses and carriers carrying massive cedar logs was seen as far as the eye could see. David was in reverence of all this and he again recognized that Yahweh had established him as king over Israel. The kingdom was highly exalted and he knew it was for Yahweh glory and the sake of the people of Israel. David and Joab worked with the people of Tyre. They drew up plans and laid out the ideas he had for the city. The fortress once known as Jebus quickly changed form and the City of David became reputable with its innovative appearance.

While they were busy with this the word also came to David that the Philistines were calling on all their tribes to gather. It did not surprise him and David knew that they would be in conflict with him. Some of the Philistines of Gath did regard him as a threat even before he became king. He knew that they did not comprehend the hand of Yahweh. How could they? David only had he's small band of men and Achish never knew that he was the anointed king of Israel. Achish use to shake he's head when David tried to tell him that Yahweh gave them the victories. Achish only saw what he wanted to see. Now all the tribes of Israel was united and had become a mighty army under David as their king. This frightened the Philistines.

Benaiah had come to him in morning telling him that the Philistines had deployed themselves in the valley of Rephaim.

David had told him that he had to speak to Yahweh. Benaiah had acknowledged he's king response and it was not unusual to the big bear of a man anymore. David walks out onto the roof of he's chambers staring out over the city. The city had truly been transformed in the last few months. David stares up into the bright starry skies. He had donned the Ephod as he always did.

"Thank you Lord for the favour that you bring. Lord, shall I go up against the Philistines? Will you deliver them into my hand?" A wind blows softly ruffling through David's beard and hair. The words come as softly as the evening breeze.

"Go up for I will certainly deliver the Philistines into your hand."(2 Samuel 5 verse 19b)

"They are coming my lord!"

Bilahim, prince of Ashdod looks at the image of Baal standing before him. As always the statue only stares back at him. He gets up from he's knees the sounds of the readying troop outside fuels he's hatred for David. How dared he enter the stronghold of their armies? The first time he had heard the name David, was at Hebron. He was not there on that day. That was the day their giant champion Goliath was defeated. The story of the young Sheppard boy killing the champion Goliath had reached Ashdod that same day.

"By Baal it had to be some kind of trickery!" He had thought to himself. Only later did he hear that the shepherd boy that killed their champion also started to lead Saul's armies against their men and had killed many skilled warriors. He wanted to face the youth himself and wipe him off the face of the earth but never crossed paths with the conceited grunt. This had continued for many months and then suddenly for a while nothing was heard of David except a rumour that King Saul of Israel wanted to kill him. Time passed and he had heard from the neighbouring tribes that an army of rogues and bandits had been gathering in the desert near Hachilah, opposite Jeshimon. He never thought anything about this until a wing of Ekrons army was attacked at the city Keilah. He had then learned that this rogue army was led by the same Sheppard boy, called David. He drew up with a group of he's men and was greatly infuriated when he heard that David sought out Achish for protection from the Israel king Saul. How could the old fool take someone like that under he's protection? He should have drawn up against Achish and killed them all! After that he did not trust Achish and loathed the fact that he gave Ziklag to David and he's men to dwell in. It also did not go by unnoticed to anyone of the Philistine tribes that since David had joined Achish he's kingdom and riches had grown and that had irked him even more! It was by he's cunning and devious bidding that the Amalekites attacked Ziklag while David and he's men were gone. He had sent a messenger to the tribe of the Amalekites telling them that the borders of Ziklag were unprotected. The messenger never returned but soon afterwards he had heard that the Amalekites invaded Ziklag. They had plundered the city and had taken all the woman children. He was shocked afterwards when he heard that David and he's men had defeated the Amalekites and got their woman back as well as the spoils of the war. He then again started to plan to kill David himself. He never got the opportunity. Shortly after the raid in Ziklag David and he's men had packed up and left.

He climbs onto the back of the black Arabian horse and canters to the front line of the troop. He stares down the valley the hatred burning in he's eyes. He had taken the first attack with the horses. The princes of Ashkelon and Ekron would take the second and the third. The spoils and the glory will be so much more when he defeats the man he hated so much. "In the name of Baal, attack!"

The hooves of the running horses thunders through the valley of Rephaim. David stares calmly at the attacking hoard and lifts he's sword into the air.

"Men of Israel! Children of the living Yahweh. The Lord is with us! As water broke out of the rock for Moses, Yahweh has broken out against the enemy at hand!"

The Israel men scream a battle cry in unity. The front line of the Philistines riders come thundering towards them. The riders are now almost two hundred paces away. David screams to the flag bearer to he's right. "Raise the red flannel half - mast!" He looks to he's left he's men's faces set in grim anticipation their hands holding the freshly cut bamboo poles. The riders are now a hundred paces from them. David gives the second command. "Raise the flag full mast!" He searches the actions of the men hiding on the other side of the valley and sees the two large bamboo poles snapping into place on the other side. Suddenly the first line of Philistine riders crashes down. It almost seem like an invisible hand had swept over them. The sound of bones breaking mingles with screaming men and neighing horses. The years that David had spent with the Philistines had taught him well. He knew that the Philistines would use the ground advantage and that they would attack with horses first. They were attacking using high ground advantage coming down the valley. They would use the speed and force of the animals they rode to crush into he's army. He had instructed the men during the dark cover of the night to lay the trap that had now flattened the riders and their animals. They had taken a thick long coil of rope that ten men had to carry and stretched it across the valley. They dug two deep holes and placed two thick bamboo poles in each hole. He had ordered he's men to secure the ends of the ropes on either side of the bamboo posts and tightened them as much as possible. The rope had stretched lowly over the valley looking like a giant python. David had then instructed the men to make a brace for each of the poles that could easily be cut through. This allowed the rope to relax and the men covered the long coil with sand and rocks. As soon as he would give the signal the men had to cut through the braces and the poles will slide back into their positions tightening the rope across the valley. It worked even better than David had hoped for and the first line of fallen horses and their riders had caused so much bewilderment and the dirt hanged thickly in the air. The second line of riders came crashing into the fallen pack not knowing of the danger that lay ahead.

Bilahim never saw the rope that rose in front of he's horse but was suddenly flung from the saddle with a great force. As he went flying through the air he caught a glimpse of the Israel men running up the hill and then he struck the ground and it felt like all the bones in he's body broke. For a moment he feels dazed and he's vision is impaired with the blood that flows from a gash just above he's left eye. He wipes away the blood with the back of he's sleeve. He stares back and sees he's fallen men and horses lying everywhere. The Israel men streamed over them like a swarm of locust. It takes him only a few moments to recognize what he was looking at was pieces of scruffy rope and realize what had caused the great turmoil and all the confusion. The Israelites had used an unpretentious rope to trip he's horses!

The prince of Ashkelon had warned him not to join the first group of attacking men but he was consumed by he's hatred for David and did not heed to the warning. He felt the anger surge to a point that he could not contain and screamed out loud while searching for he's fallen sword. He turns around to the whining sounds of the black stallion he rode on. The impact of the rope had broken both front legs of the animal and it lay kicking hopelessly with its hind legs. He sees he's sword sticking out underneath the saddle and quickly takes hold of the grip. The sword slides out easily under the saddle and Bilahim feels much more buoyant after arming himself. He's army was no longer attacking and men were dying by the hundreds by the hands of the Israelites.

"I will burn all the statues of your gods in the valley today for there is only one true Yahweh!" The voice cuts through Bilahim like a two edged sword and he swirls around. The red beard of David seems afire in the sunlight and Bilahim stares into the eyes of a man that he had hated for so long. He starts to smile "I should have killed you a long time ago you arrogant sheep herder! I thought the Amalekites would do the job for me but now I will finish what they could not do!"

David slowly twirls he's sword round and round. "I knew that someone tipped off the Amalekites when we left Ziklag and should have known it was you." Bilahim laughs at him. "I will not make the same mistake you cur! I may lose this battle but before this day is over Israel will yet again look for a new king! David keeps he's eyes fixed on any sudden movement of the Philistine Prince.

Bilahim was a cunning warrior. He grimaced now and the big yellow teeth of the Philistine gave him a further menacing look. "Saul and he's sons were weak and they pleaded before we killed them! Today you will beg me to spare your life but I will kill you slowly!" The men slowly circle each other. David meets he's opponent attack as Bilahim surges forward. He swings he's sword down at David's head but follows up with a punch directly on David's nose with he's left fist. David quickly lifts he's sword to block the attack but did not expect the force of Bilahim's fist exploding into he's face. He's vision is sullied and he shakes he's head vigorously keeping he's attacker at bay with he's sword arm. He retreats and takes a few paces back switching the sword to he's left hand swinging the blade in a wide arch. Bilahim grins at the smaller man.

"I do not know what trickery you have used to kill the oaf Goliath but by Baal you are no match for me!" He attacks again this time aiming at David's unprotected neck. David is still trying to recover from the blow on he's face. He felt the warm blood streaming from he's nose down into he's beard. He's nose was surly broken. He sees the sword cutting down and does the only thing that came to him. He moves quickly to he's right; the sword misses he's neck but cuts into he's left shoulder.

Bilahim was standing much closer to him now. David quickly kneels down on to he's right knee rolling onto he's uninjured right shoulder flanking the towering warrior. Bilahim was sure that he had delivered the killing stroke. He did not expect the smaller man to roll onto his injured shoulder. He was astounded when he's sword only cuts through the air were David was standing a few moments ago. It is a wild swing that leaves he's stomach exposed. David cuts he's sword across the Philistine belly and then reverses the stroke and stabs he's sword into the side of the warrior. Bilahim's entrails bulge out through he's tunic. He drops he's sword and he tries to keep the red mouths of the gaping wound together. He stares at David in disbelieve. David slowly rises from the ground.

"It was the living Yahweh of Abraham, Isaac and Jacob that had delivered Goliath into my hands and now He has delivered me from you." Bilahim speaks through cleansed teeth. "Yahweh? There is no other god than Baal!" David switches he's sword to he's right hand and replies before he cuts into Bilahim's jugular. "You are about to find out! Now know that the Lord is Yahweh! It is He who made us and we are He's people, the sheep of He's pasture!"

Eleazar enters King David's tent. A physician is busy treating the king's shoulder wound and crushed nose. Eleazar smiles at David. "Have I not taught you to move faster?" David grins sheepishly. "You should see the other guy." Eleazar takes a seat opposite him.

"The Philistines have retreated but will surly attack again when dawn brakes. I have posted sentries and readied the men should they try a surprise attack." David smiles at Eleazar. "There will be no further attack on the Philistines." Eleazar stares at David and wonders if he was struck on he's head also. "My king there is still almost ten thousand Philistines in the valley?" The tent opens again and Benaiah enters and takes a seat close to Eleazar without waiting for an invitation. "The wounded are being treated and the men are ready for a second attack. We are waiting on your command." The physician ties a piece of cloth over the shoulder wound and then leaves the tent. David tenderly stretches he's shoulder testing the bonds with a scowl on he's bearded face.

"Come let us talk in earnest my friends. Yahweh has spoken to me. We shall not attack the Philistines again. Tomorrow when we hear the sound of marching in the Mulberry trees then we shall advance quickly upon the Philistine." Eleazar stares at David he's eyes wide. "Who will be marching in the Mulberry trees?" David puts he's hand on Eleazar shoulder. "Always trust in Yahweh ways. Yahweh will go out before us and strike the Philistine camp with He's mighty hand and then we will follow."

Eleazar cannot contain he's uneasiness and gets up and paces the tent. Benaiah cleans the dirt under he's fingernails remarking very drily. "Yahweh has delivered us from all our enemies and now He strikes the enemy with he's own hand?" David smiles at the two men before him. They were like he's brothers. "Let me talk to you about an immense mystery. When the prophet Samuel was alive he spoke to me of things that I did not understand. He told me that one day Yahweh will sent a ruler and king like no other before. This king will come to set the captives free." Benaiah smile broadens. "Yes, you are that king David. You have united Israel and the people of Israel are prospering like never before." David shakes he's head and takes a parchment out of a bag made of Oryx skin hanging on a peg close by. "No my friends this king will not just be a present ruler but is the King of all kings and the Lord of all lords. He will give the everlasting water of life to those who are thirsty. These are the words that was kept by the scribes and seen by our forefathers. These things has been kept hidden until the exact time when it will be revealed. Some was written by Noah's grandfather Enoch when Yahweh revealed it to him before the big flood that came upon the earth." Benaiah scratches he's beard a deep frown etched in he's forehead. "Everlasting water of life?" David stands and beckons to the two men to follow him and then leaves the tent.

The men are greeted by a welcoming sound of wood crackling on a fire. They sit down close to the warmth and for a moment no one says a thing but all stare into the orange glow of the dancing flames. David picks up the parchment and places it on he's lap and opens the scroll. "The Lord spoke to me and I wrote it down. This is a future proclamation of this king of Kings to come." The orange glow of the fire shines on the parchment in David's hands and it almost seems transparent.

"My God, My God, why have you forsaken me? Why are you so far from helping me and from the words of my groaning? My God, I cry in the daytime, but you don't answer and in the night season and am not silent. But you are holy, you who inhabit the praises of Israel. Our fathers trusted in you; they trusted and you delivered them. They cried to you and were delivered. They trusted in you and were not disappointed. But I am a worm, and no man, a reproach of men, and despised by people. All those who see me mock me. They insult me with their lips they shake the head, saying "He trusts in Yahweh, let Him deliver Him. Let Him rescue Him since He delights in Him. But You brought me out of the womb; You made Me trust at my mother's breasts. I was thrown on you from my mother's womb. You are my God since my mother bore me. Don't be far from me for trouble is near. For there is no one to help. Many bulls have surrounded me. Strong bulls of Bashan have encircled me. They open their mouths wide against me, lions tearing prey and roaring. I am poured out like water. All my bones are out of joint. My heart is like wax; it melted within me. My strength is dried up like potsherd. My tongue sticks to the roof of mouth. You have brought me into the dust of death. For dogs have surrounded me. A company of evildoers have enclosed me. They have pierced my hands and feet. I can count all of my bones. They look and stare at me. They divide my garments among them. They cast lots for my clothing. But don't be far off, Yahweh. You are my help: hurry to help me. Deliver my soul from the sword, my precious life from the power of the dog. Save me from the lion's mouth! Yes from the horns of the wild oxen, you have answered me. I will declare your name to my brothers. Among the assembly, I will praise you. You who fear Yahweh, praise him! All your descendants of Jacob, glorify him! Stand in awe of him, all you descendants of Israel! For he has not despised nor abhorred the affliction of the afflicted. Neither has he hidden he's face from him; but when he cried to him, he heard. Of you comes my praise in the great assembly. I will pay my vows before those who fear him. The humble shall eat and be satisfied. They shall praise Yahweh who seek after him. Let your hearts live forever. All the ends of the earth shall remember and turn to Yahweh. All the relatives of the nations shall worship before you. For the kingdom is Yahweh's. He is the ruler over the nations. All the rich ones of the earth shall eat and worship. All those who go down to the dust shall bow before him, even he who can't keep he's soul alive. Posterity shall serve him. Future generations shall be told about the Lord. They shall come and shall declare he's righteousness to a people that shall be born, for he has done it." (Psalm 22)

Eleazar is the first to speak. "It sounds like a proclamation of a man in deep distress and not a great king." David smiles and stretches himself out before the fire. "I know and yet there is something so powerful about this man suffering and He's cry to Yahweh that I cannot explain it. It was written that He will be exalted for ever and ever and all knees shall bow and confess he's name is Yahweh!"

The early rays of the sun creeps over the valley of Rephaim. A breeze whispers through the stems of the buffalo grass. A mountain goat effortlessly climbs an almost unclimbable steep rock cliff and the sound of a few loose rocks clatters along the rocky ravine.

David and a few hundred men are waiting silently behind huge boulders of rock in view of a string of Mulberry trees is a hundred paces from them. Eleazar sits quietly thinking about the words that David had read to them the previous nightfall. He is tense but also knows that wonderful miraculous things have happened in Yahweh's presence. He stares at the moving branches of the Mulberry trees as the wind moves through them. A tangible silence seems to cover the valley. Even the wind had died down. A weighty presence fills the air and Eleazar stares at a stem of grass in front of him. It even seems like the drops of mist on the stem of grass is frozen. He looks at the men around him and the anxiousness he sees on their faces confirms the heavy presence that he also felt. He stares at the posterior of their king. He knew that David had also felt the surrounding presence but the king did not move a muscle.

An unacquainted sound fills the air. Eleazar inclines he's head listening intently and it almost sounds like the flutter of bird wings but suddenly the ambience sound increases and some of the men cover their faces. Eleazar stares at the valley below trying to envision the sounds that he's ears were discerning. He cannot see anything although the sound was inimitable! The morning air is filled with the sound of thousands and thousands of marching men. It seems to be above them and all around them. Eleazar falls to the ground too afraid to look up. The sound reaches an overbearing climax and then just as quickly as the sound had come it disappears.

Eleazar opens he's eyes and raises he's head. David stands up from the grass before him. All around him the men come to their feet some of them with bewildered scared looks on their faces. Eleazar himself hopes that the fear that he feels did not still show on he's face. David turns toward the men. "Move up to the Philistine camp. Yahweh has prepared the way!" The men march towards the camp some have drawn their swords but Eleazar sees that David had not drawn he's sword and follows he's king's example. No lookouts or calls of warning from the Philistines can be heard even when they are about three hundred paces away from their camp. Eleazar feels the same fear creep up in he's stomach as they enter the camp of the Philistines.

All around them Philistine soldiers lay dead. The look on their dead faces displays that of complete dread and distress. All the tents are flattened and the images of the Baal gods that they worship lay broken everywhere. King David turns towards the men of Israel.

"Yahweh has gone before us and has defeated the Philistine army! He has broken the armies of the Philistines as He has broken the gods that they worship! There is no God but Yahweh! This place shall be called Baal Perazim for the Lord has broken through the Philistine army like water through a wall. Give praise the Lord for He is more glorious and excellent than the mountains of prey!"

Chapter 13

The oxen bellow loudly. The cart buckle under the weight of the ark and Ahio steers the oxen down the pathway.

"Whoa now! Slow down! To the left Buri! Now keep it going!" The voice of Ahio can barely be heard above the music that the masses are playing. The sounds of fir-wood on the Lyres, stringed instruments on tambourines, cestrum's and cymbals in unity flows down the valley. The two cherubim on the top of the ark shine in the morning light. Ahio steers the oxen slowly down the path. They are nearing Nachon's house and Ahio knows that the path makes a treacherous turn to the left and therefore the slow pace. Uzzah walks beside the new cart. He had argued with he's brother that he wanted to steer the cart down the hill but Ahio had instructed him to walk beside the cart and make sure everything went well. Their father Abinadab had instructed them to adhere to the kings bidding and take the ark to the city of David. They knew that king David would one day come and ask for the ark to be taken to the city. It had been standing in their father's house for a long time. Abinadab had gone himself to speak to King David and had then returned and instructed he's two sons to prepare the ark to be transported.

A small whirlwind dances lightly on the threshing floor and loose grain of wheat is swept into the spiralling column. Ahio steers the cart expertly into the left turn avoiding a deep cleft on the right side of the path. He slowly turns back to the right. The wagon suddenly jars to stand still and Ahio gazes under the cart.

A rock lies stuck in the path of the back left wheel. Uzzah kneels next to the wagon seeing the obstacle and takes he's staff to remove it. He nudges the rock with the staff but the weight of the cart had trapped the rock between the wheel and the earth.

"Can you move it brother?" Ahio's face appears from above the cart looking a bit worried. "I think we can go over it. As soon as I call out let the oxen pull forward." He takes he's staff and wedges it against the rock. "Now pull!" Ahio swings the long whip all the way past the front oxen the sound cracking above the music. The animals bellow once more and then start to pull. The back wheel slowly starts to lift over the rock. It comes over the rock and then suddenly discharges. One of the oxen stumbles as the wagon increase in forward momentum. "Whoa boy!" Ahio has to hold onto the sides of the cart with both hands to prevent himself from falling. Uzzah sees the oxen stumble and quickly reaches out to the side of the Ark to support it. Ahio gains control over the oxen and looks backwards to make sure the ark is still in place. The music suddenly dies down and a woman start to wail and scream out. Ahio stops and stares at he's brother lying next to the cart. The fool must have slipped! He climbs from the cart and takes he's brother by he's shoulders. He's weight is heavy and Ahio slowly turns him onto he's back. He's eyes are still open and it seems like he is staring at something beyond. Uzzah was dead.

"Father! I have just received the official count from the shepherds from the north! Four thousand two hundred and eleven! It has also doubled!" Obed – Edom smiles at he's son. Since he's miraculous healing the boy could not keep still. The other stock counts had also arrived in the passage of the week. He's live stock had doubled within three months. He sits back staring at the closed door leading to the underground cellar. It is where the ark is placed. Obed – Edom stares out over the plains. He's house was not that far from the place where Uzzah had died. When Abinadab's eldest son died the people of Israel wailed in fear. Ahio refused to drive the cart with the ark. It was one of King David's guards that came knocking on he's door telling him that the it was the kings orders that the ark would be stored in he's house. That same day they had brought the ark to he's house. He was a man that feared Yahweh and kept the Lord's commandments. Although he had felt fear it was born out of a holy understanding of Yahweh the God of Abraham, Isaack, Jacob. Shortly after the arrival of the ark strange wonderful unexplainable things had started to happen.

"Go and prepare a feast my son. The Lord has truly blesses us. Invite all and prepare the fires." Obed – Edom stares after he's son as he leaves. It was pleasing to see he's son run around. Abetjar had only been seven years old when he had broken he's right leg. At first they had thought that he would completely loose he's leg. He's mother had stood by he's bed for days on end while the boy battled through a fever. It took months before he started to walk on he's leg again. The leg never healed properly and stood at an awkward angle. The years passed and many were the nights where Abetjar cries filled the house. It was not only the pain in he's leg but also the pain in he's back due to he's uncomfortable walk. As time progressed the young man could only walk short distances and had to stop and rest very often. It was two days after the ark was brought to Obed – Edom's house that the phenomenon occurred. He had warned he's family and servants that no one was permitted to enter the underground cellar. He had gone to instruct the Sheppard boy's where the flocks needed to be taken for the winter grazing. He had returned to he's house to find Abetjar lying face down on the ground in front of the cellar door. The cellar door was open and a picture of Uzzah dead staring eyes came to Obed – Edom's mind.

He bend down and with a sigh of relieve saw he's sons chest rise and fall as he steadily drew breath. He took Abetjar and gently lifted he's head. The youth opened he's eyes as if awaken from a slumber. "What happened Abetjar? Why is the cellar door open! I told the household not to enter in here!" Abetjar had stared at he's father in confusion. "I was tired and could not continue anymore. My back was hurting and I really needed to rest. I only leaned against the cellar door. I never opened the door father. I was about to continue when a terrible pain had shot through my leg. It was worse than ever. I must have fainted from the pain."

It was then that Abetjar's confused look changed into a look of surprise and wonder. He stared down at he's leg and in haste came to he's feet. Obed – Edom was almost knocked over by the boy sudden movement. "What is it Abetjar?" The youth stared at he's leg and then started to move around the room. "Father! It is gone! All the pain in my back and leg is gone! Look at my leg father!" Obed – Edom stared at the boy leg in wonder. The leg was no longer crookedly twisted. Obed – Edom walked over to he's son tears streaming down he's face. "Praise the Lord! Yahweh has healed you my son!" That was the first extraordinary occurrence since the ark was brought to he's house.

The next came when one of the Sheppard boy's came from the hills of Ramah to report a strange happening. He reported that he was sure that he's flock had increased with at least three hundred sheep during the month. All the sheep that belonged to Obed - Edom was branded the same way. The back of each sheep left ear was dyed red. The boy told him that he's suspicion grew when he noticed a ram that he had never seen before. The back of the ram's ear was dyed in red but he was sure that he had never seen it before that day. He decided to take stock of them and to he's amazement the flock had grown with at least two hundred sheep within two weeks. All the sheep had the same dyed marking on the back of their ears. Reports soon followed from the rest of the Sheppard boy's giving account of similar occurrences with in their flocks. At first Obed -Edom sat and tried to debate this strange occurrence for he was a practical man. Even if all he's ewes did procreate it would not make up for the growth in the numbers. It takes at least five months for a ewe to lamb and most of the increases came with full grown ewes and rams. Then it struck him.

It was Yahweh's doing. Everything had started to change since the ark was brought to he's house. Obed – Edom's kneels down in he's bedroom.

"Thank you for your blessing Lord."

"I have called upon the priests Zadok and Abiathar. The Levites Uriel, Asaiah, Joel, Shemaiah, Eliel and Amminadab to sanctify themselves. It was because it was not done the first time that the Lord our Yahweh broke out against us. The elders of Israel sitting in the council room nod their heads in agreement.

"No one may carry the ark of Yahweh but the Levites, for the Lord has chosen them to carry the ark of Yahweh and to minister before Him forever." David had made sure that they had specifically built the Tabernacle in accordance with the scriptures as Yahweh had instructed Moses to build the tabernacle. David also instructed the Levites to carry the Ark exactly the way that it had been done in the days of Moses. They would carry it by its poles on their shoulders.

"Tomorrow we shall go to the consecrated house of Obed – Edom to bring back the ark of Yahweh to be placed in the Tabernacle. We will give thanks to the Lord! We will call upon He's name and make known He's deeds among the people!"

Michal stares out through the palace window. The city of David is a colourful joyous place. Blue silk banners stream from every window and some are carried by the dancing hordes. The sound of trumpets thunders over the joyful singing and Michal stares at the approaching masses.

The ark of the Lord is carried by the Levites as instructed. All around the hauler's people are dancing and playing musical instruments. Michal stares in antipathy at the figure dancing before the ark. David leaps and twirls before the ark of the Lord he's linen Ephod lifting high above he's waste.

Michal shakes her head in discontentment. "How impropriate for a king! What a fool! He is uncovering himself before every servant and maid of Israel!" The Levites carry the ark to the erected Tabernacle and the sounds of the trumpets blow again. Michal looks at David as he ascends to the platform before the tabernacle. Servants carry two lambs to an altar next to the platform. David lifts he's hands to the heavens. The people of Israel quite down and David's voice carries clear over the hordes.

"Oh give thanks to Yahweh. Call on he's name. Make what he has done known among the peoples. Sing to him. Sing praise to him. Tell of all he's marvellous works. Glory in he's holy name. Let the heart of those who seek Yahweh rejoice. Seek Yahweh and he's strength. Seek he's face forever more. Remember he's marvellous works that he has done, he's wonders, and the judgement of he's mouth, you offspring of Israel he's servant, you children of Jacob, he's chosen ones. He is Yahweh our God. He's judgements are in all the earth. Remember he's covenant forever, the word which he commanded to a thousand generations, the covenant which he made with Abraham, he's oath to Isaac. He confirmed the same to Jacob for a statute, and to Israel for a n everlasting covenant saying, I will give you the land of Canaan, the lot of your inheritance when you were but a few men in number, yes, a very few, and foreigners were in it. They went about from nation to nation, from one kingdom to another people. He allowed no man to do them wrong. Yes he reproved kings for their sakes. Don't touch my anointed ones! Do my prophets no harm! Sing to Yahweh, all the earth! Display he's salvation from day to day. Declare he's glory among the nations, and he's marvellous work among all the peoples. For great is Yahweh, and greatly to be praised. He also is to be feared above all gods. For all the gods of the peoples are idols but Yahweh made the heavens. Honor and majesty are before him. Strength and gladness are in he's place. Ascribe to Yahweh due to he's name. Bring an offering and come before him. Worship

Yahweh in holy array. Tremble before him all the earth. The world also established that it can't be moved. Let the heavens be glad and let the earth rejoice. Let them say among the nations Yahweh reigns! Let the sea roar in its fullness! Let the field exult, and all that is in it! Then the tree of the forest will sing for joy before Yahweh, for he comes to judge the earth. O give thanks to Yahweh for he is good, for he's loving kindness endures forever. Say "Save us God of our salvation! Gather us together and deliver us from the nations to give thanks to your holy name to triumph in your praise" Blessed be Yahweh, the God of Israel, from everlasting even to everlasting." (1 Chronicles 16 v 7 – 36)

The people in one accordance called out "Amen!" They burst out in song and dance and the servants appointed to give the food to the people start moving in among them. Michal looks at the multitudes trying to calculate the sum of resources spent to distribute the meat, bread and piece of cake with raisins that David had had instructed them to give to the nation. Michal turns from the window. The masses will return to their houses. The men will now bless their families as instructed and David will return to the fortress to bless he's household. Michal rushes to the garden entrance knowing where David would enter the palace. She sees him approaching through the trees and she goes out to confront him.

"How glorious the king of Israel was today, who uncovered himself today in the eyes of the servants of he's servants, as one of the vain fellows shamelessly uncovers himself!" (2 Samuel 6 verse 20) David walks by Michal ignoring the venomous words that follows him. "My father would never have shamed himself like that!" David stops but does not turn around toward Michal. "I was dancing before the Lord who chose me instead of your father and he's house, to appoint me ruler over the people of the Lord, over Israel." He turns towards he's wife he's eyes blazing.

"I will be even more undignified than this, and will be humble in my own sight. But as for the maidservants you have spoken of, by them I will be held in honor." Without a further word he enters the palace. Michal turns away from the palace walking out into the garden.

"The king will see you now." Nathan follows the guard into the king throne chamber preparing the words Yahweh had spoken to him in he's dream the previous night. The message form Yahweh came shortly after the conversation he had with David about the temple.

It all had started four days ago with a man called Mephibosheth. King David had called him shortly after the ark was brought to Jerusalem. The king had enquired about the family of Saul and wanted to know if anyone was left in he's house of Saul. Nathan had spoken to some of the servants and they had brought news about a servant of Saul called Ziba. According to the other servants Ziba and he's sons where all servants of Saul. The king requested Ziba to come to the palace where the king had enquired from him if anyone was left of the blood line of Saul. Ziba had told the king that a man by the name of Mephibosheth the son of Jonathan stayed in the house of Machir the son of Ammiel.

Ziba explained to the king that it was where he was looked after, for Mephibosheth was lame in both he's feet. King David was surprised and very excited when he heard that a direct descendant of Jonathan was alive. King David had immediately sent a caravan of he's own men to fetch Mephibosheth. When the caravan returned they brought the man Mephibosheth before the king. The man with the lame feet lay with he's face on the ground and David called out to him.

"Mephibosheth?" The man had answered King David. "Here is your servant." David had walked to the man putting he's hand on he's shoulders "Do not fear for I will surly show kindness for Jonathan your father sake. I will restore to you all the land of Saul your grandfather and you shall eat bread at my table continually." Mephibosheth had bowed he's head again and answered. "What is your servant that you should take heed to such a dead dog as

I?" David had whispered something inaudible to Nathan and then gave the command to the servant Ziba to serve Mephibosheth the same way that they served Saul. The servants had then carried Mephibosheth from the hall and King David had turned towards Nathan.

"I have this nice palace made of Cedar but the ark of the Lord dwells inside tent curtains. I want to build a temple where I can place the ark." Nathan had given it no thought and spoke the words that came to him. "You can do all that is in your heart king David for the Lord is with you." Nathan had then left the palace and that night the word of the Lord had come to him. He had to tell David what the Lord had spoken. David eagerly calls upon the prophet. "Nathan! It is good that you have returned. I need to talk to you about layout of the temple. I have called upon the finest masonries and carpenters to build the temple." Nathan waits until the king finishes.

"King David the Lord has spoken to me in my dream last night. This is the words of the Lord our Yahweh.

"Should you build me a house for me to dwell in? For I have not lived in a house since the day that I brought the children of Israel up out of Egypt, even to this day, but have moved around in a tent and in a tabernacle. In all places in which I have walked with all the children of Israel, did I say a word to any of the tribes of Israel, whom I commanded to be shepherd of my people Israel, saying, 'Why have you not built me a house of cedar?' (2 Samuel 7 verse 5-7) David had not moved since Nathan started to talk. He listens attentively to the prophet. "Now therefore tell my servant David this, 'Yahweh of Armies says, "I took you from the sheep pen, from following the sheep, to be prince over my people, over Israel. I have been with you wherever you went, and have cut off all your enemies from before you. I will make you a great name, like the name of the great ones who are in the earth. I will appoint a place for my people Israel, and will plant them, that they may dwell in their own place, and be moved no more. The children of wickedness will not afflict them anymore, as at the first, and as from the day that I commanded judges to be over my people Israel. I will cause you to rest from all your enemies." Nathan takes a moment and then continues. "Yahweh will make you a house. When your days are fulfilled, and you sleep with your fathers, I will set up your offspring after you, who will proceed out of your body, and I will establish he's kingdom. He will build a house for my name, and I will establish the throne of he's kingdom forever. I will be he's father, and he will be my son. If he commits iniquity, I will chasten him with the rod of men, and with the stripes of the children of men; but my loving kindness will not depart from him, as I took it from Saul, whom I put away before you. Your house and your kingdom will be made sure forever before you. Your throne will be established forever." (2 Samuel 7 v 11 – 16)

These are the words that was spoken to me by the Lord our Yahweh." David gets up from he's throne and walks to he's bed chamber. He closes all he's curtains and bows he's head before Yahweh.

"Who am I that you have brought me this far Lord? Let your name be magnified forever saying the Lord of hosts is the Yahweh over Israel. Therefore your servant has found it in he's heart to pray this prayer. Now therefore let it please you to bless this house of your servant that I may continue before you forever; for You Lord Yahweh have spoken it."

Chapter 14

"King David has returned from Helam. I heard they killed seven hundred charioteers and forty thousand horsemen!"

The camel's mill around the watering hole, the late afternoon sun stretches the palm trees shadows over the men sitting by the small oasis. Achmel takes a drink from he's watering skin listening to the conversation of he's father and the others around him.

"He has subdued the Philistines, he has defeated Moab and even the Moabites have become he's servants. He has recovered the territory at the River Euphrates when he defeated Hadadezer the son of Rehob, king of Zobah. He defeated the Syrians at the valley of Salt. I heard that at least eighteen thousand men were killed. Israel is blessed and surely the name of King David will go down in the parchments of history as the mightiest conqueror!"

Achmel lays down onto he's sheepfold next to the fire the men voices lulling him. "He has sent Joab to destroy the rest of the people of Ammon and besiege Rabbah." The sounds of the men voices respites him and Achmel closes he's eyes. "The king has not gone with he's men? No he has stayed behind in the City." The words die away as Achmel falls into a deep sleep dreaming of becoming a warrior and serving the mighty king David.

David stares at the evening sky. Millions of stars stretch out across the desert sky clustering over the city. The full moon hangs like a giant ball on the horizon. The silhouettes of the dunes making it seem even larger. David stares over the roofs of the city. He still felt troubled about the words that the prophet Nathan had brought. He was tired of fighting and when he had returned from Helam the prophet Nathan came and told him that the Lord did not want him to continue to build the temple. The words Yahweh spoke through the prophet had upset him deeply. " You have shed blood abundantly, and have made great wars. You shall not build a house to my name, because you have shed much blood on the earth in my sight. Behold, a son shall be born to you, who shall be a man of peace. I will give him rest from all he's enemies all around; for he's name shall be Solomon, and I will give peace and quietness to Israel in he's days. He shall build a house for my name; and he will be my son, and I will be he's father; and I will establish the throne of he's kingdom over Israel forever." (1 Chronicles 22 v 8 – 10) "Solomon?" David had had six sons that were born in Hebron. He's firstborn Amnon by he's wife Ahinoam; the second Daniel by Abigail; the third Absalom the son of Maacah, the daughter of Talmai, king of Geshur; the fourth Adonijah the son of Haggith; the fifth Shephatiah, by Abital and the six Ithream by he's wife Eglah. The sons born in the city were Shimea, Shobab and Nathan. He also had a daughter Tamar. A movement on the roof of one of the houses below catches he's attention. David stares at the scene below.

A dark haired women walk to a cement bath built on the roof. She takes her long linen robe off and steps into the water. The light of the full moon shines on her unclothed figure. Her long dark hair is knotted in a bun behind her head. She innocently turns her frame towards the king and David continues to stare at her. The woman start to wash her long hair and David watches her every movement. David walks to the entrance of he's bedchamber. "Hushai!" The footsteps of the servant approaches outside the king chamber. "My king?" David walks back out onto the veranda. Hushai walks into the king room and sees the cedar doors standing open on the veranda. He walks to where the king is standing on the roof. "Yes my king?" David is still staring at the woman below. She has put on a clean white dress the sign of her purification and is combing through her long hair. "Do you know whose house that is down there?" Hushai walks over to where the king is standing and stares into the direction David is pointing. "I do not know but will find out my king." David's eye's does not leave the woman.

"Find out and come and tell me who that woman is down there."

The smell of fresh bread fills the palace kitchen and the sounds of laughter comes down the hall way. Two maid servants come rushing past Hushai and he almost gets knocked over. The girls reticently make an apology. He takes no notice of the two giggling women and continues out into the garden. He was summoned by a messenger from the house of Uriah. Hushai walks down the pathway thinking about the night he was summoned onto the roof by King David. He had gone out that night and had enquired from the servants whose house it was that king David had pointed out to him. It was the house of Uriah the Hittite. The woman the king had enquired about was Bathsheba the wife of Uriah. Hushai had gone back to the king and had given him the information. King David had paced around like a trapped bear and then suddenly he had picked up a parchment and a reed and wrote something in it and handed it to Hushai.

"Take this to the house of Uriah. Accompany the woman back here to me." Hushai did not ask any questions and had taken the parchment to the house of the Hittite. The servants of the house of Uriah had taken the message from the king to their mistress. Shortly thereafter a woman that was heavily veiled appeared with the servants. She did not say much but scrunched the king's message in one of her delicately formed hands. Hushai had accompanied the woman back to the king's chamber. When the woman stood before King David she took off her veil and Hushai was struck by her beauty. The king had closed the heavy cedar doors.

In the early morning hours he was summoned again to the king's chamber. The woman Bathsheba was waiting again heavily veiled and Hushai had accompanied her back to her house. It had been almost two moons since the king strange request. When he heard that a messenger from the house of Uriah was waiting at the palace gate he did not know what to expect. The servant from the house of Uriah stands with her eyes cast down by the guards at the palace gate. Hushai approaches her but she does not say a word and only hands a small sealed parchment into he's hands.

The parchment is addressed to the king.

He had become angry when he had first read the message. He had torn the parchment as if to tear the words that were written on it out, and threw it on the floor. He had sent Hushai out of he's chambers and paced around he's room the whole morning thinking about the situation. David stares at the heavy wooden beams in the roof. A knock on the door jars him back to the moment. David quickly picks up the torn parchment from the floor.

"My king lunch will be served shortly." David can hear the tension in the servant voice. "I am not hungry Hushai." David stares at the parchment in he's hand. He had thought long about it and the plan that came to he's mind seem like the only way out.

"Prepare a messenger to travel to Joab and ask him to send Uriah the Hittite to me." There is a slight hesitation before the servant replies. "Yes my king I will do it right away." David lies down on he's bed again. This will all be over soon and then he will go back into battle with he's men. He had many things to prepare before the Hittite returned. He took he's reed and he's parchment and started to write.

Later he called on a messenger to deliver a parchment to Bathsheba. All he could do now was to wait.

Uriah gazes at the enemy on city walls of Rabbah and stares at the heavy wooden gate before him. He wipes he's head cloth over he's tired eyes and waits for the call to attack the city walls. The last few days had been bizarre and yet momentous or at least that was how he felt. He wipes the sweat from he's forehead again and then ties he's head cloth around he's head thinking about the days that had passed.

It all started when he was summoned by the general Joab. Joab had told him that King David wanted someone to return to the city of David and report the events that had transpired on the battle front. Uriah was surprised that Joab had asked him for he had was not a messenger. He found it even more peculiar when he saw a messenger from the king and he's only logic reason was that the king wanted unswerving news coming from the mouth of he's own soldiers.

Therefore he did not question he's general and certainly not he's king. He packed he's water skin and took some dried bread and set out to deliver the news that the general had charged him with. At least he was not alone for he travelled back to the city of David with the messenger that the king had sent. After a few days travel they had arrived back in the City of David. As they came closer to the city he could not help but to think about he's newly-wed wife Bathsheba.

They did not have children but he longed to have sons of he's own. They had spoken about children but decided to delay until the wars that was being fought would pass. He did not want he's son to grow up without a father. He entered the city gates and could not help but to glance in the direction where he's house was build close to the inner city sanctum.

Joab had instructed him not to waste any time and report directly to the King. He did not even wash himself but immediately went straight to the king's palace as he was instructed. At first he was nervous but when he had entered the courts of the king he was welcomed in such manner that he almost found it a bit uncomfortable that the king took such keen interest in him. He took the position across from where King David sat and David asked him how the war was going and how the rest of the soldiers were. He had given the account of the war as Joab had instructed and answered the questions that King David asked to the best of he's knowledge. It felt very strange to sit like that in the kings company and when the king had told him to go home and wash after he's long journey, he had almost felt relieved to leave the kings presence. He had left the palace and shortly after he's departure he heard one of the king servants call out after him. The man had a package in he's hand and he handed it over to him saying that the king wanted to reward him for he's service. He had opened the package and had found a beautiful crafted Scimitar with an ivory hilt.

Uriah gawked at the gift for a long time and then he walked away from the palace in utter astonishment. He did not go home as the king had entreated. He knew one of the blacksmiths that tended the king's horses and asked if he could take shelter on a sleeping mat in one stalls. He had felt guilty for the honor that was bestowed on him by King David and yet he was merely obeying a command to bring news to the king. He picked up the gift that the king gave him stroking the ivory hilt and suddenly he's thoughts was with the men sleeping under the starry skies. The Scimitar felt heavy in he's hands and he rested it next to he's sleeping mat. He stared out into the night and before he fell into a deep sleep he's last thoughts was consumed by the striking eyes of he's wife Bathsheba.

He woke up that morning with someone calling out he's name. It was Elah the blacksmith standing with one of the king servants. He was again summoned by King David. He found it very odd that the king would ask for his presence again. He had brought the news as Joab had instructed him and was planning to depart. When he entered the king council room that morning he found the king in a rather foul mood. King David had enquired from him why he didn't go home and spend time with he's wife. It was not an abnormal question and yet Uriah did not understand the king outburst when it came to his overnight arrangements.

Uriah had explained to King David that he did it to honor the king and the men that stayed behind. He felt that he had left the rest of the men behind and all of them stayed out in the open fields facing the dangers of war. None of them had the privilege to see their wives and might even be dead soon. He was to return soon and did not want to be a stumbling block for the men on his return. The king had seemed much calmer after he's response. King David surprised him again when he invited him to stay for another day before he returned to the battlefield and have dinner with him that evening. Uriah wanted to serve he's king. He found everything very bizarre and could not wait to tell his wife about his adventure when he saw her again. He had joined the king that evening. Uriah lick over he's dry lips. He was thinking about the evening dining with the king. It suddenly seemed like it happened a long time ago although it only transpired a few days ago.

The evening was a bit of a haze to him. The king had raised glass after glass serving the delicious red wine. He's servants kept their jars filled. Before Uriah knew it he had become very drunk. He remembered that the king had jested with him and insisted that he went to he's own house that evening. The king grinned and said that it surely would beat sleeping with the horses. However when he departed the king chamber he again felt guilt ridden that he had such a good time in the king presence. He again slept in the stall that belonged to Elah the blacksmith.

Early that morning as he prepared he's journey back another servant of the king came and handed him a papyrus scroll that he had to take back to Joab. He packed the necessities for the journey and then he travelled back to the battle front at Rabbah. He went straight to Joab and delivered the scroll that he had received from the king servant. Joab had opened the scroll while he enquired about the king and he's journey. The deep sombre frown on he's commander face did not pass him by and he wondered what was written on the scroll that seemed so grim. Joab had kept quiet for wile and closed the scroll. He's commander then informed him that they would take the city under siege in the morning. He wanted

Uriah to lead the men into battle and take up the front ranks with the east wing attacking the main gate.

It had been a remarkable few days indeed and he would soon sit around the fire and recount the events that had transpired with the rest of he's men. He stood in the front ranks with his men waiting on the battle-horn to sound. Uriah looks over the rim of he's shield at the city gate of Rabbah. The battle horn sound and he draws he's sword advancing with the group of men. The city gates of Rabbah open and the army of the people of Ammon storm towards them. Uriah's heart beats faster and he utters a battle cry from he's dust worn lips. A man with an axe runs at him and he ducts behind he's shield the blow shuddering against he's left shoulder. Suddenly the man arms fling wide open, the big axe dropping from he's hands. The man falls down onto he's face in the dirt an arrow shaft sticking out behind he's left ear. Uriah stares up on the city walls of Rabbah. Archers! But why would they kill their own men? Something heavy strikes him on the side of he's neck. Uriah feels along the shaft of the arrow protruding from he's neck. A warrior with he's sword raised runs at Uriah. He desperately tries to block the blow but feels the cold steel slip into he's stomach. He feels he's legs grow weaker and the light of day start to fade from he's sight. He's head hits the ground and he feels the sand on the side of he's face. He sees the face of Bathsheba and he starts to recite he's evening with the king.

Joab gazes into the direction where the messenger that had just returned from King David had again departed. David own words that the messenger had recited was still churning around in he's mind.

"Joab you should not be upset by the passing of Uriah. The sword devours one as well as one another. Press the attack against the city and destroy it." Joab grins wolfishly in the darkness. David had judged him quickly when he had raised he's hand against Abner.

How would the king treat him now that the king had innocent blood on he's own hands?

David looks at the sleeping baby boy suckling on he's mother. Bathsheba's eyes are closed and David softly closes the door behind her.

The months had come and gone and although Bathsheba's mourning period for Uriah was not over yet he had moved her into the palace. No one ventured to ask the king questions. He's son was born the night before and Bathsheba was still weak. No one had said anything and David had kept to himself. Abigail had tried to talk with him but he refused to talk to her.

He spent most of he's time listening to the reports that came from Joab on the war with the people of Ammon. After every report David had heard he had yearns to take up he's sword and depart to the battle field. He knew why he had not yet departed to the battle field. It was the guilt of the blood of Uriah that was shed that kept him in the city.

"My king." David looks up at he's servant Hushai standing at the door. "The prophet Nathan is here to speak with you." Hushai awaits the king instruction. David seem to look beyond the servant staring into an unknown world. "I will be there now." David walks towards the stronghold throne room. Since that day on the roof he had avoided Yahweh and now he felt uneasy to stand before the prophet. Nathan had not spoken with him since the day that he had announced that David would not build the temple for Yahweh. David enters into the throne room and sees the prophet standing at the step of the throne. David walks towards the heavy cedar chair and greets the prophet with a trifling abandonment. "Nathan. What brings you to the palace?" Nathan nods he's head and walk directly towards David and stands before king David's throne.

"King David. There are two men in the city. One is rich with many flock and herds and the other is very poor. Except for one little ewe lamb the poor man had nothing."

A growing fear gropes David inside. He knows that the prophet was talking on behalf of Yahweh and he listens intently to the words spoken.

"The poor man looked after the ewe and it was brought up as one of he's own children. It ate from its own plate and drank from its own cup and the man treated the ewe lamb as one of he's children."

Nathan pauses for a moment while remaining eye contact with David and then he continues. "One day the rich man had a visitor and the rich man refused to take from he's own flock to prepare a meal for he's visitor. Instead he went and stole the poor man ewe lamb and prepared it for he's visitor."

David felt anger rising inside of him for the actions that Nathan was describing was appalling. He jumps up from he's throne waving he's fist in the air. "As the Lord lives this rich man much surely die for what he has done! Who is he?" Nathan calmly looks at the king.

"You are that man."

All color drain from David's face. "This says the Lord Yahweh.

"I have anointed you king over Israel and delivered you from the hand of Saul. I gave Saul's house and he's wives into your keeping and gave you the house of Israel and of Judah. And if this was too little I would have given you more. Why then have you despised the commandment of the Lord? You have killed Uriah the Hittite with the sword of your enemies and have taken he's wife. You have despised me thus the sword will never depart from your house."

David had not moved since Nathan had come out with the ruthless truth about Uriah. Some of he's servants that were in the chamber stare at him but he does not seem to take note of anything except the words of the prophet.

"This says the Lord Yahweh: Behold I will raise up adversity against you from your own house. I will take your wife's away from you and hand them to your neighbour and he shall lie with your wife's in the sight of the sun. You did it secretly but I will do it before the whole Israel."

David knees feel weak as he stands up from the throne. He suddenly feels like he had aged beyond he's years. "I have sinned against the Lord. What have I done! Lord please forgive me!" Nathan softly continues. "The Lord has put away your sin and you shall not die. However because of this deed you have given great occasion for the enemies of the Lord to blaspheme.

The child that was born yesterday shall die."

"The child has died. Someone must tell the king." Egmil looks at Hushai with he's demanding expression. "I do not think it is a wise thing to tell him. He has not eaten for seven days. If he finds out about the child's death he may do more harm to himself."

Hushai almost drops the wooden plate of bread he is carrying. Standing at the kitchen door is King David. David voice is not full of anger or sadness when he addresses the servants. "The child is dead?"

Hushai clears he's throat. "Yes my king." David walks over to a cement basin filled with water and start to wash he's face. "Bring me a new robe and give me some of that bread." The servants scurry out of the kitchen to do the kings bidding. Hushai serves the bread to the king. "Are you alright King David?" David takes a bite out of the bread and only nods at he's servant. Hushai clears he's throat and speaks in a gentle tone. "My king. May I be presumptuous and ask a question?" David gives a wry smile at Hushai and only nods he's head again.

"I do not understand my king. When the child was alive you fasted and did not eat a thing. Now that the child is dead you have risen from your fasting and cleaned yourself and now you are eating? " David chews the bread slowly and then he responds.

"When the child was alive I fasted and prayed that Yahweh might be gracious to me. Now the child has died. The child cannot come back to me but one day I will go to the child." David puts the bread on the wooden plate and leaves the palace kitchen. A message had come from Joab. He had besieged the city of Rabbah water supply and they needed reinforcements for the final siege.

David walks towards Bathsheba chamber. In the week that he had fasted he had thought about what the Lord had said. He prayed that Yahweh would be merciful but he also knew that Yahweh was punishing him for what he had done to Uriah. He hears Bathsheba cries as he walks down the passage and although the child death was upsetting he suddenly felt free from the guilt.

The men needed a king that would lead them into battle and he was ready to be their king again.

Chapter 15

Amnon lies on he's bed staring at the roof in he's bedroom ignoring the knock on he's door. "Amnon! I know you are in there. It is me; Jonadab."

Amnon slowly rises from he's bed to open the wooden door. The sunlight blinds him for a few seconds but he quickly turns back towards he's bedroom chamber. Jonadab closes the door behind him and follows the young man into he's room.

"What is wrong with you? You have been lying here for almost two days now. Look at you. You have become even thinner since I have last seen you." Amnon seem not to care but turns on he's side with he's back towards Jonadab.

"We have been friends for many years Amnon. I know it has something to do with the lovely Tamar." It is as if a blade enters Amnon's spinal for he suddenly sits up straight staring at he's friend. "I cannot help it Jonadab. She haunts my dreams! I cannot get her out of my mind!" Jonadab takes a chair from the kitchen and settles himself next to Amnon's bed. "I knew it had something to do with your sister." Amnon suddenly looks angry. "She is not my real sister. We have the same father but her mother is the wench Maacah."

Jonadab strokes he's hand over the side of the wooden frame of he's chair. "That may be true but that so called wench is the princes of Geshur, king Talmais daughter. You should also not forget that Absalom is Tamar's brother." When Jonadab utters the name of Absalom; Amnon angrily shakes he's head.

"Absalom! I am the older brother and yet he is favoured above me! Even in he's guises he has had the better share and people seem to respect him more than they do me. This is a hopeless situation." Jonadab smiles slyly at he's friend. "Maybe not my friend. What if you could have Tamar alone with you for a few hours? I bet you could spent them in a better fashion than this?" Amnon looks at Jonadab with hope in he's eyes. "How can I do that? My father does not allow the young virgins to spent time alone with any men. Not even her own brothers."

Jonadab laughs heartily. "Your father is not the best example to keep himself pure is he now? I have a plan." Amnon swings both he's legs from he's bed listening closely to he's friend. "When your father returns from Rabbah don't go out to meet with him. When he sends a servant to enquire why you have not come to meet with him after he's return pretend that you are ill."

Amnon looks at he's friend with questions in he's eyes. "How does that give me time alone with Tamar?" Jonadab rolls he's eyes at he's younger friend. "Your father will come to visit you to see what is wrong and it is then that you must ask him to send Tamar to tend after you until you feel better." Amnon seem uncertain but there is a well-lit hunger in he's eyes. "I don't know if it will work." Jonadab slides he's chair back into the kitchen. "Well my friend you can either be with her or you can lie here and dream about her."

The crown on he's head must weigh at least a talent of gold. The precious stones shimmers in the late afternoon sun and the men stare at it in awe. It was a hard fought battle and David had fought with every ounce in he's body trying to rid himself of the past days memories. Joab and he's men had done well to take the water supply of the city of Rabbah. The city gates of Rabbah opened after the third day of David's arrival and a large man with golden beard wearing a crown with precious stones came riding out with he's troop. The battle had dragged on for months on end and the troops looked worn.

A challenge came from the man wearing the crown and David was caught off-guard by their king's words. "I see that you have finally come from your hiding place king of Israel. Are you here to fight or to send more of your men to death so that you may have their women?"

The word was out in Israel but David never thought that it would spread so far so soon.

David response was filled with anger but also mortification. "The Lord is the judge of men and He has judged me. Lay down your weapons and you can become our servants." The king of Ammon laughed and drew he's sword. "Come king of Israel I will cut you down myself. My men will lay with your wife's tonight!" David gave the order to attack and he found himself leading he's men running at the remaining Ammon army.

David fought to he's left and to he's right ignoring the small gashes that he received; he's focus was on the large frame with the golden beard. The Ammon troop was quickly fading and soon David stood face to face with the bearded king.

As per the common war practice, when two kings face each other in combat the remaining men would stop and watch their kings battle. The Ammon king was thick in he's shoulders and he was also bleeding from a gash around he's left eye. The men circled each other. David still felt the sting of the insult that the Ammon king had flung at him. He attacked first faking a blow to the open side of the man and then swiftly twisting he's sword stabbing at the inside of the thigh. The Ammon king moved fast for such a big man and blocked the attacked easily in the same action cutting at David's unprotected head. The swords edge cut into David's scalp shearing some of the king hair.

David's anger had clouded he's judgment and he moved more warily around the Ammon king. This time the golden bearded man attacked using he's shield as a battering armament smashing David from he's feet. David's sword flew from he's hands and he quickly rolled to he's left the point of the big man sword driving into the ground where he lay just moments ago. David kicked hard with both he's feet at the Ammon kings knee. The Ammon king fell down onto he's one knee screaming in pain. David did not waste any time and grabbed the shield of the bearded man and hit him hard against the side of he's head. The Ammon king went down with a big gash of blood streaming down the side of he's face.

David stabbed he's sword through the Ammon kings heart before the man could move again. The Israel troop once again cheered him but it did not feel as glorious as it had before. Some of the men brought a crown and placed it on he's head. It was the king of Ammon's crown and now it belonged to Israel and King David. It was not the weight of the crown that felt heavy on David head. It was the look in his men's eyes that burdens his heart.

The man with the dark thick hair shakes he's head in anger.

"It was our father that had ordered you to go to him!" Tamar wipes the tears from her face. "No brother, he tricked father in to believing that he was ill."

Absalom paces the room like an angry lion. "He should have known better! He has not been the best example has he now?"

Tamar hugs her arms around her own body trying to block out the ordeal she had just gone through. "He is your own brother! I knew that he had affection for you but to go that far and then chase you away like a dirty street woman!" Tamar cries softly again and Absalom walks and hugs he's sister protectively. "Do not worry I will never forget the foul deed that he has done. He will pay for this." Tamar hides her face in her brother shoulder.

The anger that Amnon had shown after he had forced himself on her shocked her even more than the deed he had committed. He had screamed at her and then threw her out of he's house. She felt dirty and unwanted. Absalom calls on he's servants to prepare a bath for Tamar.

"I will be back sister. Do not trouble your heart anymore." Tamar looks at Absalom afraid and confused. "Where are you going brother?" Absalom binds he's thick hair with a leather piece into a braid. "I am going to talk with the king." Tamar closes her eyes. The mocking tone in Absalom's voice did not go by her unnoticed.

"I am also fuming but he is your brother!" Absalom looks at he's father not hiding the contempt. "What he has done is immoral and you want me to do nothing?" David feels the anger stir in him. When he had heard what Amnon had done he wanted to take more than the whip to he's eldest son. He knew that he would have killed him in he's anger and did not want he's own son's blood on he's hands.

"I will handle this matter accordingly. The family does not need another disgrace out in the open." Absalom stares at he's father the irritation burning in he's eyes. "The whole of Israel is talking about your murderous acts. You brought it upon yourself when you slept with that cheap woman!" David takes a step towards Absalom. "You will not refer to one of my son's mothers as cheap! I have condemned your brother exploit and will act as king but also as he's father. " Absalom turns away from he's father.

"He is not my brother. I will not forget what Amnon has done to my sister!"" David stares after he's son as he leaves he's private chambers. The Lord had spoken that adversary would come into he's house and now it had started to happen.

"Lord. I know that I have sinned. You promised that you will never leave me nor forsake me. Please carry me through this time. Please look after my children. Please forgive Amnon for what he has done and let your judgement be just. You are merciful Yahweh. Thank you for our son that is growing in Bathsheba's womb.

He shall carry the name...Solomon."

Solomon tries to pull he's father's beard with he's little fingers. David laughs and pulls he's head back looking fondly at he's son. "Enough of that you should almost go to bed now." The boy looks at he's father with tearful eyes. "No sleeping. Solm not tired!" David ruffles he's son hair. "We all have to sleep. Even I am going to sleep my little one. When we close our eyes and sleep we grow taller and taller. Do you want to be as big as me?" The small boy squirms in he's father's big arms. "Solm big as you!" Bathsheba stands at the bedroom door looking at the two men she loves so dearly. She hesitates for another moment before she lets them know of her presence. "My favourite two men." The small boy runs to he's mother with he's arms outstretched. "Mommy!" Solomon reaches out towards Bathsheba "You should be in bed my little seraph. Say good night to your father."

David kisses he's son and the boy try to climb back onto he's lap. "Come now Solomon. Let's go and see what uncle Hushai has prepared for you in the kitchen" When the boy hears Hushai's name he quickly runs towards he's mother. Uncle Hushai always has some treat before bed time. Bathsheba takes him into her arms and smiles at her husband. David stares after he's wife and son.

The Lord had made a promise that he would look after Solomon and that he would be the one to build the temple. Was it not almost forty years ago that the prophet Samuel had made a promise that Yahweh would anointed him as king? A sudden commotion down in the palace draws David's attention. He walks to the palace throne chambers and sees one of he's servants running towards him.

"My king! Absalom has killed all your sons that accompanied him and not one is left!" David grabs the man by he's shoulders. "Where did you hear this?" The servant points towards the hall entrance. "The word just came from one of the sheepshearers in Baal Hazor that accompanied them." The words of the prophet Nathan once again comes to David's mind. "Not this Lord! Please not this!" David tears he's garments and falls onto the ground crying to the Lord.

The servant that brought the news also tears he's garments in mourning.

David sits on the palace veranda staring out across the desert into the direction where he's sons had left for Baal Bezor only a few days ago. He should have known not to trust Absalom.

He had come to him two days before and requested that the whole family go to Baal Bezor for the shearing of the sheep. David had told him that he could not go and needed to tend to Solomon and Bathsheba. Absalom did not seem to be bothered by the fact that he did not want to come but insisted that all he's brother's accompanied him. "When you were young father you also tended to our grandfathers sheep. It will be good for them and they need the excursion." David had not thought much about it and gave instruction for all he's sons to accompany Absalom to Baal Bezor.

"My Lord Jonadab is back from Baal Bezor!" David turns to Hushai. "Let my brother son come forward!" Jonadab walks out onto the palace veranda. "My king. I bring news from Baal Bezor." David nods at the man before him. "Not all your sons were killed only Amnon." David stares at Jonadab in question and the man quickly continues. "Since the day Amnon had wronged Tamar Absalom has vowed to avenge he's sister injustice. We were all camping near Ephraim when it happened.

I walked out into the desert to relieve my bladder when I overheard Absalom discuss he's treacherous plan with he's servants. He told the servants to strike Amnon with their spears when he gave the signal and that the injustice towards Tamar should be avenged. I immediately realized the grave danger that Amnon was in and I rushed back to the camp as quickly as possible and tried to warn him. Amnon was merry because of the wine he drank and he laughed at me. Before I even knew what was happening Absalom servants grabbed Amnon and stabbed him with their spears. The rest us were shocked by what happened and all of us ran to our mules and fled.

A call from one of the lookouts comes to the men sitting on the veranda. "Men approaching from the South!" Jonadab stares at the approaching men. "Look the kings sons are coming! As I have said they are not all dead!" David stares at the group of men and recognize he's sons. He runs out towards them weeping in joy. "Daniel, Adonijah it is good to see you! Shephatiah, Ithream, and Shimea you are all alive! Shobab, Nathan come here and hug me!" The group men hug each other in tears and laughter. David turns towards the oldest in the group. "Daniel, where is Absalom?" Daniel stares in the direction they had come from. "When the servants killed our brother we had all fled in fear of our lives. They must have killed him also." David speaks softly. "No. Your brother was the one that planned this treacherous thing."

Jonadab joins the group of men. "My king I overhead the men when they spoke of Amnon's murder. They were going to Geshur after they killed Amnon." David calls Hushai. "Send a group of men to Baal Bezor. See what they can find out about Absalom and he's servants. If possible bring back Amnon body.

From this day I banish Absalom from entering the city again!"

"It has been almost three years since Absalom has been away from the city." The thin grey man scratches he's wispy beard. "All is working according to the plan. We must just be patient." The group of men nod their heads in agreement. "What about Joab?" Ahithophel turns towards the speaker. "I have already spoken to him. He suspects nothing. He has told me that the king longs for Absalom to return but he will not admit to it and have kept he's decree to banish he's own son. Joab did tell me however that he has fabricated a plan for the safe return of Absalom"

The man that spoke seem more at ease. "There are also some people in the tribes of Benjamin that has spoken their dismay concerning King David. They have not forgotten the murder of the Hittite five years ago." Ahithophel lets he's last sentence hang for a while and then he continues. "I want you to go back to your tribes and prepare them for a new king. When Absalom returns I will advise him on matters to gain the peoples trust."

The King war general lifts he's cup to the man sitting across the table. "To all the battles won and the ones to come." The big man smiles and lifts he's cup. "To king David, may the Lord be he's strength forever." Joab takes a sip of the sweet wine and wipes he's mouth with the back of he's hand.

"I have sent my servants to Tekoa. They have brought back a wise woman to assist me in the matter with King David and Absalom." Benaiah takes a sip of the fresh grape juice in he's cup. He has always preferred juice rather than taking strong drink. Joab looks at the battle scarred man before him. He knows that Benaiah was pondering on the troublesome matter between King David and he's son Absalom. "What has Absalom said Joab? Does he want to return?" Joab stretches he's legs out before him. "He wants to return. He has told me that although he has felt no remorse for he's actions in killing Amnon he also misses he's father."

Benaiah swirls the juice around in he's cup and then takes another sip. "What about the woman from Tekoa? What is your plan with her?" Joab leans closer to Benaiah folding he's arms across he's chest. He had hoped that Benaiah would further delve into the matter. "The woman will act as someone that has been in mourning for a long time because of her children. She will seek the king for advice. The matter will not withstand the fact that her plea will actually force the King to change he's mind about Absalom."

Benaiah puts he's empty clay cup aside and puts he's massive arms on the table. "That sounds confusing. Joab I can see that you have mulled this matter over and that your intentions are good but don't you think King David will suspect something is erroneous?

He also knows that you have already pursued this matter with a determined persistence."

Joab pours more wine into he's cup and stares into the distance. "It would be best for Absalom to return. I have heard that some of the tribes have conspired that he is the next suitable king over Israel. Rumours like that can only be dangerous in a situation like this." Benaiah smiles a rare smile. "King David will still reign for long time over Israel. I will defend he's honor against anyone who says different." Joab looks at the big man over the rim of he's cup.

"I would not want to be the man that challenges your credence."

David had dealt with more than nine different public complaints over the course of the day and he was starting to feel tired. "My king there is a woman that has come from Tekoa for your counsel in a matter concerning her sons. David takes the linen cloth from the offered basin and wipes he's forehead. "Let her enter and stand before me so that I can listen to her grievance."

Hushai gives the instruction to the guard to let the woman enter. A woman dressed in bereavement garb enters the throne room. Although her whole apparel speaks of mourning her face expresses an intellectual core strength. She falls onto her face and cries out before the king.

"Help, O king!" David did not anticipate the women sudden cry for help. "What troubles you woman?" The woman speaks to David but keeps her face downcast staring at the ground showing respect.

"I am a widow for my husband is dead. I had two sons but they fought while working in the field. The fight was serious and there was no one to part them. The one struck the other and killed he's brother."

An image of Absalom and Amnon comes to David's mind but does not interrupt the woman. "My whole family has now risen up against me and has asked me to deliver my son so that he may be executed for he's deed. I cannot allow this for if this is done there will be no seed left to carry the name of my husband on this earth. Remember the Lord Yahweh and do no permit anyone to take vengeance on my son that is left to me." The words of the prophet Nathan still echoes in the embers of he's inner thoughts. Yahweh had spoken out against he's house and since that day things had altered in he's household. He was still angry at Absalom for the act that he had committed. The face of Uriah the Hittite comes before David and he shakes he's head to clear the image.

"I have heard your plea. Go to your house and do not fear no more. If anyone troubles you send them to me for I the king of Israel has commanded it." The woman looks up at him from the ground and David cannot help but to look into her eyes. Something about her appeal seemed surreal. "My king may I put another matter before you?" David nods he's head. "You may." The woman gets up from the ground. "We will surely die and become like water spilled on the ground which cannot be collected again." The king nods in agreement. "You are a wise woman and those words are true." The woman bows before David an act of acknowledgement and gratitude. "You have heard my plea today and you have acted as an angel of Yahweh concerning what is good and what is evil. You have not condemned my son although he had committed a foul deed. May the Lord our Yahweh be with you."

The words the woman speaks touches David's heart. Joab had also tried to speak with him regarding the return of Absalom but he would not hear anything of it. Suddenly it dawned on him. Joab! "Woman. I want to ask you a question and I do not want you to hide anything from me." The woman shakes her head in agreement. "Certainly great king." It suddenly all seem so clear to him. "Have my general Joab asked you to come and speak to me? Is he's hand in this matter that you have brought before me?" The woman takes a deep breath and David sees the answer in her stricken face even before she gives words to it. "You are wise my king and I will not hold any truth from you. Joab did approach me and he told me all that I spoke with you. He asked me to do this for you are a wise king and have discerned this matter that have been before you."

David beckons toward he's servant. "Hushai ask Joab to come before me he should not be too far off." David turns back to the woman. "You have acted wisely. Go now and may the Lord Yahweh bless you." The woman leaves the palace and Hushai returns with Joab. "My king you have asked for me." David looks at he's general. There had been so many killings in the past years. He had never passed any further judgment on Joab when he had killed Abner. He knew now that judgment would still be passed but not by him. He had too much blood on he's own hands. "All right Joab; I grant you this. Go and bring back Absalom." The general falls down on he's face before David. "My request have found favour in your eyes my king. You have granted your servants request. I will travel to Geshur today."

David lifts he's hand. "Let him return to he's house but he may not see my face until I ask for him."

Chapter 16

The early morning sun rays touch the top of the dunes and shepherds take their flocks from the city gates. The men from the other cities seeking the council of the king had already started to gather at the city gates of David. Absalom walks forward onto the platform at the main gate. The horses pulling he's charioteers neigh nervously. The men accompanying him calm the horses down. Absalom turns towards the waiting people and faces the man in the front. "What City are you from?" A man with a colourful robe steps forward. "I am Hitarja from the tribe of Benjamin from the city of Hebron. I have come to speak to the king about the Philistines that invade my grazing area near the mountain of Gilboa."

Ahithophel had given Absalom clear instruction what to do with the people arriving at the gates to see the king. Absalom smiles inwardly. When he had arrived back in the city it was Athithophel had taken him under he's council and had introduced him to some of the elders of Israel. He was also invited to some of the meetings that these elders had called. People started to take note of him for Ahithophel gave him many advice surrounding the council of the elders. Ahithophel had instructed him to use he's time wisely in he's father absence. He's father still refused to see him and Absalom found that he's disdain for he's father had grown over the years. Two years had already gone by since he's return to the city and Athithophel had told him to be patient.

Absalom lifts he's hand to quite the man before him as well as the rest of the people seeking council from the king. "I am

Absalom, King David's son. The king is currently indisposed and therefore he cannot tend to your matters." A groan goes up from the ranks for some had travelled as far as Damascus to speak to the king. "Do not be troubled. I have been appointed as judge over this land. Anyone who has any suit or case can come to me. I will hear it and bring justice!" He looks at the man standing before him. "Do not be trouble for I will send a war party to defend the land of your fathers!"

"The time has come. Go to your father and ask him if you can return to Hebron."

Ahithophel rubs he's palms together. "My spies are ready and they have been acting as informants. When you return to Hebron the people will announce you as king over Hebron and the tribes of Israel will reunite behind you." Absalom slams he's fist on the door in frustration. "I have sent my servants to Joab so that he would come to me that I can send him to my father and speak on my behalf. He has ignored my calls."

Ahithophel nods he's head in agreement. "I have been your father counsellor in the city of Giloh for many years. He has always sent Joab to do he's bidding. Do not get angry. Joab will come to you before the sun sets tomorrow." Absalom had learned to trust the words of Ahithophel and he steadily sits down. "How will you make this happen?" Ahithophel smiles wryly. "The man needs a reason to come to you. Let's give him a reason. Your fields are next to Joab's right? Tonight we will send your servants to set it on fire and he will know that the order came from you."

Absalom pushes he's hair back from he's brow. "He is going to be furious but that will definitely get he's attention. I will call on my servants to go there tonight."

Joab was furious. He was already in bed when he's servants came and awoke him screaming that a fire was burning in he's fields. He quickly got dressed and rushed out to the fields. They struggled into the early morning hours to get the fire under control. He's anger was roused when one of the servants came and told him that he had seen Absalom servants set fire to the fields.

Without washing the grime of he's face and clothes he sets of towards Absalom's dwelling. Two servants greet him at the door but Joab pushes past them. "Absalom I want to talk to you! Absalom!" Absalom comes out of he's room still yawning and rubbing he's eyes. "Why are you making all this noise so early in the morning Joab?" Joab stands with he's arms folded before Absalom. "You know why I am here! Why did your servants set my field alight?" Absalom yawns again and sits down on a silk pillow.

"O, that. Well for one, now I have your attention." Joab takes a step towards Absalom. "Don't play games with me boy." Absalom looks at he's father war general with mild interest. "I am sorry about your fields Joab. I have asked you twice to come to me but you have ignored me. I need you to go and speak to my father." Joab still seems angry but says nothing and continue to glare at him. Absalom face becomes more solemn. "Why did I come back to the city Joab? Why didn't I just stay in Geshur? My father has not spoken to me for two years!"

Joab shakes he's head at Absalom. "Do not play coy with me! I have seen you at the city gates. There are many that come to you for your judgment over their matters. I see the people kissing your hand and there are a lot of rumours that is going around." Absalom seem to ignore Joab's last remark. "I have children that cannot see their own grandfather. He has not even seen he's gran daughter since she was born." Joab feels the anger fade away and sees the hurt in Absalom's eyes. "Please go and speak with my father Joab. If he sees any iniquity in my eyes when I stand before him he can execute me." Joab turns around and walks out of Absalom's house and stops at the door.

"I will go to your father for your daughter sake. You owe me for the field that you burnt down."

Bathsheba hands softly strokes David's bearded cheek. She nestles into the embrace of he's arms enjoying the time spent with him. David's eyes are closed. He thinks about Absalom's request and visit. Bathsheba interrupts he's thoughts. "You forgave Absalom and gave him permission to return to Hebron?" David pulls Bathsheba closer to him. "He came to me and asked me to forgive him. He told me that he had made a vow with Yahweh when he was still in Geshur."

Bathsheba lifts her head onto her palm of her hand resting on her elbow and stares at her husband with a frown. "What vow did he make?" David opens he's eyes and looks into he's wife's beautiful face. "He told me that if Yahweh had allowed him to return to city that he would serve Him diligently. He has grown quite popular with the people and he wants to take he's family to Hebron." Bathsheba lays her head back onto the silk pillow.

"I do not trust him. He has been dealing behind your back. You know that he has appointed himself as judge over the land and given advice over matters that the king should tend to." David strokes he's wife's hair and smiles at her. "He is my son and I have allowed it. He has found favour with men and has been introduced to the elders of Israel. It has given me more time to spend with you and Solomon. Besides Ahithopel my advisor form Giloh has spent time with him."

Bathsheba sighs. "You know that neither Absalom nor any of the others would be the next king. The Lord has spoken he's words over Solomon. He should be the next king." David takes a deep sigh. "I know but that is something that we do not have to think about now. Solomon is still a child and I am not stepping down as king yet to make way for the next generation."

A knock at the door interrupts their conversation. "My king!" The tone of Hushai voice sounds urgent. "What is it Hushai?" Hushai quickly continues. "A terrible thing has happened! Absalom was announced king in Hebron!"

David jumps out of he's bed as if stung by a hornet. "Absalom? David staggers but the hand of Bathsheba steadies him. "Hushai. Call on my generals and meet me in the throne chambers." He quickly puts he's robes on he's mind racing. How could it be? Absalom king? David rushes to the throne room.

Joab, Benaiah, Eleazar and the other war generals are already gathered. David greets the men he had fought and bled with. Joab steps forward. "My king the people of Hebron has announced Absalom as king. I have heard that some of the Israel tribes in the city hearts have rejoiced at this news and an uproar has started outside the palace walls. Athithopel has conspired against you and stands with Absalom"

David's mind races in different directions as Joab continues. "He has assembled he's charioteers and he's group of men and they are heading this way with a large portion of the tribes that have joined him." Absalom had deceived him. He had deceived all of them! That was why he had been meeting with the men at the gates. Athithopel had been conspiring against him. He had a lot of power especially with the elders of Israel. All along. The tribes of Israel were also in two minds. There was a lot of talk after the death of Uriah. Absalom had always resented him for the situation with Tamar. Absalom lied to him about he's vow with Yahweh. The Lord had told him through the prophet Nathan that someone in he's own family would rise against him. David turns towards he's generals.

"We must leave the city immediately." A loud murmur arises from the ranks before him. "Gather your families. Absalom had planned this treacherous thing over four years and has almost the whole Israel behind him." Benaiah speaks softly and yet there is an underlying foreboding tone in his voice. "Not all of Israel. We are your servants and will do what you command!"

"I do not understand why my father would also leave the ark in city? According to the priests Zadok and Abiathar he had commanded them to bring it back."

Athithopel takes Absalom by he's elbow. "He was afraid that the men carrying the ark would slow him down. Why worry about it? We have the ark of the Lord and Israel will be content with it." Absalom sits down on he's father throne. "I have heard that when my father travelled over the brook of Kidron that the people of Israel wept when he was leaving the city." Absalom turns towards Athithopel. "I have not won the hearts of all the people in the city yet. He's mighty men had gone with him and I am sure he is already busy with a plan to take back the city." Absalom prompts his father old advisor. "What council do you give me in these matters Athithopel?"

The Giloh advisor smiles he's crooked smile. "You are right. Not all the people have yet turned against your father. We must make them see that the hand of Lord is with you." Absalom shakes he's head. "I never made a covenant with Yahweh. How can I prove something that is not so?" Athithopel sits down next to Absalom. "Your father has left some of he's concubines here at the palace. Everyone knows that the prophet Nathan had said that the one that will arise against your father would sleep with he's own wife's in the sight of Israel." Absalom stares at the advisor the genius of his suggestion developing in his mind. Athithopel steadily continues. "I have erected a tent on the top of the palace roof. Go now to the tent and sleep with he's wives in the sight of Israel.

The people and the elders will see that the words of the prophet came true and it will strengthen the bond with the people."

David and the people with him continued their exile away from the city. They had reached the foot of the mount Olivet. They were walking barefoot and David had covered he's head as he started to ascend up the mountain. All the people followed the king's example and covered their heads as their king went up the mountain.

The king needed time alone. David weeps as he ascends up the mount Olivet. He thinks back on he's younger years when Saul was after him and he and he's men had stayed in the wilderness. He thinks back on he's days spent with Jonathan. The sweetest memories suddenly seem like the days when he was a shepherd boy tending he's father flock.

David stops and falls onto he's knees. "Lord. You have always protected me. You have never left my side. You protected me once when I was in the wilderness. Please protect us now. I know that I have sinned when I killed Uriah. You had told me that this would happen over my family. I ask that you turn the council of Athithopel to foolishness."

David hears someone approaching. "King David." The familiar voice of Hushai calls out to him. David sees he's servant approach. He's coat is rent and he has dust on he's head as a sign of lamentation. "Benaiah told me that I must come up here and meet with you?" David nods at he's servant.

"Hushai you have been in my service since the day I arrived in Hebron. You are more than a friend to me than many others. You know that I have sent Zadok and Abiathar back to the City with their sons and the ark?" Hushai nods he's head.

"Yes my king; the men have been talking about your decision." David stares out over the mountain tops. "I want you to return to the city and council Absalom."

Hushai eyes stretches wide. "I do not understand my king?" David rests he's hand on he's servants arm. "I have asked the Lord to guide me in this. You must return and give him the council that I will give to you. I send you back so that we can defeat the council of Athithopel. If you need to give me important information you must give it to Zadok and Abiathar. They will send their sons Ahimaaz and Jonathan to share your information with me.

Go now. The Lord will be with you."

The elders of Israel are gathered in the palace with Absalom. The rest of Israel where crowding the streets and all around the walls of city of David to hear the council of their new king.

Absalom had gone and slept with he's father's wife's in front of the whole Israel. As Athithopel had predicted the people of Israel as well as the elders had approved of this according to the word of the prophet Nathan. Talk of war with David among the people was eminent. Absalom had decided to call all of Israel together for he's first public council as king. He points at he's trusted advisor Athithopel. "Speak out before the people of Israel and give your wise council in the matters before us."

Athithopel bows slightly before Absalom. "My lord; Let me choose twelve thousand men on this day and we will go out after David this night. We must go after him while he is weak and running from us. I will take them men after him and we will only kill him. We will give the rest of the people the choice to come back and serve you or we will kill all of them." The words are met with head shaking in agreement and the advisor continues. "There will be no further wars for all people will then live in peace under your rule my king." The nods of approval can also be been seen by the elders and Absalom smiles at he's advisor.

"Once again your wise words have brought unity." An interruption at the back of the palace hall brings Absalom to a stop.

"Yahweh save the king! Yahweh save the king!"

A man with tattered robes and dust on he's face fall before Absalom feet.

"Hushai? Why are you not with my father? What are you doing here?" Every eye was now focused on the figure before the king's throne. Hushai had been in King David service since he's reign in Hebron. He had earned the respect of the elders as an advisor over the years and the people sat quietly waiting on King David advisor to speak. "I have come to serve the one who Yahweh and all the people of Israel choose." Athithopel spits on the ground before the dust worn man.

"Be careful my king. I smell a traitor!" Absalom addresses the man prostrated before him. "Is that true Hushai? Is this the respect that you show my father who has also been your friend? Why did you not go with him?"

Hushai keeps he's head on the floor. "My king I have served your father all those years. When he had asked me to bring the lady Bathsheba to he's chambers he had also put my name in shame. I have stayed with your father out of duty but when I heard that you were made king my heart rejoiced. Now I have come to serve the son as I have once served the father."

Absalom sees the approving nods of the elders in palace at the wise words of Hushai. He decides to press the matter at hand. "You have heard what Athithopel has advised us to do. What do you say in this matter?" Hushai lifts he's head from the ground. "My king; the council that Athithopel has given you is not good at this time."

Athithopel steps towards Hushai. "Traitor!" Absalom lifts he's hands. "Wait! Let him speak." Hushai turns he's head towards the elders. "I only say this because we all know David and he's mighty men. When I left him he was like a bear that had lost he's whelps! He will not stay encamped in one place and will hide in a cave or some valley and you will not find him. If you send our people out after him he will surly attack them and strike them down for he is a man trained in war. He had dwelled the outskirts of the city for many years and the battle ground is in his favour."

A loud murmur arise from the elders and Hushai wait for the noise the quite down before he continues. "I say that the whole of Israel must gather from Dan even to Beer-Sheba so that we will be as many as the sands of the sea. When your father hears this he will flee and hide. We will find him and he's men hiding in a city like he did long-ago. We will then take ropes and bind it around the city and pull down the city walls. None of he's mighty men will be left and no one will say that you have sent them into a slaughter because you chose all the men of Israel to stand against David and not just twelve thousand."

Absalom can see by the expression on the elder's faces as well as a cheer that had gone up in the palace that the people had heeded to Hushai council. "You have spoken very wisely." Absalom turns towards the elders and the rest of the people. "The Lord had brought this man back to the city to council us in these matters.

We will follow the council of Hushai for he has spoken wisely."

David and he's men had travelled to Bahurim and he was surprised when along the way the servant of Mephibosheth, Ziba met with them. The man stood beside the road with a caravan of wild donkeys with bread hanging from the saddle bags. "What are you doing here and where is your master?"

Ziba bows before David. "I have come to bring these donkeys so that your royal household can ride on them. I have brought you food and water." David accepts the kindness. "Thank you faithful servant but what about your master?" Ziba looks at David nervously. "When he had heard that Absalom had become king he had ordered me to leave. He told me to take what I wanted for he believed that the elders of Israel would restore the kingdom of Saul and grant him more riches. I have taken these donkeys and food to honor you King David."

David puts he's hand on the servants head. "All that I have given Mephibosheth I now give to you." Ziba again bows before David. "You are the true king of Israel. May I find more favour in your eyes."

As they approached Bahurim a man comes out of one of the houses and starts to curse David. He picks up stones and threw it at the king as well as David's men. Benaiah draws he's sword but David stops him.

"Wait."

He turns towards the cursing man. "Who are you and why are you acting like this." The man did not seem bothered by David's men and cursed as he spoke to the king. "My name is Shimai! I am of the family of Saul! I have waited for this day a very long time! The Lord has now returned upon you all the blood that you have shed of the house of Saul! The Lord had taken your kingdom away and He has given it into the hands of Absalom."

Abishai the son Zeruiah, Joab's brother also draws he's sword. "My king why do you let this dog continue to curse you like this?" David looks at the cursing man and the rest of he's men. "My own son is seeking my life because the Yahweh had commanded that it would be so. Let this man curse for it may be that Yahweh has sent him to curse me like this today. Maybe Yahweh will look upon me and my affliction and use this day of cursing and turn it around for He's good."

David and he's men left the city. The man called Shimai kept on cursing David until he left the city. They set up camp just outside the city of Bahurim. David was extremely exhausted. Just before he fell asleep he prayed silently.

"Yahweh. Come to me soon. Please hear my plea of anguish."

The morning broke and as they were breaking camp one of the lookouts called out. "Two men approaching from the South!" David climbs onto the rock face next to the lookout and stares down at the two figures. "That looks like Ahimaaz son of Zadok and Jonathan son of Abiathar!" David climbs down the rock face to meet the approaching men. "Greetings in the name of Yahweh! What news do you bring?"

The two men greet David and without any further hesitation they bring the message from the city of David. "My king; Hushai had instructed Absalom as you had told him to do. Yahweh had given Hushai favour above the council that Athithopel had given him. He has instructed every man from Dan to Beer – Sheba to gather and pass over the Jordan! Your servant Hushai have advised that you and all your men do not stay here at the folds in the wilderness but also cross over the Jordan."

David gathers he's generals around him. "We shall travel to Mahanaim and wait until Absalom has crossed over the Jordan."

The next day they travelled to Mahanaim and they were met by one of the elders of the city called Barzillai a man about eighty years of age. "My king David. I am Barzillai the Gileadite from Rogelim. It is an honor to serve you. You and your men will be supplied with all that you need. Stay as long as you need in the city." David took the old man by he's hand and bowed before him. "May the Lord bless you for your kindness. I shall not forget you."

The men supplied David and he's men with bedding and bowls and articles of pottery. They brought wheat and barley, flour and roasted grain with beans and lentils. There was honey, curds, sheep and cheese for David and he's men to eat. They were hungry and David was thankful for all that they received. Yahweh still provided even under duress.

That next morning David and all he's men gathered with the followers that had come with David to Mahanaim. "Absalom will come with many charioteers. We will wait for them at the edge of the woods of Ephraim. They would have to travel through the woods of Ephraim and the charioteers will slow him down. We will wait for them in the woods and then ambush them. The Lord Yahweh will go before us." David calls Joab, Abiahai and Ittae the Gittite. "You will circle around the woods with your men. Should any one come upon Absalom do not harm him. He is still my son and I will deal with him. I will go out before the men in the middle of the wood."

Joab looks at King David. "My king it is not wise for you to go out in front of the men. The people of Israel do not care for us and our lives are of no worth to them. If they see you in the front lines they will do everything in their power to kill you for your live is worth ten thousand times more." David sees he's other generals shake their head in agreement.

"You are precise. I will not go out before the men but remember be gentle with my son."

Absalom and all the gathered men of Israel had crossed over the Jordan. They were now in the land of Gilead at the edge of the wood of Ephraim. He's appointed general Amasa had reported that he had received a message from Hushai. They had found Athithopel dead in Giloh. He had hanged himself.

Absalom felt no remorse for the old fool had served he's purpose and it was because of the council of Hushai that they were advancing. "King Absalom. We have arrived at the wood of Ephraim. We shall travel through the woods towards Mahanaim." Absalom does not really care if they travelled through the woods or over the ocean. No one could battle against the hordes that was gathered with him; not even he's father and he's mighty men.

"Tell the front runners to open up a path through the woods for the charioteers. We will follow as soon as it has been cleared." Amasa acknowledges Absalom instruction and bows he's head and then heads off towards the front ranks of the army to give instruction to the generals and the axe men. Absalom could not wait to see he's father's face when they met in battle. He's father had commanded the army of Israel over fifty years but did not make use of the charioteers the way that he had learned in Geshur. He would show him today! He will ensure that the legacy of he's father and he's mighty men come to an end.

The sound of axes shopping into the wood comes from the front and Absalom slowly steers he's charioteer along the edge of the wood. The men start to go into the woods of Ephraim. He waits as they clear the necessary lumber for them to enter with the charioteers. The sound of the cutting axes suddenly comes to a stop. A scream fills the air and then suddenly a battle cry sound from the woods of Ephraim.

"Yahweh is our defence!" Absalom reigns in the leather throngs of he's charioteer.

"Death to David and he's men!" Absalom draws he's sword and enters the clearing that the front men had hacked away. Men are attacking from all sides. Absalom swings he's sword to the left and the right he's horses whinnying wildly in the heat of the battle and turmoil. Wave after wave they attacked and yet the men of David kept them at bay. Bodies were starting to pile up and soon there was a heap of bodies covering the forest floor where the trees were hacked away. Absalom's bloody sword clung to he's hand. He's horses had been cut down and he's chariot overturned. The men of Israel kept on battling bravely but it seemed like an invisible hand stood against them and more Israel men went down. Absalom did not see he's father in the midst of battle. The battle had started in the early morning hours and had continued right through the day.

Late that evening Absalom heard a trumpet blow. The remaining men were retreating. "How can this be? We have outnumbered them by far!" A mule without its rider comes running by closely and Absalom grabs its reigns. He climbs onto it and start of towards the Jordan River. He will go back just beyond the wood clearing and regroup with he's men. A warrior jumps out into the path of Absalom and swings at him with he's sword. The attack seem half-hearted and he easily blocks the attack with he's sword. The mule is spooked by the sudden appearance of the warrior and the panic stricken animal runs into the bush. The mule runs wildly; and branches strikes Absalom face and blinds him momentarily. Suddenly as if a colossal hand plucked him from the saddle he is jerked from the mule with a force by he's hair. He comes to an abrupt stop he's feet hanging from the ground.

Absalom looks around him. He was hanging from the branches of an Oak tree. He tenderly feels where the branches of the oak tree was entwine into he's hair and tries to free himself. The mule had continued its wild flight into the bushes and was whining now as it continued its crazed flight. Absalom again tries to untangle himself from the branches but every move he makes seem to worsen he's quandary.

The warrior whom had caused the donkey to flee wildly, appears in he's fringe view. He walks slowly towards him and comes to a standstill in the pathway way just below him. The soldier holds a javelin in he's hands but does not advance towards him. Absalom state of helplessness is replaced by a feeling of antagonism. "Come and finish it!" The warrior turns away from him. "Your father does not want you killed. I will find help." With that he disappears down the pathway. Absalom holds on to the branch above him, trying to lessen the pain in he's scalp thinking about the last words of the soldier.

"Why would he's father still not want him dead?"

Joab wipes he's sword on he's tunic. He stares at the bodies lying scatter in the wood. There were a sea of bodies and in some areas it was difficult to make out between the trees and the piles of bodies. At least twenty thousand men had died. A warrior comes running out of the dense forest calling he's name and Joab quickly turns and raises he's sword.

"General Joab!" Joab lowers he's sword. It was one of he's own men. "I saw Absalom captured! His hair entwined in the branches of an oak tree. He was still hanging from he's hair when I left he's side." Joab grabs the warrior by he's shoulders. "What do you mean you left him there? Why did you not kill him when you saw this?" The warrior seems confused. "King David had clearly given he's instruction that he should not be killed." Joab knew that as long as Absalom was still alive that he would try and regroup. It was David who did not want to see the truth that Absalom despised him and would continue he's rebellion until the king was dead. He knew that Absalom chose Amasa as he's general over he's armies and as long as Absalom reigned it would stay like that.

"Show me where he is." Joab and some of he's arms bearers follow the young soldier. As they come around a bend they are greeted with a pair of feet kicking wildly in the air. Joab walks right in front of Absalom. The king son stares violently at Joab.

"You!"

Before Absalom can say another word Joab plunges a javelin into he's heart. Joab takes another javelin from he's arms bearer and repeats the action twice. Joab turns to he's men. "Finnish it!" They take their spears and stab it through the body of Absalom until he's body hangs lifelessly. Joab stares at the figure and then commands he's men to cut Absalom loose.

"Take he's body down and cast in that large pit we passed on our way in the forest and cover it with rocks." Joab takes out he's battle horn and blows loudly on it. The sound carries through the wood. He's army would hear the sound and return from their pursuit after Israel. Absalom was dead and the war was over.

Ahimaaz comes walking down the pathway with soldiers behind him. He stares at the body of Absalom lying next to a large pit at the edge of the wood. "What happened here?" Joab shrugs and turns towards the working men. "He attacked us and we defended ourselves." Ahimaaz notices the leaves and twigs stuck in Absalom's tangled hair. "Does King David know that he's son is dead?" Joab shakes he's head. "I will sent one of my servants to bring the news." Joab calls a man standing close by and young a Cushite comes bowing before him.

"Go and tell King David that he's son is dead." The Cushite bows again and then start running in the direction of Mahanaiam. Ahimaaz muses for a while still looking at the lifeless body before him and then start to walk in the direction of the city Mahanaiam. "Where are you going?" Ahimaaz stop and turn back towards Joab. "I will run behind the Cushite that will bring the news of Absalom death to the king." Joab throws he's hands in the air. "Why would your run after the servant that I have just sent to bring the dreaded news? I advise you not to be foolish and take this news to the king. The news will not bring any reward!"

Ahimaaz ignores Joab admonition and turns around and start to jog in the direction the servant had disappeared calling over he's shoulder. "I told the king that I would bring him news of his son no matter the rudiments thereof." Joab shakes he's head in disapproval and turns back towards he's men.

"Make sure that you lay a very large heap of stones in the pit so that no scavengers can get to he's body."

David sits between the two gates of the City of Mahanaiam. He stares into the distance in the direction of the woods of Ephraim he's thoughts turning back to he's younger years when he had gone hunting with Jonathan. The watchman on the platform on the city gates suddenly cry out. "There is a man running alone toward the City!"

David gets up from he's chair and stares in the direction the watchmen is pointing. "If he is alone then he is bringing good news!" He's eyes trace the figure of the running man approaching quickly. "My King there is another man running close behind the first man also coming from the east!" David turns and sees the other lonely figure approaching the city. "He must also be bringing news." The watchmen stare at the second approaching man. "I think it is Ahimaaz approaching from the East." David smiles at the watchman nodding he's head in agreement. Both men are now in view and Ahimaaz seem to be the fitter of the two for he overtakes the man that led and arrives first breathing heavily.

"King David. Blessed be the Lord our Yahweh who has delivered you from the enemies who has raised up against you. We have won against Israel!" David's merriment seem well disguised and Ahimaaz dreads the next question. "How about Absalom is he safe?" The Cushite that Joab had sent also arrives before the king. Ahimaaz cannot bring it to he's heart to tell David about Absalom's death. "Joab had sent me and the servant standing before you and when I left there was a great tumult but I do not know what it was about."

Come and stand here by me that the servant of Joab can speak. The Cushite takes a deep breath and start talking. "My king. There is good news! Your armies has defeated the Israel army and they have drawn back over the Jordan River." The Cushite had not heard the question that David had asked Ahimaaz. David sees that the Cushite did not hear he's question and prompts him. "Is my son Absalom safe?" The Cushite misreads the king anxiety and speaks with pride when he replies. "May all your enemies that rise up against you end up like him."

David face becomes ashen. He does not utter a word. He slowly turns towards the city gate and starts of in the direction of he's chambers. Ahimaaz calls out to him. "King David!" David voice comes out as a hoarse whisper filled with heart ache.

"My son Absalom, O my son if only I had died in your place."

Joab takes he's horse by the bit and steers it towards the watering pit in the middle of the city. The Cushite that had brought the message to the king approaches him.

"Have you deliver the message to the king?" The Cushite salutes he's general. "Yes general I delivered the message as you have ordered me to. The king was deeply moved when I told him of the death of Absalom and he started to weep." Joab stares at the Cushite in disbelieve. "He wept?" The Cushite licks he's lips nervously. "Yes general. The people says..." Joab encourages the messenger to continue. "What does the people say?" The Cushite looks troubled but finishes he's sentence. "They say that it seem like the king would have been more pleased if all the people that fought for him today had died instead of he's traitor son Absalom."

Joab scratches the side of he's head. "Where is the king?" The Cushite points in the direction of David's chambers. "He has gone to the chambers that the elders had prepared when we arrived my general." Joab starts of towards the direction the Cushite had pointed. The image that David was portraying was not a good one. He needed all he's men to take advantage of the situation to go back to the city. He's city! The city of David! Every moment that they spent outside the city created the opportunity for someone else to take he's place as king.

Joab knocks on the king's door. "Who is it?" The voice of David sounds thick with emotion. "It is I, Joab my king." The wind picks up and Joab can barely hear the kings reply. "You may enter." David sits on a wooden chair staring at the opposite wall. "The men have returned and would like to see their king after the glorious victory."

David continue staring at the wall and the words are almost imperceptible. "My son Absalom why did you have to die?" Joab tries to hide the annoyance in he's voice. "The men fought for you today and you disgrace them by weeping for the man that slept with your wives in front of the whole Israel and drove you from your city? It seems that you would have been pleased if your men died and Absalom stayed alive."

David lifts he's head but says nothing. Joab anger stars to show in he's voice as he continues he's aggrieved words. "You have humiliated all your men today!" David turns towards he's general he's anger also flaring. "How Joab? Did they lose their son today?" Joab shakes he's head in anger. "These men have fought with you since your youth! In their actions they have saved the lives today of the rest of your sons and daughters and your wives! It seems to them that you love those who hate you and you hate those who love you!" The words seem to bring some inkling of reality to the king and Joab presses his advance.

"We should journey back towards the city of David. Go out and speak to your servants and the men that fought for you. Lest they lose heart and none will stay with you for another night." David slowly rises from the chair he sat on. Joab approaches David and wipes off the tears on the king face with he's sleeve. He seemed a long way from the warrior that defeated Goliath and the grey in he's beard had not eluded Joab. David seem to rise from he's wretchedness and also wipes he's cheeks with the back of he's hand. David walks out of the house in the direction of the city gate. The lookout blows the rams-horn and a call goes up in the city.

"The king is sitting in the gateway!" A great roar goes up and men approach the king in the city gates to come before David.

The debate had gone on for more than two days and many of the elders seem annoyed. An elder with a balding hairline addresses the people in the council room again.

"Yahweh has been with King David and have made him a mighty warrior. King David has saved us from the hand of all our enemies, from the hand of the Philistines and he fled because Absalom was he's son and he did not want more bloodshed. It was us that anointed Absalom for we were misled." A clamour rise in the chamber as the elders once again start to debate the words that the bald chief had spoken. The doors of the chambers open and the priests Zadok and Abiathar enter into the council room. All the elders turn to the two men entering the room.

Zadok stands in the middle of the room before the group of men. "We have been sent by King David to speak this matter before you." The bald elder that that spoke to the rest of the group now addresses Zadok. "What words come from the king?" Zadok clears he's throat.

"The king wants to know why you are the last people in Israel still debating he's return? The rest of Israel have granted that king David is still the rightful king. Thus says the king. "You are my brothers. You are my bone and my flesh. Why then are you the last to bring back the king?" (2 Samuel 19 v 11)

Zadok turns to the new appointed general Amasa. "The king speaks these words to you Amasa. Aren't you my bone and my flesh? God do so to me, and more also, if you aren't captain of the army before me continually instead of Joab." (2 Samuel 19 v 13)

One of the elders a small man with a crooked back speaks. "Is it true that King David wept for Absalom?" The rest of the elders sits quietly and listen. "Yes it is true. He wept like any other father would weep for the loss of he's son." The elder's converse among themselves and the bald man addresses Zadok. "Tell King David that he and all he's men must return to the city."

The mist lies thick on the river Jordan. The footfalls of the approaching men rise Plovers from their nests in the river beds. They fly away screeching their high pitched calls over the marching men heads. David and the men come to the edge of the river Jordan. A ferryboat appears like a Hippo out of the mist and the voice of Ziba the servant of Mephibosheth greets the king from the mist. "King David. I have come to take you and your household across the river."

Benaiah steps away from the king. He had drawn he's sword expecting an ambush. A caravan approaches the men and the old man from the city of Mahanaim steps out of a chariot. "Brazillai you have come to cross over to the City of David with me?" The old man approaches David. "I have thought about your offer to return to the city of David but I must decline. I am an old man. What good is it for me to go with you to the city?" David takes Brazillai's hand. "You have looked after me and my men when I was exiled from my city and now I will look after you." The old man smiles at David.

"My boy no one accept Yahweh looks after me. I have heard the songs of men and women and yet I can enjoy it no more. I have tasted good food and drink and yet today I cannot discern the taste between an apple and a fig. I am old and I will die in my City. I bring this man before you." A young man steps forward. "He's name is Chimham. Bestow all the goodness that you wanted on me on him." David hugs the old man and then kisses him on he's forehead. "It shall be done. May the Lord bless you forever more."

David and he's household climbs onto the ferry boat and cross the river Jordan. As they come closer to the other side yet another man's voice rises out of the misty morning. "King David! It is me Shimei! Please have mercy on me! I have sinned!" The ferry's bottom hits the sand bank on the other side and David steps from the boat. The man that swore and cursed him in Bahurim and threw him and he's men with rocks lies with he's face down in the sand before him.

Abishai, Joab's brother draws he's sword and steps out towards the man. "No Abishai!"

Abishai hesitates at he's king voice. "Has this man not cursed you? Shall he not be put to death?"

Shimei crawls with he's face down before David. "No one shall be put to death today. I am the king and have I not the right to decide whom I may have mercy on?" David turns towards Shimei. "I forgive you. You shall not die. Go in peace."

Shimei stares at David in disbelieve tears falling down he's cheeks. "Thank you my king. You are truly a king of Israel. A man after God own heart! May the Lord demonstrate He's mercy on you as you have shown mercy on me today." David and he's household and all he's men start their voyage and by mid-afternoon they arrive back in the city of David. Every man, woman and child greet the king with song as he passes along the way.

"The king has returned! May Yahweh bless the king!"

Mephibosheth hair and beard is un-kept and David almost doesn't recognize him. David had come back in to the city the day before and stood before the elders of Israel. All had blessed him in the name of Yahweh. David had given instruction to he's servants to prepare a house for the concubines that he had left behind. They were he's wife's no longer but it was not their fault for what had happened to them. He gave instruction that they were to be looked after but that no other man would ever enter into their house again.

After that he had called on Joab and he had told him that Amasa was to retain he's position as the head chief over the king's armies and that Joab would be he's second in charge. As David had anticipated the old veteran showed no expression and bowed low and then left the kings chamber without a word. Early the next morning a messenger had come to he's chamber and had told him that Mephibosheth had asked for a meeting with the king. He had a busy schedule and agreed to the proceedings. Now Mephibosheth was brought in and David look at the untidy man before him.

"Why did you not flee from the city when Absalom had besieged it?" Mephibosheth looks at the king with remorse on he's face "I was deceived my king. I was promised a donkey to ride on to go out of the city but no one brought me one."

David looks at the man sitting before him with a stern expression on he's face. "You have deceived yourself. I have already decided that all that I have given to you to be divided between you and you servant Ziba for he has served me well." Mephibosheth stares at the ground in shame. "I was wrong my king. Let my servant Ziba take all that you have given me for I do not deserve it." David dismissed the remorseful looking man and Mephibosheth servants takes him from the palace.

Next Amasa enters into the throne room. "Amasa. Please give report of the rebellion in Israel." The appointed general bows before he's king. "Yes my king. A man called Sheba a Benjamite had stirred up the people to follow him." A servant carrying a tray of fruit enters the room and puts it before the men. "I have also heard that many have followed this rebel." Amasa ignores the salacious fruit in front of him. "Those men that have followed are deceived by their greed and empty promises that Sheba has made." David takes a fig from the tray and stares at it. "Assemble the men of Judah for me within three days and come back and be present yourself."

The exile out of City had also been hard on David's family and he spent time with them especially Solomon and Bathsheba. After three days Amasa had still not returned as the king had instructed. David called on Abishai and Joab. "I have instructed Amasa to gather the men of Judah and go after the rebel Sheba but he had not returned yet. There is still a lot of uncertainty among the people of Israel and this man Sheba can do us more harm than Absalom had." Joab remained aloof in the conversation and Abishai responded before David. "We will take the men and pursue him my king."

They next morning they left the City with the some of the mighty men and travelled to Gibeon. It was here that Amasa and he's troop met up with Abishai and he's men. Abishai did not waste time with proper greetings. "Where have you been Amasa? The king have been waiting on your return." Amasa face is dust worn and he looks tired. "We ran into an army of Philistines and had to fight our way out." Joab approaches Amasa. Since the day king David had announced that Amasa would retain he's position as chief over all the generals he's hatred had grown towards David and Amasa. Joab deceptively embraces Amasa. "Are you in good health my brother?" Amasa is taken by surprise by Joab's action. "I am tired be we are ready to move towards the city of Abel."

Joab does not release Amasa but with he's right hand he quickly grabs the general by he's beard. With he's free hand he had slowly drawn he's dagger out of its sheath. "Abel you say?" Amasa gasp in pain and surprise. Joab had made a quick cut across he's throat with he's drawn dagger. Joab releases Amasa beard. Amasa grabs he's throat but wordlessly topless to the ground. The rest of the men come to a standstill when they see the body of Amasa in the road. Two warriors move he's body out of the way and put a garment over him. One of Joab men standing close to the body turn to the men. "Whoever favours Joab and is for King David follow Joab!"

The men leave the body of Amasa and continue their journey towards the city called Abel. They came to the City of Abel early the next morning and Joab instructed the men to break down the Southern wall to enter into the city. A call rang out from above the wall. "Joab! Joab! Listen!" Joab looked up above the ramparts and saw a woman staring at him. She spoke again. "Are you Joab?" Joab nodded and called back. "I am!" The woman now beckoned towards him. "Please come near that I may speak to you!" Abishai grabs he's brother's arm. "Be careful brother, it may be a trap!" Joab walks slowly to the rampart. "Are you Joab?" Joab looks up into the face of a woman with bright blue eyes. "I am." Joab's men all move closer to the rampart. "Hear the words that your maidservant has to say before you enter!" Joab silences he's men. "I am listening."

The woman continues. "In former times people would come to the City of Abel to seek guidance and solve their disputes. I am among the peaceful and faithful in Israel. You seek to destroy a city and a mother in Israel? Why would you swallow up the inheritance of Yahweh?"

Joab answers her he's voice booming out. "I can hear that you speak with wisdom old mother. I am not seeking to destroy the city but we are looking for a man that has rebelled against King David and that is taking refuge in Abel. I shall break down the walls if I have to but I will find this man!" The woman calls out over the rampart. "Who is this man?" Joab answers. "He's name is Sheba the son of Bichri and he has raised he's hand against King David!" For a moment all is quite then the woman voice carry down to them. "Wait down there, we will throw he's head down to you!" Joab looks at Abishai and he shrugs he's shoulders. "We will wait until the sun sits in the middle of the sky and if you have not kept your word we will break down the wall!"

Joab and he's men waited and they did not have to wait long. Before their shadows had moved much along the ground the woman call came again from the ramparts. "Now leave our city." A few moments later the head of a man they now assumed was Sheba rolled in the dirt before their feet. Joab looked at the face above him. "The Lord bless you for the wisdom that you have shown!" Joab gave the instruction and the trumpet sounded in the distance. "Let us return to city and the King!"

Chapter 17

"We have done as you have commanded my king. The servants have just finished with the numbers." Joab opens a papyrus scroll and reads it out before the king's council.

"In Israel there are eight hundred thousand men who fights for you my king. In Judah there is five hundred thousand men who stand for you my king."

David sits back on he's pillows. He's heart was troubled. He had given Joab the instruction to go out to all the tribes of Israel from Dan to Beer –Sheba to count the people and whom he had found favour with. It had taken them more than two moons to do this and in this time he had thought about he's intentions. Was it not Yahweh that had blessed him and delivered him from all he's enemies? Bathsheba had come to him a few days ago and had added to he's troubled heart.

"Why have you done this thing? Why have you given Joab instruction to number the people and find out who favoured you as king?" David had been busy looking over the plans that Solomon had drawn up for the temple to place the Ark when Bathsheba had interrupted him. He hesitated before he answered and when he did the answer sounded as dismal as the action that he had taken.

"I want to know how strong my army has become. Why do you ask this of me?" Bathsheba had looked at him and bemoaned. "Your army? David this is the Lords army. Had you forgotten who had brought you out behind your father's sheep?" David had gotten angry. "You do not have to remind me woman! I know who I am. I

305

am King David!" Bathsheba had turned around and left him alone in he's study.

He could not sleep that night. The words that Bathsheba had spoken made him roll around restless in he's bed. Even Joab had also warned him not to do such foolish thing and yet he prevailed against he's better judgement. Joab had returned with the news that the count had been completed. He had given the figures as the king had ordered and yet instead of joy he felt condemned in he's heart.

"O Yahweh! I have sinned greatly in what I have done! I pray please take away this iniquity for I have done very foolishly!" He tossed and turned throughout the night and could not find peace. He woke up the next morning with a heaviness that he had perhaps felt when he had sinned against Yahweh and took Uriah's life. The servant Hushai walks into the chamber looking worried. "My king the prophet Gad is here to speak with you." David feels he's legs go numb and he holds onto the wall to support he's own body weight. He gives the instruction for everyone to leave the throne room. "Send in the prophet." Gad's sandals echo through the empty hall as he enters into the throne room.

"King David. The word of the Lord came to me last night. Thus says Yahweh. Choose one of these for yourself that I may do it to you." The silence in the throne room is almost over powering.

"Shall there be seven years of starvation in your land.

Or shall you flee for three months from your enemies while they pursue you?

Or shall there be three days plague in your land?

Now consider what Yahweh has said and answer so that I can say it to Yahweh." David bows he's head strands of grey hair falling over he's face.

"I am in great distress. Please let us fall into the hand of Yahweh, for He's mercy is great; but do not let me fall into the hand of my enemies." Gad leaves the throne room. "So it shall be."

The wailing of woman awoke David from he's restless sleep. The sun had not yet risen and David struggles in the dark to light a lantern. A plague had broken out from Dan to Baar - Sheba three days ago and at least seventy thousands people had been reported killed. David puts on he's tunic and he's sandals and walks from he's bedchambers. There was no servants to been seen anywhere in the palace. Yahweh hand was heavy on Israel and the fear that David felt was overpowering and made him feel mortified.

David walks down to the throne room. A figure moving in the dark stops him in he's tracks. "Who walks there?" David lifts the lantern high in the air. "It is me. Gad my king. The Lord has sent me to tell you to go down to the threshing floor of Araunah the Jebusite and to erect an altar for the Lord. Go and let the elders of the city accompany you."

David sits down on the cedar steps. "Will the Lord withdraw the plague from the land?" No answer comes. Gad had again disappeared down the hall way. David readies himself and calls on he's servants to get the necessary supplies for the altar. He gives Hushai instruction to gather the elders to accompany him to the threshing floor.

The elders responded with the urgency that David had foreseen. He explained to them the instructions that the prophet Gad had given him and soon all of them set of towards the threshing floor of Araunah the Jebusite. All of them were wearing sackcloth as a sign of their repentance. It was still in the early morning hours. No one walked in the streets. As they continue down towards the threshing floor he hears wailing of woman come through some of the wooden windows of the houses. The whole city was covered in darkness and an unprecedented cold pressed down with a heaviness and despair.

The men continue to make their way towards the threshing floor. David approaches the area owned by Araunah. Movement overhead captures he's attention and he lifts he's eyes towards the heavens. David stop abruptly and one of the elders bump into him. When the elder lifts he's head and stares into the direction David gaze was fixed upon the daunting reason was evident. The king kept on staring at the heavens and the elder felt his legs give way involuntary screaming out. "We will surly die!" David does not seem to hear the distressed voice of the elder and the commotion that followed soon after the elder fell down behind him. David felt his own legs go numb and he also fell face down on the ground he's whole body shaking uncontrollably.

Standing above them between the earth and the heaven was a winged being with a sword drawn over the city. David closes he's eyes and calls out in a voice sounding in great distress. "Yahweh! I was the one that gave the command for the people to be numbered. I am the one who sinned. These people what have they done to deserve this? Let your hand be against me and my house."

A voice comes from the heavens.

"It is enough. Now restrain your hand."

David slowly lifts he's eyes and sees the angel of Yahweh putting back he's sword into its scabbard. The voice thunders out again from the heavens.

"Now come!"

David slowly rises from the ground and walks up the path towards the threshing floor. A man and he's four sons stood in the early morning hours threshing wheat. When the man looks up terror shows in he's face. He's four sons run away screaming and hiding behind a wall. David looked behind him and he saw the angel of the Lord still visible standing between heaven and earth. The man falls down on he's face and David gently touches the man by he's shoulder encouraging him to get up. The man did not move and David address him.

"I know that you fear because of what you are witnessing and you should for the living Yahweh who created such being is much higher and greater than our understanding." The man does not move a muscle and David continues. "I need to buy the spot of your threshing floor so I can build an altar for Yahweh, that the plague that have befallen the people may be stopped."

Araunah shakes he's head in fear. "The place is yours my king! You do not have to buy it from me. I will also give you these oxen as a burnt offering to Yahweh. You can use the threshing sledges for wood and the wheat as grain offering. "

David takes the man by he's shoulders and gently prompted him to lift himself from the ground. The Jebusite rises but does not lift he's eyes in the direction of the angel of the Lord. David calls on he's servants and turns to the ash stricken face Jebusite. "I will not just take the land form you. I will surly buy it for the full price."

He turns to he's approaching servants. "Give this man six hundred shekels of gold by weight." Araunah seem at a loss of words but bows before the king and respectfully responds. "That is much more than the worth of this land." David did not answer back but gave instruction to he's servants to build the altar and prepare the oxen. Soon the altar was erected and the slaughtered oxen was placed upon it. David bowed down again with the elders and called out to Yahweh. "Yahweh of Abraham, Isaac and Jacob please have mercy and forgive us!" The heavens open up for a moment and fire descends onto the altar burning the oxen that was placed onto the altar. David gets to he's feet. "Yahweh again showed mercy and withdrew the plague from the land of Israel and answered with fire from heaven!

Praise the name of the living Yahweh!"

The snow in streets of the market turned the City into a spectacular wonderland. Solomon drew the bearskin around he's shoulders and rubbed he's hands together for warmth. He continued staring at the Shulamite following her every action as she returned to the market place in the early morning hours. "She is as a lily among thorns." Solomon thinks to himself as he stares at her shining hair in the morning sunlight and drinks in her beauty with his gaze.

Every evening she was brought to the king's palace and would depart again early every morning. He had taken noticed of her every time he was around. When she came to he's father room in the evening he was sure she took note of him too. He knew the arrangement that was between the girl and he's father and also that she was still a maiden. It was Hushai who had explained this to him giving him the detail of her purpose.

The conversation between him and he's father servant happened unexpectedly one afternoon when he was again absentmindedly staring at the lovely Shulamite. Hushai had interrupted he's thoughts then.

"Yes young man, she is a beauty and might be your wife one day." Solomon words came stumbling out and he sounded like the caravan merchants parrot that he had seen in the market plain. "Uh...no I was just wondering how my father was doing?" Hushai had laughed at him and took a seat next to him. "Sure you were and that is why your mouth was agape?"

Solomon face had reddened feeling embarrassed by he's undisguised behaviour and that it was so obvious that he ached for the girl. But she was he's fathers! As if Hushai had read he's thoughts he spoke gently to the youngster. "Your father has grown old and as you are aware this winter is specifically cold. When a man enters your father season you will find that the blood does not run as hot through the veins as they use to." Solomon had tried to interpret if the old servant had intended a double meaning to he's statement and again he blushed when he saw the spark in the old man eyes.

"This is a remedy that the king Achish had used and told your father about when he was still under the Philistine King services. A man uses the body warmth of a younger woman to warm up he's old bones. I know that she is still a maiden because your father requested it to be so and so she shall remain. She shall be finished with her duties at the end of the winter season." The conversation took another turn and Hushai looked more serious. "I am aware that you have spent much more time in your father presence in the last few months." Solomon thinks about the past few moons and the conversations he has had with he's father.

He's father was growing old now and David had made it clear that he would be the next king of Israel and not one of he's older brothers. David had then taken out a parchment and started to explain to Solomon in detail that he should build a temple for the tabernacle of the Lord. David spend a lot of time and explained in a meticulous way the exact detail of the temple construction. It was at one of these planning sessions that Solomon had come to the king's bed chamber that he saw her. Just before he could knock on the door it opened and the most beautiful woman he had ever laid he's eyes on had stepped out of the room. She looked him straight in the eyes and when she realized that it was one of the kings sons she quickly bowed her head. Without any hesitation Solomon had spoken to her and the words spoke blurted out without him thinking twice. "You are the most beautiful woman that I have ever lain my eyes upon." She had not responded but stopped and tilted her lovely head in he's direction. She kept looking at him with eyes that must have looked right into the depths of he's mind.

"My name is Solomon, who are you?" She had then again kept her eyes down cast and answered him. "My name is Abishag my lord I am one of the king servants." Solomon could not get her lovely face out of he's mind the whole day. Shortly thereafter he's father had gotten he's men together to draw up against a Philistine invasion on the borders of Gob. The king left the city. Solomon had followed the girl when she went to the market place. She met with other young ladies and they stood and talked for a time. She stood out among the other woman. Solomon felt he's heart race every time she laughed. She was surly aware of he's presence and looked into he's direction once or twice.

"She is quite lovely isn't she brother." Solomon jumps up from behind the stall he has been peering from at the Shulamite. "Adonijah! What are you doing creeping up behind me?" Adonijah combs he's fingers through he's thick hair. "I should be asking you what you are doing staring at our father's wife."

Solomon feels the anger rise in him. Adonijah was Absalom's brother and Bathsheba had warned him that he was should be careful of the devious man. There was rumours that he was reconvening the people of Israel to proclaim him king when

David had died. "She is not our father's wife. She is only a servant." Adonijah hisses in he's ear. "The king might just be interested why you have such curiosity in one of he's servants. I won't forget the Shulamite my little brother and maybe soon she will belong to another."

The older half-brother pushed into Solomon with he's shoulder and Solomon only stared after he's half-brother as he disappears into the market crowd. When he turns back again to seek the face of Abishag she had disappeared.

The bronze helms of the Philistines shine brightly in the morning sun and it is almost blinding to David. He stares out over the plains of Gob. Was it almost sixty years ago that he faced the Philistine giant Goliath?

A big man walks out from the front rank of the Philistines. The battle scars show on he's thick arms and he's moustache is streaked with grey a sign of he's age. "I am Ishbi – Benob! I am the son of Goliath!" He stares at David with he's loathing in he's violent eyes. "You old man have defeated my father with your trickeries! Now face me that I can revenge my father you old dog!" David's anger arise and he draws he's sword.

Benaiah steps out before the king. "No my king. He is much younger than you. You have not been in battle for some time now. Let me kill this ranting Philistine." David ignores the petition from Benaiah and pushes he's hand away. He stares at the warrior before him. "I am King David the servant of the true Yahweh! It was not trickeries but the living Yahweh that gave me victory!" David steps out towards the Philistine he's sword ready in he's hand. The Philistine approaches him slowly. Although David was older he was still one of the most renowned warriors in the whole of Israel. David silently prays. "Yahweh. You are my rock and my fortress and my deliverer; you are my strength in whom I trust. My shield and the horn of my salvation, my stronghold and my refuge; My Saviour, You save me from violence."

The Philistine rushes in at him and takes a mighty swing at David. He's axe gleams in the sun as it swoops down at he's opponents head.

David jumps backwards and stumbles over a rock. Although he is completely off balance it is the rock that saves he's life. The axe swirls past he's head. David regains he's balance and jumps up he's sword raised again.

The Philistine had expected to decapitate David and when he missed he was also off balance. He spins around and raises he's axe above he's head coming at David like a wounded mountain bear, screaming obscenities. "Where is the trickery now? Where is this Yahweh of yours? "David awaits the rushing Philistine he's knees slightly bend. The Philistine swings he's axe in a wide arch this time aiming at David's midriff.

David rolls he's wrist he's sword ricocheting the full blow of the swinging axe. The force of deflecting the axe numbs he's arm and he also feels a warm feeling down the side of he's arm. He stares down at he's shoulder and sees a deep gash. The axe had not totally missed. The Philistine army start to rant wildly following their warriors jeers. "Where is your Yahweh now?"

David hears Abishai, Joab brother and Benaiah voices above the noise. "Yahweh is your rock! He has defeated the Philistines before and again he will defeat this Philistine!" David stares at the man before him. "I call upon you Yahweh who is worthy to be praised! So I shall be saved from my enemy. Let me fight this last battle with dignity and glory be on to your name forever!"

A strong wind picks up of the desert floor and blows directly into David's face. An old but familiar feeling sidles inside he's body and a sudden burst of energy runs through he's tired muscles and he feels as light as a feather. The Philistine sees the gust of wind picking up and mistakes David's action as being blinded temporally by the sand.

He takes the advantage and again rush in swinging he's axe overhead. He swings he's axe directly at David's head certain that it was a death strike but only strikes the air where the old man's head was just a moment ago! The Philistine feels a stab in he's thigh and then a blow against he's head that makes him go down in the sand on he's knees.

David had rolled to he's left when the Philistine had attacked and had quickly cut he's sword through the Philistines inner thigh. He had hoped to hit a main artery. He then jumped to he's feet and struck the Philistine on the side of he's head with the blunt end of he's sword. It all happened so fast that the Philistine army had completely gone silent for a moment as Ishbi – Benob hits the sand on he's knees.

David's head rushes and he suddenly feels faint. He's legs start to shake and he is short of breath. He kneels down onto he's one knee trying to catch he's breath. The Philistine gets back onto he's feet shaking he's head groggily. He turns and sees David struggling for air on he's one knee. He walks towards him very unsteady on he's feet and raises he's axe. Excruciating pain explodes in he's lower abdomen and he stares down at he's stomach. The blade tip of a sword protrudes from he's stomach. The light fades away and he falls with he's face on the ground.

Abishai draws he's sword out of the Philistines back. He knew that the Philistines would attack seeing he's act as being deceitful in the rules of war. The Philistine's hordes scream in anger. Benaiah draws he's own axe the huge blade reflects in the sunlight. "For Yahweh and King David!"

The mighty men of David rush into the Philistine hordes. David slowly arises from the desert floor with Abishai's help. "Are you alright my king?" David answer comes softly.

"In my distress I called upon the Lord, and cried out to my Yahweh. He heard my voice from He's temple, and my cry entered He's ears."

Bathsheba knew that the presence of the prophet did not always bring good tidings. Nathan now stood before her in the absence of David telling her what she dreaded. "Have you not heard that Adonijah has invited all your brothers and all the men of Judah to a sacrifice and that he is proclaiming himself king?" Bathsheba stares at the prophet Nathan in astonishment. "When did this happen?" The prophet takes a deep breath and wipes sweat of he's brow before he again address her in the throne room. It was very peculiar without the audience of King David.

"They are already making toasts to the new King by the stone of Zoheleth. He has invited all except Zadok the priest, Benaiah son of Jehoiada, the other mighty men of David and me. Mother of Israel let me give you advice so that you can save your own life and the life of your son Solomon. Go to the king and tell him immediately!"

Bathsheba did not waste any more time and went directly to king David bed chamber. Since he had returned from the war with the Philistines he had not gotten out of he's bed. She knocks on the door and young servant opens the door. She walks into the chambers and bows before the King. The man lying on the bed looked old and frail. The green piercing eyes was the only thing that still looked the same. David rises himself on he's pillows.

"What is the matter Bathsheba? You look in great distress?" Bathsheba takes the hand of David into her own kneeling next to he's bed. "My King, by your own words you have said that Solomon would become king after you." David nods he's head and Bathsheba uses the encouraging nod explain their quandary. "Adonijah has gone and invited all of Israel and Judah to a sacrifice and has proclaimed himself king!" David stares at he's wife and then without hesitation he asks for the young servant to send for the prophet.

A short moment later the bedchamber door opens again and the prophet Nathan comes into the room. David address the prophet without any greeting. "Is it true? Has Adonijah proclaimed himself king?" The prophet nods. "The whole of Israel is gathered with him but the people eyes are still on you to appoint the rightful king." David closes he's eyes for a moment before he answers. "Call on Solomon to come to my chamber. Also send for Zadok and Benaiah."

When all had arrived David addresses Solomon before all the people in the room. "My son, soon I will rest with my fathers. Be strong and prove yourself a man. Keep the charges of the Lord our Yahweh. Walk in He's ways and keep he's statutes and commandments. All he's testimonies are written in the laws of Moses. Do this and you will prosper in all that you do." A slight breeze blows over the lanterns in the room and the flames flickers elatedly. "This is my charge that I give you. You know that Joab has done and that he must be punished for he's deeds. He has killed Abner son of Ner and also Amasa son of Jether. Do according to your wisdom and do not let he's grey hair go to he's grave in peace. Remember to show kindness to Brazillai the Gileadite for he was the one that gave us food and shelter when we fled from Absalom. Also see that no one touches Shimei the son of Gera for although he cursed me he had come down to the Jordan River and ask for forgiveness."

David lays he's hands on he's sons head. "Solomon build the temple exactly as Yahweh had instructed and obey the command given by Yahweh.

I bless you as King of Israel in the name of the Lord our Yahweh."

David turns he's eyes to the two men standing at the door.

"Benaiah and Zadok come near. Zadok take with you my servants and let Solomon ride on my own mule and take him down to Gihon. There you and Nathan must anoint him as king over Israel and blow the horn and then say. Long live King, Solomon!"

Benaiah booming voice fills the room. "May the Lord Yahweh of my King bless Solomon like he's father and also more!" David smiles at he's old war companion. "We have been in many battles together my old friend. You will be the captain over the chiefs when I am gone. Follow the instructions of my son Solomon as you have followed my instructions."

Benaiah grips the hand of David a tear rolling down he's bearded face. "Now go and do as I have commanded." The men leave the room and David calls Bathsheba to he's bed. "As I have sworn before the Lord our son Solomon will sit on my throne in my place." Bathsheba holds David's hands in hers. "Now take the scroll by my bed and write down what I tell you."

"Why is the city in such uproar?" Adonijah claps Joab on he's back. "Surely all have heard the news and they are rejoicing for I am King!"

A young man comes rushing towards their table. Adonijah raises he's glass. "Look it is Jonathan the son of the priest Abiathar. He must be bringing good news." The people sitting at Adonijah's table all wait on the young man to speak. "I bring news from the city. King David has anointed Solomon as king over Israel!"

Adonijah drops the cup from he's hands. "The priest Zadok and the prophet Nathan have anointed him with Benaiah and the mighty men of Israel." Jonathan wanted to say more but Joab held up he's hands.

"Listen!"

In the distance a horn blows and a chorus comes through the night air growing louder and louder.

"Long live King Solomon!" The guests sitting at the table look at each other with fear on their faces and start to leave. "Wait! Where are you going?" Joab grabs Adonijah by he's arm. "Come we must flee for Solomon and the mighty men of David will surly kill us!"

Thousands of people had gathered outside the City of David before the new anointed King's throne. The mighty men of David stood on each side of the throne and Solomon stands before the people of Israel.

"King David has died."

More wailing arise from the crowds but Solomon hold up he's hands and speaks out very vociferously over the people of Israel.

"These are the last words spoken by King David."

He opens the scroll that he's mother had given to him.

"David the son of Jesse says, the man who raised on high says, the anointed of the God of Jacob, the sweet psalmist of Israel:

Yahweh's Spirit spoke by me. He's word was on my tongue. The God of Israel said, the Rock of Israel spoke to me. One who rules over men righteously, who rules in the fear of God, shall be as the light of the morning, when the sun rises a morning without clouds, when the tender grass spring out of the earth, through clear shining after rain.

Most certainly my house is not so with God, yet he has made with me an everlasting covenant, ordered in all things, and sure, for it is all my salvation, and all my desire, although he doesn't make it grow.

But all the ungodly will be as thorns to be thrust away, because they can't be taken with the hand, but the man who touches them must be armed with iron and the staff of a spear. They will be utterly burned with fire in their place." (2 Samuel 23) Amen!"

Epilogue

(1 Chronicles 29 verse 26 – 30)

Now David the son of Jesse reigned over all Israel. The time that he reigned over Israel was forty years; he reigned seven years in Hebron, and he reigned thirty-three years in Jerusalem. He died at a good old age, full of days, riches, and honor; and Solomon he's son reigned in he's place. Now the acts of David the king, first and last, behold, they are written in the history of Samuel the seer, and in the history of Nathan the prophet, and in the history of Gad the seer, with all he's reign and he's might, and the times that went over him, and over Israel, and over all the kingdoms of the countries.

Printed in the United States
By Bookmasters